*Lionheart*

James Maclaren was born in Warwick[...] International Relations at King's College London and served for twenty-five years in the British Army as an infantry officer. Afterwards he turned to journalism and teaching and spent most of his life abroad in Europe and the Far East.

His first two novels are available on Amazon. *The Dolphin Men* is an historical fiction novel looking at the dark world of a corrupt policing and political establishment in London in the nineteen sixties. *The Arms Merchant* explores the mechanisms and complexities created when the worlds of post-cold war espionage and eastern European mafia crime collide. *Lionheart* follows his tradition for examining the dark ruthlessness of corrupt power in which the personal can be ruined by the ideological and which can leave even the safest of democratic systems vulnerable to corrupt distortion. Maclaren's fascination for how slight twists of fate can produce the most dramatic consequences and his storytelling talent provide an important contribution to the thriller genre.

*By the Author*

The Dolphin Men
The Arms Merchant

# LIONHEART

James Maclaren

First published 2022

By Maclaren Associates Limited

Penhurst House

262 Battersea Park Road, London, SW11 3BY

Paperback edition published Amazon 2023

All rights reserved

© James Maclaren, 2022

The right of James Maclaren to be identified as author of this work has been asserted in accordance with Section 77 of the Copyright, Design and Patents Act 1988

This book is sold subject to the condition that it shall not, bey way of trade or otherwise be lent, resold, hired out or otherwise circulated without the publisher's prior consent in any form of binding or cover other than that in which it is published and without a similar condition including this condition being imposed on the subsequent purchaser

*To a little girl who is my love*

*One Chinese watches a thousand; a thousand Chinese watch one.*

*Communist proverb*

*"England, bound in with the triumphant sea Whose rocky shore beats back the envious siege of watery Neptune, is now bound in with shame, With inky blots and rotten parchment bonds: That England, that was wont to conquer others, Hath made a shameful conquest of itself."*

*Richard II - William Shakespeare*

*"I can't bear Britain in decline. I just can't. We, who either defeated or rescued half of Europe, who kept half of Europe free, when otherwise it would be in chains. And look at us now."*

*Margaret Thatcher, 1979*

## CONTENTS

You can't go through here ..................18
I don't want flowers ...........................41
Learn, learn, and learn ......................62
When did you last eat chocolate? ....................85
Tell me what you want ....................108
Everyone is good communist… .....................131
The Girl ...........................................155
There is no law against antiques....................174
The country is full of patriots .........................199
Marxists get up early in the morning .............222
We always clap for birthdays ........................249
What do you think they know? ......................271
A land fit for a king .........................................298
Down in darkest Lambeth .............................325
I'm just a sleeper...........................................352
Sunrise ..........................................................379
Arise ye workers… ........................................402
Run.................................................................429
Then raise the scarlet standard high..............444
Escape ...........................................................459

# PROLOGUE

**Downing Street 9th June 1983**

A SCENT OF FABRIC and flowers lingered in the room, a faint aromatic fingerprint. Offices, of greater grandeur, prestigiously placed and from which the prime minister could oversee the affairs of state existed, but this was her preferred. She liked that it was small, intimate and had not evolved from random decisions of history, or the bland modernising conformity of government committees.

On arriving in Number 10 she had been depressed. Rows of Whig and Tory statesmen, let their iron gazes of disapproval fall from gilt frames upon those entering their fiefdoms. Deep in the bellies of the house, she toured grand but gloomy state apartments that had provided powerful stages for the theatre of government. They seemed haunted by the ghosts of the nation's past, the echoes of war, alliances, and treachery the high drama of history seemingly infused into the very plaster of the ornate ceilings. These places felt stagnant and decayed, she thought, a dreary reminder of the country whose fortunes she had vowed to reverse.

Change must begin here, she resolved.

The study had become her first project and the clubby battered leather sofas and the unloved dark hunting prints of her predecessors had been ordered away, replaced with softer contrasts of colours and style that pleased her. Small water colours from a well-known eighteenth-century English artist decorated the pale lemon walls. At this time of year the trees in the Downing Street garden would break the sunlight causing it to fall through the windows in a speckled pattern and the light summer breeze would carry the delicate perfume of roses and honeysuckle into the room.

Tonight, dawn and the sun were hours away and the heavy curtains were drawn tight. Only the ivory-silk glow from table lamps lit the room. Except for a petite but heavy carriage clock that gently chimed two hours past midnight, the room with its tasteful richness was in silence.

She was the only occupant, a woman as famous as any politician before her, her face and manner instantly recognisable for the boundaries she had broken with her sex and for the radical—many declared ruthless—medicine administered upon a sick nation. She sat stiff backed at her desk, with legs neatly tucked away under the chair. Her shoes had slipped from her feet and her ankles were delicately crossed. Using a heavy black fountain pen, she wrote in graceful strokes. Despite the hour, the favoured blue wool Aquascutum suit, selected at five the previous morning still looked pressed and fresh and the coiffured hair, remained an elegant signature.

Pausing the pen nib, her calm gaze lifted to look around her. In her mind came the roll call of the long line of prime ministers who this room had hosted, who had sat here before her; chosen men—she was the first woman—men who had led the country, first to gather its empire and greatness, then to summon its power to save a continent, before finally being forced to confront and nurse a forlorn decline and the painful struggle with its own identity.

Earlier, the doleful peals of Big Ben had marked the closing of the polls. Reform had been her victory cry four years earlier and reform on all fronts had been her mission. Only tonight, her plans lay broken, broken by political change, swiftly, ferociously, and with the cruelty of the tropical storm delivered to smash her plans to driftwood on the sand. The building like the country would have no transforming light reaching into its corners. The tired extravagant rooms and society with them, would stay unchanged and this small space, she thought, remained alone as her small achievement.

Democracy was messy and unpredictable.

She had conceded defeat an hour ago. A short message of congratulations delivered by phone to her political adversary. It had been an awkward, stiff exchange. A short formal conversation that followed long-standing convention, a formality intended to drain rancour from the political battle and draw a polite line under the insults, claims, and prejudice, allowing the process of transition to be handed over briefly to the civil servants. She had been gracious. *Congratulations...the contest is yours...I wish you and your government every success...* The words seemed hollow in retrospect. She was a political winner, and who in the world of politics longs for their opponent to achieve success?

In return the tone of the victor had been compassionate. *Thank you for your service to the country...I look forward to seeing you in the House...* The sincerity or otherwise of each other's words mattered not. Two minutes, that was all, just an exchange of two minutes to restore dignity to the political brawl and pass the baton of government to new ownership. But beyond the politeness both had understood that as a political force she was no more.

The last time she had confronted the scruffy small man, who would now succeed her, had been across the floor of the House and had been a bruising affair even by the standards of the Commons. Each of them had known that her authority was to be tested, that the forces of the left and right they represented would challenge each other for the loyalty of a nation. His easy eloquence, a liquid cadence that came straight from nineteen-fifties academia had played well. His mocking barbed wit describing the collapsing state of public services to the delight of his uproarious backbenchers, who, scenting blood waved their order papers ecstatically, slapping each other's backs, mercilessly taunting the furious, sulking, silent government ranks opposite who could only glower in reply.

Sitting impassively, arms folded, she had listened with forced composure, attempting to ignore the merciless arrows directed her way. When it was over, her advisers moved to reassure her. *Don't worry Prime Minister...the public will not be persuaded by easy promises...* She had disbelieved them.

She had counted the political shadows gathering around her. The steely self-belief and purpose that had propelled her to the summit of power, past envious legions of men ill-disposed to her ideas and often her sex had begun to diminish. Each day had become more of a test to summon the strength to confront the political waves that drove her ideas towards the rocks.

A cruel pack was hunting her.

Like old lovers helplessly parting ways, she observed the people's trust in her fade, the early years optimism replaced by mutterings of discontent. Others, supporters, and enemies alike, had also seen it. The myth she was ageless, timeless, and cast-iron damage-proof had been broken and the blue eyes, once filled with unsatisfied menace, had dulled. A recent cabinet secretary, pompous and bitter, sulking in early retirement, had cast his opinion. *There's that smell of death in the corridors*, he had whispered knowledgeably to confidantes in club land over brandy. *Won't be long now.* The gleeful sneer had found its way to her ears.

And the cruel pack had won.

There would be remorse, of this, she was sure.

She was fearful now, fearful for the naive ideologue of false compassion towards the people that would follow. Powerful shadowy forces were lurking, eager to embrace a regime that would first consolidate and then extend their grip on society. She had seen the reports, grimly read the files on some of the most radical politicians in the country, fumed at the radicalisation of the country's universities, driven by the influence of their academics and she had watched the lurking strength of the unions, hungry for power and control, gather their strength. The country had become awash with money from the Soviet bloc, KGB money, feeding political evangelists with their armies of organised acolytes.

Inwardly, she grimaced at the ideas her successor had paraded before the unwitting people. Dismantling the nuclear deterrent, abolishing the House of Lords, withdrawal from the European Economic Community. She hated the prospect of the country crumbling, fearful of where such ideas might lead.

An ideologically run state sliding deeper into authoritarian rule.

Was that possible?

Yes, she feared it was.

The tide of change she had promised was retreating fast.

Now there were people to inform. Warn.

She glanced at the clock which now said two-thirty. On the note paper in front of her she had written a shortlist of just three leaders:

The President,

Chancellor and,

Secretary-General.

Too late or too early for the second two names on the list. Berlin and Brussels were still in the depths of night. Washington was four hours behind.

She thought of her friend and political ally.

The president was a man who liked to retire early and was usually in bed by ten. Tonight, she thought, tonight he would have remained awake to see whether the world leader he considered his greatest ally had come through the sternest of political tests, to defy the unimpressed polls. On her desk was the picture of them together on a cold Washington day in December, standing on the steps of the Capitol. In the image he was smiling broadly, the handsome features of a man that critics in their ignorance had written off before history held the chance to judge. The twinkling eyes and warm twisted mouth, that gave a permanent smile, the hairstyle, full, slicked, and American, and the outstretched wave of the arm, caught in the sweeping presidential pose, a gesture that spoke to a camera with the practise and ease of the actor he had been.

'You are through to the White House Prime Minister.'

A click, a pause, and another voice; female, American, efficient: 'Please hold for the President ma'am.'

He did not keep her waiting his voice coming at once onto the line. Despite the distance of the Atlantic Ocean between them the mellow Californian tones of her friend came to her clearly.

'I have the news. Obviously, I am sorry.'

She was pleased that her senses had been correct.

'We knew it was probable,' she said by way of explanation.

'You've spoken to the other guy?'

She confirmed she had. 'Yes, it's done. By tomorrow he'll be here.'

'You people move quick; I'll give you that. Well, I'll talk to him soon, I guess. Let's see what he has to say.'

The call turned to warm exchanges of regret and personal goodwill. The sadness in his voice was beyond doubt. The rich drawl of the West Coast accent and easy manner which many took for genial incompetence, but was not, lifted her a little. He did not disguise the farewell behind the words, which they both chose carefully, aware that the call would be turned into official, if confidential, transcript on both sides of the Atlantic. There must be no tainted witness to their shared thoughts. From the diminished pulpit of the back benches, she did not expect the savage brawl of the Commons with its heat and noise to have any appetite to heed her fears, but the president had made it clear that the stages of Princeton, Harvard and Dartmouth would await her. There, her warnings for the political darkness approaching would have an audience.

It would not be enough.

She and the president understood that without their shared ideals, hopes, and cooperation, the Americans would draw away, taking their power and energy elsewhere, already weary of a Europe awash with complacency and idealism, contemptuous of peoples who had forgotten their wars too quickly and who openly despised the brash confrontationalism of the Americans. To the American mind, Europe seemed oblivious to the dangers gathered behind the Iron Curtain, a monolithic machine that contemplated Western Europe as a bear might prowl the edges of an isolated settlement scenting for weakness.

After replacing the receiver, she thought of how her friendship with the president had been tested. How much of her fate and that of her country rested with the decisions and actions of others beyond her control.

Did it need to have been like this?

The Falklands.

The small outcrops of storm-washed rock that peeked above the ocean waves of the Atlantic on the far side of the world and a diplomatic wrangle over ownership that had burst into conflict as a South American dictator gambling a rickety political future with military adventure.

It started there, she believed, with the U.S. decision not to support her decision to retake the Islands. The country had been forced to the role of a jilted lover cast ungraciously and without warning from the shared bed. Starved of sustenance from their closest ally, the British fleet had set sail, its commanders aware of how firmly its arms were tied. A brave but unequal counter to the Junta's adventure.

In the White House, the president had tried, she knew that.

She had provided a few short and sharp phone calls as the conflict developed to remind him who his real friends were.

But the Senate hawks had wheeled gleefully to deny him. Anti-British factions in the CIA and the Pentagon—there were plenty in both departments—had leaked details of the secret attempts to help the British. As the Task Force pounded south in heavy roiling Atlantic weather, the president's envoy exhausted from the shuttle diplomacy had delivered the unwelcome message that: "*...with deepest and solemn regret, the United States would not support the United Kingdom militarily or diplomatically.*". She thought him weak with his plans for shared sovereignty.

In her mind she could still picture the General; handsome, tanned, stiff-backed, his features stony faced and tight lipped with embarrassment, almost standing at attention a few feet from this desk. His message delivered, he had listened silently and awkwardly to her furious admonishments. She knew he was in league with her own Foreign Secretary and his department of smug over-educated fools, all of them happy to surrender their souls to the Devil if the agreement was written eloquently enough.

It was for these slippery mandarins, pompous officials in their elegant suits, who unblushingly glossed over their failure to predict the crisis with whispered plans for compromise that she reserved her greatest wrath, furious with the Foreign Secretary's languid assurance that they: *Could solve the crisis with diplomacy.* She had openly scoffed. *Diplomacy.* To this day no one had explained to her how you solved an invasion by *diplomacy.*

But she realised from the moment the words left his lips they would all have their way. Her fury, frustration, and anger, nothing more than theatre as the weak frightened fools collapsed around her, the pursuit of righteousness paralysed with the sum of their fears.

A single brave Argentinian warplane hopping across the waves, weaving through the pickets of destroyers and frigates to send the British aircraft carrier to tumble and turn to the bottom of the cold depths had decided the mission to recover the remote stormy islands. She had known then she was asking too much. The iron will to proceed was broken. The Fleet had been recalled back to its ports. Now as her thoughts flew to that time, she shook her head and passed her fingers across her brow to swipe away the memories. Just to think of that pale blue flag with its yellow sun fluttering above the windy rain slashed rocks made her blood boil and her heart sank thinking of the lonely island people looking out to the winter waves which boomed and whooshed against the shoreline still waiting for the ships and marines that would never come.

She continued the short discreet notes to the Secretary General of the NATO military alliance, the German Chancellor (who she disliked) and the Secretary-General of the United Nations. In them she confided, to varying degrees, the concerns she had shared with the American president. She contemplated a note to her French counterpart but decided against it. The man was a boastful indiscreet fool who would merely mock her words, unable to suppress his glee at her departure. Instead, she would send something diplomatically meaningless. She also decided it could wait a day or two, for she was sure his Gallic ego would recognise the snub of a message sent from an ex-prime minister.

The centrality of the transatlantic mission, the community in which she believed: *shared blood, language, culture, and values*...had suffered irreparably. British introspection and American doubts invited other influences to weaken and undermine cooperation; social, economic, and political forces, corrosive and damaging that rapidly rusted away at the joints breaking the rivets of the alliances that had kept Europe safe since the devastation of a world war.

She blotted the notes carefully and placed them in the empty tray for collection.

Beyond the drawn curtains she knew the night watchmen of the press pack were gathered, waiting in a patient huddle illuminated only by the single gloomy lamp above the Number 10 entrance. When dawn reached into the street, their numbers would be reinforced. A clicking, clacking, and scribbling press hoard who had waited for her final words throughout the short, excited night. Later in the morning on the warm sunny Downing Street steps and freshened with a change of clothes, she would give them her final sombre statement as prime minister.

Then, finally, the last act would take place, the short drive to kiss hands with the Sovereign and with all formality complete the title of prime minister would leave her.

Then?

Then, nothing.

There was not even enough time or achievement for a decent memoir.

The dark intentions of rising political forces that she had been warned about, the secret files prepared by a fearful establishment detailing their links to foreign powers, the people, their plans, the money, these would remain locked for the day the terrible detail needed to be used. Of these she would say nothing.

Neither would she talk of the plan she hoped would roll it back.

There was a light tap on her door. It broke her thoughts.

'It's time Prime Minister.' The figure of Crawford her loyal assistant her face drawn and sympathetic, looking tired and unhappy herself, stood in the doorway dispatched from the outer office reminding her she still held responsibility with final duties that must be discharged.

One last review of her desk.

For the first time she noted how even more tidy than usual it was. The leather-bound blotter was clear and everything official had been removed with care and efficiency by an unseen hand. In the early hours when the fervour of the fight has passed, hopes dashed, dreams realised, there is within the inner workings of government, just the briefest of skips, well-greased points shift and the political train smoothly changes tracks without waking the sleeping citizens who, with their votes cast and duty fulfilled, await their destination.

But even in the fury of a bitterly fought election the affairs of state must continue, and she had lost none of her diligence in reading her boxes, her grasp of detail was unmatched across government and respected even by her opponents.

There had been classified files in the tray. One had particularly interested her. An intelligence report on the changes in the hierarchy of the Soviet Union' Presidium. A promising more youthful politician, circling close to power, a reformer that the Kremlin watchers had briefed her might be useful, someone with whom they believed there could be common ground from which to break the East-West impasse. She had been struck by the picture she had been shown, the face of a man which seemed to express humanity and not the solid drab stiffness of other Soviet leaders, handsome humorous features with warm eyes that twinkled, and a self-confidence untroubled by the port wine birthmark that spread like a jam stain on his forehead.

She had read the previous reports, carefully collated, cross-referenced with sources and comment from other departments that informed her of his speeches, internal Party alliances and his personal tastes for music and food. She had studied with interest underlining the sections that intrigued her most, and that she wanted to know more about. The latest report had been brief saying only that he had been removed, exiled deep into the Soviet wilderness to be hidden in the endless grey soil of the country's bureaucracy. Shame, she had thought. An opportunity missed.

It would be someone else's problem now.

She collected her purse and began to leave, straightening the cushions on the sofa as she did so. She held the door handle and turned to look back into the room. It was unmoved by her departure and waiting for the next page of history to turn. Then she opened the door and disappeared into the corridor beyond.

She had held office for just a single term.

*Perestroika,* the word, and its meaning remained unknown to her.

She would never meet Mikhail Gorbachev.

***

## JAMES MACLAREN

---

DOCUMENT COVER SHEET

STRAP-1

TOP SECRET

(Classification)

Unauthorized disclosure will cause exceptionally grave damage to UK national security.

| MEMORANDA | COPY NUMBER | 1 of 7 |
|---|---|---|
| ORIGINATOR: | PUS(H) ▓▓▓▓ | |
| TO (PERSONAL FOR): | PUS (MOD1) ▓▓▓▓<br>DDG (BOX20) ▓▓▓▓<br>DE (STRAT) ▓▓▓▓<br>▓▓▓▓ | |
| COPY TO<br>(COMMITTEE):<br>(Sec to circulate) | CAB. ▓▓▓▓ (Sec)<br><br>U.S FE-CM ▓▓▓▓ (Sec) | |
| DATE: | 29 Jul 1987 | |
| OPLAN | M/89/0177 LIONHEART | |
| SUBJECT: | Future Political Leadership of the United Kingdom. | |

REMARKS/HANDLING INSTRUCTIONS

This document is disseminated for personal action addresses ONLY. The originator will not authorise ANY political or further department dissemination.

Wider distribution will compromise the long-term objective of returning the democratic political order and system of the UK in the event of change to the current political and Executive arrangements.

# LIONHEART

> **TOP SECRET**
>
> **CABINET OFFICE**
>
> 70 Whitehall London SW1A 2AS   Telephone 071-270 0101
>
> Ref. AO91/1049
> From ▮▮▮▮▮▮▮▮▮▮▮▮▮▮▮▮▮▮▮▮▮▮▮▮▮▮▮▮▮▮▮▮▮▮▮▮▮▮▮
> 17 July 1989
>
> *My Dear James*
>
> **Telephone Conversation - LIONHEART**
>
> Thank you for the meeting at your home on the 11th May. Since then, events have moved swiftly, and it is clear that following the General Election result the Government will be compelled to meet union demands for major constitutional and electoral reform. Experts agree that once in motion this will be difficult to reverse and the changes to not only our domestic system of government but also our vital strategic relations with other nations will be radically altered. A shift to an alliance with those countries of the Eastern Bloc and falling into the orbit of the Soviet Union may only be a few years, perhaps months away.
>
> In accordance with our contingency plans you should now, with the support of our allies, activate LIONHEART. The Committee retains its faith in you to act as the future political focus for this process and to undertake such measures as agreed in the Directive to restore a democratic political system when the opportunity presents itself. The OPLAN allocates you the code name: CLOUD BURST.
>
> I am copying this letter to ▮▮▮▮▮▮▮▮ U.S State Department. The LIONHEART Committee's work is complete and the committee has been dissolved. I will make arrangements for the destruction of all domestic department references to LIONHEART.
>
> *Yours ever*
>
> ▮▮▮▮▮▮▮▮
>
> Mr James Dugdale MP
> Poachers Retreat, The Manor, Reepham, Norfolkshire

\*\*\*

# CHAPTER ONE

*You can't go through here*

**Lancashire Present Day**

'WHAT'S YER BUSINESS HERE?' the police constable asked in a voice that was low and surly without a hint of respect. 'The road's closed.'

Above, thick cloud, darkening ominously as the afternoon edged away pressed down onto the Lancashire earth. A tough wind bustled off the Dales to roll through the gash of the Irwell Valley. It sent rain in plumes like a grey net film across the countryside.

It was the first Thursday in November. The false summer of October with its afternoons of soft haze and clinging mist was gone now, replaced by colder shorter days filled with the smells that said winter approached. Across the fields, hedgerows and distant woodland had already been stripped bare and the earth either side of the road were recently ploughed. Gulls, blown inland squealed and wheeled in their search for worms in the turned wet soil.

## LIONHEART

Fifty metres down the country road lay a dark broken shape. Harry Gates could see even from this distance that it was a body, one that was badly crushed and smashed.

'What happened here?' asked Gates not deterred by the officer's manner.

The constable didn't reply straight away. He was young and stood easily with bored discipline behind the blue-white-blue incident tape that stretched across the country road. He could have found shelter under the dripping birches that lined the road, but Gates suspected that moving from his position could earn him a reprimand that would be more uncomfortable than the rain. A crackle of radio static spat from his receiver which hung from a shoulder strap worn as a bandoleer.

He chose not to immediately acknowledge Gates' question. Instead, he turned and with the disdain that can come when youth is licensed with generous authority studied the new arrival coldly.

The constable's frosty eyes saw a man with untidy black hair turned silver by the rain, cheeks with blotched tiny broken veins, like a miniature map, a sure sign of alcohol and an indifferent diet. A carelessly tightened tie frayed at the knot peeped out from the top of a shapeless overcoat that glistened at the shoulders from the persistent drizzle. Slightly overweight with scuffed down at heel black shoes that were from the city, the visitor to his cold sentry post looked knocked about by life and out of place on a wet afternoon in a valley town.

The young policeman's working-class vowels turned the question back. 'Who's asking?' Cupping his hands, he breathed warmth onto them, autumn breath floating from his chilled lips. 'For the record like.'

Gates nodded agreeably and in his resigned state of patience fished inside an inner pocket, rummaging around, before pulling out a crumple of papers and cards.

'Here you go,' he said cheerfully and handed over his press identification. He made sure he kept the small red Communist Party book visible as he did so.

The policeman noted both. He took his time studying the card.

The brusqueness, Gates had expected. The constable was little more than a youth, the red skin of healing acne had blossomed as a raw blotch on his chin, while the whisper of hair on his lip indicated daily shaving was still an optional approach. The bulk of a regulation blue greatcoat disguised awkward gawky features that the improved rations of the police barracks had not yet filled out. It gave him, thought Gates, a slightly comic look, like a young boy in borrowed clothes dressing up as an adult hero. But he knew the officer would have a gun, an issue Makarov attached to the thick leather utility belt that held the coarse uniform trousers above his thin hips. Probably he had even fired it in the last few days, on the range. Policemen were required to practise their firearms proficiency regularly.

Their knowledge of the law less so.

A plod, concluded Gates. A beat officer of minimal training, a willing pawn who knew nothing beyond his oath of loyalty to a Party he could only hope to be a member of. In previous times, thought Gates, he could have been a security guard somewhere, patrolling a supermarket aisle for would-be shoplifters.

But when a policeman asks you for your papers you did not argue.

Sight of the small red book issued only to members of the British Communist Party had brought a mollifying effect. This was usual. It unfroze the suspicion people held for strangers and attracted a grudging respect rather like people used to have for honours and titles before such decadent entitlements were flushed away, swept down the drain with the rest of the system's historical and elitist baggage.

Heraldic clutter and self-important pomp that no longer held meaning or interest, the Party had declared.

Gates almost felt the officer's manner warm a little. The suspicion and disdain reserved for the average citizen evaporating slightly. A beat officer was unlikely to have achieved Party membership. In state organisations such privilege came only with much higher rank. Within the lower orders of society membership was restricted to very few. It would be granted mainly to symbolise loyalty. A reward for exemplary service of some kind, perhaps with one of the youth movements. Alternatively, membership was reserved for powerful family connections.

Nepotism was an institutional career track.

'It wer hit and run comrade,' the acne recovering youth announced, handing the press card back to Gates. His voice had taken on some comradely respect. 'Reet there as you can see.'

The Lancashire accent was fierce and from nearby. Gates' own roots were here in the Dales, and he could place a phrase to a village or a town with accuracy. A Lancashire accent was like that, very precise and localised. He guessed the guy came from some small rural community close by, perhaps near the large market town of Radcliffe but more likely slightly further away, towards Bury just a few miles on to the north.

Both men looked towards the crumble of rags and limbs that glistened slightly in the wan light. Gates thought the body to be that of a man.

He wanted to be sure.

The young constable would have grown up there, basic schooling, nothing by way of travel, the drudgery of a state agricultural employee awaiting his future before the attraction of authority and lure of excitement had drawn him to the vast Moss Side police training centre and the sprawling ugly mass of Manchester that lay a few miles distant.

'That guy wer walking his dog, seems like a van or truck went directly for him. High speed. Took 'em both. He wer just walking down the road from that sunken lane beyond the wood.

Knew owt about it I'd say.'

It was just speculation. He had not been at the scene long and had no idea for how much time he would be left out here in his sentry position. He was stood on the narrow road that led out of Great Lever, an unremarkable community that balanced on the lip of the valley. It was a village of sorts, established for the milling community two centuries ago and built along a single street without the benefit of design or planning. There was an ugly flat-roofed local store run as a franchise by a supermarket chain with a two-pump petrol station alongside. The village had no centre to speak of, no gathering place that would provide a clock or statute to the glorious dead to act as an historic reference point. Instead, a spired church, primary school, and community centre, all constructed from local dark gritstone were evenly spaced amongst the row of cottages over the distance of a mile or so. At either end the community withered into bleak countryside with its fields and woodland. 'No one is to go down that road,' his sergeant had told him. 'Brass are on their way, they'll deal with this, stay owt their way and do exactly what they ask.' Until now there had been no one and nothing had happened. There was no sign of the 'brass' and the locals had fled, retreating into their small homes, anxious not to draw attention to themselves.

Gates remembered this area as a kid, visiting on rare days out with his parents. It had changed. The old woodland had been savagely cut away to create open farmland. A short tramp to the east across the fields and a scramble down through the undergrowth of the valley sides would find the fast, flowing rivers of the Croal and Irwell. Close to this spot they collided in a teeming froth, tumbling past the overgrown ruins of cotton mills and abandoned pit workings. Once a beauty spot, it was now blighted by coke dust that sprinkled the trees flung by the winds from the opencast pits that worked the Manchester Coalfield. Each year more of the countryside was consumed, turned into bleak, dull-brown man-made canyons in which great mechanical teeth worked away at the earth.

'WITH SOCIALIST PRODUCTION FOR A BETTER TOMORROW', was that a Russian or Czech slogan? He could never remember. It didn't matter. Coal was in demand across the Socialist nations and coal miners were paid three times the national wage.

Gates looked a second time down the road, more carefully, and this time saw a smaller crumpled pile that was the dead animal. It rested a full twenty yards beyond the crumpled pile that was its owner, flung by the impact through the air to land there. He wasn't close enough to be sure, but there was a definite spread of crimson around the scene and most of the animal's limbs were twisted into odd angles.

Some impact. Forty miles an hour at least.

This was no accident.

Broad daylight as well.

'Mind if I take a look?' He saw the hesitation in the officer's face, prompted no doubt by the fear of harsh and unreasonable authority and he lifted a twenty-pound note from his pocket. 'I'll be very quick, I promise. Use this to treat the family.'

It was the way of the world.

It was too tempting.

'Thanks,' said the policeman, who had no family to treat.

Perhaps he had joined the police to avoid the army, thought Gates, many did. Those poor brutes conscripted into service were rotting in the Russian wars in Afghanistan, Africa and even it was rumoured on the Chinese border, locked in conflicts and bloodshed they neither understood nor cared for. He had heard the quiet rumour amongst his journalist colleagues that Soviet manpower was running low, and the Kremlin would be seeking increased support from the other Warsaw Pact nations, even the ones supposedly protected by treaty.

Was it true? He believed so.

You saw the veterans occasionally, many with devastating injuries, limbless, shocked, left largely to their own world. You knew better than to ask their story. The system laid flowers at commemorations, politicians dabbed at moist eyes and the newspapers bought out their most solemn epithets. But the grieving and rage was left for the families who wanted but received no answers.

Only the families.

'You must be very quick Comrade; there's an Incident

Team on its way,' the officer hissed in an anxious voice, 'just a couple of minutes, please.'

Gates raised his hands in an open gesture of understanding and the policeman pocketed the twenty deep into his overcoat. Together they ducked under the tape and walked briskly the few yards to the scene.

A short, determined flurry of rain driven in by the stiff breeze belched out of the valley and the cold heavy droplets smacked against the tarmac, then just as suddenly the outburst settled, to continue as a soft drizzle. Gates' hair became plastered to his forehead, water trickled down his neck. He didn't notice, too distracted, by what he was about to see.

He was fifty-seven years of age and had been a reporter all his adult life. Once he had been quite a good one. But while his best years may be behind him, the lure of the unexpected, something intriguing, even in these cautious times, where journalistic bravery was in short supply, was difficult to resist.

They reached the broken body and Gates looked down to inspect the corpse.

He was shocked. More than that he was curious.

'Now that's a mess,' he said softly, almost to himself, feeling slow excitement spread through him like a nervous thrill.

The body was that of a big man, difficult to tell whether it was muscle or fat that gave him his size. It lay face downward in an unnatural pose that was both spreadeagled and curiously foetal. The wide pool of blood that spread from beneath the shape emphasised the lifelessness of the shape.

It was badly smashed most of the bones appeared snapped and crushed. The blood was mingling with the rain to spread in a greasy dribble outward across the tarmac and the head was turned the wrong way a crushed matted dough of blood, tissue, hair, and brain matter. The one eye had been pushed out of place wrenched around to where the temple should be. It was open and staring up at the rain-filled sky like a black glass marble. One large hand, the fingers burst open stretched above the head, close by lay a thick gnarled walking stick that must have been flung from the man's grasp.

'Oh Christ,' said the constable and managed to reach the side of the road before throwing up his lunch and breakfast into the grass.

Gates crouched down closer, taking care to avoid the blood that threatened to seep under his shoes. Gates wondered what the final moments must have felt like. One moment, the soft sprinkle of rain on your face, the smell of the fields and the sound of the wind teasing the trees then, shock, a split of noise, flash, blackness, and silence.

'Do you know who it was?' he asked over his shoulder, ignoring the retching sounds and heaves that only came under control when the young lad's stomach was finally empty.

The policeman pinched his nose between thumb and finger, snorted violently and shook his head. He was wiping his mouth with the back of his hand and did not want to appear ignorant, but he had been told nothing. Just where to stand and with orders to prevent anyone using the road until someone said different. There was something about the way the corpse had been pulverised that made him feel sick again, but he worked hard to control it. He was embarrassed at his display of weakness in front of a civilian.

'Probably a quick death once he had been struck, lots of damage.' Gates was speaking mainly to himself. As a crime reporter Gates had seen his share of dead and maimed corpses. More than this callow youth in uniform. Manchester was a violent place, second only to London. 'Who found him?' he now called over his shoulder to the officer who watched him gingerly.

'Not sure Comrade.' He may have remembered Gates' generosity and felt some information was called for. 'But I believe it was an anonymous call.'

Gates pulled his phone free and took a picture.

'What are yer doing?' the officer hissed, alarmed, 'no one said anything about pictures.'

'Don't worry Comrade, I won't be using it. Just a personal record.' Gates brushed aside the complaint and took another shot from a different angle. 'No idea what happened?'

'Don't ask me Comrade, not my job to speculate.' The constable swore and hopped to one side as a mix of undetected blood and rain reached his shoe. 'Shit.' The queasiness that followed the vomiting had not left him, the pulped body was too close, and he gulped and swallowed to control the impulse to vomit again. 'What vehicle did that?' he asked.

Gates already knew, but he said nothing. There were no vehicle skid marks, therefore no brakes. There were no vehicle fluids either. An impact like that from a saloon car would collapse a panel, damage a radiator, spring a hose. Someone had pointed a heavy, very heavy vehicle at a man and a dog they knew would be there and drove it at them fast and deliberately. After being hit the body had been crushed under the wheels, probably more than once. You had to do that in a hit and run—if you needed to be absolutely certain. The impact itself, even at speed, was often not enough. Unconscious, yes, seriously hurt, certainly, but instantly dead? Not always. The only way to make sure was to crush the organs.

The dog twenty feet away was broken but basically intact. Gates assumed the initial impact had killed it. Poor brute just got in the way, he thought.

Whoever did this wanted to make sure the target was dead, beyond doubt. Why a hit and run and not a gun, why this mess? Deliberate perhaps, avoid the ballistics? Or to make it look clumsy and amateurish. There was no way to tell.

This policeman pulled on Gate's shoulder. 'Come on Comrade, let's go or there will be all sorts of trouble, for you and me.'

Gates, ignored him, clawing a few more moments to memorise the scene. He could see the man had been middle-aged and was wearing a thick expensive outdoor coat, the sort worn by the affluent during autumn country walks. Thick, well-stitched material that would hold a crushed body together preventing the flattened torso from spilling its ruined organs onto the hard surface of the road.

Just as well, Gates thought.

From what he could make out from the clothes, the pulverised body was that of a man who shared few of the hardships of everyday folk. That probably made him a person of particular interest.

Over the crest, a little way off, appeared the rhythmic strobe of blue-red-blue lights moving at speed, bouncing off the trees to form a moving tunnel of flashing light that headed their way like a wave on the contours of the road. The radio on the young policeman's lanyard chattered loudly and from the trees that lined the road came the angry raucous noise of rooks driven from their roosts by the disturbance.

Time to go.

With reluctance, Gates accepted the constable's urging to return to his position. Back at the incident tape Gates decided to wait awhile and see what happened next. With difficulty in the rain, he lit a cigarette and offered one to the kid who shook his head. Twenty pounds would go a long way beside his meagre police wages. But allowing Gates to get near the body had been a risk and Gates thanked him for his understanding.

They stood for a while, Gates smoking, the young

policeman looking around the area, a little embarrassed at his display of weakness, unsure how to reassert his authority. The opportunity was not long in coming. After a few minutes the officer stiffened and looked over Gates' shoulder. A middle-aged woman in raincoat and headscarf was cautiously approaching along the pavement. She shuffled as if trying to merge against the background and be inconspicuous, hoping no one would notice her. Gates saw that she looked worn and pinched, the coat was buttoned tight to her neck.

'What do you want?' said the policeman, moving to bar her way. 'Thee can't come this way love.' The tone was gruff but not completely unfriendly. He inclined his head to the blue metal sign in the centre of the road with the words: 'POLICE INCIDENT'.

'I-I live down theer. My home is that way.' She pointed through the incident tape. 'The bus dropped me off in town.' Her voice was a squeak of nervous explanation. 'The driver was saying the road wer blocked. I have t' get back to the house, he'll be wanting his tea.'

'He was reet. There's no way through. Police business.' The brusque manner was back in place, his voice losing the initial sympathy.

'But there is no other way through...' she began to protest, 'what's happened? Can't you take me past it?'

'That's enough, I can't. Thee'll just have to find another route or wait.' His tone had become impatient. He didn't like his orders being challenged. Bullying women pedestrians was more his style, thought Gates, obviously he had already forgotten what he looked like a few minutes previously.

She looked at the policeman for a moment. Gates wondered whether she was going to protest further and plead more. But he saw the defeat in her eyes, and she obviously thought better of it, there was no point in arguing and she turned reluctantly back towards the village. The shopping bag looked uncomfortably heavy, and the woman wore shoes that were flimsy and soaked.

The policeman shrugged. Indifferent to her problem. How she returned home or prepared her evening meal was no concern of his.

The rain had eased further. Above them only a pale puddle of brightness behind the low cloud now resisted evenings onset. From the chimneys of houses thin drifts of charcoal smoke had begun to rise into the sky and the smell of burning wet coal drifted over them. No one had come out to see what was going on, investigate the presence of the police cars and the white incident van that was cordoning the scene around the body.

Thin beads of rainwater dripped from the brim of the officer's helmet.

There had been no offer of tea to relieve the damp chill from the locals. The Police used to be popular in rural parts. Years before the constable was a Friday evening gleam in his father's eye, Gates thought, cordon duty would be relieved with offers of cake and drink, empathy from locals who saw the police as part of their community.

People kept their distance now.

If only this kid knew, he thought.

Authority was something to be wary of and avoid.

'No description of the vehicle?' asked Gates.

'Not that they have told me Comrade.'

Every curtain in the nearby houses was firmly closed and Gates knew they would remain so.

There was nothing further to be learnt here. Gates was irritated with himself. He realised he had come to the wrong side of the cordon. In the fading light he could see there was more activity on the far side of the body. Forensics and detectives had arrived from the opposite direction of the road. He could see two figures in white suits with hoods and a group of three plain clothed officers who stood a little beyond them. They were too far away for Gates to see any detail and he briefly flirted with the idea of heading back to his car and working his way across to the far side. But he dismissed it quickly. The only route was through country lanes and by the time he had negotiated the local traffic build up caused by the incident and then made his way through the countryside to arrive from the other direction, it would be dark. There would be little to see, and the police would have tightened control of the area.

He cursed his luck at his decision and may now have to find any further information the hard way.

He had one last idea. A piece of information that may be useful. Something worth knowing.

'Do you know who is investigating?'

The officer brightened at this question. He *knew* he should not be talking to the press. Punishment for giving information to anyone was severe. But hey, this guy was a member of the Party, a loyal citizen like himself. Anyway, the press in these parts were not really controversial, they reported events faithfully impartially. Not like those foreign papers, the ones from America, Canada, and the few neutral bits of Europe, now he would say nothing to them, they just print ugly lies about the country and its friends and allies. But this guy came from the *Manchester Herald*. The *Herald* was a solid strong paper with honest national values that could be trusted.

'London's taken it on I heard. Special Branch are sending someone senior to take charge. He's on his way up by chopper. In the meantime, local boys have been told to keep the scene preserved.' He jerked his head towards the group of officers and white suits who stood in conference close to the body that had become a dim ugly lump in the afternoon gloom. 'Make sure no one, but no one goes past you.' He remembered the words his sergeant had said to him. 'This is one for the Specials, don't mess up, we want no complaints from up top.'

'Comrade Assistant Commissioner Hallam will be giving the orders.' He gave the information with some pride. Tonight, in the barracks after supper when he had properly dried out, the officer would sit on the end of his bed, polishing his boots and would tell the story to his mates with delight. One of the first on the scene, he would proclaim. There at the scene, when the most powerful policemen in the country arrived.

He would obviously keep silent about the bribe from the reporter and the loss of control of his stomach.

The radio crackled and he fumbled the earpiece working it more firmly into his lobe. From somewhere a superior was issuing instructions.

Gates thanked the constable, said goodbye, and turned away thrusting his hands back deep into his raincoat pocket. The police officer retrieved a battery-operated blue flashing beacon from the side of the road which he carefully placed on the centre of the carriageway and switched on; the rhythmic blue strobe growing stronger in the falling gloom. When darkness came, he did not want the same roadside fate befalling him from a pissed-up local full of beer or vodka.

Gates slowly returned down the road back towards the edge of the village and where he had parked the battered Fiat 124.

From somewhere behind him, a little distant, came the clatter of a generator being started, an incident tent being erected. Shouts and calls of more men being directed.

He paused.

His brain was telling him to think a little more about how he had come to be at the scene.

The tip-off of a fatal hit and run had come at 2:10 pm. The telephone call had come straight to his desk at the *Herald*. A good, experienced reporter who never lost sight of the basics, he had glanced at the clock and noted the time. He did so again and saw it was now 4:10 pm. The officer told him he had been there since 2:40 pm, but he also said that he was not the first on the scene. A patrol car had responded initially, and he, the officer, had been drafted in as back up to relieve them, scooped up from his patrol duty in Chatterton as rapid uniform reinforcement to do leg work on an incident cordon. Gates subtracted the timings in his head. Supposing it took thirty minutes to round up and deploy the foot soldiers after the patrol cars had responded, that meant the first response vehicles were discovering the body at about the same time as someone was making a phone call to Harry Gates' desk at the *Herald*.

Possibly the call had been made to his desk even slightly before.

By whom?

Why would they tip off a journalist? And why him personally and not simply ring the news desk? Why did they want him there so early in the incident, immediately after it had happened?

The call had been anonymous, quick, untraceable. Someone who probably knew the telephones into the *Herald* were monitored. Just a male voice, accented but not local, somewhere further away. More Yorkshire. On a hunch Gates was going with Leeds, but that was a big city with its own variations of accent. He could be wrong.

*Someone wanted him here to see this. Was he part of some plan?*

The people who lived here were farm workers mostly, mixed with old folk who had managed to hang onto their homes, despite the land and property re-purposing laws. No one around here was going to say a word to him or talk to the police. It was a closed rural neighbourhood that protected itself, kept its head down, didn't make waves.

In these parts, Manchester, under ten miles away, was a foreign country.

Soon the police would begin door to door enquiries seeking information and witnesses.

There wouldn't be any. Information or witnesses.

Probably why whoever was responsible decided on this location and this method.

So, *who* called him at almost exactly the time the person on the road was being rammed by a large vehicle?

His own car was close now, close enough to see the edges of the doors that glowed crimson with rust.

There was another piece of information that was of interest to Gates.

Hallam.

Hallam was a Special Branch officer. Senior and clever. He reported to superiors far away in London where he prowled the corridors of real power. A road traffic accident or even an average murder was of no interest to this man. Politics and subversion were his area.

Not a man to get on the wrong side of, particularly with the anti-sedition laws as they were. Highly driven and ruthless. Certain people thrive in authoritarian societies. They relish the order, the ability to make decisions in the polar world of black and white. Hallam was one of those. Gates knew him only by reputation. As the chief crime reporter on a major regional newspaper for fifteen years you get to know a lot of people in the security world. Hallam moved in the rarefied upper atmosphere of the powerful elites. He was a watch dog of the States' secret affairs whose brief fell across the whole of the state security community and, it was rumoured, he had the ear of those far beyond the country's shores. Even more senior officers moved carefully in his presence.

Strictly speaking terrorism fell within Gates' reporting responsibilities, but both he and his editor knew better than to bother the paper's readership with reports on the occasional nuisance blasts at barracks, power shortages and ambushes on military patrols in the north. Such news travelled in careful hushed messages between people who trusted each other. Somehow the people knew but no one need admit to reading about it in a newspaper.

A wolfish grey dog, its long pink tongue lolling wetly, began to follow him at a short distance. Its moist snout began twitching and sniffing close, trying to sense whether he was a source of food.

No, the *Herald* did not report the actions of rebels; its staff, like Gates, all carried their party cards.

But this still begged the question...if Hallam and Special Branch were overseeing the investigation—

Then who was the body lying on the ground?

Did Gates want to know more? He wasn't sure he did.

He was thinking about this as he started the engine and began to drive away. On his left he began to pass the woman moving slowly dragging her shopping back into the centre of the village. He hesitated, sighed, and began to pull over. The dog had transferred its attention to her. The traffic would be bad, the roads narrow, and he guessed it would take him an hour to work the detour.

He lent across and wound down the window and called across to her. 'Hello love. Hop in, I'll take you home. I am sure there is a route we can use.'

She hesitated, unused to the kindness of strangers, but the hesitation was brief. She squeezed herself and her shopping into the small front seat of the Fiat and the smell of wet wool and old vodka drifted across to him. Pushing the car into gear they drove away in a cloud of blue exhaust smoke.

## JAMES MACLAREN

The hungry dog realising their escape briefly growled in disappointment, and stared with suspicious wet eyes before loping away, returning to its surly search for food.

***

# CHAPTER TWO

*I don't want flowers*

**The Manchester Herald Newspaper**

THE NEWSROOM HAD THE look of a football stadium after the final whistle when the players and crowd had drifted away leaving only grounds staff to sort through the debris. It was past six o'clock. Too early for the cleaners and bins and floors were overflowing with lunch debris, paper cups and screwed up balls of copy paper. Most of the hacks had filed their copy and drifted away for the evening, except for the sports staff who worked hours no one outside their team could understand. A few researchers and assistants were still at their desks buried in searches of the Internet or scurrying around with paper and data disks. The large open plan area was strip lit from heavy fluorescent fittings that buzzed and hung from the ceiling on chains, functional furniture was arranged the length of the room in identical lines with partitions that formed small cubicles and the floor was covered with grey carpet tiles worn shiny by heavy footfall. Two noticeboards ran the length of one wall, although

Gates had never seen anyone pin anything to them or even pause to read any of the yellowing paper. The office chairs were old and creaked horribly when sat upon, unequal to the punishment of careless use.

Gates noticed the glass fronted offices of the editor and the censors on the far side of the open plan suite were still lit. That was not especially unusual, he thought, but something about the day's events made him think about why. Inside, under the lights he could see his shirt-sleeved editor, young and harassed, prowling his floor space, a mobile phone pressed against the side of his face. A man who lived alongside stress as intimately as a lover sharing his bed and destined to die young nursing the paradox that came from balancing personal preservation with a duty to the truth.

Looking into the glass fronted office, it crossed his mind whether something was already known about where he had been and what he had seen. What if…what if… But he decided to dismiss the idea as too fanciful, even for these cautious times. There was caution and there was paranoia. Even in a society made heavy with the weight and reach of the Party, the Party that demanded so much knowledge and obedience from its citizens, it remained possible to operate unnoticed in the shadows of the bureaucracies with their suspicions and rivalries. Even the efficiency of the surveillance state they all inhabited was unlikely to have translated the events of the afternoon into a flag against his activities—at least not yet. But Gates walked a line, and he knew this.

His own cubicle was halfway down the newsroom on the outside end of a line of three similar positions and next to a window. Not that this offered much of a privilege, the window at the end of his desk was long, installed at ceiling height and frosted. It was on the wrong side of the building to catch any morning sunlight. The unloved spider plant inherited from a departing colleague that hung precariously to life at the edge of his desk was a daily reminder of this.

Tossing his car keys onto the desktop he shrugged off his wet coat and draped it over his chair. He groaned realising his shirt felt damp, water must have soaked through the outer garment's shoulders. Outside, dusk had fallen across Manchester and with the approaching darkness came heavy drops of rain that smacked against the glass. Flicking the desk lamp on he saw the half dozen yellow sticky notes with untidy biro writing randomly attached to the desk and he settled himself into the awful swivel chair moving the half-filled paper cup of stale coffee into the bin. The chair gave the usual groan of protest, and he leaned forward to peer at the notes wondering if he should be interested in any of them.

From across the room in the direction of the sports team there was a yell of laughter and triumph, someone winning a casual bet or a jocular argument between friends. Keep it down someone demanded, an irritated complaint, I'm on the phone. Get a life Comrade, came the good-natured reply.

'How did it go?'

The voice came from across the desk, and he realised that Lucy was still working. A round young face peered round at him from across a large computer monitor the dimensions of which easily hid her. She was diminutive and of uncertain shape due to the large baggy roll neck woollens she favoured wearing whether winter or summer and shoulder length chestnut hair fell loose over her shoulders. Her dark eyes were set above rosy cheeks and they peered through thick framed round spectacles balanced on a pert pretty nose to give her a geeky and cute look. Pinned through the wool of her sweater the small red enamel *Komsomol* badge she always wore, shone like a bright faithful star on her breast.

It was a useful reminder. *Be careful what you say and who you say it to.*

'Sorry love didn't see you there, what's going on? Any reason for you to still be working?'

'No, just tidying up some text in a piece.' She shook her head, her hair dancing like a loose curtain. High cheekbones with smooth skin that dimpled when she pulled a face. 'Thought I would hang around and see what you came back with.'

That was one way of putting it, he thought. She was nice-looking, round youthful features unsullied by age that needed no effort for the skin was still smooth and unlined. But the small enamel badge told its own story. Gates knew she was in her late twenties, and in her bag was the same Communist Party card he carried in his pocket. The difference was, he thought, she was the real deal. A millennial who knew the world only as it was now. No one is rewarded with Party membership just for being a good student Communist.

Gates decided to be coy and see how much she wanted to know. 'You work too hard. You should relax more.'

Lucy made a brushing dismissive gesture with her hand, as if to say: *you know how it is.*

'So, what was it?' she asked, returning to the question.

Her smiling eyes held kindness, she was always friendly, the cheerful dutiful junior, they were colleagues although he was twenty-five years her senior, both Party members who had served loyally in their roles. But was there an edge to her look that made him cautious, something inquiring beyond professional curiosity? She had been there when he took the anonymous call. It occurred to him that he might be walking into a trap with her questions. Lucy was a believer, after all. He would be wise to take no chances. The unwary answer could quickly ring a lot of bells.

*Great Lever, you need to be there. Something you need to see.* He didn't have the chance to ask who was calling. Instinctively he had listened reaching only for a pencil.

'Just a hit and run, no ID. Cops not really giving anything away. I guess we'll have to wait for an announcement.'

*There'll be a cover-up. Your chance to get some facts right.* Then the line had clicked shut and Gates was relieved he had not had time or been asked to respond. He had said nothing that a transcript might choose to construe against him.

Perhaps it was his imagination and he tried to banish the idea. Being a member of the Party does not automatically make you an informer, there was no reason to think she considered him anything other than a loyal comrade—which he was. She looked at him for a moment, the eyes behind her glasses cool. For a moment he thought irrationally of Kate. What did *she* have to do with anything? Nothing except recalling the cruel appraisal that she used to expose his weaknesses, lay the past and his failure bare to mock him. That was not Lucy, that was a wife from before that used him, asserted her superiority to reduce him to the status of acolyte. Then Lucy smiled in reply and her gaze dropped. She switched off the terminal in front of her. The enquiry was over, and it was time to change the subject.

'A crowd have headed off to the pub, the game in Moscow is showing,' —she reached for her coat on the back of her chair——'the sports desk has put some dosh behind the bar. Will you go?'

Gates hesitated then remembered the fixture. Manchester City were playing a semi-final in Moscow against Spartak Moscow. He was not really into football, especially the major international competitions which to his mind were rigged anyway. One of the two Moscow teams had won the European Championship for the last five seasons, probably because they always had the best players in Europe and never seemed to play away from home—neither of which seemed likely to be a coincidence. If that were not enough it would be a brave set of officials who disappointed a home crowd. *The emperor's new clothes*, no one says anything. Still, the match was a big event, yesterday's television had shown the Manchester team heading off to the airport with the professional swagger and large smiles that went with the job, fans and reporters lining the route cheering them on. Gates would happily bet everything he owned that they would return tomorrow after a glorious defeat. The hacks on the sports desk across the room would write of a thrilling plucky game that the visitors were unlucky to lose, but which ultimately the better prepared and more talented Moscow outfit deserved to win.

Why does socialism find football so compelling, he wondered? A game that attracts tribalism, collects loyalty in adversity…and more. It's not just a game, it's a culture that with its egalitarian ideals can draw allegiance, he decided.

He shook his head and feigned disappointment. 'Sounds fun but I have a few things to do.' He thought he should probably go. Non-attendance at semi-professional social gatherings could attract attention, but his mind was elsewhere.

'What about you?'

Lucy had zipped her full-length coat with its fake fur collar.

'No, off to cover the Regional Party meeting. They're electing new representatives to the City Council. It starts in an hour.' She sounded genuinely regretful at missing the match and socialising with colleagues. She checked and closed her bag. 'Bad timing, but duty first.'

Gates managed not to outwardly grimace. To call the arrival of new council representatives an election was a stretch. There was unlikely to be any opposition to the nominations.

'Oh, bad luck, but that's important work, I hope it goes well.'

She smiled a, we-both-know-that's-not-true smile, and said: 'Well goodnight, Comrade, enjoy your evening.'

They knew each other well, however, end of day formality in the office was normal.

'Yes Comrade, good luck with your assignment. I will read it tomorrow no doubt.'

He plugged a note of enthusiasm into his voice and watched her exit down the central isle fluttering small words of farewell to the few remaining occupants busy under the fluorescent lights as she went.

Lucy was a team player and popular with all of the newsroom.

Gates sat there for a short while and looked at his emails, mostly circulars and announcements of the type he did not need. He thought about his earlier trip to the Irwell Valley and the scene of the hit and run. His mind was uneasy. Was he supposed to do anything? He phoned the police information press desk and received a polite but firm reply from the information officer that: *…regarding the 'incident' the* *investigation is ongoing.* He added that there might be a press release in a *day or so.* Gates got the impression that any form of press reporting was not necessary—or probably welcome. There was no more to be done and he decided to wait, wait for whatever came next. With a final look towards the editorial team offices and the harassed editor glued to his phone he switched off his own computer and desk lamp. Then with a series of less enthusiastic good nights than those offered by Lucy he headed out into the Manchester rain to find his way home.

HE walked quickly out of the building and across the wet street towards the open ground that served as a car park. A car horn sounded close by, and he looked behind him back across the darkened road. In the shadow of a shop doorway, he saw a muffled figure of a man in black coat and baseball cap standing, sheltering from the gentle fog of rain, but who seemed to be looking his way. Gates stopped, somehow alerted by the figure, and from the safety of the far pavement tried to make out the dark shape.

Then a bus passed between them and after it had gone, he saw the man had emerged from the doorway and with collar turned against the rain and hands deep in pockets was slowly walking away from him, his shape soon lost from the orange puddles of the streetlights by the hurrying crowd.

'FLOWERS?' called a middle-aged woman from behind her cart of limp looking roses. She was sheltering beneath the fading green awning buried in an old shapeless overcoat watching Gates leave his car. 'For your girlfriend?'

Gates called back with a grin, 'I'll be so lucky.' He had parked the Fiat which creaked with tiredness on the road and hurried through the rain across to the row of Victorian terraces converted long ago and in which his three-room apartment, shared with an extended family of mice, was perched on the top floor.

The woman had offered her flowers from the opposite side of the street where there was a small untidy park into which no one with sense would venture at night. At the entrance along the railings were a line of flower stalls or shoe stalls or tables sheltered under faded canvas of whatever pieces of cheap household wares could be found and sold. Every day they were manned by the platoon of wizened and weather-worn women who eked out a top up to the state pension that froze them in impecunious circumstances. The Neighbourhood Committee of local party busy bodies had been trying to get them moved for what seemed like years objecting to their ant-social presence. They kept drifting back and a mixture of resignation and apathy meant they were now settled as a permanent feature.

There was a cackle of a laugh from the women in reply to Gates' riposte. The stall owners had seen Gates enter and leave the terrace a thousand times and never with a woman. He had no need of flowers nor for that matter the jumble and junk heaped on the wooden carts. But there was no harm in trying.

They sat on their wooden stools and watched him fumble for a key on the unlit doorstep.

Above him a few windows were lit. In the flat beneath his own he could see the shadows of a man and a woman moving behind thin curtains. On the ground floor the sound of a classical radio concert faintly floated out, a melancholy piece possibly Chopin, he wasn't sure. From somewhere came the thunder of a toilet flush and the hideous gurgle of pipes obliterating the piano recital's light cadence as the plumbing drained through the building.

Inside, the hallway was dark too, the light bulb overhead had popped three weeks ago. He went through the post peering close to filter out the two letters and a marketing circular addressed to himself. The letters went into his jacket pocket and the glossy circular he chucked on the hall table pile which would grow until someone had the wit to dispose of it in bulk.

The hallway and staircase smelt of Jayes cleaning fluid, cabbage, and curry, following the aroma led him to the stairs, the cord carpet underfoot was worn thin and shiny. As he passed the first floor came the sound of the couple who lived beneath him their shadows now turned into words, arguing, their baby's cries unheard. A woman's voice: *You lazy shit, help me. Pick her up.* Her husband's angry reply: *Go to hell, I've been working all day, she wants you.* From somewhere else far away a dog yapped, its cries for attention universally ignored. The overcrowded apartments had long ago gathered immunity to the sounds of frustration and anger.

From there past two sharp corners and after an ill-lit ascent, he left the couple's harsh words behind and found his way to his front door at the top of the house.

There wasn't much inside, a small sitting room with a worn and gruesome sofa, a chipped bureau, a few meaningless pictures, a flat pack bookcase and a large old television. Two doors led off to the bedroom with its iron bedstead and the small bathroom, while through a partitioned arch on the other side off the room was a kitchenette.

In the eighties, he had bought the house as a renovation project in the Whally Range area of the city, intending to renovate one floor for himself and let the rest of the property out as apartments. It had been a fashionable area, very up and coming, and he had been pleased to have made a sound investment. Over time the law had changed, slow incremental changes to private ownership that eventually required him to handover the property for families. Soon after, the street had turned to hard times, drab and tired, a place for workers, most of them a payday away from ruin.

At least he had managed to keep this top floor retreat as his own.

In the kitchen he found vodka and poured a generous measure into a thick tumbler with chipped glass and returned to switch on the television before dropping himself onto a sagging sofa. The screen gave out a blue grey glow, there was a nightly news programme playing, in which the newsreader sat in front of a large graphic of the country its borders filled in with the colours and shape of the Union Flag. The dark suited announcer read the items in a languid Oxbridge voice that was like soft wood being polished.

*...pollution was falling, air quality has continued to rise.*

Gates inwardly scoffed at this; the low shrouded haze settled above the city that greeted the morning sun each day suggested differently. People would believe it, he thought, because people believed when it was too hard to argue.

*The Soviet ambassador at the United Nations had complained vigorously in a security council meeting about American naval aggression in the Mediterranean, after Soviet Navy vessels had chased off one of its nuclear submarines from near the shared Cyprus naval facility.*

The nightly obsession with America and its aggressive interference in the affairs of the Pact continued.

*...the prime minister is preparing with cabinet colleagues for next month's Warsaw summit and is being urged to press for a stronger say in the use of British troops being used in the Alliance wars.*

Good luck with that, thought Gates.

*...the date has been agreed between Buckingham Palace and the Supreme Council for the coronation of the new King which will take place on 1st May next year. Our reporter is...*

It was remarkable, thought Gates: No one has ever really

questioned how the Royal Family had survived the reforms and changes of three decades. In a socialist utopia, how does such a symbol of national class privilege remain as the Head of State? Perhaps some things were just too embedded into a nation's DNA to dispense with. What else? Fish and chips? Soap operas. These and other odd quirky aspects of British life seemed immovable and weirdly remained. Yet, he thought, much had disintegrated and turned to dust under the force of ideological change.

The BBC news was longer these days, announcement after announcement. Foreign news with reports of threats by enemies of the state and its Warsaw Pact allies and then wondrous revelations of technical achievement in the science labs of universities, dramatic increases in industrial production, fresh trade and economic alliances which brought a promised horizon of peace and prosperity ever closer. All read with the same measured educated tones and the pure well-dressed vowels of Shaw and Kipling. As the newscaster's words filled the room, he found himself thinking about how he had arrived at this place in his life. The decisions, mistakes and events that nudged, shaped, or properly shoved him into this existence.

A car pulled up outside with a single high-pitched squeal of worn brakes. The engine stuttered to a halt, and he could hear the jabbering of voices and the buzz of a doorbell that wasn't his.

In eighty-nine he recalled the same newscaster voices

dryly bringing news of the first Soviet navy ships to be stationed in the south coast ports. The Future Cooperation talks taking place in London shortly afterwards and then in ninety-four the news that NATO was to be disbanded. The Americans forced to withdraw back across the Atlantic Ocean.

At the time such developments excited him, and he wrote as much in his daily column. He remembered an earlier time in eighty-seven, when as a young ambitious reporter, at the house of a Party mentor whose word and favour he fawned over, he received the invitation to meet and shake Premier Chernenko's hand during the Soviet leader's visit to the Labour Party Conference. Gates had preened with pride at the recognition. The night he was introduced he had shared his privilege—drinking heavily with other journalists and activists—and his alcohol mused thoughts had been contented: *The benefits that would come now true socialism prevails. Being part of building a better society. More just, kinder, honest, and equitable.*

You never reach the horizon.

There was some sort of argument taking place on the doorstep below his window. Raised voices and the sound of a milk bottle smashing. Then a banging of car doors and the breathy hoarse cough of a tired engine being bullied away down the road, gears grinding as it gathered momentum.

*In other news the new Soviet nuclear-powered aircraft carrier Admiral Kastonov is exercising with British and French warships in the Atlantic. The Atlantic Fleet flagship will pay a fraternal visit to the French port of Brest when the exercises conclude...*

He left the television on and sipped his vodka remembering the letters in his pocket. There was a surge of excitement, an electric shock of anticipation at the realisation when he saw the one was hand-written and carried a Polish postmark.

Sophie.

He finished the glass slapping it down on the coffee table and ripped open the thin air mail envelope and fished out the three flimsy sheets of loopy biro writing. His excitement was child-like, the earlier dour thoughts that had consumed him briefly vanished as he contemplated news from his daughter.

"Dear Dad..."

She did not write often, or maybe she did, and the letters just did not get through the system. He had no way of telling nor any idea whether his letters reached her or not—she never referred to them or made mention of his news. It was supposed to be a university, a cultural programme, *Sociology, and the Marxist Way*. Such a description was generous.

"*Hope you are well...*"

He did not count the weeks or the months anymore. Youthful exuberance and idealism on a student newspaper. He had warned her, but young people seldom listen do they. Unafraid, and they think they can change the world and the world won't bite back. They choose their friends with carelessness, their causes with fearlessness and their words with naivety.

He had thought like that once.

Different times, different directions.

"*Life is really good here, food is great, and I still have the same room mate Cecile from Oslo...*"

One idea too many and that was that. Summoned to explain and selected for re-education. In theory a course—in practise detention. Was it three years? He thought for a moment and realised it was.

"*...learnt so much here, the tutors are excellent.*"

And so, it went on. He read the rest dully learning nothing and a feeling of numbness and helplessness chased away the excitement of receiving her letter. Campus life, the routine, meals with friends and tutors, evening quizzes, sporting competitions, so little time to relax but she didn't mind and how helpful and kind everyone was. She was sorry she did not write more but she was so very busy.

Always a letter, he thought. A rare Skype call and never an email. He had asked her once why? but she had not answered.

He crossed to the window and glanced out into the road below, He could have sworn he saw the silhouette of the man earlier in the rain. He moved the curtain gently to get a better angle, but when he looked again, he saw nothing.

Hours later in the darkness of the night when sleep would not come, he lay there on the sunken mattress in a room not much bigger than the bed itself and wondered when they would let her go and what she would have become when they did. The images circled around his mind until his thoughts burned out and a restless sleep finally prevailed.

So absorbed was he by the descent of his thoughts that he did not hear the quiet shuffling outside and it would be morning before he realised that the top landing outside his attic flat had been host to the soft careful footfall of a visitor.

HE woke at eight, remembered where he was and rubbed his eyes. They felt like he had grit in them, the night had barely refreshed him. When finally, sleep had come it had been filled with the dream of Sophie, a much younger Sophie, exhausting, full of energy and fun. She was asking him questions about the world and life, puzzling over his explanations as she sat in his lap sucking her thumb contemplating and sometimes puzzled by his answers. Then the image began to fade into a tunnel he could not pull it back from, he reached desperately with his fingers to bring her to him, trying to find a limb to cling on to, secure her, but it was useless, and her face became blurred and then white, and the cold companionship of morning crept back.

The apartment felt chilly and in bare feet he padded across the thin carpet to the kitchenette where he flicked the switch on the electric kettle. He could see from the small window that the day was grey and overcast, in the direction of the city a haze hung low. Despite the BBC assurances he guessed the air quality would be poor and that he should really wear a mask.

On the far side of the street below the woman were already back at their crude wooden stalls organising and arranging bunches of flowers amongst piles of household bric-a-brac they had collected from somewhere. For no reason he noticed a man in a leather jacket and baseball cap absently rummaging through the boxes of plastic and metal and then the call of the boiling water took him back to his morning routine.

Mixing some coffee granules in a cup he headed to the bathroom. He ran the tap for a minute before lukewarm water began to flow and he leaned towards the mirror while he waited. What he saw wasn't pleasing, there was a pallor and blotching of age and the unchecked effect of gravity about his features. Without enthusiasm he lathered his face with soap and began to shave, carefully skirting the rash of skin on his neck rubbed raw by his shirt.

In his bedroom he dressed, finding a clean shirt, knotting a red-brown tie, and pulling on the same fifteen-year-old jacket and scuffed shoes from yesterday. He was at the door reaching for the handle when the phone rang. He hesitated, but only briefly then turned to pick up the receiver from the wall.

'This is Gates, Comrade.'

'Hello Harry.' The female voice was Lucy, behind her he could hear the chatter and noise of the newsroom. TV monitors, hum of conversations and a shouted order demanding attention. 'Are you on your way to the office soon?'

'Yes, but is anything wrong?' Gates reached into his pocket

for his third cigarette of the morning wondering why she was calling him at home.

'Not wrong, important more like. There's a press conference at Police HQ. It's been called at short notice for nine-thirty. They went directly to the editor sounds like an important announcement and they're rounding up the hacks. I think Comrade Miles will want you to attend. He was looking for you. I told him you knew and were already on your way. Was that, okay?'

Gates thought of the young editor already pacing his office irritated with a day that had barely begun.

The hit and run? He wondered.

'Yes, thank you, on my way now, I was just leaving in any case. Oh, can you tell them I called in, let them know I'll be at the police headquarters.' He was genuinely grateful. If the editor was looking for you it was good to know. She didn't have to call, others wouldn't.

Lucy promised she would.

He replaced the receiver and spun back towards the front door, fumbled for his key only to drop it on the mat. It was just as well he did because as he knelt down, he saw the cheap white envelope that had been slid under the door in the night. He looked at it for a second, without quite knowing what to think.

Not regular post. Too early, and anyway post was delivered centralised downstairs.

Then the urgency of getting to the meeting caused him to

scoop it up and put it in the inside pocket of his jacket and he hurried from his flat, past the flower sellers and over to the Fiat that sat in a defeated squat at the side of the road.

It was starting to rain. The man in the baseball cap watched him silently, then hunched his shoulders and buried his hands in his pockets to walk across the dog fouled park.

***

# CHAPTER THREE

*Learn, learn, and learn*

IN NINETEEN SEVENTY-NINE HARRY GATES was twenty-three years old. He had a new journalism degree from a northern university, one hundred pounds in his bank account and an angry sick widower of a father whose steel worker pension kept him in cigarettes, food, an abundance of self-pity but nothing else. He had one other thing: a job offer from the *Daily Mirror* in London. He carried the letter in his pocket wherever he went and probably read it thirty times a day.

It was a time, Gates remembered, of economic darkness, when securing a job was no mean feat and he had sufficient wits to understand that it was less his academic achievement, an average degree from a middle-rank university, than his undergraduate activism which had secured him such a coveted appointment. A visceral zeal for political reform had caused most of his youthful energy to be spent advancing the message of the Socialist Workers Party to anyone that would listen and to many that didn't. An opportunity to work at a London paper was in most part recognition for his political loyalty, a reward, an invitation to contribute to the struggle against a new political order. The arrival of a dangerous reforming leader armed with an ideology that would be hard to confront had left him angry and frustrated. Rather than simply fume, this job would give him a platform reaching far beyond student meeting halls. Within days of the letter arriving, he was on the train south to London and ready to serve his new masters.

Now he was far older, and the world looked a good deal uglier.

In the driver's seat of his car, he opened the letter and read the short, typewritten note. He thought for a moment and then tore the single sheet up into the tiniest pieces he could before replacing them in the envelope which went back into his inside pocket.

Outside on the street, one of the women at her stall was singing loudly, her crackly old voice still strangely sweet as she entertained her friends and tried to attract passing interest.

Proper disposal would have to take place later.

Thankfully, the car started, it could be tricky on damp mornings. But today the cylinders belched into life with a throaty cough. By driving quickly and closing his mind to the avoidance of potholes, he made the police press conference with barely five minutes to spare.

A STATUE to the city's war dead guarded the entrance to the

police headquarters. The bronze block of a soldier flinging himself into battle stood four metres high. On the plinth black leaf script set out in neat rows the names of those fallen in the service of the nation. The last three names were bright and new, having only been added in the last month. Those entering the building would have to divide in waves to pass round the monument at the base of which were heaped the fresh wreaths of poppies piled in a red blanket that rippled in the autumn air in grateful tribute.

The building was a brutalist monolith that sat on the edge of the city's civic administration and shopping complex, a warren of tired concrete and dirty glass. By day the secret squares, dead ends and grimy passages were colonised by gulls, at night they were home to rough sleepers. Away from the immediate police precinct, graffiti provided urban decoration.

Inside the building, Gates showed his press card at reception, signed his name, and hung the visitors pass around his neck. He followed the small group of other arriving hacks up the stairs to the second floor and the press briefing room.

A smartly dressed attractive female official in pencil skirt and white blouse stood at the door checking names from a clipboard. She flashed a business smile at Gates and pointed towards double doors.

The briefing facility was really a large repurposed and windowless conference room, reorganised when necessary to accommodate press announcements. It had bare walls save for a line of police posters arranged in a gallery that urged citizens to report suspicious behaviour, donate to police charities and set out as a reminder to the general population, as if any were needed, of the frightening prison tariffs for offences such as pickpocketing, shoplifting, and black market selling.

It was from here that the police announced significant arrests or briefed the press pack on forthcoming operations. Today the room was a little over half full, the various reporters had spread themselves out across the dozen rows of seats, with companionable nods to each other as newcomers arrived. The mood, Gates detected, was not brimming with excitement at the summons.

Stupid, thought Gates. We're all going to write much the same thing. But he sat apart, nonetheless. It was preferable to the combination of zealot like applause or dry smirking that accompanied official events such as this. His paper, *The Herald*, was firmly in the zealot brigade and lyrics that did not sing in harmony with the tune did not sing for long.

Waiting for the conference to begin, he took out his phone and read the online edition from last night searching for Lucy's piece on the city government congress meeting. He knew she would have worked hard on it and wanted to be able to congratulate her when he got back to the office. Technically it was a strong piece, tightly constructed with a good word range and descriptive flair that took a dry unappealing subject and gave it some life. The facts it contained were predictable, infant mortality rate down, prosperity rising, education standards improving, and it included news that four talented and deserving new members had been appointed by the Northern Party Congress to the Municipal Committee of Manchester.

The only thing Gates actually believed was that coal production was up—any visit to the vast opencast scars to the north of the city could confirm that. Nevertheless, she was a good kid and under the circumstances that made her what she was, deserved credit for the efforts. He knew the editorial staff liked her work, she never gave the censors a problem, and she would be promoted soon.

The opening of the side door interrupted his thoughts and four senior officers in uniform accompanied by a lone civilian filed into the room and took their seats on the slightly elevated stage area. They sat behind a long desk in front of the force emblem, that was an impressive example of socialist heraldry comprising a vector drawn family, laurels, hammer with sickle and a star. It filled a large backdrop behind them.

From the platform one of the uniformed officers cleared his throat.

'Good morning Comrades: welcome to this Greater Manchester Police Force press conference and thank you all for coming.'

The opening remarks came from the most highly ranked officer, an assistant chief constable, seated in the centre of the panel, an officer known slightly to Gates. He was somewhere in his late forties, lean and fit looking, smart in his crisp white uniform shirt. He introduced his colleagues sitting either side of him, all of whom except the one civilian Gates also knew.

Party, Gates assumed. A high-ranking official, the unseen political hand of the Greater Manchester Police, attending to quietly guide proceeding and remind anyone who needed to be reminded who was in charge.

No Hallam, he thought. Somehow Gates had connected this press conference with the events of yesterday and now wondered whether he may have been mistaken to have done so.

The senior officer began to speak in a loud authoritative voice that suggested good news, an important success that people would want to know about.

'Today, I have an important announcement to make. Yesterday two police tactical teams from the Northern Terrorist Command supported by undercover officers raided a country house outside the village of Lydgate forty miles east of Manchester. This raid,' he continued, his tone confident and pleased, 'was as the result of a long-term surveillance operation that has been conducted jointly with specialist officers from other forces and other agencies. A number of specialist military units were also on stand-by and available.'

Gates thought how youthful the officer looked, how pink and without blemish his cheeks were. Chosen for the camera, he thought. Is it only me who has noticed the tiny beads of sweat which followed his hairline?

He's lying, thought Gates, but knew he could not fathom the reason.

A murmur went around the room, the assembled reporters muttering excitedly at this news. The officer allowed the announcement to sink in, ensuring he had their full attention.

'The raid was designed to trap and arrest dissident terrorist elements who have been preparing further acts of terror in their campaign against police, military, and civilian targets across the north of the country. Intelligence has suggested that their latest target was a planned attack on the nuclear reprocessing facility at Sellafield on the Cumbrian coast.'

First, he had heard of a terror campaign across the country, thought Gates. It had the impressive urgency of immediate fear and threat, but that very eagerness to shock at once, in Gates' eyes made it suspect. There were incidents, some serious even, but a campaign? There was little evidence of that. In any case what would be the point of attacking the vast atomic complex that was home to the reactor waste of most of Europe's nuclear power plants. That would be a mindless act of sabotage without rationality. Perhaps exactly the perception the authorities wish to give.

The public need to understand that terrorists were irrational, dangerous, a threat to order. While the government and police were good, dependable safe.

This was usual and predictable messaging.

'During the raid, a significant exchange of gunfire between a terrorist group and the security forces took place.' He paused the explanation presumably to allow the tension to heighten. His face became pleased and beamed with satisfaction. 'I am happy to report that there were no security force or civilian casualties. Regrettably, the terrorists represented a clear and present danger to the lives of officers', and all were killed during this exchange.'

The officer now stopped and learnt across to confer swiftly with the civilian in a low whisper his hand across the microphone. After exchanging short nods of agreement, he turned to speak again.

'I can today confirm that one of the terrorists killed has been named as James Dugdale.'

Dugdale, the name was familiar, it rang a distant bell, a name he knew but had not heard for years, but an echo from somewhere. What does he have to do with anything? thought Gates.

The unnamed civilian patrolled the faces of the journalist's seeking confirmation that the news report had been received and understood.

'Dugdale was a dangerous and determined terrorist and the architect of a number of serious and credible terrorist plans. He was the leader of a formidable organisation resolved to work against the interests of the state. His death makes the country a far safer place.'

An announcement that made for a suitable outcome. There was a lot of chattering now and rapid scribblings on reporters' pads. Gates could hear the scratch of pens on paper and the clicks and beeps of recording machines.

The officer spoke further giving more details of the operation and when he had decided he had given them enough, sat back and paused before inviting questions. When they came, they were qualified with proud endorsements and congratulations to the security forces for their skill and bravery. All the questions concerned the tactical details. *How many shots were fired? Have all the terrorists been identified were there any other leads the police were working on?*

An organisation? No one is asking about it. What is this organisation Dugdale was in *charge* of? What were its aims, how did it pose a threat? Where did it find its people?

The room was poorly ventilated and even with less than twenty people had become stuffy and warm. Gates felt the need for fresh air. He had heard enough. There would be no tough questions for the police because even if the press assembled here wanted to think of them, they wouldn't dare ask them, let alone print them. An unknown terrorist organisation taken out by heroic police and security forces and the death of a hunted man, whose name Gates only vaguely recalled, but whose face would be, by the evening, on every newspaper and computer screen in the country, where he would be described as a sworn and most dangerous enemy of the state.

There was nothing more to be learnt here. He decided to slip away.

He had other business.

The note.

A door opened and closed. A camera flashed and an assistant moved a trail of audio cable to a better position.

Voices in the room continued: 'The assistant commissioner will take another question, yes, there, at the end, Peter...the Chronicle...take it away.'

*Sandywell Green. Park entrance. 11:30am.* The instructions. They had been typed and unsigned.

He checked his watch. Just past ten-thirty. Gates put his notebook away and slipped from his chair around the back of the room.

It was with relief that he found himself in the open air away from the confines of the police headquarters. He realised he had left himself short of time and would need to hurry if he was to be at the appointed meeting place. The exit away from building was via a walkway of ugly concrete ramps. On the walkway a man and a woman stood together on the steps outside. They were close, romantically close. She was attractive and slim with a tight high ponytail that danced with her lover's kiss. Was she looking his way? He thought her glance followed him over the man's shoulder as he passed. He turned left onto Old Mill Street walking towards the Markets District near the Northern Quarter. When he was near the terminus, he could lose himself amongst train passengers and shoppers.

*James Dugdale.*

Back to his days on the *Mirror* in the eighties, Gates remembered Dugdale as a Tory politician, one of the last until membership of that party was made illegal. He had been part of the rear guard, a few retreating speeches and rallies that had come to nothing as the increasing ripples of socialism and then the deeper waves of outright communism had washed across the country's political and social landscape. He had assumed that Dugdale, like many others, had been shipped off to one of the re-education camps along with most of the right-wing intelligentsia, spending time in Hungary or Poland to *re-orientate* their beliefs before a quiet return on license to find their property and financial assets stripped and their family dispersed.

That may or may not have been the case with Dugdale.

The Fiat was parked two hundred yards away, on a main street, outside a butcher's shop. He decided to leave the car, realising it would be slower to edge through traffic than walk. There was something else. A feeling. A butcher was outside his shop arranging trays of offal and sausages, pink fatty meat, with little globules of blood. His mind went back to the body smashed on the road the previous day.

Squashed and burst fingers on the blood-stained asphalt. He pushed the image away.

There was no escaping the realisation that he was creeping into something dark and ugly.

The events described at the conference returned to his thoughts. A police raid on a remote house away from any publicity. Did it even happen? If it did there was nothing to say it took place yesterday; it could have been weeks or months ago. Certainly, he was aware of dissident political activities that happened across the country, and he knew of the partisans with their irregular acts of military defiance that had occurred in the north of the country. But most of this had come to nothing. State Intelligence and its surveillance system was omnipresent.

Total. The grip was too tight.

Gates had heard that over eighty thousand people were held in the special re-education camps in Poland and Hungary, most for what were called *anti-British* activities. This treatment did not include the psychological harassment and detention of individuals that took place. The disruption of family life, blackmail, surveillance, thuggery, destruction of reputation, tactics all designed to cause a loss of will not to conform. The organisation that put them there was a vast network of government operatives, police and thousands of collaborators and informers supported by a technical collection network of closed-circuit television, audio, big data internet monitoring and wide area surveillance by increasingly sophisticated fleets of drones. Organised resistance was impossible.

It was all designed to demoralise and snuff out political opposition before it could coalesce into something harmful or dangerous.

But no one talked about it. You just lived amongst it.

And kept your head down.

If a raid on some organisation had taken place, a terrorist cell cornered and eliminated then the unspoken unreported evidence and rumour would swirl around. Consciously ignored perhaps, but it would be there.

There had been none.

And it raised the question, *why* the authorities needed a distraction?

Gates was being followed.

How did he know? He had no idea.

It was a just a feeling he had had since exiting the police building and arriving at street level and he was certain of it now. The woman with the ponytail, something about her had alerted him, causing a frown to fall on his face and he had felt his pulse increase.

It had happened before and normally would not have worried him unduly. Journalists were often subject to spot surveillance checks even those considered loyal to the Party. It kept the whole industry of surveillance going and made sure the possible curiosity of a reporter did not cause them to wander off track. Probably yesterday's visit to the hit and run was being followed up. The young policeman's report of his arrival at the scene of the hit and run would have filtered into the system along with his telephone enquiry to the press desk.

But it was more concerning now. Was it a trap? A test? Or

was the surveillance connected somehow. Going directly to the rendezvous, he judged, was too risky.

He turned west in the opposite direction down Portland Street back towards the city centre and the busy streets of deadened public spaces with their waiting crowds and gently quickened his step.

He needed to lose the tail.

WALKING smartly and regularly checking, Gates soon realised he was right. Released from the romantic embrace, he thought he glimpsed the ponytailed girl walking parallel to his route on the opposite pavement moving easily but briskly past shoppers and walkers. The man was nowhere to be seen but was most likely working his way along a parallel street to get ahead of him, ready to let the woman break away. Were there others? Possibly. Difficult to do much without at least three or four watchers and almost certainly a car team keeping a safe distance. He lengthened his stride. The watchers weren't always that good, the best teams were in the security service and no doubt were busy with higher priority targets than errant journalists.

It was time.

He turned suddenly into a side street next to a dry-cleaning shop, walked ten metres and then slipped into an alley behind a line of terraced houses. Increasing speed, he used the alley to double back on his original route hoping its exit would be into a parallel street.

It was.

He was back on Portland Street looking towards the city centre.

She was gone.

At least she appeared to be.

As he approached the central square, he could see it was busy. A crocodile file of children was being led by an adult, a teacher, their excited chattering voices happy to be released from the classroom on a day out. Roaring cars and vans circled the square filtering and joining the continuous flow, sometimes slowing—sometimes not—for the pedestrians who darted between the street furniture.

*Don't be too obvious. Don't let them think you are trying to get away.*

The tram station was opposite on the city electric line. Gates bought a one-pound ticket and lingered around the covered stop until the train approached. He boarded it and then, just as the doors sighed shut, jumped off, and sprinted over the metal footbridge to the other platform. He almost ran into a gorilla of a policeman standing on the platform, immobile, solid like the Rock of Gibraltar. His hard eyes looked a full six inches down on Gates.

'Careful, friend,' the policeman hissed. 'Slow down.'

Gates mumbled an apology and slipped past the Goliath and disappeared into the waiting passengers, leaving the policeman shaking his head and muttering slightly.

A minute later he boarded the south-bound tram, only to quickly exit at the Central Coach Station. From there it was a short cut through the side streets to find himself on the canal side embankment. With the broken brickwork of abandoned factories and out of control undergrowth for cover he followed the north bank heading away from the city. Beside him the quiet, greasy still of the waterway gave off a fetid smell of machine oil and gasoline.

He was sweating from the exertion but was pleased with his nimble footwork. After a while he paused and waited under a bridge for three or four minutes, but it was a working day, and the towpath was empty of people. Even the vagrants who made this area home seemed to be somewhere else. When he was sure that no one had followed him into the alley he continued his way alongside the canal and began to retrace his steps east back towards the meeting point.

Madness, he thought. Why get involved? No one is making me.

He felt momentary anger inside him against whoever was pushing notes under his door, luring him to traffic accidents, following him around the city. Whatever they want these people are persistent.

A vision of Sophie, her worn face but still with the soft beauty of youth sitting at a desk in a bleak bare classroom far away faithfully transcribing slogans from a blackboard came from nowhere into his mind. *'LEARN, LEARN, AND LEARN...'* The old popular wisdom that every good communist knows, timeless phrases from Lenin memorised from early childhood and later imprinted as mantras into the thoughts of those who needed reminding of the need for obedience and loyalty. *'PEOPLE OF THE COUNTRY UNITE...'* A furrow of concentration on her brow as she focused on getting the words right.

Then.

A further vision of himself from long ago.

The hissed enraged words from his long-departed first wife circled in his head: *What have you done, you stupid zealot, you, and your pathetic Party. You have destroyed us, all of us.*

He had let her go at the time unconcerned at her anger. They were lost to each other, the undergraduate lust and energy gone in a strange dawn of realisation of what they each were and where they belonged. *They use people like you to do their work sing their slogans. Then when they have all the power and the people are worthless, they will spit you out with the rest of the proletariat.*

The fury had bought her voice to a whisper and then she was gone.

Gates hadn't cared. There was already somebody else.

He had been a good loyal servant. Now he was too old for this. All he wanted was to quietly finish his time, gather the meagre pension that was a reward for a lifetime of socialist journalism and hope that the system might tire of keeping a daughter it did not need in interminable punishment.

He wanted the vision of Sophie which haunted him day and night to end.

But he did not turn back.

He walked for twenty minutes leaving the canal towpath to pass a parade of brick shops selling hardware, groceries, and clothes. He couldn't be sure but judged he had been successful and was now alone. After a time, he left the high street and headed into a network of terraced streets with broken pavements and small patch gardens.

There was a tannery somewhere. The wind pulled the smell of quicklime, animal hide and rotting water across the streets. It was a student district, the packed ghetto of dwellings home to the pimply boys and fresh-faced girls flirting as radicals which the government briefly tolerated while in their undergraduate years before pressing and crushing them back to conformity.

The young women wore odd combinations of clothes and even dyed their hair purple and blue; the men had allowed their hair to grow, wore denim and often sported the large white lapel badges with the name of their youth movement—Sovereign—scribed in red. A political inspiration to youth until its leaders were carted off to the camps and it had slipped from view. Gates had heard it was starting to become popular once more, particular in London where demonstrations had begun again, growing in size. Discontent about conscription to the Pact wars, an underground trade in banned American music, the circulation of subversive magazines; activities all carefully watched by the police and Security Service. Graffiti had been scrawled in spray paint on a garden wall: 'A BETTER TOMORROW'.

There was little traffic here, just a few parked Skodas and Austins, occasional passing students and mothers pushing prams.

He stopped a passing woman to ask directions. She was young and wore a coat that was thick but old and pushed a battered pushchair that looked like it had served a couple of generations. She wore no make-up, and the eyes were uncertain until she understood what he wanted was only a harmless enquiry. She gestured behind her, flashed a quick nervous smile, and hurried on relieved to be free of an unwelcome encounter with a stranger.

He was close and two streets later found himself at the entrance to a small area of enclosed green space: Sandywell Gardens, announced a small, cracked sign. There he began to wait uncertain as to what would follow. It did not take long to find out. A battered white Volkswagen work van that had seen better days pulled quietly alongside the kerb.

He realised he was not alone after all. Turning he found himself facing the girl with the ponytail.

'Nice try. Now get in,' she was already opening the side sliding door. 'There is someone who wants to talk to you.'

Too surprised to refuse, he moved towards the van.

Gates wondered whether the shock showed on his face.

THE driver was a bulky burly man wearing a leather jacket and he wore a fluorescent waistcoat. He was pretty sure it was a different guy to the one sharing her embrace earlier. The woman, who he now saw was young, groomed, even more attractive than his glance in the street had told him, indicated the interior of the van and slammed the door shut after him. The rear was crammed with tool bags, lengths of plumbing pipe and he wedged himself against an old sink basin the redundant taps jabbing into his side. The vehicle pulled off and Gates awkwardly twisted around trying to get comfortable. He considered saying something but suspected he would not get answers. He also realised his mistake, although an understandable one, in assuming that the man and the woman were a police or Security Service surveillance team.

He had also assumed he had lost them.

Wrong on both counts, he thought. They knew where he was going all along. They must have thought his efforts at attempting to lose them absurd.

They van began to twist turn and roll and Gates assumed they had left the main roads and were probably probing deep into the villages fringing the Lancashire dales. After thirty minutes of bouncing along the vehicle slowed and turned into an entrance. Gates could vaguely hear the crunch of slow-moving tyres on gravel. After the engine had stopped there was a short pause before the sliding door rattled open violently and the girl stood there waiting for Gates to clamber awkwardly out relieved to be free of the company of the sink unit. He stood on a driveway and looked up to see a rambling mournful house that dated from somewhere in the early nineteenth century rose. It had an uncertain shape and had, he supposed, once been imposing with eaves and steeples, but now looked unkempt: the Georgian stone defaced by weather, its large windows eaten by rot, and encircled by marauding snakes of ivy. The sunken pathways had been extensively encroached by weed and were covered in fallen leaves.

'We're here,' announced the woman. 'Follow me.'

The driver stayed in the driving seat not looking back as Gates fell in behind her, around them the restless whistle of the breeze through thick leaves was the only sound. He followed the young woman who ignored the large front entrance porch and strode around the back of the house. Gates had thought the exterior of the house ugly, and it had seen better days but inside he found himself in a spacious stone kitchen that was pleasantly warm and smelt of recent cooking. There were solid dressers, pans and ladles hanging from pot racks. A farmhouse table of scrubbed pine sat on flagstones in the centre of the room and an iron wood-burning stove that pumped out heat was at the end.

Standing next to it was a man in a much used and battered waxed jacket, baggy brown corduroy trousers, and sturdy brown shoes. He was making tea in a scene that looked like he was enjoying a break from pottering amongst the roses. His big-boned frame turned as Gates entered and he put him in his early seventies, but obviously still fit and sprightly moving easily, his hands quick and his feet nimble, probably at home, thought Gates, on a dance floor or tennis court. The man's silver hair was brushed back, and he had warm fleshy cheeks, with sharp blue eyes that spoke of intelligence and good health. His chin had been freshly scraped with a razor so that it gleamed slightly. There was the look of breeding and confidence about him that comes from education and strong family stock.

'Come in and sit down.' He said, turning to greet the new arrivals. 'Gates, isn't it? Nice to see you, so pleased you agreed to come.' There was something frustratingly familiar about him, an old memory that wouldn't quite reveal itself; Gates searched in vain for a name. 'How is the newspaper trade in these modern times?'

He had begun the conversation as would old friends greeting each other after a long interval without contact, his enquiry accompanied by a broad smile and twist of the lip that may have been amusement. From somewhere in the house could be heard footsteps on wooden floors, doors closing, and Gates assumed more people unseen were watching and waiting, making sure they were undisturbed. He wondered what lay elsewhere beyond the heavy-set door and imagined cavernous rooms filled with dark portraits and furniture covered in dust sheets.

His host transferred a teapot, steam gently circling from the spout, from the Aga to the table. 'I assume you would both like tea, come and sit down, make yourself comfortable, please. Miranda, would you fetch some cups and be Mother?'

Gates sat at the table and the man did the same while Miranda assembled an odd collection of mugs. Gates wondered what would come next.

His host waited until the girl, now introduced as Miranda, had taken a seat herself and poured the tea.

'Did he give you any problems,' he inquired of the girl.

Miranda shook her head. 'He went walk-a-bouts,' she said without smiling. 'C- for effort.'

The host smiled. 'Don't be too harsh on him, it shows he is not without some resource.'

A shaft of speckled sunlight fell through the window to briefly spill warmth and light across the table before the fickle day moved on and the room was left to the fragments of low light from ancient side lamps.

'Let me introduce myself. My name is James—James Dugdale. I think you may have heard of me?'

***

# CHAPTER FOUR

*When did you last eat chocolate?*

'POLITICS IS A DIRTY business Dugdale.'

It was an observation the Chief Whip gave to every newly elected member during their first conversations in the Palace of Westminster. It had taken quite a time for the party's senior disciplinarian to get round to meeting all members of the new class of 1979.

While Harry Gates was celebrating his employment offer at a London tabloid newspaper, a landslide election victory saw the government benches in the House of Commons chamber turn blue, a flood propelled by a political force not seen in a generation and one possessed with a personal mission to dismantle socialism. Such a storm of change gave the government enforcer long days and evenings working the bars and tearooms, checking the nooks and crannies of the Palace of Westminster ensuring that his new flock of bright-eyed law makers, all eager to begin a fresh progressive era of British politics were aligned, orderly and obedient; schooled in the rules that would guide their coming roles in public life.

Amongst his new charges, he allocated an extra thirty minutes with a gin and lemon in Annie's Bar to James Dugdale. The new MP was cut from the right cloth, a reformer with skills in business and law who was also a leader, someone able to command attention and provide light when most were generating only heat. A good orator, who had proved able to reach people with wit and common sense. He had run a sharp campaign successfully overhauling a stubborn Labour majority in a Norfolk seat.

The doyen of the party sipped his gin. 'But most of all politics is about loyalty,' he had continued. 'I'm just like a school prefect really; you only get good or bad news from me.' He had spoken with a twinkle in his eye and broke into a grin. 'Nothing in between I'm afraid.' At sixty he was old enough to have seen war service in Europe and he knew good men when they crossed his path.

The Chief Whip had already briefed the newly installed PM. One to watch, he told her. His own assessment was second term junior minister, cabinet rank by the end of that parliament, then who knows.

Fate, with all the fickleness of its finger would intrude.

None of this would happen.

For a time, the political career of James Dugdale did not disappoint, and the Chief Whip was pleased that his intuition had been well founded: 'What did I tell you,' he confided to

Cabinet friends, 'she'll want him for greater things soon.' His colleagues did not demur.

He had watched Dugdale gain early selection for membership of the powerful Home Affairs Committee, applauded some strong speech work, ensuring it gained approving nods from No 10. Like other members on his side of the house the Chief Whip made sure he was in the Commons chamber for the much-anticipated droll clever question that provided a mischievous highlight for his colleagues during Opposition debates. He recalled an occasion in the tearoom when the PM had dropped by and paused for conversation with Dugdale to discuss his questioning of immigration policy in committee the previous week. The favouring of attention for five minutes had bought envious glances that would not be forgotten. She was not in the least put out by the report she had received that the permanent secretary had left the committee room quietly smarting from Dugdale's forensic questioning. As she moved on from their exchange, she had let her view float lightly in her wake: *We must keep officials on their toes.* And the Chief Whip had caught the twinkle in her eyes that conveyed mutual understanding. It was clear to all that Dugdale was among the future chosen.

Occasionally such misty memories seeped unbidden back into Dugdale's consciousness. When they did, he would sweep them away irritably refusing to dwell on them. He disliked such reminisces as sentimental and without purpose. The world had changed greatly since those days, there was no going back—at least like that, to a world of parliamentary intrigue and manoeuvring.

The Chief Whip was long gone, banished along with all of his former colleagues with their jealousies, ambitions and talents. They had all disappeared in a blood-red sunset of change that had fallen upon a country unable to escape the doldrums cast upon it by forces too ruthless to resist.

GATES watched as the older man sipped his tea. The fridge hummed noisily, and a tap dripped. Dugdale ran a hand with long fingers across the smooth tabletop, his lips pursed slightly as he contemplated his words. They had never met, but Gates recalled Dugdale now.

From another existence the facts of the man's life filtered through to him. Son of a baronet, who lived life with the late-night whiff of cigars, brandy and the scent of other men's wives while abusing a much younger wife of his own. It had been widely rumoured she found comfort as the mistress of a cabinet minister. The frailties and insecurities of both parents safely concealed by the social order and conventions that only the ruling class of the English would recognise. His father lived long enough to see the young Dugdale collect his rowing blue at Cambridge and then shortly after shot himself in his study to conceal the gambling debts and an embarrassing illegitimate pregnancy the scandal of which would have finished him. Two years later his mother died of alcohol and loneliness and Dugdale from the wreckage of a dysfunctional family—but with the enormous gift of class patronage—made his way first into the law and then politics.

There was a time when Gates would have despised such a man. Now he was just curious. The previous ideological and social gulf between them had lost all relevance.

'You want to know why you are here of course,' Dugdale said, as he returned the hot mug of tea to the table. 'That's not a surprise, sorry for hauling you in like we did.' He paused. 'I can explain, but I would very much like to know if I can rely absolutely upon your discretion.' He paused once more and looked directly at Gates. His blue eyes glittered like a cat, and he spoke with the captivating drawl of the better English boarding school. 'And maybe your curiosity? We have been wondering about you for a little while and now certain events make me think you could be useful to us.'

'At the police press conference this morning, they said you were dead,' Gates said, not very pleasantly. He shifted in his seat gathering his thoughts, avoiding a direct answer. 'How do I know you are really Dugdale?' He felt thirsty. Nervousness, he told himself.

Dugdale lent back in his chair. 'Well let's turn that around. How do you know who they have claimed to have killed is who they say?' he said, his face amused. 'Happily, I assure you I am here and what they say is not true. Quoting Twain is a cliché, but we can say with some safety that reports of my death are exaggerated.'

It was a poor attempt at geniality which Gates ignored. 'There was a police operation yesterday. Who was it against?'

'If you say so.' Dugdale's voice held puzzlement which may or may not have been genuine.' He tilted his head to one side as he spoke: 'Of course I can think of lots of reasons why they might want me dead. And an equal number of reasons why they might want others to believe I am a goner.'

Gates shook his head, he realised he had been caught off guard. Obviously, the police had their reasons. Disinformation was regularly useful confusion. But it did mean that they knew about this man and in some way considered him dangerous, a threat. This thought woke a nagging fear which he suppressed refusing to allow it to surface. A threat to whom?

'However, there was a road traffic accident, hit and run.' Dugdale went on with some gravity. 'A serious one, a man died. You were there. Why do *you* think the authorities would want to report one incident that *didn't* happen and not report one that *did*?'

'So,' Dugdale's long slow smile made his face become handsome and young, 'do I have your discretion. You might find what I have to say interesting.'

'Will you answer questions?'

Dugdale was shaking his head even as Gates began to ask the question. 'I doubt it, not many anyway. There are people, others, to protect, but all the same...you'll want to hear what I have to say.'

Gates was momentarily unsure. Dugdale paused catching Gates' eye. He realised he was on uncertain and unfamiliar ground. The fear of consequences rose within him. He knew that to continue meant there would be no going back. Years of keeping his head down, playing the good socialist, writing the lines the Party expected, describing events the way they demanded and turning a blind eye to the information that they would not want known. All of that would count for nothing, swept away. Realising he would not be able to *unknow* anything that this man told him, it occurred to him that if this meeting ever to come to the knowledge of the authorities...

It did not bear thinking about.

'Why me? What is it you want? I'm simply a journalist. I can't help you.'

Dugdale settled back in his chair, Gates' reluctance to commit to anything seemed not to disturb him. It was as if he had a channel into his thoughts, knew the anxiety that Gates was feeling but also understood the curiosity, the investigative urge that any journalist, however lapsed or compromised feels. 'I'm not sure that is true. You might consider yourself insignificant, but you may have a value we can use.' Dugdale pursed his lips. 'Miranda, tell Mr Gates what we know about him will you. Don't spare us the details.'

It was the first time she had spoken properly beyond the

brief brusque instructions of the journey and the dismissal of Gates' street-surveillance ability. She looked tough—as well as attractive—and he guessed she knew how to handle herself. Gates found himself mildly surprised at the accentless cut-glass English of her words. Flawless vowels that seemed to mock and made Gates wince as with no notes she began an unwanted and uncomfortable examination of his life.

First, the early childhood near Rochdale, middle son in a steel worker family. An elitist detour to a grammar school concealed, but not refused, by his minor shop steward father, the hypocrisy something of a family embarrassment to be hidden as a secret shame. From there to an undistinguished university career gaining an English and Politics degree. By contrast to his indifferent academic studies his time was blended with first class socialist activism, enthusiastically applauded, and supported by the left-wing tutors the universities had become stuffed with. Journalism beckoned and the move to Fleet Street opened for him.

It was all there she and Dugdale proved they knew his life. Political reporter on the *Daily Mirror,* Assistant Editor at the *Morning Star...* Even wrote a couple of speeches for 'Red Ken' during the day when the Greater London Council was a 'thing' and was never far from a picket line or protest.

Gates recognised the narrative well enough and ignored the mocking edge to her voice.

'Usual workers' propaganda posing as pretty average

reporting but became quite connected in the then Labour Party and its Militant Movement; lots of friends there and for a while in quite high places.'

The marriages Miranda described without bothering to hide her contempt. There was a brief university relationship, ill-matched in personality and beliefs, entered more as a rebellious act of defiance possibly motivated by the anger of his youth. It didn't last long. A relationship failure quickly followed by a second marriage, to a new partner Kate, a Party comrade who shared his protest and his bedroom. A firebrand free radical, all sex and anger. The union had gone well for a while, quite the 'Red' pair, mixing in elevated company, but the activism and hedonism extended into her bed which became something of a comrade meeting place. Miranda twitched her lips slightly, whether from sardonic amusement or disapproval, there was no way to tell. Gates remembered what someone had said to him once, someone he didn't like and who didn't like him, taunting him wanting to hurt. *Having a terrible marriage is like having bad breath, everyone knows.* They had all enjoyed that, many of the circle in which they moved pulling up front row seats for that horror show. A couple had even joined the cast, thought Gates, not holding the cruel jibe against the would-be tormentor.

'There was however an offspring,' she said. 'A girl—Sophie. We can come back to her.'

Gates grimly ignored the reference to his daughter. His palms had become sticky. Miranda would not be stopped.

'Delighted in print that Britain's colonial past was rewarded with the Falklands defeat, even penned his paper's letter of congratulations to the Argentinian Junta. One of your earliest acclaimed pieces we think.' She paused. 'Do you recall?'

'It rings a bell,' murmured Gates. Inside he felt unsettled and forced down an urge to try and walk out.

'I think I remember that piece,' added Dugdale stirring his tea absent-mindedly. 'I'm sure the Junta was most grateful.'

'Enthusiastic supporter of Britain's withdrawal from NATO and the relinquishing of the Atlantic connection with America. Stood on the dock at Portsmouth and welcomed the arrival of the first Soviet flotilla to make use of British dockyard facilities. Applauded the success of the Italian Communist Party in forming a government and urged a similar political revolution here, which we kind of got, although a bit less flashy than the Italian version. More British Leyland than Ferrari. Came about with a few speeches and a vote.'

Gates wanted no further judgement. 'Fascinating,' he said protesting sharply and found himself colouring deeply, cringing in anger at this cruel mocking of his past. He glared towards Miranda: 'That's—'

Dugdale stopped stirring and raised a finger to cut off the interruption before Miranda resumed, her voice calm and unruffled by the interruption.

'Continued to come up in the world, loyal party member looking forward to a bright future under the Soviet-UK treaty and presumably you believed mission accomplished when Parliament finally voted itself into oblivion in favour of the Supreme National Assembly with its Council.'

She waited to see if Gates would react again. He did not. He now sat quiet, receiving, not willing to argue the bitter history, his concentration began to focus on Dugdale, sharp focus that asked why this man's attentions had fallen upon him.

'So now there is a change,' Miranda continued with infuriating patience. 'At some point in the late nineties something goes wrong, regular falling out with colleagues, alcohol makes a significant appearance, and the divorce has become extremely messy. Kate decides a senior member of the London Central Committee offers a more promising lifestyle and perks. She now enjoys fewer revolutionary tastes we understand and is more into cream carpets and expensive expressions of abstract art in North London. Mr Gates here heads north to Manchester, probably just before being fired, his political connections having apparently sided with the connected and more entertaining Kate, and he takes daughter Sophie with him.

'Scrapes a job staying in journalism but no promotions, repetitive work on a regional paper, the crime brief. Hardly any Party engagement, even had to be reminded to pay his local neighbourhood subs—'

Gates wanted a cigarette.

'You know it all.' He couldn't have left Sophie with her mother. She cared little for the child and Gates had known at some point they would clash. The child was feisty and stubborn. Better with him where he could protect her. That was a laugh he thought. Look where his protection had landed her. 'Now explain *why* you feel the need to know so much about me?'

Dugdale put in: 'How is Sophie Mr Gates? Have you heard from her?'

The briefest of winces on Gates' face answered his question.

Gates opened his mouth ready to growl his angry rebuke, but wisely closed it keeping his temper. 'She's busy. I guess you know why,' was all he said.

'I suppose the guilt thing may come from you thinking that your own quiet political disillusionment encouraged her to be a little indiscreet in her own handling of authority. Am I right?'

Gates suspected that there may be truth in that. 'I have no idea,' he said dryly.

A couple of years back, and with gritted teeth, after they had taken her away, he had appealed to Kate for help, swallowing his pride to beg for her to be returned. She had just looked at him as he stood in the doorway of the smart North London Victorian terrace, dull eyes pale with disdain.

*Probably serves her right,* her voice unconcerned and cold. *She can come back when she has leaned her lesson.*

What turns a woman into a monster like this, he had thought. How does that happen?

'You kept your Communist Party membership?' Dugdale

was saying, 'was it a favour for old times' sake? That was nice of them.'

'I conformed. Now, shall we talk about what you think it is that I can do for you?' Gates asked dead-eyed. 'And more importantly, why would I?'

Dugdale was looking at him, thinking about how to proceed. He seemed to decide that the verbal fencing should finish, that it was time to get down to business. 'Suppose I was to say to you that change is going to come to this country again,' he suggested in a tone of one proposing a remote option from many available. 'Don't ask me how or when there's a good fellow, but a change that will come soon enough. There are plans, powerful plans made by serious people.' He looked away at some point across the room. Then went on gravely, as if he had come to the end of an obituary where the honest conclusions on man's worth can be found. 'The firebrand in you has cooled, we are of the view you may even welcome change yourself.'

Gates was suddenly quite lost. *Who is 'we'?* he thought.

'"We"? What is this? There is a brotherhood?'

Dugdale chose to ignore the sarcasm. Instead, he jutted his chin across the table towards Miranda who sat silently, her mug of tea untouched.

'Maybe not quite what you think. But how do you explain Miranda finding you, bringing you here safely?'

Dugdale looked intently at him. 'The political duels from

your side and mine are ancient history now, they've have been played out. You had your victory, but people and the country has had its answer.' He lent back and folded his arms. There was an air of patiently reciting a well-rehearsed argument. His gaze was unblinking. 'Did you believe that after people like you delivered this country into the control of authoritarian zealots that patriotism would die, that people would *give up* wanting their country, their way of life, their freedoms? That's just not the way it works.'

'Well, the people chose, but I'm listening.'

'It was only time before the changes in our political systems that you and others achieved would come to be reversed. This is what I am talking about.'

'*How?*'

'Let's just say we believe it's possible to bring about change, possible to act with common purpose across society reverse many of the political and social changes that have been imposed upon us.'

There was a stillness to his voice and Gates found himself a little lost, unable to understand fully what he meant. It sounded like Dugdale was talking about treason and his thoughts flew to Sophie again. *I am all that she has left, anywhere.*

'Resistance? That's been tried. It failed.'

'Not in the sense you mean,' said Dugdale firmly. 'And not like those foolish hotheads, old soldiers, and students, which have appeared from time to time. No, that approach is far too crude to succeed. No,' he said with punch. 'I am talking about something far more subtle, *assume* control rather than seize it. It's not a coup d'etat, it's an infiltration. This is the long game we are engaged in.'

'And what makes you think this would work?' Gates' tone was doubtful.

There was a short pause, Dugdale's eyes once more took on a cat-like gleam.

'When was the last time you ate chocolate Gates? I mean *proper* chocolate that tasted of coco and milk and not like plastic. You remember, like the pure sweet bars you had in your youth. Come to it, when was the last time you saw pastries or anything that wasn't low grade meat and vegetable in the shops? Bought something to wear that you liked rather than needed.

'Have you wondered why you have to search for toothpaste and when you have found it wondered why it leaves an antiseptic burn in your mouth or why the only washing machine you can buy is a repaired one? Been to a hospital lately? Would you want to? When was the last time you watched a news item that made actual sense, that you didn't have to force yourself to believe? Matters are coming to a head; they have been for some time; the people are nearly ready to make better choices. They just need leadership through the choices and out of the confusion.'

Gates was unsure about that. He was unbelieving,

confused by what he was being told: 'The people have enough. Their needs are catered for. State schools, hospitals, a better standard of living than most of Europe. What we have—'

'Really? You think so?' Dugdale cut him off, suddenly angry. 'We dig coal, so we don't have to buy it from the Russians at enormous cost to our economy and environment and congratulate ourselves on being energy self-sufficient. We have good universities that produce smart science that we no longer turn into anything. But where do the guts of your smart phone come from? Not anywhere near here. California, by the way, finds all of its power from renewable sources, wind and solar. In Canada over seventy per cent of cars are electrically powered. How long do we keep that type of progress from the people?

'We adopted extreme socialism, or most of it, but never put in place the complete command economy. Typically British, we even had to compromise on revolution. Our socialists thought we could keep big business but tell it what to do.

'We're failing. You realise how the standard of living you talk about is paid for? The country only survives on enormous U.S. and Japanese loans. What if they were to call those in? Who would step in? The Soviets?' He scoffed at his own suggestion. 'I don't think so.'

'The party is too strong, the control and grip too deep, they will hunt you down like all the other feeble Resistance groups that have come and—'

'The Soviet Union is weaker than ever before,' Dugdale interrupted him, his voice a long groan. 'The Americans ally with the Japanese to squeeze them economically in the Pacific and with the Canadians in the Atlantic. The Chinese are slowly bleeding them dry with their wars in Asia and out compete them with state capitalism. The cost is beyond them, over thirty per cent of the national wealth of Alliance states, including this country, is spent on the military. Despite shipping a great deal of their client states food and raw materials back to Russia, we understand there are winter food shortages and unrest in Moscow. How long before that is the situation here, I wonder.'

'And that will stop them?' retorted Gates. 'You are talking revolution. They won't hesitate to crush you.' But he realised his reaction had been expected.

Dugdale shook his head in mild disagreement as if lecturing a stubborn student whose idealism is a barrier to understanding, whose emotion crushes pragmatism.

'You think? Anyway, we prefer to consider it a counter-revolution. Consider this: there are very few Russian forces stationed in this country, what there is, are mostly navy and air force. They can't afford to station combat forces here, they're too busy being chewed up on the Yalu River. Do you think our own military will act against its own people on the orders of Moscow? I don't. Anyway, they have had enough of being forced into doing the Pact bidding. Too much blood and waste, it won't take much to turn the loyalty of scared conscripts.'

Gates thought about what Dugdale was saying. 'You really think,' he said. 'That the people will support this?'

Dugdale had risen to his feet. 'With just a little momentum, yes.' He saw the look on Gates' face. 'You're too pessimistic, too invested in the belief system you are—were?—part of,' he said. 'Look at this generation.' He began to pace the stone floor of the kitchen and nodded down towards Miranda who had been listening impassively to the exchange. 'They don't want this anymore. They have the same zeal and the passion that you and others had in the eighties—more probably. Except they are less misguided, probably more ruthless about ideas such as sovereignty and freedom. They just haven't had the luxury of protest that you did.' The last sentence was delivered as a tart admonishment.

Gates said nothing. He looked at Miranda as if for support. Did she go along with all this? But she just returned his look coolly, her eyes without friendship or interest.

Both men thought about their exchange for a few moments.

'How does it work? How do you intend to take back a country? Without a revolution.' Play devil's advocate, thought Gates, take him at his word. 'The party is hardly likely to hand over power and they have plenty of support. You expect to pull off a bloodless coup?'

Dugdale shook his head slightly. 'No, I didn't say bloodless. There will be some who resist, and we will have to...deal with them.' There was a pause as he considered. 'But you are right you cannot just run up a new flag and declare victory. It must be something that will be recognised, it must have legitimacy. If we can control most if not all of the major institutions, the media, the unions, the armed forces then the Council and by extension the Party realises it is helpless. Then it's a question of timing, choosing the moment. Put simply we give the Council of Ministers no choice, we isolate it. Ours will be a velvet revolution, a soft transition of power that will not require the people to spill blood in revolutionary warfare.'

'That level of influence, that reach, you can't possibly have achieved that?'

'A few years ago, when the experiment was young you would have been right. Far too difficult to organise too many institutions and organisations to influence and control, difficult to gather up the allegiances and create the trust. One of the curious ironies is that in an ostensibly strong single party system it's a lot easier. You just have to know which part of the nervous system to squeeze and apply pressure to. Do that and the whole thing shudders to a halt.'

Gates scoffed: 'You make it *sound* easy.'

'That wasn't my intention, but you have to believe Gates.' There was a deep subtle expression on Dugdale's face. 'But yes at least soon. Look, we came to the scene late as far as socialism is concerned. We weren't part of the old Stalinist idea of a European land barrier to Mother Russia. We were recruited, actually we volunteered ourselves, to become part of the global project for influence. Most of it we did ourselves. There were no purges, no show trials. The system of government changed but the institutions didn't, they weren't fundamentally reformed they were redirected. The Judiciary for example, it's still independent but behaves very carefully with its authority and independence.

'The point will come when we can take control of those organisations. Announcements made, proclamations given, organise in the open, all coordinated and then crucially the people will see that change has arrived. Once there is the support of the people it's all over for the Council. They will either accept they no longer have a mandate and voluntarily hand power over to a new administration, or...they will appeal for assistance to Moscow.'

'And what would *they* do?'

'Well then we are in the hands of friends with their immediate offers of support and so on.'

He was vague, thought Gates, and who the 'friends' were and what their 'support' was, was not a subject Gates expected him to go into.

'If our assessment is right,' Dugdale continued, 'Moscow will accept the *fait accompli*. Just too difficult for them to do anything about.'

'Why is that?'

'National character for a start. They see us as a querulous, stubborn island people, aggressive when pushed. Clever and stoic. They always thought we would be too difficult to control, unable to accept the indoctrination that other continental countries succumbed to, and they didn't really need us. They've left a good deal of our art, culture and social habits alone, less rigid control of civil behaviour. Oh, plenty of changes yes, but none of those ghastly mass games they waste so much time on in Czechoslovakia or the awful torch-lit parades the Germans love so much.

'Look, they don't need to. Most of Western Europe has become one big cornfield broken up by steel manufacturing and coal mining. They have what they want there. A complete continent of natural resources with internal lines of communication running back to the East.' Dugdale began to chuckle. 'It's well-known in certain circles that our current leaders after gaining power, had to plead with the Soviets to let us into the Pact in the first place, Moscow thought we would be more trouble than we are worth. When the time comes, with powerful support to the cause, there will be a face-saving climbdown.'

But Gates shook his head. 'Madness,' he breathed.

'After that, a government of national unity for a few years, new constitution, one has already been drafted by the way, updated bill of rights and in time the forming of political parties will be allowed, then the country can begin to return to how it was. An economic basket case of course and it will take years of aid, but that will come. A decade perhaps a little longer.'

'And does this plan work for all of the nations? What about the Scots and the Irish?'

'Ah…well…yes there will be issues there,' Dugdale observed thoughtfully.

The question seemed to bring on a particular stillness in the conversation, and Dugdale bunched his hands in a reflective posture under his nose. A silent acknowledgment of the complexities that awaited.

How has Dugdale existed all this time, thought Gates. There was much about this man's life he would never know. Presumably, a life in exile, working grand proposals for the restoration of national greatness. Was he a hero who future generations would celebrate? A romantic schemer overseeing the plans for national salvation, harnessing the assistance of others; Americans, Canadians, others. Or was he simply their pawn, a fixer for others. How does he maintain this lofty cheerfulness, some sanity even, knowing that all the time your life is a precarious thread that could be snapped at any time? For all his doubts about what he had told him, he found himself reluctantly impressed by the man.

'But that's for another day. Well, they asked for independence for long enough,' he responded after some time, 'I doubt that what they got was what they wanted though. Maybe the future Union will be smaller than the one that was broken up. Anyway, let's not get ahead of ourselves, a long road to travel first.'

'Why have you told me all this? What's to stop me reporting everything to the authorities?'

The soft knock on the day was timely. Dugdale looked at Gates for a time and did not answer. Then he walked across the kitchen reaching the inner door that led into the hollows of the house. Opening it he spoke quietly for a few moments to a dark tall figure that Gates could not quite see. From somewhere beyond came the sound of music and Gates noticed it for the first time. A pop tune from a few years ago, a syrupy melody popular with younger people played on the radio incessantly before being replaced with newer taste. It reminded Gates that they were not alone in this place.

'Let's walk,' said Dugdale. 'It's so difficult to enjoy the outdoors without being disturbed and we're quite safe here, at least for a while.' He closed the door, the footsteps of the guardian receded, and the music faded.

***

# CHAPTER FIVE

*Tell me what you want*

IT WAS A FICKLE DAY that alternated between sun and brief showers of rain. Leaving the kitchen, they were rewarded, for a while at least, by afternoon rays of weak sunlight that fell in strips between a line of chestnut trees solemnly bounding one side of the long grounds. At the rear of the house was a small sunken garden, home to creeping dark moss and a cracked old sun dial. A wooden bench, sodden and blistered by rainwater faced south across a large open paddock. The lowered courtyard would likely catch the sun in summer giving the area a light and pleasant aspect, but autumn had turned the stone slabs damp and it had become a trap for the mouldy leaves blown in by the wind and which now clung as mush to their shoes as they walked.

The two men followed a narrow path that wandered towards the chestnuts before falling away into countryside. They walked awkwardly unused to each other's stride, unsure of the pace the other found comfortable. For a while neither spoke but breathed the damp air and listened to the wind grapple with the trees.

'Why did you want me to see that hit and run?' Gates chose different words to repeat the question he had posed to Dugdale before leaving the warmth of the kitchen. 'Sending me there was your doing?'

Dugdale pursed his lips, and his eyes regarded the ground in front of him. There was no denial or confirmation. Instead Dugdale said: 'It's a critical time this country is entering. So much of what will take place requires belief. Belief usually comes from what a person can see with their own eyes, in much the same way that truth for the most part relies upon what people experience.

'Take this conversation with me, a man officially proclaimed dead. After speaking with me do you do? Take what you have learnt, and inform the authorities whose truth is different from your experience?' Dugdale was mustering persuasiveness, presenting his logic as unarguable. 'If you did there would be two truths. But your truth becomes dangerous—especially to you.'

'And the hit and run?' Gates repeated, again in bewilderment and wondered why every question required a philosophical answer.

Dugdale said nothing for a while, and then: 'Truth and belief are everything Gates. You saw something that wasn't a fiction. Something that may make you begin to realise where our choices should lay.'

Gates wanted to confirm what he had begun to suspect. 'You killed him?' Wasn't it obvious? He thought.

'Yes—yes, I'm afraid I did arrange for it to happen, I had no choice. He had become a concern.'

'Who was he?'

'His name was Burns, Len Burns, know him?'

Gates thought for a moment, the name familiar but briefly eluding him, lost in the whirl of recent information, then memory returned. 'Yes. The union man? A big wheel. Number two in the Amalgamated Electrical and Mechanical Engineers Union.'

Being number two was an impediment to recalling the name. Who remembers who the number two in a state organisation is?

'That's him. A powerful figure. Having him at the centre of union power has allowed a number of opportunities.' He looked up at the sky dolefully. 'Unfortunate,' was all he said.

'Why? He...he... was he your man? Working for you?' The idea genuinely shocked and surprised Gates. He supposed it was not impossible that there were high level officials in the Party who were disenchanted at the state of the nation and its affairs. It just seemed unlikely.

From the trees came the rustle and soft groan of the wind.

'Yes, and you'll understand he was deputy to the General Secretary, and you know who that is.'

Gates did. The received wisdom was that there were five

men in the country whose power went beyond all others, almost untouchable. That wisdom included the view that none of the five were the prime minister. Such power would be derived mostly from close connections to Moscow. Joe McBride, the Union's General Secretary, was widely understood to share Politburo holidays on the Black Sea.

Dugdale continued: 'Burns was a rival for the leadership of that union next year. Having gathered quite a lot of regional delegate support he was predicted to oust his boss and become the new General Secretary. They hated each other of course—it is a union with fraternal friendship after all—but we know how they work. Surprisingly, given the world we live in, he actually had a good chance of doing so.'

He had thrust his hands deep into the pockets of the wax jacket, his chin had dropped in thought.

'You realise how powerful that organisation is? two million plus members. He was one of us and when the time was right his appointment could have given us unnoticed and almost complete control over many critical workers able to stop and start the economy as and very probably when we wished.'

Glancing around, Gates saw the tangled hawthorn bushes, overgrown grass and puddles of wet leaves that swirled around their ankles. When the sunlight appeared, it seemed to yaw around them creating patterns of gloom and light. His mind wrestled with what he was being told.

'Burns had been a success story, making his way to a

summit of power that could help make change a reality, no longer simply a dream of men growing steadily old with their hollow plans to return to an old political order. He was one of our levers for change.'

'Then why was he killed?'

Dugdale appeared genuinely anguished, hesitant, uncertain how to answer this: 'He was like you really you know, began much the same way, same age, same politics, perhaps the same bitterness in later life when he realised what his beliefs had led to. But it seems his loyalties were at best divided, he had become involved in complex affairs and rivalries and it's likely he had been compromised; it always starts with the small things, personal indiscretions—an easy weakness to begin with. Oldest trick in the book of course. Powerful man falls for the pretty little tart planted in his office and they find out what they can, uncover his indiscretions.'

'An office affair by a powerful union boss leading to his downfall?' Gates shook his head doubtfully. 'That seems unlikely. There would be no union bosses left.'

'I agree. She was just the start, and being corrupt—well, few people with any authority aren't anymore. So, they lay a few more traps, financial, personal, and so on. Sex and money, it's always sex and money. It was like that in my political days and will be for as long as we have politics. His boss was not going to go without a fight.' Dugdale hesitated. 'Anyway, there was a plot to discredit him, bring forward excuses to undermine him as a successor. A corruption case was being prepared. We know this. It would have got very messy. At some point the police and the various agencies would have become involved.'

'So, then the danger would become that he could lead them to you?'

'The shot at the top job was no longer certain. We knew he might be arrested soon. All very regrettable.' Dugdale's strides lengthened, his hands thrust deep into the pockets of the waxed jacket and Dugdale looked towards the tops of the swaying trees that seemed to mesmerise with their dance. 'It was a predicament, but one that did not have to lead to his death.'

'So, what changed?'

'Word reached me that the position was worse than political compromise and blackmail but that he had possibly been recruited by Special Branch. If that was true, it was potentially disastrous. I couldn't confirm it, but I could take no chances.'

'You are saying there was no choice? You had him killed on a possibility?'

'Yes. If he was working for Special Branch, he was a danger. If he wasn't, well to be blunt he was no longer of great use to us. No, he was doomed either way. I regret that, but there it is,' Dugdale responded regretfully. 'He would have talked at some point, they all do.' Dugdale paused in his stride. 'You know what they could have done to him.' Dugdale shook his head, a slow gesture of regret. 'Deeply unpleasant.'

Two floors below the Police press conference briefing room where Gates had sat were the holding suites. Cells and interrogation rooms that existed largely as an open secret, referred to in dark ghoulish humour, their purpose and the events that took place inside was one of the dark mysteries of powerful state security agencies relieved of accountability to all but the highest Party authority. Gates knew they were there, even knowing a few people who had spent time in there, albeit only for a few uncomfortable hours. Sent there to shake them up, remind them of the reach of the System and who was in charge. Dugdale was right.

Without question.

The state security apparatus had multiple levels. At the very bottom were the ordinary beat police—coppers, they stood guard at the football matches, organised the traffic, rounded up the drunks laced with beer and vodka who caused trouble at the bus stations, and pulled in the youths attempting to avoid conscription. In this organisation were also the investigative branches that sought out those responsible for violent crime and robbery. The conventional police worked with but were separate to the Internal Security Police who provided the muscle for public order, SWAT teams and the guarding of critical facilities. Stripped of most accountability and merged into vast regional bureaucracies, serving the public had become an old idea.

At the top were the highly secret intelligence agencies, the Security Service for domestic intelligence work and the foreign intelligence agency that hardly anyone knew about and who did their work unseen from their monolithic London headquarters. In the middle were the Special Branch. Officially police but with long arms that stretched across otherwise formidable boundaries they were to all intents and purposes an autonomous force. They ran the informer networks that stretched and coiled like veins in a body across society, its industry, local Party structures, they were there in every major city or town. They looked for the terrorists, the traitors, the disloyal. Coming to the attention of the Special Branch was bad news. Very bad news indeed.

Hallam, the policeman at the scene of Burns' murder was Special Branch. They only concerned themselves with those the state feared or did not trust.

'Of course, if the allegations made against him were true, he may already have been a source of information to those in authority and would be ready to try and do us damage in the future,' Dugdale said.

'So, you set the dogs on him just in case your plans may have been spilled. That sounds bad, but why bring me into all of this?'

Dugdale had been evading the question since first bringing Gates into the kitchen. The background, the situation, the theatre of Gates' past all designed to delay the suspense, or draw Gates into the dilemma with the vice-like lock and mechanical advantage of a piranhas jaw from which retreat was impossible.

'I need to know whether the allegation he was working for Special Branch was correct. We don't know if he was a traitor to our mission or not. Without knowing it may not be safe to proceed as we plan. If he was working for Special Branch for how long and what had he given them? He can do no more damage, but I need to know what he has done.'

'You had a man killed as a precaution without knowing the truth and you think I can discover whether you were correct?'

Dugdale nodded. 'Something like that, yes, sounds callous I know. But you have to understand what is at stake.' He didn't need to see the look on Gates' face, he knew what the other man was thinking. 'Look, the men that died in that police and military raid yesterday. They knew nothing of Burns' death, crazy right-wing zealots already compromised and then picked out and coldly eliminated to divert everyone's attention and probably to cover up the loss of a valuable and highly placed asset? So, no moral judgements on my decisions here please.'

'You think that's what the raid and the announcement of your death was all about?'

Dugdale breathed deeply. 'Who knows for sure, but very possibly. It does suggest they know more about their enemies than we have given them credit for and that makes knowing the truth about Burns even more important.'

Christ, this guy Burns must have been in very deep, thought Gates. He peered around at the tangled hedgerows, the strands of blackberry twisting and wriggling through the stout spikes of hawthorn hedges with their autumn red berries, so poisonous to humans but a winter feast to field mice and voles storing their energy for the raw force of winter.

'If State Security knows who killed him, why do they not just say so?'

'To know that we would have to ask them—which we can't of course. My own view is it's to spare their blushes with the Party. People like McBride would have had their own design on Burns' future. They won't like the security boys trampling on their ground, they would in all likelihood be furious at the prospect of a Special Branch informer in their senior ranks whatever they had begun to think of Burns. I doubt the Party has much comprehension of our intentions as Hallam and his colleagues may suspect. Hallam will want to keep it that way.

'But, without more knowledge, I am unable to say to allies, those to who we owe the opportunity to reclaim the country and say with certainty: "We can proceed, there are no leaks." And without such assurance they will be reluctant to support doomed seditious plots that just make the cold war colder and give no benefit.'

'If he wasn't working for Special Branch?'

'Then I ordered the death of an innocent man who was already heading for trouble with his Party masters, and I will have to live with that knowledge. Speaking practically my guess is they won't be keen to make a martyr of him which a death at the hands of terrorists might do. They will invent and create a far less glorious route to his demise than he deserves I'm afraid. Whatever it is will be designed to make the matter go away as soon as possible. Lose the mess in a union war, everyone's used to that kind of thing.'

Dugdale was unpicking an entangled thorn branch, delicately easing it free from the lock it had gained on a wooden stile into the next pasture. Gates watched him, wondering when the thick and menacing thorns would strike back at the ungloved hand.

'McBride was already quietly briefing officials on Burns suspected corruption activity and some not very nice criminal links before we acted. He can rely on Special Branch not wanting to be on the wrong side of a general secretary with friends in Moscow. They will want to save face at losing a valuable asset, so they'll go along. After all they're supposed to protect the Party, not make trouble for it.

'The problem that leaves,' Dugdale continued absently, 'is it doesn't help me understand what Burns was involved in and what it means for our plans.'

'And now you are uncertain who you can trust.'

'Precisely. That's why I want you to do some investigation for me.'

The thorn finally found it's mark and Dugdale retreated sucking a wounded thumb from the painful stab. The allusion to the current situation probably not lost on him. Crossing the stile would wait for another day.

'Investigate the corruption angle. Support the Party. While you do that see what you can discover about his relationship if any to the Special Branch.' Dugdale held out his hands almost in an appeal to the skies. 'We can comfortably rely on the rivalries and distrust between the Party and its own security apparatus to leave some confusion for a while.'

'There is this "we" again, what is this organisation you keep talking about?' Dugdale had also referred to "...in time". What did that mean? Was something about to happen? Beyond these fields and trees, Gates thought, are people, factories, and schools. A whole world with its dramas, fortunes, and sadness, but Dugdale stands here and calmly talks of plans to throw it all into turmoil. Raise a new political order. But with what?

Gates decided he didn't understand what was this revolutionary organisation that Dugdale was part of. He could see the allusion to sleeper cells, maybe just individuals, buried in government departments, its institutions, unions, businesses, the armed forces. A covert ecosystem, invisibly networking, while it gathered strength. Was it carefully preparing to unseat the political order that had previously defeated it? How could it have remained undetected as Dugdale suggested?

'None of that need concern you right now,' said Dugdale, with gentle force.

'Okay, but do they know about you and what you do, what you intend? From what you say, it seems they suspect.'

'Possibly, to a point. But the tradecraft of all of this was planned a long time ago with a lot of thought and preparation. It's not the wartime escape committee you might think. The authorities expect and are prepared for the more obvious blunt expressions of resistance, the attacks, assassinations, it's what authoritarian governments prepare for. Groups such as the one they eliminated yesterday are useful. Terrorism is camouflage, believable, manageable, something to coalesce popular support around. What they are really up against we rely on them never realising until it is too late.'

'What will happen now?'

'Depends upon what if anything they have discovered including information gained from Burns. The people I answer to will make the judgements.'

Of course, when he thought about it, it made sense, the leadership of whatever Dugdale talked about would be elsewhere, the 'allies', Gates assumed.

They had come to a small bridge, no more than a thick plank of wood across a tiny brook that gurgled beneath grass. Dugdale tested it out with his foot, rocking it gently.

'But they know about you, or why make an announcement you are dead.' Gates said.

Dugdale shook his head. 'Yes, my name is known.' Dugdale seemed to find the idea amusing. 'And I am the hare they chase. But my real role, well we doubt that they know that, if they did then we would never have got as far as this conversation. It would have all been over. In any case getting near to me would do them no good.'

'How is that?'

Dugdale lost interest in crossing the rickety bridge, the appetite for risk chastened by the victory of the thorn. They lingered a little in the gully, as if the effort of questions and words required their limbs to pause. For a few moments, the silence between them was grave.

'Because they would never take me alive,' said Dugdale with calm finality.

They could have continued following the brook towards where it met a thin tree line. Instead, they stayed in the dip of land that became valley pasture its contours flattening and widening away from them. The meadow swayed, disturbed only by the rustle of a fresh breeze.

'I'm not the leader of this, I'm the fixer or the personnel and communications manager in this enterprise. I make sure the right people are in the right place, connected as much as they need to be. A bit of recruitment, when necessary, some troubleshooting when required. The game, the Grand Game…well, that is really played elsewhere, by others.'

'But they rely upon you, the Americans I assume. You are the key to this.'

'To a point. That's why I need you to help me. I can't investigate this, there is no means to carry out that kind of work…'

Gates did not react and Dugdale went on: 'I want to believe that the removal of Burns doesn't make a great difference, that plans can continue. But I do need to be sure.' His voice had gone quiet.

Something in Dugdale's words caused Gates to think there was more significance to the man's concerns, but he had no idea what that could be.

Their walk down into the open hollows of the land meant the house had dipped from view hidden by the bank behind them. For the first time Gates became aware that Miranda was twenty yards behind them above them on higher ground standing at the corner of the tree line, her gaze patrolling the scene around them.

'What do you think I can do?'

'Discover something, something that might be of use to me. Confirm or deny what we cannot. Find out whether Burns had become a traitor to us or just a tool being used in a union and state power struggle. You're a journalist, it's your job to investigate crime, corruption and you have connections.'

The idea, the request, if that was what it was took Gates back.

He looked back at Dugdale, his face showing disbelief at the idea. 'It's not that easy…journalist, yes, but if I start sniffing around matters of national security, the Party's politics, I won't last five minutes.'

'Are you so sure?' Dugdale's words turned smooth. 'Look,

whatever Special Branch were really up to, it will suit them and the Union to bury the death somehow, corruption scandal probably, publicly at least. We can rely on the bureaucrats fighting it out for a while. The police won't trouble you if they think that is your angle,' Dugdale continued mildly. 'After all corrupt officials are fair game for the press, scrutiny is to be applauded. In the course of that see what you can uncover for me.'

Gates grew more uneasy at Dugdale's suggestion. He didn't like the logic but that didn't mean he couldn't recognise it. He looked away, uncomfortable.

'Should I appeal to your sense of patriotism—perhaps suggest you have realised earlier mistakes—and wish to atone for the errors of your earlier career that helped bring us to this point. You must feel the consequences of what you have been part of,' he insisted hesitantly, although his tone told both men it would not be enough.'

Gates nearly laughed out loud. The risk, danger, the stupidity of becoming involved in revolutionary plans. To be squeezed between the deadly plans of zealots and idealists was madness.

'It's not something I want to be involved in.'

Dugdale's persuasiveness was not finished. He had more. Winning a point was about framing the words differently. 'You are involved already. Your employers, not to mention the police, are going to expect you to write something about a brutal hit and run, even if it's only what they want you to say. I also suspect that Special Branch are going to wonder what you were doing at the scene of a murder,' said Dugdale.

Gates felt the wet grass seep into his shoes and tried to make sense of his emotions. His chest felt weak, and he felt anger that he should be forced into something he wanted no part of it. The wars were gone, and he was a crippled foot soldier simply wanting to be left alone in a quiet place away from the noise of battle. *They use people like you to do their work sing their slogans. Then when they have all the power and the people are worthless, they will spit you out with the rest of the proletariat.* The words from his younger self again. This time they became cautionary advice no longer castigating him.

'What if I say no? What if I want no part of this?'

Dugdale stopped and turned abruptly. He looked surprised, as if Gates was being naive, stupid or both. It occurred to Gates he may be used to dealing with people who had greater courage, principles driving convictions all qualities that went beyond self-interest. He is wondering, thought Gates, if he has misjudged me.

'That would be a disappointment, but not unexpected.' His voice changed, the political sophistry gone, the words now carried blunt punch. 'But before you say no there's something else you should know. A clever man, a man I admired,' said Dugdale carefully, 'once told me I would only ever get very good or very bad news from him. I'll pass that same advice on to you now. The bad news is over there.' He jutted his chin over Gates' shoulder to where Miranda stood. 'She doesn't like your type very much; her father was a general, a very good one, highly distinguished service. Unfortunately, towards the end of his career he was not considered reliable, not even trusted to be put into well-earned retirement. So, they made up some sedition charges and hanged him.' Dugdale let the general's fate sink in. 'Not surprisingly she is extremely loyal to me, to this cause and she is very, very efficient. The Americans trained her for a year or two, they can really be very good at that sort of thing.'

The threat needed no elaboration. Burns' death pointed to the fate of those with too much knowledge. Rather proves my point, thought Gates. These people who claim to be patriots throwing off oppression, proclaiming freedom and liberty. Are they any better, or just the same thugs with different ideas? He really couldn't tell.

'This needs to be cleaned up Gates, and you can help. Find out what was going on and we can all move on to a better place.' For a moment he looked at Gates, his face an awkward appeal. 'Personally, after your performance in life I thinks it's the least you can do. You have a duty, we all do. But more importantly you have a daughter in a gulag they call a college because of a system you helped to create.' Gates stared at him for a while, not in the mood to challenge Dugdale's opinion. 'Do I count upon your support? Yes? No?'

Still Gates did not answer. His mind was on a crushed

body, very real; a police briefing, probably fake; a young cold woman who had bought him here, also very real; and Sophie whose face sometimes slipped away but who provided the only real purpose in his life.

Without warning Dugdale turned and began to stride back up the hill, leaving the path to make a direct line across the wet grass back towards the rear of the house whose angled rafters came back into view. He looked at his watch and Gates sensed a new urgency had come upon the man, that enough time had been spent on this explanation. It was time to move on to new tasks. Gates quickened his pace to keep up.

'And, if I agree, what is the good news?'

Dugdale stopped and looked at him calmly. Gates had a sense of what a good politician he must have been all those years ago. Smoothly, effortlessly caressing people while at the same time causing them apprehension and nervousness, the ability to intimidate without revealing a threat. He felt something and looking down he realised that Dugdale had gripped his hand, a handshake that was firm, a physical connection that briefly tethered them together.

Dugdale's blue eyes glittered again and what he said bought Gates to an involuntary stop, his ears disbelieving: 'Sophie, your daughter. If you agree, I can get her back.' His face turned stony, and the eyes became a little cruel. 'If you do this, I can make her safe.'

MUCH later, alone in his apartment, Gates sat without lights, next to open curtains letting the dull moonlight of night drip in. He ignored the chill, was grateful for the rarity of still darkness and tried to make sense of what he had learnt and found his heart racing, his breath a little short. It was like an illness had come upon him, but he recognised it as fear and anger, the suppressed regret at the beliefs of his earlier life taunting him. A lifetime of existing on his wits and by rules he had conditioned himself to follow, rules created by the state that demanded you conform out of fear with no chance of turning back.

*You're not interesting enough and certainly not important enough,* Kate, the second wife had taunted him viciously all those years ago. *You can take the girl, go back to your northern hovel.*

She was right, in her cruel way. There were smarter more driven people around. People more ruthless and committed, people who saw ideology as opportunity not a force for good. Those people would win, and Kate would be among them. Had he been guilty of seeing life too idealistically? No one was indispensable to the cause—he knew this now. The corruption of power with the vanity it creates is as corrosive as the strongest of acids. It had not needed Dugdale to tell him so, in the solitude of his mind he had told himself: You know it's corrupt, you know you don't matter. What more evidence do you need than a twenty-three-year-old daughter being sent to rot in a Polish re-education centre. At this point the most important cause for carrying on was Sophie, a victim of the society he had been a small part of creating. This realisation in the moments like now, when he let it in, formed a pool of guilt which drove sleep away.

Was Dugdale's way any better?

Was he right?

Was there really any chance to reclaim a country, restore an old system with its values of liberty and freedom? If it did, would it actually be much better, sufficiently improved to justify the risk and the probable loss? The old system had changed for a reason.

He lit a fresh cigarette from the butt of the previous filter and watched the blue smoke curl afraid to leave the warmer apartment air for the night outside. It's not about ideology, he thought, it's not about duty or putting things right. It's simply personal now. Caught on the possibility of Sophie's freedom? The emergence of hope. Never mind the big ideas, they no longer interested him and could be left for others to claw and fight over. Look after your own, put your own interests first. Follow the opportunity don't leave the possibility to save her on the table, time to ignore the dangers and do something that was right. The paradoxes were endless and were circulating endlessly in his head.

Dugdale was asking him to investigate a murder in which there were no innocents.

Asking him to take risks attempting to extract information

from ruthless men and dangerous organisations.

In the name of what?

'We are not far away, do remember that,' said Miranda, as she left him at a train station on the east of the city. It had been a precaution to take the Metro service back into Manchester, slipping back from the commuter belt. In the middle of the day the coach was only half-full, but it stank of sweat and tobacco smoke. Gates had occupied a worn greasy window seat looking through black window grime at the industrial outskirts and thought about what he had been told.

What choice do I have anyway, he said to himself?

In the evening gloom slumped in the lumpy horsehair chair, it still seemed to make no more sense and he looked down at his hands focusing on the cracked skin around his nails. Can I do this? Inertia, doing nothing had always seemed the best option, solid down the line non-controversial, reporting your master's voice.

But that was before Dugdale's offer to rescue Sophie.

Miranda had passed him a card, a plain white business card of a shop. 'That's your contact. Go there if you need to tell us something. Buy something silver over a hundred pounds, that'll get our attention. Can you do that?' Gates nodded. 'No phones, no emails everything is at arms-length. If we need you, we'll be in touch.'

Later that night when sleep finally claimed him the dream assailed him again. The same bleak classroom with the same young people dressed alike in grey coveralls siting at desks. In the middle, Sophie, her hair cropped, and face scrubbed and pale. Once more his mind made him watch as she wrote the words from a blackboard, following them faithfully, a furrow of concentration on her brow, eyes fixed on the chalk text her lips miming the words as the pen scratched them out onto the paper. The dark variations of the cruel unwanted dream that played over and over.

Earlier, her image had been there when he and Dugdale had returned to the kitchen table of the old crumbling house. Miranda had made more tea and they had sat across the mugs and looked at one another.

'What do you want to do Gates. Either way your life now changes.'

He wanted that image gone.

Gates had lit a cigarette and twirled the packet with his fingers on the table. 'I'll find out what I can.'

\*\*\*

# CHAPTER SIX

*Everyone is good communist...*

**London**

'THAT STUFF IS A heart attack on a plate.'

Tom Shiner laughed at Gates' sarcasm and washed the bacon in the egg anyway. He considered combining the delicious mix with the buttered toast for an extravagant mouthful. Instead, he opted to extend the pleasure of the fried breakfast he was not paying for. The toast, he decided, would go well with the hot tea that steamed in a mug on the Formica tabletop.

'You offered to pay; it was an opportunity too good to resist.' He looked across the table at his old colleague. 'Can't remember the last time you were in London. How're things with you?'

They were in a cafe close to the Balls Pond Road near the Dalston Junction overland station. It was a gem of a place, hidden in the shadow and grime of the main motorway A10 link road, difficult to reach unless you knew it was there. The area was cordoned by elevated motorways and the cubes and vertical rectangles of tower blocks reaching upwards and which could be accessed only through urine-soaked subways that marooned the poor and the elderly in their aerial slums. Lodged away was this forgotten space of an old London, overlooked by the central planners as the money for concrete ran out or their attention shifted elsewhere.

It was a good place; Gates could tell immediately. The kind those in the know keep to themselves.

Shiner knew of it of course. As a Londoner by birth and a local resident by choice he prided himself on knowing where to eat and drink. Over the entrance a gaudy rectangular sign grimy with the dirt of the hurtling traffic above ticked red neon in a constant circular pattern like a clock. The Turkish manager had fixed it there to attract trade. Gates wondered why, glancing around there was no shortage of clientele. But all were busy with their plates, newspapers or talking. Combined with the regular whoosh of steam from the kitchen and yells of two waitresses pirouetting with trays containing fried food that still hissed with heat there was not much chance of being overheard. Lord knows where the manager got his supplies from. Shiner told him he used the place often.

'Not eating yourself?' asked Shiner and probed towards Gates' plate with the blade of his knife to where the eggs and rashers were untouched. 'Coffee alone won't do it. Your suit looks like it's been slept in, and you look like a decent meal wouldn't do you any harm. No one looking after you I take it?'

Gates gave a grim chuckle and rolled his eyes. 'How is that likely to happen?'

Some people change little with the passing years, thought Gates. Of all of the pack of journalists that used to write for the *Mirror,* the *Worker* or other socialist dailies, they were the only two left—at least that he could think of—and Shiner had definitely fared better. The droopy folds of middle-age suited him, still sharp faced and sharp eyed. Then as now he had thick long blond hair flicked back over his ears, the mouth remained quick to smile. They had been on the *Mirror* together as cub reporters. Shiner had more talent but less zeal. To him the experience of political reporting had been a game rather than a calling. Still first with a joke and first to the bar, meeting deadlines by a whisker, his copy brightened by the effect of gin and lemon.

Today he wore a cricketing tie under a linen jacket, the type journalists would once have worn on middle east trips to war zones or African famines. Shiner hadn't left the country in years, no would consider him for an exit visa. Gates remembered a memorable long-ago Saturday, a charity match at the Oval, *Lobby Journos* versus *Backbenchers* and Shiner's determined well supported seventy-five not out at the crease to take the game.

Gates could still hear the laughter and cheers that continued into the last and longest innings then played in the bar.

He had been popular, perhaps too much so. Kate had called him: *a charming, clever clown,* to his face across the table at a smart dinner party in a North London suburb with people who pretended they had ideals rather than money. There had been smiles and laughter, no offence taken. But Gates had seen the flinty look in his ex-wife's eyes and knew what that meant. There were one too many clever remarks at people's expense, some of which found themselves into snide print. Shiner had a habit of teasing those he probably shouldn't, those whose thin skins bruised too easily. He had more brains than most of them and they knew it. They resented it at first and then came to hate him for it. He had lasted a little longer than Gates, hanging on while the adrenalin of radicalism shaped itself into a new order and conformity and then he had found himself slipping towards the fringes of his trade, passed between papers, the by-lines and credits steadily becoming shorter.

Now, he never wrote under his own name. Officially freelance, he provided the material for success to others, mostly and more lucratively as useful information for journalists seeking the salacious gossip that could thrill or be used for revenge. There was always a market for that, even in a state-controlled media industry.

Shiner made it his business to know about people.

He knew a lot about a lot of people.

And information can be traded.

At the next table, a man in a yellow high vis jacket read

from a newspaper and loudly lamented the previous evenings performance of Arsenal against close rivals Tottenham Hotspur. He gave the manager three matches, he said in a disgusted voice, then he was for the chop.

'Trade is still good?'

'The work suits me,' said Shiner. He bit into the bacon and chewed briefly. 'No more crawling around a number of functionaries who pretend to be newspaper editors.'

'Pleased to hear it.'

'Allows me to eat in places like this.' His eyes scanned the busy cafe with its peeling walls and a helplessly greased ceiling fan. Then he chuckled. 'The indiscretions of our elites, it's positively bourgeois. A self-licking lollipop of a business. Someone always pays for that.'

'No thoughts of a quieter life?'

'You mean run for the hills, go north like you did? No, not really. This is my town remember. Despite the bastards who run it and what they do.'

Dangerous words.

Shiner saw the look and laughed. 'Don't worry *'Comrade'*. It's not Orwell yet. We are safe here. That's why you came right?' His face turned serious, quite suddenly. 'I was sorry to hear about Sophie, Harry, truly sorry. I know what she meant—means to you. That heartless bitch Kate could have done something, she has the connections. She wouldn't help?'

'Sooner the better,' the man in the yellow jacket was saying over the top of a huge mug of tea, 'Spanish idiot has been a disaster.'

Gates crunched the buttered toast, brushed breadcrumbs from his tie and shook his head. 'It happens,' he said simply.

He had arrived at Euston Station just after seven that morning, the journey flying by in a single hour. The coaches were busy, and Gates had stood as the silver bullet of a rain ripped across the English countryside. One of the socialist successes, prestige infrastructure construction unconcerned with planning permission. His editor had only partially surprised him by allowing him to follow up a lead in London. Gates had gone into his office directly on his return to Manchester after meeting Dugdale. It's corruption in a union at the very top, he explained. I think it could be big. I understand a union boss has been killed, the police aren't talking yet, but they will. I need some answers about why and who is involved. The editor had nodded thoughtfully. On the whole, Harry liked the man. He worked the system pretty well, kept the censor off the hacks as best he could and wouldn't pass up the opportunity to take a swipe at corruption. That was sound enough journalism and probably the best that could be asked for.

'I still need five hundred words on this Dugdale incident the police are boasting about, it'll be front page tomorrow.'

Gates sensed the press announcement from the police on Dugdale's killing had not excited him either. But the story was expected to be out there. 'By 8 pm, on your desk, I promise. We can use the police images.'

He had been tempted to take a day off, hide the trip to London, keep the whole project away from any scrutiny, but had quickly dismissed the idea. Too many cameras, too many electronic access barriers, too much risk. Better to go with a legitimate purpose—at least officially.

'I was surprised to get your call. You know what you're doing I take it? This is fishing in some very dark waters Harry.' Shiner's eyes were grave and held concern. The days at the *Mirror* were long ago, but they had shared some good times. 'But here you go.' From his inner pocket he pulled two sheets of paper. 'There's probably more, but this is what I have to hand.' He saw the questioning look on Gates' face. 'This is with my compliments. You can owe me sometime.'

The sheets were typewritten. There were some black and white photos embedded as large thumbnails, some text and a tabular record of dates and places.

Shiner said: 'Busier than some, not as busy as others.' He continued eating, eyes down over his plate while Gates studied.

The image in the first thumbnail was definitely Burns, it matched the stock photograph in the *Herald's*, *Who's Who*. He guessed it was taken recently at a meeting. A publicity shot perhaps. Burns was in half-profile, business suit, seated at a meeting table, leaning forward, his forearms extended, hands clasped and looking calmly towards the lens. It was a powerful face, confident, it could have been a shot of a party official, managing director, or of course what it was, a senior union leader.

'The picture underneath is the girl,' said Shiner his mouth full of food. A simple passport type shot showed a pretty face, dark-haired and blue eyed, at least a quarter of a century younger than Burns. Lush lips and a soft neck. She looked sweet, innocent incapable of deception.

Yet that is what it was.

'This one gives you the idea better.' He turned the folder discreetly opening it and Gates saw the picture of a man and women disembarking a railway carriage. The man was Len Burns, the woman, the girl in the passport shot 'Annie Freedman, aged 26,' resumed Shiner, 'comes from Kent, Maidstone to be precise. She works as an administrator-come-secretary in the London headquarters. That's all I know really. But not difficult to work out how they got together.'

'How did you—'

'Put two and two together?' Shiner laughed. 'Actually, I have this sort of crap on a lot of people. Our leaders and betters lack imagination, they're pretty predictable in their habits. The political class take their wives to the Black Sea and their mistresses to Paris. I pay a guy who knows the faces to hang around the Eurostar entrance on a Friday afternoon. Pound to a pinch you'll see someone noticeable sliding off for the weekend. Usually, the girl is not with them but will be somewhere close.' He paused and smiled. 'Funny thing is they always come back together, a fond short kiss at the taxi rank and they go their separate ways. Never fails. After that it's just a bit of joining the dots.'

'How long have they been seeing each other? Do you know?'

'That, I don't. But you can see they were first spotted three months ago. So, at least that long. It could be more of course.'

'How often do they meet.'

Shiner shook his head. 'This stuff is of passing interest, not surveillance, so this is just useful collectibles. You'll see a couple of reports of meetings in hotels. They all like the Millennium, so they've been spotted there.' He pointed to the paper he had handed Gates. 'There's a flat in the Barbican he uses when in the city. Most Party men keep their mistresses away from these weekday places. Too risky. Wives use them when shopping. They tend to know when a female rival has been nesting there, there must be a smell or something. But may be worth checking.'

'Outside of his private life have you anything of interest regarding his work?'

'You mean the nomination for secretary-general?'

'Yes,' said Gates lightly, as he passed the plate of toast across. 'Know anything about that?'

'Only that Burns is the surprising favourite to win. He's popular and influential with the local committees in the regions. The current guy has been too interested in his Moscow connections, trips to the Baltic States and pulling the government's strings back home. Everyone thinks he is old and tired. He has left Burns a pretty free hand to run and organise things internally as he wants. And he's done that well, he's popular, and the big man has no doubt recognised his mistake.'

'Any idea how he might put the situation right? Rig the nomination process?'

Shiner looked surprised and his face took on an expression of mock outrage. 'Who rigs an election in this country. Let's be sensible. We just don't have them anymore—at least important ones—no, Burns was clever.' He became serious. 'The nomination and voting machinery are in his hands. They only have one every five years. He's spent that long getting control of the nomination colleges and putting the process together. He knew what he was doing, they used to call it gerrymandering in the old days, remember?' Gates smiled and nodded. 'The only problem is the emergence of some corruption allegations which they are going to try and hitch Burns to, but unless they find or create something significant that will be no more effective than accusing him of adultery. When they are all at it who seriously cares?'

The rest of the material was useful, addresses, some phone numbers a few other of Burns contacts. His home address outside Great Lever, which Gates already knew.

Shiner looked up and studied Gates, his scrutiny thoughtful. 'What's your interest Harry, why do you want to know about this guy?'

Gates hesitated but concluded that Shiner would know soon enough. Anyway, he was a goldmine, and he might need more favours.

'Burns isn't going to win any nomination to replace McBride, Tom, he's dead. Killed in a hit and run three days ago near his home.' He watched Shiner's face change to a look of surprise. 'Police are keeping quiet about it at the moment.'

'Holy fuck!' Shiner lent forward, genuine surprise on his face. 'You're serious? Who? Do we know?'

'Don't know,' Gates was being half truthful. 'Probably the police and the union are deciding that between them right now. When they get their story straight, there'll be an announcement.'

'And your interest?'

Gates shrugged, forced to continue the deceit. 'There'll be some tale about Burns being corrupt, something to make it go away. Unlikely anyone will answer for it. I am just trying to write a piece that's more than an announcement and better than an obituary.' He suddenly felt hungry and scooped a slice of the untouched bacon into his mouth. 'Can you get me this girl's address? Is she in London?'

Shiner nodded. 'Give me an hour or so. I'll text it to you. Okay?'

'Fine.' Gates hesitated once more. 'Listen, I need to know something else. What do you know of James Dugdale?'

'The guy the police reported they killed a few days ago.

Planning an attack on Sellafield?' He saw Gates nod. 'A little, not been around for years. Ancient history, one of Thatcher's pets. I remember him of course. Ended up being detained for a few years. Last I heard I think he was in Canada. Isn't there a colony or something out in British Colombia for his tribe?' Shiner paused while he thought. 'Rumours of course. Rumours he might be involved in a conspiracy against the government, the Party. That idea has been around for years, a plot by the deep state years ago to bring back the old democracy.'

'What do you think to that idea?' Gates offered impassively.

'What the idea or the existence of a plot?

'Both, I suppose.'

Shiner looked at Gates carefully, as he considered the question, his mouth in mid chew. 'Alright, if you're asking. It's an interesting idea, but after a number of years of digging around in the political dirt of this country I've yet to see any evidence of it.' He continued to look at Gates thoughtfully, but Gates said nothing.

'I will admit the announcement of a death of a little-known radical seems strange, it's the actions of a spooked state. Anything you care to share?'

Gates couldn't be sure, but Shiner seemed not inclined to believe the police announcement of the man's death. Like him, he probably suspected a 'media-look-over-there' planted story.

'The announcement was probably a way of the police

diverting attention from Burns death,' Gates said cautiously. 'But you never know I suppose.'

Shiner had finished his breakfast and moved the plate to one side, spreading his hands on the Formica tabletop. He wasn't one to give up on acquiring information so easily.

'So, these events are connected.' He probed his teeth with his tongue easing bacon free from his molar. 'I don't really follow the news on the latest terrorist threats, they come thick and fast. I had assumed the announcement about this Dugdale was another inter-agency turf war, 'keep off my grass'. It's a cat fight for resources, you show a threat and better still demonstrate you're dealing with it, it's more difficult to take your job and your resources.'

'Probably just that,' Gates lied. 'I'm concentrating on the union corruption, but I thought the linkage, if any, to Dugdale might be interesting so, I thought I'd run it past you.'

Shiner did not look convinced, but let it go. 'Occasionally there is a rumour of some of the old crowd coming back to the country. Apparently, they get in via Switzerland or Sweden, false papers using the neutral routes. Quite what they are up to no one really knows. They don't try to make trouble themselves. I assume it's a little rabble-rousing, distribution of useful funding, false paperwork, that sort of thing. Maybe it's more than that, if so, you should be careful where you go with this my friend. Do you want to see if I can find more?'

Gates didn't reply, thinking he should now drop the subject.

One of the waitresses appeared to clear plates and they waited until she had moved out of earshot.

But Shiner continued in a low tone: 'Be careful Harry. I can tell you are involved in something. If there's more to Dugdale, well…we go back a long way, and I would be happy to help.' His eyebrows raised in an arch and Gates felt his friend sensed something of his mission. 'But don't go too far out on your own. Give me a ten-pound note?'

The request must have caused Gates to look surprised and Shiner grinned. 'Don't worry it's not a demand for payment, I'm not that cheap.'

Gates did as he was asked and slipped a battered note from his wallet across the table. He watched as Shiner slid the note under the butter knife. With a pen knife he made a small tear and then ripped the note in two. He passed one-half of the note back to Gates.

'If you get this back, then get in touch. There is always *Sunrise*, I keep her on the estuary.'

Gates nodded. The old hulk of a retreat, a Dutch barge Shiner kept on the jungle fringes to the east of the city.

He would have liked to ask more; he was becoming drawn into a conversation that it was unwise to have.

'I have to go, he said.' He took a five-pound note from his wallet and waved at the girl.

'Come back soon, Harry. It's been too long.'

Outside they both buttoned their coats and shook hands.

As they parted, on impulse Gates asked: 'Knowing people in the Party as you do the good, the bad and the opportunistic, was Burns a good communist do you think, reliable?'

'Everyone's a good communist Harry,' said Shiner. 'But good communists only do what clever communists tell them. You've read your Marx.' And he padded off down the street, the thunder of traffic above drowning his farewell.

THE only person on the third floor of the Barbican apartment building was a cleaning woman. She was large and black, her ample rump balanced upon clog shoes came into view as Gates climbed the final few stairs. She was swinging a mop across the floor and talking to herself in a language Gates didn't recognise but stopped when she became aware of the footsteps behind her. She looked at him suspiciously as he edged past her unsure whether to return his greeting. He found the door to Burns apartment a little further along the corridor and wondered what to do next. It was solid and he had no key. He didn't even know whether it was occupied. There was no bell, so he tapped gently and listened against the woodwork.

'He's not in, love, haven't seen him since last week.'

The cleaning woman had circled the mop to a halt and was standing watching him.

Gates thought quickly. 'Oh damn,' he muttered in audible frustration and tapped his jacket pocket. 'I'm from his office. Is he not back yet? He wanted me to collect a parcel and I have papers from him.' He looked at his watch. 'I can't wait for long; Union headquarters is waiting.'

'You work for him?' she asked, her gaze took in Gates hair and threadbare suit. He looked an unlikely asset to a powerful official.

'Of course, shall I ring him?' He held out his phone and twisted his face into an earnest look.

She hesitated, weighing the odds, her manner softening ever so slightly. 'Tiss alright dear, not the first time he's left something but you're the third in as many days. The girl yesterday and the young man before her had their own keys. I'm the one that do his cleaning,'—the accent was pure Caribbean—'he said he would be back as usual. If it's really urgent I suppose I can let you in.' She fished in her thigh pocket and produced two Banham security keys on a ring and held them out. 'Be quick mind.'

There is a way of offering an item, a curl of the fingers that says not yet. Gates realised this was a transaction not a favour and with a you-got-me grin he pulled five-pounds from his wallet thanking her for her trouble and extracting a promise that this was between them.

'I'll be downstairs in number 12,' she called in her song-song lilt as she began to descend the stairs leaving him alone in the corridor. 'Drop 'em off with me when yer finished dear.' The soft crump of her flat shoes on the tiles receded.

The locks worked smoothly, and Gates found himself in a

good-sized sitting room with an open plan kitchen at one end. Floor to ceiling windows ran the length of the living area, and to one side was a study alcove area with a large desk. The furniture was Scandinavian blocks, the floor light wood with grey rugs. There was a utility about the place that spoke of occasional comfortable use. Two doors led off the main room, one to a bedroom just large enough for the substantial bed and a windowless bathroom of chrome and white tiles that smelt of old cologne.

On the large square coffee table was a pile of periodicals and trade magazines. Across the floor trailing under the sofa from the electrical outlet was a computer power lead, the male connector left loose on the floor. A discarded computer disk was on the low table.

But no laptop.

*The girl yesterday and the young man before, both had a key.* So, not the first person here? thought Gates.

What was he looking for? He wasn't sure, something that might give a clue to Burns' activities away from his union role, he supposed.

He started with the study alcove. There was no computer on the desk, just a banker's lamp, a tarnished silver cigarette box, and desk tidy. It was a pedestal desk, English reproduction mahogany, out of character in a quirky tasteful way with the rest of the apartment and there were drawers to the floor. He quickly went through them finding nothing. The top drawer had been clumsily prised with a flat blade by someone who didn't know what they were doing. Gates could see how the barrel of the lock had been eased down, scraping the varnish, and chipping the surrounding wood.

Definitely not the first person here.

He slid the drawer open and as he suspected it had been cleared of anything of possible interest. Except…a plain white business card. An antique or bric-a-brac shop in Manchester. Gates recognised the address. It was the same card Miranda had passed to him. He decided to pocket it.

He sat on the swivel office chair and placed his hands flat on the desk. Who had been here? Special Branch, Security Service, someone from the union, maybe even Dugdale. The latter he didn't think so. Quickly he went through the bedroom, checking drawers and cupboards, even ducking under the frame of the bed. But it was all clear. It didn't make sense all of those would have been more thorough, systematic and destructive.

It was evident that whoever had been here either knew what they wanted, or only had time for a very quick look-a-round. A real search, one intent on finding clues would take hours.

He went back to the desk.

There he was surprised to find Burns' passport in one of the pedestal drawers. Gates flicked through it and saw it was still current. There were plenty of stamps, mostly Eastern Europe, a couple to Sweden and some visits to Switzerland. It told him nothing and Gates was about to give up. He knew that he needed to return the key before the cleaner became suspicious. He was wondering if there was nothing here of interest anyway.

For no real reason he slid his hand under the drawer that had been forced. To his surprise he felt paper, an envelope held by parcel tape to the underside. Pulling it clear he found himself holding a large manila envelope. It was unfastened and unmarked except for the tape diagonally placed across each corner to hold it to the underside of the desk.

The photographs were of Burns and a woman in bed. Their pale bodies writhed on white sheets and the camera angle taken from alongside the bed showed their faces and bodies clearly, down to the beads of sweat that lined their flanks. The girl's face, inclined towards the camera, was twisted, and screwed in some shots, her neck arching beneath the pressure of the man's body arms spread above her head. In other shots she sat astride the man's middle-aged belly, her long thin arms supporting her weight each side of his head, dark hair hanging down towards his face. In the last shot both appeared spent, and she lay with her head on his stomach, fingers curled into the thick black hair of his chest her eyes directly into the lens of the camera.

They were cold clinical images of intimacy, pictures shot through a dispassionate lens hidden from the subject's knowledge.

The next series of photographs confused him. They were surveillance shots taken at street level through a long lens, he assumed from a car. It was of Burns dressed in a summer suit climbing the steps of a building. The series captured him leaving the roadway and entering the glass sliding door. He wondered what their significance was but at first glance there was none.

It was the final shots that caused the breath to leave Gates' lungs.

Two young men standing naked in a room. It was difficult to be precise, but he guessed they were about twenty years of age, but no more. One of the young men was bent over a table resting on his elbows. His contorted face was easily visible, his short hair wet from exertion and there were string beads of sweat on his forehead. The other youth stood behind him, his hands gripping his lover's hips firmly. Gates could see the lean muscles of the young man's thighs and arms defined, tensed, and pumped.

Blackmail it is, Gates thought, although he did not yet know why.

Gone, along with the contents of the drawer. It confirmed his suspicion that whoever had been here had come with a purpose to collect not to discover. There was no point in remaining longer.

He locked the front door behind him and turned into the corridor.

Outside on the stairs he met the cleaner lumbering with the

tools of her trade back up the stairs.

'I waz jus cumming to find you. Wondered where you had got to,' she said giving him a worried look. An entrepreneurial approach to key-holding carried risk and she was fearful she may have misjudged the opportunity.

'Sorry, my phone went,' he said. 'Had to answer it.'

'Where's the parcel you wanted, the papers?'

'Ah, that was the phone call. A mix up. They may already have been collected. Probably the caller yesterday. Did she say who she was?'

'Oh, we didn't speak dear, she's a regular, has a key, I just saw her going in.' She seemed to reflect on the event now Gates had referred to it. 'She looked scruffy too, in a bit of a state if you ask me dear,' she added carelessly, unconcerned at any offence Gates might have taken. 'Seemed upset. Did he say what time he'd be back?'

Clearly this was a woman who let nothing past and had an eye for detail and not one to hold her feelings back, thought Gates. 'Who?' he asked.

'Yer man, Mr Burns?' she cried, exasperated with his slowness.

But Gates was already on the move. 'Later today,' he called over his shoulder and took the stairs two at a time out onto the pavement and filled his lungs with the chill London air.

THE apartment was a puzzle. Someone had been there, and

they had a key. Why hadn't the police been there? It would be perfectly natural after a murder to search his city apartment seeking clues, it was an investigative standard procedure surely. There was only one organisation that could stop them—that would be Special Branch. Why hadn't *they* searched the apartment? Was it because they didn't need to?

Perhaps.

So, what was it that whoever had been to the apartment had been collecting? He assumed it was collection because that would explain why the pictures were there intact, undisturbed, presumably where Burns had hidden them. They wouldn't have been difficult to find, which meant they weren't looking for them—or didn't care about them. So, what had they been looking for? A computer, papers of some kind, something else?

He didn't know.

He was drinking bitter coffee in a cafe a few streets away. The Barbican was a smart area, and the coffee was over-priced, but Gates needed a little time to think and collect his thoughts. He turned to the question of what the shots of Burns in the street and the two unknown boys meant? They were incriminating somehow, which suggested blackmail? Was this Special Branch forcing his recruitment as Dugdale feared or just part of the smearing of Burns by McBride the union boss, McBride, trying to incriminate him as Dugdale hoped?

The pictures of Burns and the girl were probably less important.

Sex with an office junior. So what?

It was the others that counted. Something that put pressure on Burns.

Something that could be used to give up Dugdale's secrets?

Possibly. Too many questions unanswered.

The cafe was quiet. He rang a mobile number and waited for it to be picked up. Checking his watch, he saw it was 12:18 pm. A soft female voice answered: 'Lucy Swan,' then, 'Oh hello Comrade,' as she realised who the caller was.

'Hello Lucy, how's the office?'

He heard her chuckle. 'Same old, same old. How is your trip to London?'

'Fine, thanks. Listen Lucy, I'll be quick. Can you check whether a Annie Freedman is still employed by the AEMU?'

'I can try. Where would she work, the London HQ?'

'Yes, she is involved in the corruption case, I'm looking into. She lives in London, in the Paddington area. If you can find anything else out about her that would be great.'

'I can see she's on social media.' Her voice slowed, her brain focusing on thoughts, not words and Gates could visualise her typing into a search engine and reading as she spoke. 'A couple of the usual sites, twenty-six years old, half-Portuguese, is that right? And she's in the phone book. Let me put what I can together. I'll call you as soon as I have something.'

'Appreciate it, Lucy. I'll be back in the office tomorrow in case anyone asks.' Gates rang off and decided to finish his coffee and wait where he was until Lucy rang back.

***

# CHAPTER SEVEN

### *The Girl*

**London**

CROMWELL TERRACE RUNS NORTH to south for half a mile, through a sprawling grey housing estate. It's a main thoroughfare that cuts through a maze of cul de sacs and speed bumps and is close enough to Paddington railway station to hear the platform announcements and squeal of locomotive brakes on the final few feet of track. Annie Freedman's address was in one of the old fifties apartment buildings halfway down.

The block was six floors of apartments, brick faced with external access walkways at the front. The lines of windows looked worn but solid as did the London Metropolitan Authority red brickwork which was blackened by traffic soot but overall, the area was less run down than Gates expected. The background rumble of the elevated motorway and the rush of trains departing and leaving mingled with the horns of local delivery vans squeezing through the carelessly parked cars and vans.

He found the apartment address that Shiner had texted him on the second floor. The front door was black and flaking, there was a plastic bell push that didn't seem to work so he rapped the large, tarnished knocker loudly. A minute passed before Gates heard a security chain rattle free, and the door opened on its chain. He caught the glimpse of the young face of a woman that he recognised from Shiner's photograph.

'Miss Freedman, may I talk to you?' He smiled at her. 'I won't take much of your time.'

The girl's face was as close to the gap as the chain allowed, her expression uncertain and wary, her dark eyes were slow and sleepy, and Gates could smell wine, cigarettes and perfume. Expensive brand, he thought. She didn't look like a girl with money, a lover's gift?

'Who are you?' came a nervous reply. 'What's this about?'

'My name is Harry Gates, I'm a reporter, with the *Manchester Herald*.'

The face disappeared and the door slammed shut.

Gates waited a minute, then took one of the photographs of Burns and the girl in bed from his jacket pocket. Folding it over, being careful not to crease it, he slipped it through the letter box letting it fall to the floor. Then he stepped back, lent against the outside balcony lit a cigarette and waited. On the ground far below a group of boys began to kick a football between a garage wall and a car. An angry shout disrupted their game and Gates heard them laugh then return a stream of obscenities before selecting another vehicle as the goal. The ball crashed into the doors of the car with venom.

It took three minutes. Then he heard the soft plop of the bolt slipping back off its chain and the door slowly and cautiously opened. There was fear about her face, as if he were a bailiff making a final call on a pressing debt. For a short while she looked at him, then her eyes darted beyond and around him peering to see if he was alone. She was small, not much over five feet. Long dark hair fell over a blue t-shirt to the middle of her back. She wore denim shorts with ripped hems on top of her bare shapely legs with smooth olive skin and no shoes. She was a looker, but today, Gates thought, she was not presenting at her best.

'What do you want?'

'I want to talk to you Annie—not about that photo—I want to know about Len Burns. Help me and I won't use any information about you. But if you don't answer my questions, then other people will start asking about you and him.' He tapped his jacket pocket containing the photos to emphasise the point. Her face held worry and resignation and Gates thought how confused and frightened she looked. 'And if they do that's not going to help anyone, is it?'

She thought for a moment then reluctantly she pulled the door open and made room for him to pass through along the short corridor and into a small sitting room. A corner sofa took up most of two of the walls, a small dining table stood opposite.

Above the table on the wall a television hung not quite straight and from behind it a jumble of electrical cables fell to the floor. There was just room for a low, chipped and marked pine table piled with fashion and celebrity magazines the covers ringed with coffee stains and on top like a triumphant flag planted on the peak of a notable mountain, a three-quarters empty bottle of white wine. Another empty bottle rolled under the table as she failed to step over it. She flopped onto the sofa and pointed to the dining chairs opposite. Gray silver clouds pregnant with rain filled the muntin gridded window. Around the room on the walls were over-sized film posters in black frames, the only decoration in an apartment cluttered with youth.

'What do you want to know? What are you going to do?' she asked, her voice feverish.

'Look, I'll come to the point,' he began apologetically. 'You and Len Burns were lovers, that's obvious. I want to ask you some questions about your relationship. Can I ask how long you had been seeing each other?'

She hesitated. Then with reluctance: 'A while. Nearly a year I suppose.'

'You worked in his office? You worked for him?'

She had lit a cigarette as soon as she sat down using both hands to steady the lighter. But the cheap paper was burning fast, the ash tottering ready to fall. He took it from her and stubbed it in a glass ashtray next to the magazines.

Again, the hesitation. 'Just an administrator. Nothing

special, nothing important. I just helped with the paperwork, filing, ordering the stationary, that sort of thing.'

Earlier Lucy had called Gates with information about the girl. She had got the job just last year, under qualified but with great references. Taken on by the personnel department and placed in Burns' extensive outer office. A plant? Gates had asked. Lucy had spoken to the recruiter. She had apparently been surprised at the appointment. The recruiter had thought the girl nice, sweet but a little dim. Very probably, Lucy agreed.

'Was it planned?'

'How do you mean?' she replied dully.

Was she being coy or did she really not understand the question. 'Meeting Burns, becoming his mistress. Did someone tell you to get close to him? How did you get together?'

She said nothing and swallowed the last of the wine in her glass. She pulled a face suppressing the acid taste of the cheap wine.

Then: 'A bar. One used by office people after work. He had a roving eye. We all went there regularly and I just put myself in his way. It wasn't difficult and I wasn't the first.'

'And you were told to?'

'Get close? Yes. See if I could find out who he met, who he knew, where he went perhaps. Listen in on phone calls, get him to become indiscreet. Anything like that.'

'What were you promised, or did they force you?'

She pushed back a strand of loose hair which had fallen in

front of her eyes. 'Nothing really. A little help with my parents, pensions, medical, a little money.' Her voice broke a little and she looked around searching for the cigarettes. 'The alternative if I didn't, would be to make life difficult for us.'

Her compliance belonged to both a threat and a reward, thought Gates. 'So, you did what they asked, spied on him?'

She shrugged. 'Yes, but it wasn't like you think. Although…it was at first. It didn't work out as they planned.'

'Now, you tell me, what do *you* mean?'

'He was expecting something of the kind, I think. He was waiting for them. He knew he had enemies, but he let me in anyway.'

Gates was puzzled. 'Why would he do that if he knew you were going to deceive him?'

She laughed at that. 'He was clever, very smart. I think it was a bit of a game to him. He was called the 'boss' you know, by everyone in the office or close to him, he was called that for a reason. He knew how they worked, knew how to play the system. He laughed it off: "Don't worry love."' She mocked Burns with a surprisingly good Lancashire accent, '"It's better I know who it is. You just do as they ask, I'll look after you.", thought he could control the situation I suppose, and control me, something like that anyway.' She shook her head as if to clear some internal confusion. 'He once said he saw me coming, he was pleased it was me, but I don't know, we never really talked about it. Just accepted it really.'

'And what about the people that asked you, put you close to Burns? Did you tell them that he knew, knew you had been put there?'

She shook her head.

'Why not?'

The girl gulped and shook. Although it was only lunchtime Gates guessed she had begun to drink early, her breathing burbled, she was technically drunk only fear keeping her sufficiently sober and he knew he would have to tear information from her, a rambling, confused admission that he would have to piece together like a jigsaw with pieces missing and no box with a helpful image to compare the pieces to.

'Could you get me some water?' She had realised the alcohol filled her belly, her throat was shrunken and shrivelled, she had trouble holding back the reflux that at some point would spill from her.

Gates rose, glad of the movement and went into the kitchen.

'In the fridge,' She called, 'there's a bottle.'

There was and not much else. The fridge smelt and the surfaces in the tiny kitchen were cluttered with mugs, make-ups, saucepans and opened packets of food and envelopes.

'Here you go,' Gates said cheerfully handing her the glass and he watched while she drank the fizzy water thirstily. He could see it provide some immediate relief. 'Now,' he continued, encouragingly, 'why did you not tell your handlers that Burns knew about you?'

'I—I didn't know what they would do, too scared, I suppose. Scared where that would leave me if I couldn't do what I was told. Anyway, he was good to me, said he didn't mind, that he understood. He made me feel safe, protected. It seemed safer to go along, pretend.' She drained the glass and made a face. 'Oh God, it's a mess. I'm sorry he's gone,' she said quietly, a whisper, more to herself than Gates, leaving him wondering whether the sorrow was from personal loss or the demise of a protector able to save her from the wrath of a cruel system. 'How did it happen?'

'Annie,' Gates' voice continued to be coaxing, gentle, 'tell me, how do you know he's dead?' She nodded, 'There's been no announcement. Why are you here, at home, and not at work?'

Refreshed by the water she returned to the wine and poured the remaining liquid into the glass. 'Someone came to the office yesterday; I didn't see who. Then my supervisor, called me, told me to go home and stay there. Len was supposed to be here yesterday. I got worried when he didn't show and rang his number. Somebody answered, but it wasn't him. I knew something must have happened.'

'Who was it that answered?'

She shook her head. 'I hung up straight away. How did they do it?'

'He was involved in a hit and run,' said Gates and saw

Annie's face wince with pain. 'He was murdered Annie,' he added, almost to reassure her. 'It wasn't an accident, it was quite deliberate, but he didn't suffer, it was quick, probably instantaneous.'

'That's good I suppose,' said Annie, and reached for her cigarette, took two puffs, and shuddered in distaste. Her complexion had turned a shade paler.

'Tell me again, tell me clearly, who told you to get close to Burns? Who are we talking about? Why did they want this information? Or was it just to embarrass him?'

'I really can't talk about that,' she said hoarsely. She was beginning to shake; the tears were coming closer.

But Gates felt that the suspicions she had shown when he arrived were beginning to crack and break. He sensed there was a need to unburden herself, redeem or resolve her fears? He had no idea. She was confused he could tell that, completely out of her depth, floundering as cruel forces overwhelmed her. Her words had bought forward Gates' own memories of feeling desperate and helpless when the forces of the state began to tighten their grip on his own existence. He remembered his feelings as he realised he was losing Sophie. The despair as he floundered trying to keep down a journalist's job while the forces he had helped summon, began to crush the link to the only love he had remaining. As he watched this girl's despair, he recalled the people he spoke to, the numbers he called, the friends he approached and the messages that were not returned. The sense of helplessness and loss flooded back. The fear that one was falling from a very high cliff with people watching in plain sight and no one was there to step forward to catch and save him, avert disaster.

What this girl was going through must be so much worse. Dark forces had gathered around her.

Gates collected his thoughts and returned to the present.

'Try Annie,' he said gently. 'Perhaps I can help.'

'You can't,' she whispered. 'They'll kill me.'

'Was it someone from the union or someone else, from the Party perhaps?'

She wiped a tear from her eye with the back of her hand and her cheek glistened with moisture. 'I thought it was.' She sniffed into a tissue. 'I really thought that was all it was, just the union finding leverage, keeping tabs, that sort of thing. It seemed harmless. But it wasn't.'

'Did you know he was being blackmailed Annie, did he tell you or did you find out somehow?'

She nodded again, her eyes brimming with the gathering tears which she wiped with her sleeve. 'Yes, I knew. His mood changed suddenly, he became worried, anxious, I hadn't seen him like that before. He could get angry, he had a short fuse, but I had never seen him like this. He was afraid.'

'Did he tell you who was blackmailing him? Something to do with the Union, trying to make him give on the leadership bid?'

She shook her head. 'No, that wouldn't have worried him. This was something else.'

'And what else did he say?'

'Len told me not to worry, that he could keep me out of it, that if I kept quiet my parents and me would be okay. He would make arrangements to get me away.'

'Did he tell you how? And why would he do that?'

She shook her head. 'He never said. Just that escape was possible, he would arrange it, I never learned anything more than that.'

'Is that why you went to the apartment yesterday, to find a way out?'

Her laugh was choked and bitter. 'It's too late for that now. But I knew he kept money there, dollars as well as pounds. I knew where. I went for that.'

'What did you want the money for? What have you done with it.'

'Parents,' she said. 'It will be no use to me anymore. They will need it.'

Gates said nothing. They both realised it was probable she would be arrested soon. The parent's future when that happened was uncertain. She had been pulled into something deep, deep and complex and beyond her comprehension and ability to escape. Would they kill her as she feared? It was possible. Young women went missing regularly, she would become just another victim of crime, a statistic with no connection to anything or anyone.

'Was there anything else in the apartment? Did you take anything else?'

'I don't know about anything else; I just took the money. I don't think Len would have minded that. He would have given it to me if he knew. Anyway, he kept anything really valuable in the safe. I only saw him open that once.'

There was a safe, Gates thought, and kicked himself for such a poor search of Burns' apartment. Not that he could have done anything about it, but it made him wonder if there was anything else he had missed.

'What about these pictures Annie?' He spread the images from Burns' apartment across the coffee table. 'Do you know anything about them? What do they mean? Do you know who they are?'

She shook her head. 'Nothing. Nothing at all. I have no idea. He said there were pictures of us, pictures that were being used against him. Doesn't surprise me,' she said, her words slurred from the wine. 'Bastards. Put them away for God's sake.'

Gates left them there spread on the table; he pushed the other images forward. 'Are you sure Annie?' He pointed to the picture of Burns climbing office steps and the two lovers locked together. 'Where could this be? Who are these men?'

She pulled a face. 'No idea, I really haven't, please put them away, I don't want to look,' and she turned her face away.

Gates left them there. 'When did he get these pictures,

when did he become afraid? Tell me about that.'

Annie raised her arm limply pushing her long hair back across her forehead.

'About four months ago I suppose, not longer.'

'Are you sure about that?'

'Yes. Now put them away, please.'

Burns shuffled the pictures back into a pile and returned them to the envelope. Annie drank more of her water. The room darkened as outside black cloud passed low over the building.

Gates had to soothe her, reassure her, he had begun to glimpse what she knew, he had drawn the thread loose. He was determined to ease it further, draw it all the way from her consciousness.

'Did you try to stop informing on Len, get away from them?'

Her parents live on a single income. The mother is an immigrant from Portugal apparently, cleans to make ends meet, Lucy had reported. Father is disabled, war wound, disciplinary problems during military service made him ineligible for a pension. Probably she sends them money, seems pretty devoted to them. 'I spoke to her mum, she visits regularly,' Lucy added, 'they're very proud of her.' The leverage of family, a classic tactic to force compliance. The bonds of family, isolation of hope into the success of an offspring. Of course, she had no choice, the parents waited for her, depended upon her. They would have known that.

Annie rubbed the flat of her hand across her face,

smearing snot and tears that still flowed freely. She dabbed at her nose feebly with the saturated tissue. 'No, I had no choice. They told me my parents would be looked after if I helped. If I didn't...' she shrugged.

Her voice was cracking, the memory and thoughts were flagging, addled by fear and alcohol.

'Who?' Gates asked gently 'Who made you?'

'They're not going to look after me, are they?' She looked up raising her eyes to meet his. They were wide with fear, the tears gone like a curtain replaced with a certain dread. Realisation as to what Burns' death meant, the implications and consequences that would soon fall upon her. 'He's dead and I'm fucked, so fucked.'

Gates had no idea what to say. A few moments silence passed between them. Then the girl's head gradually rose, a slow crinkly smile gathered at the corners of her mouth.

'You could help, I've helped you,' she said slowly. 'You're a journalist, help me in return. I could be good to you.'

For a short second Gates was lost. He wondered what she meant.

'Help me, please.'

Then she was on her knees in front of him. He realised too late what she meant. He saw her eyes become glazed. He felt her hands on his trousers, her hair fell across his lap, she was trying and failing to open his belt.

'I'll do anything you want, anything at all...I promise...'

She was on him, reaching for his face her arms became locked around his neck, planting wet kisses on his cheeks, trying to force his knees open to get closer against him. But the kisses were poisoned with salt from her tears. He could smell the cheap wine and expensive perfume. After twisting his face away and fumbling with his hands he found her wrists and pushed her gently away.

'Stop it, Annie, please Annie, please...don't, there's no need, I don't want that. That's not going to work. I would help if I could, but not this. You need to be strong. Do you understand?'

She raised her head and looked up at him. Her eyes were wet shining swimming pools. Realisation came into them, and her face changed, reality returning. She pulled back sitting on the floor, resting against the sofa with her knees drawn up.

'You're right,' she said, passing her hand over her face and searching for the cigarettes again. 'Forget it.' She made it sound like a rejection, and not one of the kind types.

Go, he told himself. Leave her. She's unstable. She had been used, a tiny irrelevant pawn in a game of secrets and coercion. Used for her looks, her insecurity and vulnerabilities cynically played. She was right, no one was going to look after her. But her depth of depression and fatalism puzzled Gates. There was more, he was sure. He decided to draw her back from contemplating the future.

'What was Burns like?' Gates asked, knowing he was repeating himself slightly, wanting a route to engage with her.

The question seemed to help her regain some composure.

'He was clever, he knew so much, confident like some men are and he could be generous, oh I know it was just sex really. He was...well, he had tastes and he made me do things I didn't want, I didn't like, but I tried, and I think he was pleased. He was sweet, actually I think he cared.' She shook her head. 'He even promised to look after me and my mum and dad.' She looked at Gates with a wide stare that was almost an appeal. 'Who does that in this crappy country?' It was an open disbelieving question. 'But he did. I even think he meant it.'

Gates looked at her summoning sympathy. 'Annie, I really need to know who you were working for, was it for the police, the security services? If you tell me, perhaps we *can* make them leave you alone, let you and parents go on in peace. Why don't you tell me what happened? Tell me what you know about the blackmail.'

He came home one evening, said Annie, she had been waiting for him. His face was grim when he arrived, black clouds filled his features. She had asked what the matter was, frightened of the answer he might give her. He didn't want to tell her and had gone straight to the drink's cabinet pouring himself a very large scotch which he gulped before refilling. We need to be careful, he said, I'm in trouble. He was furious, said Annie, I mean really furious. She had been scared. Is it your wife? She had asked. That had caused Burns to laugh to laugh bitterly at the question, as if the idea was absurd. Which it probably was.

*No one is worried about that*, he retorted. No this is actually serious. She had tried to soothe him, calm him down, did he want to eat something? She had made food anyway. Over dinner, picking her moment, she had asked again. He was calm now but brooding darkly, picking at his food swigging at a whisky glass which he regularly refilled.

'Finally, he told me about the blackmail, the pictures, he didn't say what they were, but that I was in them, he said it was probably all over,' Annie explained. 'I realised then it was not about the union trying to bring him down, I realised then it wasn't them using me.'

Burns did not say more just brooded and drank. Annie had sat quietly watching his mood deepen. In the end, when the whiskey bottle was empty, they had gone to bed but sleep had not come. In the middle of the night, he had taken her roughly without affection, without asking, an animal coupling, him desperate for relief, she had lay there, almost motionless, anxious not to anger him.

'I have to have the rest, all of it, Annie,' he repeated. 'If I have all of it, even if it's painful, perhaps I can help.'

Her mouth was slack, a smear of saliva at the corner of her lips dribbled onto her chin. 'You can't do that,' she whispered. 'These people don't go away. He just said I should do it if I wanted my parents to be okay. I didn't want to, but I had no choice.'

The 'they' had become a 'he'.

'*Who* was this person, Annie?' he asked quietly. 'Do you know?'

When it was over Burns had laid back bathed in sweat, his chest heaving eyes open and staring at the moonlit ceiling above him. Annie had felt her cheek swelling from the last blow. She felt uncomfortable and damp but dared not move while he lay still and silent. Finally, she had summoned the courage to ask: What's happening? *Who*, who is doing this to you? Burns had been bitter: the same fuckers who are using you, had been his response. Annie had wanted to know what he would do. But he had lay there still and quiet. 'Nothing,' he had replied. 'We do what they ask us. We have no choice.' At dawn, when she woke, he had gone. They didn't speak about it again, but he was not the same after that night. He became withdrawn, easy to anger.

'And then, Annie,' he whispered gently, coaxing, 'did anything happen after that?'

She had seen Burns less frequently after that, each time his mood a little darker. '"Don't talk to anyone,"' he says. "It'll be fine. You just do as they say."' These people scared him, and he wasn't someone to scare easily. Whatever they had over him and wanted him to do was serious and powerful, she was sure of that.

'You're sure you're right, this wasn't the union bosses playing dirty, trying to undermine him?'

She shook her head and gave a bitter laugh. Her voice

strengthened and her tone became firmer. 'No, no, not the union. I told you, I thought they were at first, that's what Len believed as well, I think. I wish it was, Len could have dealt with that. He could have made it right.'

'How do you know they weren't?'

She started to cry again as if her reservoir of tears was infinite. Full fat drops that trickled down her cheeks choking her words. She remembered the last time the man had been here. A large man towering above her with a powerful frame. He had stood close, gripping her arm, squeezing the flesh until it hurt, unsmiling Slavic features, cruel brown eyes with hot breath easing from his fleshy lips. She had smelt his lunch, strong meat with garlic.

'Because he spoke Russian,' she said.

AT Euston, it was too late for the last Manchester train, so he bought a ticket for the next morning. Then in a cheap hotel he lay on his bed and stayed awake most of the night. He thought of the girl and her dead lover trapped and tormented without escape forced to endure a life of fear. Through the thin walls he listened to the shudder of the plumbing, far-away phones and the shouts and calls of dark streets.

***

# CHAPTER EIGHT

*There is no law against antiques*

**Manchester**
GATES FOUND A BANK OF phones boxes and chose the one that worked trying to ignore the stink of stale cigarette smoke and urine.

He tutted impatiently while the electronic tone rang out, unanswered, but let it ring for a long time before hanging up, relieved there had been no connection. Unlike the heavily controlled mobile network public phones wouldn't normally be monitored but there was always a chance the call information could be retrieved if someone wanted to. Gates had purposefully left his mobile phone on his desk and would claim absentmindedness if anyone asked why. He preferred cold calling anyway.

Across the street was a convenience store with some crates of bread stacked on the street. Inside was a coffee machine and he bought two rolls and a cup of the weak piss of liquid that dribbled out of the machine. The coffee was, as expected, disgusting but the bread proved surprisingly good, warm, fresh, and filling. He had returned to Manchester that morning without breakfast and was hungry and needed food.

While he chewed, he wondered whether he was being followed himself. It occurred to him he had probably become a person of interest to a number of people, drawn into a web of something he did not understand. The emergence of a Russian connection to Burns had unnerved him further. Certainly, their involvement spoke to Dugdale's fear for Burns' loyalty. If they had been controlling Burns, then they would be watching what happens after his death.

That probably meant that sooner rather than later they would be watching him.

His best defence was therefore to do what newspapermen are expected to do. Investigate and report.

On arrival back in Manchester there had finally been a response to his press request for information to the Police on the death of Burns. The press office had called him at his desk just five minutes after he had taken his seat and had confirmed the union official was the victim of a hit and run. The investigating team were keeping an open mind on the cause and motive at present and that no further details were being released at this time—out of respect for the family—was the official answer. Off the record they believed the motive was linked to internal union corruption, a falling out amongst thieves.

He recognised the crudely planted narrative forming.

Blame the victim. Create an unvirtuous circle and shield it with smoke and suspicion. Wait for any fuss to die down, rely on short memories and people keeping their head down. Without fail the whole process will move on and become removed from consciousness.

Lucy had been there when he took the call. She had looked at him across the desk. Large spectacles balanced on the end of that pretty nose.

'You going to follow this up?' she had asked.

Behind the inquiring casual tone Gates wondered, just for a second, if there was a small flash of something unexpected in her eyes. Compassion, concern, or enquiry? There was no way to be sure.

He had drummed the desktop with his fingers, his answer ready. 'For a while,' he murmured, and had gone on to mutter something about the corruption rumours he wanted to check on. 'Probably won't come to anything,' he said, not sure whether his attempt at downplaying the story was convincing. 'But it should be investigated, it's our responsibility,' he added, then realised that he sounded a bit too pious.

But Lucy appeared not to notice, she had simply agreed and returned to her typing, the plastic keyboard clacking rapidly as her fingers danced across the keys.

Outside, the street looked normal. Early fog lingered and the day was cold. A tired looking woman with a pushchair dragging a reluctant infant by its hand passed him by, an old couple clasping each other were feeling their way towards the distant tram stop, two squealing girls tottered on heels into a clothes shop and a schoolboy, his head empty of everything but mischief, skipped his way home at high speed for an early lunchtime.

Gates finished the bread dropping the paper bag into a waste bin immediately followed by the untouched coffee which he regretted buying.

He recalled the conversation with the press office. He had asked if there was a press embargo. The reply had been immediate and firm.

'No, Comrade, but anything written should have its facts checked with this office first, the press officer had cautioned in a severe tone.'

He guessed Hallam's people were by now in touch with the *Herald's* editor. Checking on his movements, his sources, maybe already having a discreet word with Lucy. Accepting the invitation to visit the scene of a man's murder was a normal instinct for a newspaper man. However, his curiosity had dragged him into an entangled situation he would normally want little part of. Even if Lucy could be trusted, which he doubted, he didn't want the kid involved.

That's why he had now tried to ring Burns' wife from a call box. Leave as little trace as possible from the office while he tried to figure more of this out.

'If you need any help Comrade, I am happy to assist.'

He had smiled at his colleague and assured her he would not hesitate to ask, before grabbing his jacket and heading for the newsroom entrance.

Since last night, the fragments of what he had learned had circulated continuously—

Dugdale: *I can get you Sophie back...*

Miranda: *We'll know where you are...*

And then for some reason he could not understand, an unconnected echo from a distant father: *Don't get too big for yer boot's son, yer come from nowt and there's folks that will send yer back to nowt.*

Where did that come from?

That blunt graceless scorn offered instead of praise after his father read the *Mirror's* job offer letter had created rage and left a taste, one he had never been able to remove. Bitter jealousy, from a washed-up man. He had dismissed it. They had talked only occasionally since then.

Gates' car started with trouble, the engine wheezing into life like an emphysema patient greeting the day. Finally, the cylinders caught and turned over as he knew they eventually would and he pointed the Fiat to head out of the city, trying to avoid the potholes wincing as the shock absorbers bottomed out against their stops when he failed. They might now be called Fiats, he thought, but there was no doubt these vehicles were made with Volga steel and put together with a tractor wrench. He drove for thirty minutes leaving the grey Manchester suburbs behind finding himself again on the winding B-roads leading out to the area of Rossendale. Sandwiched between the West Moor and the main Pennine range was the Irwell Valley. Across the steep-sided gash in the moor the Lancashire land softened in the gloomy morning air the city fog replaced by winter mist, and the village of Great Lever with its mean rows of terraces once more came into view—so quiet after the din of the city. The big trees had turned brown. Carpeting the verges of the road, their autumn leaves were falling, oak, ash and the fiery foliage of dogwood. The birds were leaving, and the days would become shorter.

He stopped to ask an old man the way. The surly short response and a vague whirl of the arm confirmed he was going in the right direction, and he carried on to the far side of the near-deserted town. The fork to the right came just before where he had approached the police roadblock two days previously and he nearly missed it. A mile from the outskirts of Great Lever next to an old woodland copse he found the gates to the gritstone farmhouse set in the tall roadside trees that lined the lane, with moist autumn fungus clinging to their bark like slime.

THE large house that was the Burns' family home was set back—an attractive rectory house of substance that was detached and walled. At the front there was a view only of the road, but Gates could tell that at the rear the scenes would rest over the eastern side with fields and woods to the horizon. The larger towns of Radcliffe and Bury lay that way. Too far to be seen. A compact Volkswagen, too small to be an official car, was parked outside but there were no other vehicles and Gates wondered whether police interest had already moved on. The gates were open, and he left his own car to one side of the gravel drive and walked towards the front door.

The two-storey building probably dated from sometime in the early 1900s and was substantial. It was no surprise to Gates that someone of Burns' status was well looked after. A quick survey of the area, and he caught sight of the CCTV camera set on a four-metre pole set away from the house and cunningly semi-concealed amongst the roadside trees to point back towards the front door and cover the driveway. A casual visitor would be unlikely to see it, you would need to be looking. Somewhere, not far away, a chainsaw was chewing wood, the smell of burnt fuel and fresh sap hung in the air and he noticed a large garage outbuilding to one side with what he assumed was a woodshed behind. Oily two-stroke smoke belched in small clouds above the moss on the roof. Cutting winter fuel, he presumed.

A wooden porch was nestled in a tangle of twisted rose bushes. He pushed the old-style doorbell and waited. For a few moments there was no response, then a shadow of movement appeared behind the glass of the rectory door which was opened cautiously. A middle-aged woman wearing an apron who Gates took to be a housekeeper appeared at the door and asked in carefully rehearsed English who he was. The accent was eastern European, probably Polish, he thought, and he asked if he could speak with Mrs Burns. Was she at home? The woman looked at Gates a little blankly, so he gave his press and communist party cards, and she disappeared back inside. She wasn't gone long and on return she showed him inside and into a large empty drawing room at the front of the house. The modern furnishing surprised him. Polished hard wood floors, square Nordic-style tables, and low-slung chairs. The style was from the GUM store in Manchester, the privileged furniture floor where the exclusive Scandinavian import products were available. There were no books, he thought. None of the clutter of a family living area. Not much about the room seemed personal, just a few pictures. It looked formal, a room to receive visitors and the woman muttered that Mrs Burns had been resting but would be with him shortly and then he was left standing on a cream rug awkwardly wondering whether he should sit or await an invitation.

Margaret Burns appeared a few minutes later, closing the door behind her and walking over to shake Gates' hand. She clutched a small white handkerchief which she used to dab at her freshly powdered nose. She handed back his cards, sniffed into the handkerchief and gestured for him to sit and asked if he would like coffee. 'I can get Mrs Grazwya to make some.'

He declined the coffee and perched himself on the edge of the leather-covered armchair.

'I assumed there would be interest from the media Comrade,' she said. 'This is a difficult time for us, but of course I understand that the nation's press has a job to do.' Composing herself and interlocking her hands and placing them in her lap, she asked: 'What do you want to know?'

She wouldn't really want to speak to the newspapers, Gates knew that. But in her world, you didn't snub anything or anyone that might be connected to the Party. Gates guessed even without the enormous grief she was dealing with she was feeling vulnerable and exposed. An uncertain future had appeared. He wondered whether anyone had coached her on her lines?

Making sure all the stories dovetail correctly together.

'Mrs Burns. I am truly sorry for your loss. I am not here to cause any trouble. But your husband was an important official, there is a public interest in reporting his death and its circumstances...I know it's not a good time, but I hope you understand.' He was glad he had not phoned. Calling unannounced often gave you the chance to catch someone unaware, the urge for confessional release that follows grief dropping the guard and causing words to slip. 'I was hoping you could give me some background on your husband, family, home life, that sort of thing?'

Inside his words, he wondered about his reasons for coming here, what did he expect to find or learn? Partly of course, such a visit would be expected as part of press duties.

But he hoped it might provide some detail, some insight into what Burns had been doing. Some clue as to where exactly his loyalties had taken him.

He looked at the woman as she sat opposite deciding that Margaret Burns had aged well and a few years ago she would have turned heads. Mid-fifties Gates guessed, a once slim figure now fulsome at the hips but with legs that were shapely and would still attract interest, although she was hopelessly ill-equipped to deal with the youthful softness of Annie Freedman. The dress she wore had probably been pressed back into service by the circumstances. It was black silk and tight with a neckline that was low. The inch-too-small size made her impressive décolletage a little obvious. But he realised on scrutiny that the face had aged, she looked at him with glassy blue eyes that were dulled and framed by auburn hair that crept with fine strands of grey and makeup that had been applied carefully but slightly too thickly. At the corners of her mouth thin creases were pulled tight like surgical stitches and a cloud of over-sweet scent hung around her, Gates found it cloying. He also decided she was on drugs. Tranquilisers probably. Her eyes looked a little too glassy and glazed, the lips sleepy. There was a vagueness about her. Like she was in the room, but her mind was elsewhere. At that moment the housekeeper appeared holding a sherry glass which she deposited at Margaret Burns' elbow. She carefully sipped the crystal glass protected by a paper napkin to avoid smearing it and listened patiently to her answers to his first obvious questions about her husband.

He was a good man, she told him, who worked hard, earned his position. He came from the bottom, from a working-class family and who qualified as an electrician, then decided to try and make a difference to other people's lives. Well, that can make people envious and jealous, can't it? So, yes, he had enemies, rivals. He had to be tough with them, can't let people stand in your way, can you? Some people can be a rabble, always wanting to cause trouble. He was very well thought of in London, she added hurriedly. They loved his speeches. We were lucky, we went down to join him every couple of months. At the apartment? Gates inquired casually. She looked vague and said something about friends, Central Committee friends, her voice lowering to a whisper. A suspicion passed Gates that she may not know of Burns' apartment or at least preferred not to. Did Gates know London? But he loved us, thought the world of his boys and Claude, our dog, so, so terrible...who would do such a thing? What did Gates think?

She took a photograph frame with a family picture of the four of them on a beach. Pärnu in Estonia, she explained. A holiday after a fraternal workers' conference. We were very happy. It was a lovely time. We were very close.

He wondered if she had any clue; soon they would begin to smear him with corruption charges, attacking his integrity and character. Did she have any idea how the machinery worked to protect itself? She may have to rethink that loyalty a bit.

Gates hadn't noticed the picture when he arrived and now looked at it with interest. In the frame, Gates saw a heavy-set man with large jowls wearing sunglasses. He was pictured at the centre of a family huddle a fleshy but powerful arm around his wife. Black hair, heavily oiled was slicked back and thick eyebrows rose like hedgerows above the glasses. Beside him in bathing trunks stood two boys somewhere in their early teens, youthful hollow chests with large grins and scruffy hair filled with salt and sand. Mrs Burns, fulsome in summer patterned cotton, rested her head on her husband's shoulder. Behind their broad smiles, under a blue sky with dumpling clouds a calm sea lapped at a long empty beach curving away into the distance. Now was not the time, thought Gates to make any reference to office indiscretions. He had little doubt that she knew, but powerful man can do what they like, sleeping with the office staff is a hardly a rare event, and for the cuckolded wives, ignorance with privilege kept the status quo intact.

The picture for some reason created a small awkwardness, a silence to be filled, so Gates asked how they had met, and a swift unexpected smile passed like a breeze across her face, and she gushed her response.

'Oh, it was wonderful. We were so happy. It was in the eighties; Len was invited to head the local Party Workers' Committee. I was a secretary in one of the branch offices of the TUC at the time. I became his assistant and well...well, you know how these things can go. He was very busy, and full of energy. There was much reorganisation to do after the bad years. Putting things right after that woman had gone.'

Thatcher. She could only be referring to the former political force that had vowed to extinguish socialism from British politics. Still the raw hatred that the name of the ex-prime minister could conjure after three decades was never far from the surface of society.

'There was so much to do after the damage she did and Len worked so hard to give the workers what they wanted, what they deserved.'

He did that alright, thought Gates, reflecting on the change that came after her departure, the building of the state with its vast bureaucracies and powers, renationalisation of industries and the forming of new foreign allegiances all undertaken in the name of the people. They all did. Everyone must be very pleased with the outcome.

'Of course, he was not alone,' she added hastily, correcting any impression that her husband had acted out of any personal pursuit. 'He was just one of many brave and decent socialists, who have given us so much,' and she dabbed at the corner of her eye.

There was a slight swish of silk and stocking as she sat back down, and her skirt slipped a little too far up her thigh. She didn't appear to notice, distracted by her own story. Then Gates noticed the two bottles of pills on the small wine table by her chair which confirmed his earlier thoughts. The heavy scent masked Mrs Grazwya's loyal application of the sherry bottle for most of the morning.

'He was very well thought of, even then,' she was continuing, 'he was young, but he knew Jack Jones and Scargill quite well, such great men. Heroes to our Socialist cause, don't you agree?'

He replied that he did. Then he asked what she knew of the hit and run incident?

She frowned and gave her answer quickly as if on unsafe ground rushing through what he presumed she had been told. The police haven't said much, but they have been very supportive she immediately added. Hit and run, revenge for something Len did, they said. He had been investigating corruption. 'But I don't know anything about it,' she said quickly.

Gates had the impression she spoke without true conviction and he continued looking down at the picture which he still held. The frame was old, sterling silver with ornate curled corners. The back was slightly loose, the tiny sliding retaining clips bent. Looking around the room Gates felt it looked odd, a little out of place in a room that was sparse in the way of other photos or ornaments.

'Are you sure that's what you *believe*?' Gates suggested.

She looked cross but did not challenge the question directly. 'Well, that's what they said why wouldn't it be true.'

'Was that a regular walk your husband took with the dog.'

Gates asked. Oddly, the question seemed to cause tears to form and begin to brim in her eyes. The reference to a normal routine perhaps or maybe the recollection of the Estonian holiday, he couldn't be sure.

Grief can bring a cathartic condition removing risk or caution from a person's words. Gates wanted the confession that he was sure was close to revealing itself.

Her nod of reply was almost a shake. 'Yes, it was his normal walk when he was at home. Through the small wood and round to the edge of the village. He was usually gone just under an hour. I suppose someone who wanted could have known that.'

Gates nodded thoughtfully. Then he said: 'He was tipped to become the new General Secretary next year. Do you think that would have given him enemies?'

She had lit a long filter cigarette. Gates could feel her trembling like a greyhound after a race. A fissure of apprehension appeared, the layer of makeup cracking.

'Oh no Comrade, I mean definitely not amongst the leadership. Len and the Council had the greatest of respect for each other. Why, Comrade General Secretary McBride phoned me only yesterday to give me his and the Union Council's condolences.'

I am sure he did, thought Gates. Pension and benefits. A widow's gold. Mind your place. Or else…

'Did he have any theories as to who would want to do such

thing.'

'Well, I wouldn't know, you would have to ask him that,' she replied a little tartly. She had finished the cigarette quickly and looked around to find the packet which was on the side table next to the pills. She lit a second long filter without offering one to Gates.

'Was he away a lot? I mean with his work. Did he travel?'

'Some, there was more recently. He had to visit a lot of branches up and down the country. Talk to regional committees that type of thing. London of course, he commuted for part of the week.'

'What about you Mrs Burns. Do you have any different theories on who might be responsible for your husband's death?'

Her eyes flickered, her blue gaze avoiding his. 'I think the police are right. It was criminals in the union. Some jealous stupid thugs who have crossed my husband in the past. They must be terrible, wicked people,' she said with a helpless bitterness. 'I hope they will get justice. They will find them Comrade, I am sure.'

Gates was still holding the silver frame lightly fingering the shiny edge. He hadn't seen silver in a long time, at least not quality silver, hallmarked like this one. He recalled the silver cigarette box in Burns' apartment. Both tarnished, in need of care and cleaning. Who collects a rare item of silver and doesn't clean it? *Purchase something that will get our attention.* The pawnbroker card that sat in his pocket and Len Burns' desk.

Gates had never asked Dugdale how important Burns was to his plans. He knew little of espionage tradecraft but thought it strange if an inner circle of plotters relied upon shop purchases for communication. Such a system bristled with imponderables that suggested a peripheral actor to Dugdale's cause. How many where there like that? Gates wondered, people of resource or influence positioned around the country in its institutions and businesses, given a glimpse of what may take place and then silently kept in reserve waiting to be called.

'Did he talk about his work, share some of the burden?'

'Not really Comrade, it was very complicated with a great deal of pressure. He didn't like to trouble our family home with it.'

Gates was forming the impression that Margaret Burns had little interest in her husband's work, at least beyond gratitude that it provided her with access to the reserved floors in the GUM Department Store. Then he suddenly felt irritated with himself for being unfair. There had been a lot of references to family life, how close they were, what a good father and husband Burns had been. He couldn't decide whether Burns had been trying to protect them from the authority he served or had been helping a cause that would bring about a better life for them?

He was no closer to knowing.

'But there are other theories, it's been said that terrorists may have targeted your husband. What do you think of that?'

'Oh, I don't think so,' she said hurriedly. 'My husband had nothing to do with those people—nothing at all. No, much more likely to be thugs, crooks with a grievance against Len,' she declared.

'How did he seem recently? Had he been in good spirits?'

Was there the faintest of hesitations? 'I know he had a great many responsibilities that preoccupied him but nothing more than usual, I think. He liked to keep busy and was very conscientious.' She smiled, looked a little coy and then added: 'But it was our anniversary next month, he had promised a surprise, a holiday somewhere. He made it sound nice. It's quite remote here you know. We were both looking forward to that. He wouldn't say where, just that we would all go away. He did like his surprises.'

A careful man, thought Gates, a capable man, not someone to give up easily, not someone to put his family in peril if he could help it. It was possible he had prepared a fall-back for the many unpleasant contingencies he found himself facing; escape papers and money; a false travel plan to buy time, clues to be left behind to confuse a pursuer. Burns would know the system and probably had the resources. Annie Freedman had spoken of escape, Margaret Burns now described a surprise holiday.

Then in the manner of an afterthought she asked: 'Are you married Comrade Gates?'

The question startled him, it was unexpected, and he bowed his head as he answered. 'No longer, I'm afraid,' he replied absently. 'Forgive me this is such a nice piece, has it been in the family long?'

She noticed then that he was still holding the silver frame. The question seemed to confuse her, and she shifted, pulling, and straightening the skirt back down across her knees and held out her hand for Gates to return it.

'No, no, not long at all I suppose. My husband had a weakness for old things, antiques. There is no law against it,' she added hurriedly. 'He would occasionally bring something home.' She sniffed in what have been disapproval. 'I don't know where he got it from, it wasn't a taste we absolutely shared.'

She was right, there was no law against antiques although the acquisition of items for values sake with no practical purpose was considered widely as socially decadent.

'What about outside the union and Party. Did he have many friends or colleagues, hobbies or interests perhaps?'

She shrugged and her face clouded. Gates assumed there was much she did not know about her husband's activities.

'Not really…as I said, he was busy with work, he was a very dedicated man.'

'What about visitors,' Gates pressed. 'Has anyone come here to the house? Did anyone come to see your husband recently?'

She glanced down avoiding his eyes and Gates sensed the

weakness in her with greater clarity. The woman who wishes to know nothing but has stumbled upon uncomfortable truths. There was something, Gates thought. She doesn't know much, but she knows something. And what she knows I think scares her.

She passed a hand across her face, as if wiping away a cobweb, a memory. Gate kept his features neutral.

'It would be very helpful Mrs Burns,' he said, without saying why. 'Perhaps colleagues who worked with him? Or others who had business with him?'

'Possibly. He liked to work in his study late. Occasionally a colleague would bring papers…or…they would need to brief him on something that had happened somewhere.'

'Do you know who these colleagues were; one, two people, the same person perhaps?'

Did Margaret Burns sense the thrust of Gates' questions—realise that there was more to his purpose than character background? Did she notice him lean forward to engage her more intently. Probably not. The glazed look and vague tremble gave Gates an almost *deja vu* feeling. It was Annie Freedman all over again. Two women sharing the same man and for both of whom the consequences of their relationships would be terrible.

'I don't know Comrade; I am usually in bed quite early. I take a pill, I sleep badly.'

'It would help a great deal Mrs Burns,' Gates repeated, making a sympathetic look, trying to sound like it did not really matter, only a small detail filling in a little gap, adding completeness. He pretended to focus on his notebook in which he scribbled meaninglessly with a pencil, the feigned indifference coaxing Margaret Burns subtly to reveal what she knew. 'Perhaps you can you remember the last time there were visitors?'

She nodded, and suddenly looked crestfallen, her eyes began to brim with tears and Gates could see the first softening of mascara ready to drip down her plump cheek. The tiny crow's feet at the corner of her eyes squeezed tighter. The grief, alcohol, pills combining to loosen her thoughts, weaken the guarded discipline that was all that prevented her sharing whatever she knew. The memory of an event that she could not bring herself to admit had significance but which she found could be recalled only with considerable effort.

'There was something I thought strange.' She sniffed the words slowly. 'Slightly out of the ordinary…last week, two nights before the…incident. Two men came late at night.'

Gates composed a look of mild interest and made a note.

'And you didn't know who they were?'

She shook her head, gulping slightly, a stifled sob racked her bosom testing the silk of her dress. Her reaction seemed stronger than expected to the memory of an unexplained visit. A visit that disturbed her, raised a question she did not want answered. She shook her head once more, her eyes wide trying to contain her nervousness. 'As I said it was not sufficiently unusual…look Comrade perhaps we should end this here I think—'

'Please, Mrs Burns,' Gates cut in. He looked at her with a smile. Her brain was dulled slightly, now something would slip, he was sure, and he was familiar enough with the human condition that could bring people to the cusp of confession. 'I really am just trying to help.' Leaning forward he summoned yet more sincerity. 'Mrs Burns, it wasn't an accident that killed your husband. Now, the police think it was something to do with the union, and—' he raised his hands, '—probably they're right. But if we can help them get to the truth, wouldn't you want that? What can you tell me? I promise it need go no further.' Momentarily Gates hated his pretence. He was lying to her, lying to milk just a little more information, but his guilt was short-lived.

She looked at him in silence for a second her composure returning slightly. 'All I can say is that the next morning he seemed different. Nervous, frigid, distracted. He was not a man to frighten easily. I really hadn't seen him like that before.'

Gates again pretending to write a note. 'That must have been upsetting to you,' said Gates, gently keeping the mood. He remembered the CCTV that looked across the drive half-hidden by trees. 'You have a security system at your home, there are security cameras around the house.'

She nodded and looked mystified, only vaguely aware of what he was asking.

'They work at night, infra-red? Does it record?'

She nodded once more and pressed her lips together preventing words.

'It would have recorded that visit, wouldn't it?'

'Yes. It did.'

'Who visited your husband the night before the incident Mrs Burns?'

'It was the police or state security or someone like that.'

'And have the police taken the recording? After the *incident*?'

Again, she nodded, her composure slipping, the effect of grief, pills, and alcohol breaking down the act and this time it became more obvious that behind the mask of grief there was fear. Perhaps she was frightened for the practical consequences of what would follow her husband's murder, house money, status. But Gates suspected an even greater fear. He sensed the large shadows that filled her mind, and he knew she considered herself in real danger. But from whom?

'How can you be sure who it was?'

'After the incident one of them came back and asked for the tapes. He and another colleague searched my husband's study, our bedroom, this room, everywhere. But they didn't stay long; they were in a hurry. They took the security tapes and left.'

'Did you see the recording, Mrs Gates, before the police removed it as evidence?'

The handkerchief was bunched to her lips. Her voice was a sob. 'Yes. My eldest son Jason. He looked at the system immediately after the accident. He showed me. I recognised the officer who came back.'

Gates thought about what she had said. 'What did they say when they returned?'

She gave a simple shrug. 'Only that I should not report or talk about their visit.'

'Not even to other police?'

She simply returned his look without answering. The eyes now dry and open gave the answer.

'Where's Jason now, Mrs Burns, I'd like to speak to him.'

'Oh, I'm not sure that's a good idea. I don't think you should.' She was beginning to recover herself; doubt and caution was returning to cover loose words. 'He's cutting wood in the barn outside. He's been doing it for two days now, he won't stop. But please don't upset him. He and my husband were close. They spent a lot of time together. He has taken it very hard; he wants to be by himself.'

'How old is Jason?'

'Just twenty-four last month. He is training as an apprentice; my husband arranged it. He's very different to my younger son you know, chalk and cheese.' She dabbed at her eyes again and pulled hard on the cigarette. She was thinking of their future, he thought and how uncertain it had become. He could also tell a full tearful flood was not far away. 'My younger son Hugo is more sensitive, introspective, closer to me perhaps.'

'I am sure they will be a great comfort to you Mrs Burns.'

He nodded towards the photo frame replaced on the mantelpiece. 'They look fine young men.'

She nodded, accepting the words, but they passed her by, and Gates could see there was little more to learn here. She had slipped into herself. He was keen to make his excuses leaving her to her pills and grief.

'Mrs Burns, sorry I should leave you to your family, you have been generous of your time.' Gates felt sorry for her. She was frightened and knew she now had no protection; she was at the mercy of others. 'One last thing. You said it was the same officer who visited your husband before his death who removed the security tapes. I don't suppose he identified himself?'

She shook her head, and sniffled muzzling her nose in the damp handkerchief, her composure returning slightly. 'No Comrade, he didn't. I'm sorry,' she added rather unnecessarily, and Gates turned to go. 'But my son knew who he was.' Gates turned half back. 'Jason said he was very senior, and from London, Hallam I'm sure was the name Jason said, an assistant commissioner, I think.'

After Gates left, Margaret Burns reached for the refilled sherry glass, a sweet accompaniment to the small pills she gathered up and swallowed.

***

# CHAPTER NINE

### *The country is full of patriots*

IT WAS WITH RELIEF that Gates left the house full of perfumed grief and escaped into fresh air. He followed the noise of the chainsaw tracing it to the rear of the garage. Through the trees that bordered the road he noticed the sleek shape of the black BMW saloon. There was a muffled surge from the engine and the vehicle smoothly began to cruise back towards the village of Great Lever. A Branch car, he realised. Only they were arrogant enough to advertise their presence with the high-powered expensive German imports. Not much chance of keeping his visit discreet after all, he thought, and it confirmed his earlier notion that he was now under surveillance himself.

He walked through a narrow gap between large shrubs and there attached to the rear of the garage he found a spacious woodshed open on one side. Inside, the far wall was stacked high with cut and seasoned logs ready for winter fuel. A battered but powerful bench saw was at one side of the shed, next to it a log pile of freshly cut mature trunks presumably dragged from the nearby copse. The floor was covered in wood chippings and sawdust so thick it lay like a deep blanket of moon dust that was soft underfoot. In the centre of the shed was a tall powerful young man in t-shirt and worn jeans. He was bent over a sawhorse forcing a chain saw blade though a log. Despite the cold damp of the day the t-shirt was soaked with sweat, the wet dust forming a golden-coloured crust that covered his arms. There was an aggressive dangerous appearance to him which caused Gates to pause. As he approached the young man gunned the chainsaw one last time and then let the engine die away in a splutter. The saw fell idle to his side, and he glared at Gates with cool grey eyes.

'Who are you?' He spoke with a Mancunian accent—alert, suspicious and without friendship.

Gate put him at about Sophie's age, perhaps a little older. His hair was cropped close enough for the pink scalp to show through the dark fuzz. He realised that the holiday picture Margaret Burns had shown him was older than he had thought. Gone was the tousle-haired skin and bone teenager with a toothy self-conscious grin enjoying a sandy beach on a warm day. This was a muscular adult version who had a look of sharpness about him.

'Hi, are you Jason? I am sorry to hear about your dad, Comrade. My name is Gates—Harry Gates. I'm a journalist, the *Manchester Herald*. I was just speaking with your mother and hoped to have a few words with yourself.'

The younger Burns turned fully to face Gates. The

chainsaw hanging loosely by his side.

'Press.' The word on his lips held contempt and he looked far from impressed. 'Look mate, we have said all there was to say to the police. This is not a good time, why don't yer clear off and respect our privacy?'

'Please, a few moments only. Just background Comrade, your father was important and respected.' Gates appealed. 'Your mother is very upset, I wondered whether we could talk about him a little?' He did everything he could with his voice to signal goodwill. He fished in his pocket and offered the younger man a cigarette.

'Look around you,' his eyes pointed to the floor and the piles of wood shaving.

Gates waved the cigarette packet at him anyway. 'Looks damp enough to be safe if we're careful.'

Jason shook his head again but told Gates to go ahead. He reached onto a shelf to find an old empty jar to use as an ashtray. On the shelf, Gates could see heaped entanglements of workshop junk in amongst which was what looked like military scrap, old, small calibre shell casings, a bent deformed helmet that may have been Chinese, some leather work; ammunition, medical bandoleers and what could have been a bayonet with scabbard.

The younger Burns looked at Gates a while longer, his face remaining hostile but giving way to the reporter's persistence. He swung the chainsaw onto the bench and removed his heavy work gloves. He then turned and lent his back against the work surface and regarded Gates evenly. 'What do you want to know?' He gulped water from a large plastic bottle, his Adam's apple working like a piston as the liquid slaked away the wood dust. Gates could see the resemblance now, the same square solidness of the mouth and jawline as his father, a face without the wear and less knocked about by life but with the set of a street fighter. No heavy jowls yet, but with the decades they would come.

Steam rose from Burns' shoulders as the heat of his exertion vapourised the sweat. On one arm he glimpsed the small rectangle of a tattoo, the obsolete Union flag, the divisive barely tolerated symbol banned in public places for the reference to old allegiances, but stubbornly still used by many of the old, stubborn, and radical to proclaim heritage. He lifted the shirt to wipe his face and Gates noticed the crease of a rugged, wide scar that ran as a violent livid blue river across his stomach. Gates looked back to the military junk scattered on the workshop shelf.

'Nasty wound Comrade, how did you come by that?'

'Work benefit of serving my country.'

Of course, he would have completed conscription. Gates wasn't sure whether the reference to serving his country had been sincere or ironic. 'How long did you serve?'

'Depends how you count the time. I was waiting to start an apprenticeship when my call-up came through. You might just mean the six weeks training I got before flying to a place in Asia I've never heard of and the two months on operations before some Chinese artillery shell did this? Or you could include the six months in hospital, one-month rehabilitation and a train fare home from a grateful government? Which, is when my army time technically finished.'

It was not an uncommon story. The slide into frontier wars, campaigns to shore up authority in the remoter parts of the alliance challenged by ethnic tensions, fierce competition with the rising might of China. Those who thought distance and no obvious national interest were protection against involvement had been proved wrong. The young men of the country were paying the price of political allegiances.

'I'm sorry Comrade, I didn't know about your service, your mother didn't mention it.'

'She blanks it out, doesn't like to think about it.'

'What about your father? Did you talk about it to him?'

'A little, he understood more.'

'The police think that your father may have been killed by persons in the union, corrupt criminal elements. What do you think?'

Burns for a moment said nothing. Then he inclined his head. 'That's their job to find out ain't it.' His tone contained an aggressive edge. 'If that's what they say happened, then that's what happened.'

'You don't think so?'

'Not my place to say otherwise, like I said Dad was in charge of anti-corruption. In a few months he might have been in charge of the Union itself.' He made a harsh laugh. 'You make a lot of enemies when you put yourself in that position.'

'What do you know of his enemies or for that matter his friends?'

The younger Burns looked at him sharply. 'Why would I know anything about any enemies or friends? What are you trying to suggest?' His features were cool and sharp, his words defensive. 'Don't try and put words in my mouth. Just say what's on your mind why don't yer.'

'Alright I will.' Gates risked a smile before asking: 'I want to know what was going on with his work that required the attention of Special Branch visiting his home at night? What do you know?'

If Gates' knowledge of the visit surprised him Burns made a good fist of hiding it.

'Probably nothing more than you. I'm just the son remember.'

'Your mother told me you were close. That you and your father shared a lot of time together.'

'So what? Doesn't mean he told me anything.' He looked at Gates.

'Fathers and sons share ideas, help one another. Your father seems like a man who would be a big influence upon you. Wasn't that so?' Gates asked the question lightly, attempting a further smile, careful and alert to the younger man's aggressiveness. There was no smile in return. Did he just not like journalists or was there a reason for the prickliness?

'Political ideas you mean? Well, we didn't. Look what are you after? I haven't got nothing to tell you about Dad's work or who he was involved with. He didn't share that stuff with us, and we didn't ask.'

'Okay, okay, it just seemed you may have some insight. As I said fathers talk to their sons, don't they.' Hardly a universal truth. He and his own father had barely shared anything. Maybe this was obvious because Burns scoffed, and his mouth twisted in suspicion at Gates banal attempt to probe a relationship.

'She doesn't know what she's talking about. She gets confused easy,' the young man scoffed. 'It's happy families in there, thinks we're both teenagers, never talks about anything real. Hates that we've grown up. We'd be the little boys forever if she had her way. She still hangs on to him.'

He jerked his head in the general direction of the house and Gates assumed he was talking about the younger brother. He remembered the photograph from earlier and wondered what changes had come *that* young man's way since the scene on the Pärnu beach.

'So, you were closer to your dad than your brother was?'

'Aye, I suppose I was. He was his own man. Made his own decisions. Said what he wanted—within reason,' he added. He looked down at the floor, pushing the sawdust away from him with his boot.

'You admired that?'

Burns' look was angry. His reply was acid. 'Why not? Of course, I did. Something wrong with being proud of yer father? Weren't you proud of yours?'

The comparison caught Gates off-guard. He saw the young man's expression and decided to evade. 'Well, it's difficult to answer, I'm not sure...' He stopped and considered telling the truth. Giving the young man an insight into how not all parents are heroes to their children. When uncaring coldness is met with bitterness and withdrawal until a wall is built that can't be climbed even if you want to try. 'We don't all have luck with our parents,' was all he could think of to say. 'But that wasn't your father, was it? Yours cared about you.'

'He was a good man, a patriot, there's not enough like him about. What they did to him was awful.'

What's a patriot? thought Gates. Isn't the country full of them?

'In what way Comrade, tell me?'

Burns shrugged and looked uncomfortable. 'I just mean he was trying to do his best for people and the country.' He scowled at Gates. 'And he was just trying to look after this family.'

Gates hesitated at that. 'There were rumours Comrade...' he saw more flashes of anger light up in the young man's eyes.

Burns jerked his head back. 'What...?'

'No offence Comrade, it's a private matter. Rumours of a

girl...? I don't intend to use them—but...but others might. I'd like to put—'

'You write any lies and filth about my father, and I swear I will chew you up like one of these here logs, is that clear, *friend*?' He jabbed a thick finger towards Gates.

Gates raised his hands in a disarming gesture. 'Perfectly,' he said. 'I understand perfectly,' and he took a step back. 'It's just...just that someone will, and I only want to help you. Maybe there is a way to stop your father's reputation from being attacked. Think what it will do to your mother?' Gates did not wish to dwell on the interplay of his actions. Charting the relationship between his reassuring words, angled questions and what he would go away to write was to invite a distasteful self-analysis. A confusion of contradictory motives that he feared to contemplate.

The young man's anger didn't go but uncertainty came onto his face. It was clear he was well aware of the rumours. Suddenly he looked deflated, as if realisation was coming upon him. Gates sensed an internal turmoil, something different to expected grief.

'When did anyone from the press want to help anyone? There was nothing, he wasn't a saint, who is? But he was as good a man as the rest of them. He wasn't like a lot of them with bit of power, lecherous drunks trawling London night-clubs and cat houses. He put us first. And if anyone says different, they are liars.' The defence of his father seemed to make him slump slightly. Taken away from the physical activity of the labour of cutting logs his mind seemed to be turning to contemplation of the situation. 'We're probably fucked anyway. What does it matter?'

'Why's that Jason? What do you think is going to happen?'

'They will be out to get him. Starts with rumours and stories, then some kind of investigation: corrupt elements, an internal dispute, they will say at first. His role will become larger until he was in charge of the rot and when they've finished rewriting what went on all of this will go.' He jerked his head again towards the house. 'No more sympathetic words, he will be forgotten and added to the long list of criminal subversives working against the state. We all know how it ends, even her, no matter how much she begs.'

Gates did not argue. The ability of the state to turn upon its own was just part of the system. Everyone just accepted it and hoped it would not be them. He looked at the son and saw only dilemma.

'Your mother said policemen visited your father the other day. A late visit that was caught on your CCTV cameras. You showed her the images.'

The young man shrugged and swigged again from the water, big thirsty draughts. 'No big deal. Dad was responsible for discipline inside the union. Probably something to do with that.'

'Late at night, by a senior Special Branch officer? Isn't that odd?'

Burns just shrugged, but retorted: 'How do you know he was Special Branch? No idea, you tell me.'

'I don't, but you did, you told your mother the officer's name. How did you know who he was?'

The slip had caught Burns and for the first time he dropped his eyes, his answer uncertain: 'Did I? Dad must have mentioned it, I must have heard it from him when he was talking about work.'

Gates said nothing. Something was not right all along and now it had become obvious. 'Of course. That must have been it.' He rose from the workbench against which he had been leaning. 'Look I'm sorry for what happened to your father, I hope it works out for you all.'

Burns looked surprised at the departure and his face showed relief. Gates turned to leave. 'But before I go, there is one thing I know.' He turned back and looked at Burns evenly. 'I know you're lying to me.'

Burns flushed angrily.

'Who do you…'

'Commissioner Hallam you told your mother. Well, *that* isn't a name known to the public. He certainly wouldn't appreciate it if it was. So, how would you know who he is let alone recognise him from CCTV footage. That's a bit strange, yes?'

'Fuck you! What…'

Gates walked across the workshop back towards Burns. 'Special Branch don't investigate union corruption. Perhaps there was some other reason for such a high-powered secretive visit. Want to share what you know? It's off the record.'

Gates was aware the young man's grip on the chainsaw had tightened. It was no longer roaring and spinning but would make a useful club against his head.

Burns shook his head. 'Nothing I want to share with you Comrade.' His wide pale eyes were fierce with anger.

'Do you make a habit of reviewing all the CCTV tape, was that something you just like doing? Or did something make this visit worthy of inspection?' Gates paused, then: 'Look all I'm interested in is why your father was killed. If you can help with that, that's all I'm after.'

'Like I said Comrade, nothing.'

'Okay, I've got the message.' He held up his hands. 'I'll leave you be. But remember others won't. I thought your father was a decent man, you may need a friend in the not-too-distant future.'

Burns hesitated and some of the tension subsided. 'I was upstairs, I heard them come in,' he said. 'I didn't hear what they wanted when they arrived. I just saw there were two of them they went into dad's study.' He swigged more water; Gates heard it glug down his throat.

'Something made you suspicious, didn't it? I mean beyond a visit by plain-clothed policemen that would be a worry, right?'

'He wasn't just a Branch man. He had someone with him, a Russian. Russians visiting your house late at night, that's not a good sign.'

Gates could agree with that. 'Are you sure?'

'Very. He stepped out to use his phone. Didn't know I was on the landing above.'

For a moment Gates considered trying to persuade him to say more but decided the young man had said all he was likely to. There was more, he was sure. But did he need to hear it? It sounded like he had enough.

'Okay, that's fine, I'm going. But if you want to talk that's how to reach me.' He handed over a card.

And that would have been it. Conversation over a useful piece of information gathered and Gates would have left.

Turning to go he was aware of movement at the woodshed entrance, and he came face to face with another boy. Younger, less developed than Burns, gangly and with awkward limbs. He had pale grey eyes, a soft almost feminine mouth and tousled unruly hair that curled over his forehead. Despite the physical differences the resemblance between the two was unmistakable. Gates understood immediately that the younger boy before him was Hugo, the younger son.

The young man looked surprised when he saw Gates but averted his eyes deciding to ignore him and called past him to his older brother. Mrs Grazwya had made lunch did he want some? It was in the kitchen.

Gates continued to look at the young man, taking in the features, the line of his limbs and knew he should probably have realised sooner.

It was the natural connection if you thought about it.

Sometimes you fail to see the obvious, Gates thought. He hadn't considered a family link when he had been searching Burns' London flat. ...*looks after this family*, Jason had said earlier.

The photographs. The two lovers.

Without doubt this was one of the young naked men in the photographs.

Outside it had begun to rain. Gentle penetrating drops. The black tiles on the roof glistened under a film of rainwater that ran across them. Above low, dark clouds were scudding across the sky. The gravel on the drive had turned slick and silver rainwater fell in long strips from the guttering on the eaves of the house. Leaving the two young men to their grief, he walked towards the little Fiat. As he did, he noticed a curtain twitch on the ground floor. He thought it might have been the pale face of Margaret Burns watching him.

But the face had gone before he could be sure.

WITH nothing further to do he drove back into Manchester. In the *Herald's* offices he went to the canteen which at this time of day was almost empty. There he stared out of the rain blackened window. A rainstorm was moving across the city. He had made it to the offices before it unleashed properly, the first hard drops beginning to hammer at the pavement as he scooted for cover. He thought about the meeting with the Burns sons. Was Jason Burns telling the whole truth. Had he learned enough to confirm their father was working for the Russians? It seemed so. The girl was nothing. An office affair Burns could bat away in an instant. But a homosexual son? That was different. There were strict laws on such behaviour. Under the law deviancy and degenerate behaviour could attract significant jail time, a long spell in re-education—if he were lucky. Habitual offenders could even find themselves the subject of reversal experimentation.

Burns was ruined and he had known it.

His son realised it as well. He and his brother were dead men walking, the family faced a future as outcasts, their father disgraced and no longer able to shield them.

Had Jason been honest with him. Not completely. Gates was certain there were more. But what could he expect? The young Burns would hardly be ready to open his heart to an unknown reporter.

What was left? The story of course. A story that would be expected to support the Party line. A story of internal corruption that kept everyone who read, owned, or even controlled the *Herald* happy.

A story he would have to write.

Because if he didn't someone would ask why not.

He took the stairs to the newsroom and his desk and there began to type. He felt ashamed of his methods in squeezing information, first from Annie Freedman, then Margaret and

Jason Burns. He wondered whether he should do the decent thing and try to lose the story. He decided the risk was too great. Too great for him and more importantly Sophie. The story was his alibi. The story would keep him safe for a while.

Forcing his mind clear of the ugly thoughts that filled it he began to type. Outside the rain intensified and the click of the keyboard was lost in the noise of a filthy night that would keep even wolves from prowling.

THE young woman sat on the toilet seat in her small bathroom and sobbed trying to stifle the gulping convulsions that threatened to overwhelm her. She clutched at her arms, her body shaking, and she hugged herself tightly. Her vision had become unfocused and blurry at the edges. As she sat amongst the untidy clutter of towels, cosmetics, and soaps, she realised she only had minutes before the men outside became too alarmed or impatient and forced their way in. They had promised her she would be safe; that no harm would come to her or her parents. She had, had no choice but to comply with their demands. They had lied.

Of course, they had lied. Everyone lies, she thought bitterly.

Five minutes ago, there had been the hard impatient knock at her door. She had been expecting them. Since she had learnt of her lover's death and that reporter had visited yesterday, Annie Freedman realised it was only a matter of time. There had been no choice but to wait, there was nowhere else to go, nowhere to run.

They wanted to clean up the traces.

With Burns dead she had no further value.

The Englishman had done the talking, but the Russian was in charge. The same Russian who had been there at every debriefing which followed her meetings with Burns. She had recognised his authority as he lent against the door. His heavyset frame barring the only route out of the cramped little flat. He had enormous fists; she knew that she had seen them. Now they were thrust into the pockets of his raincoat and his dark eyes set deep in the broad Slav face looked at her with fish-like coldness.

Some months ago, she hadn't been able to believe her luck at the job in Burns' office. A colleague she barely knew, young and sharp-suited had approached her, flirty conversations had led to talk of career and the future. He had casually told her of an opportunity in the office of an important official and had convinced her to apply.

'Might as well try,' he said over a friendly cup of coffee, his cheerful enthusiasm had been catching. 'I hear the money's good, and you never know your luck in a raffle.' He told her he knew someone in the headquarters personnel office. He would put a word in. And he was as good as his word, because he did just that.

She had been so excited at being offered the position; she

had never questioned how the offer of help had come about or why someone had been so keen to help her. He hadn't even asked her for sex in return for the favour. The day she learnt she had the job she phoned her parents and bought two new cotton blouses for wearing at the office. 'It's more money,' she had told them. 'I'll increase what I send you.'

It had all gone well at first. The work was interesting, she was given responsibility, and everyone treated her well. She knew the official in charge was an important union man and he had smiled at her on the first day, welcomed her and soon was giving her small personal tasks to complete. She had blushed when one day he had said he liked the way she wore her hair. That night Mr Burns had been on the television, and she had felt important, recognised, valued. She rang her parents and told them to keep an eye out on the news programmes. That's my boss, she said proudly. After a few weeks the former colleague had called her and insisted they meet for coffee.

'There's something we need you to do for us Annie,' he had told her. He was all smiles and with a soothing voice, warm like wood, that at first, she had liked. Now as she listened to what he said she was not so sure.

'Who is us?' she had whispered, apprehension growing. It would have been easier if he had just asked for sex.

He had leaned towards her, breathing softly, speaking quietly. 'Get close, Annie, very close to Mr Burns. He likes you; he looks at you. You need to tell us what he says in the dark of the night. Run the odd errand for us, keep an eye on his apartment, let us know his movements. That's all, we'll do the rest.'

'Why would I do that? What if I don't want to?' The words had come trembling slightly forced from her lips by a pounding brain struggling to understand how she had been coaxed into this position. Stupid, so stupid. Of course, the job was not real. The truth dawned on her. They had just used her.

The colleague had sat back and regarded her. 'Jobs can be temporary, new ones can be hard to find,' he murmured almost absently. 'Invalid parents are difficult to feed. They need caring for. Up to you of course.'

So, she had.

She had fed them what she could find. Scraps of paper from his desk, phone calls, timings, visitors to the offices. She had met her handlers when they demanded, the Englishman did the talking with the occasional guttural intervention from the Russian. A hard-looking man in a bad suit. She carefully recalled for them the details of Burns' business, his associates, his conversations, and thoughts, much of it acquired in the quiet of the night when she lay against his exhausted damp skin, her own body sore, tender and bruised.

Each meeting had left her shaking, anxious inside, fearful for where this would end.

Now Burns was dead.

They were in her flat now: 'You're going to have to come

with us Annie,' the Englishmen had said.

She had always assumed he was a policeman but there had never been an offer of identification. She hadn't attempted to protest. She knew it useless. Instead, she had begged for a few moments to go to the bathroom use the toilet. She needed to pee badly, she said. The men knew fright when they saw it, they were used to fear, knew what it could do, didn't want the mess on the journey and to her surprise, the Russian had nodded to his colleague, and they let her go. There was nowhere to run to. Better than her pissing in the car.

But they had underestimated her. That was a mistake.

Gathering herself, she thought fast. She had prepared herself for this moment. Once she left the flat a deeply uncertain but without doubt unpleasant fate awaited her. She knew enough about Burns; she was a loose end. They would not want to risk her telling anyone what she knew, who she had been working for the names she had been told to memorise when searching his desk or briefcase. Worse, she thought of what might happen to her elderly parents trapped in their own small home. She could not allow that. She knew what she had to do.

Annie had told herself it could not be forever. She had let the man do what he wanted. That had been bad enough. It was odd that despite that with him gone, she felt a deep sense of loss and so vulnerable.

Naked.

There was something else she could not allow.

She ran her hand across her belly. Although it was early, she felt sure she could feel the movement in there. The tiny foetus gathered from a few cells and which only she knew about was growing fast. She had wondered how it would work, how she could help it cling to life, enter a world it was never intended to see. The baby had been her escape plan. Pregnant she was useless to them and worthless to Burns. Perhaps he would have given her a little money to disappear. She had heard that had happened to others. Guilt and irritation at the inconvenience. Take the unwanted bastard away. Then she could have been free. Her parents would have helped her raise the baby; she would have found a way to manage.

You always find a way.

It was not to be.

She was out of time.

Annie pulled the cord from her towelling robe on the back of the door and looped it over the stainless-steel rail that went into the ceiling and which she used to hang washing to dry over the bath. She knew the rail was fastened firmly into the ceiling joists; she was short and not very heavy. With luck it would do.

Then she climbed half onto the edge of the bath and wrapped the other end of the cord four or five times around her neck. There must be a little slack, she thought but not too much, keep it loose for the drop. She kept wrapping as she balanced herself carefully raising herself carefully to her feet, knees bent, holding the wall for support until the cord was almost taut but with enough slack to let her fall. With her dexterity stimulated by fear, she managed to reach the toilet cistern with her toe and pressed it to make it flush. She hoped the sound of the water would give her a few extra seconds before the men next door would be alerted. It must be now, she thought, only seconds before they burst through.

Don't be a coward.

You must do this.

She carefully rose to her full height on the edge of the bath gained her balance and stretched out her arms. There paused like a tight-rope walker she let the final thoughts of her life fill her mind.

To her relief she was finally free of the images of her sweaty grubby encounters with a man old enough to be her father who had treated her as a plaything, an object to be used. Encounters that caused her to weep and scrub her body with soap for hours after but without whom she felt strangely alone. Instead, her final thoughts were of the small baby inside her belly that would grow no more and remain unaware of the cruelty that existed in the world, then the image changed, and she saw a garden and a swing, an image from years ago in her childhood. The day was cloudless, and an endless mellow blue sky stretched above her. A cheerful handsome man who she recognised as her father laughed as he pushed her into the sky towards the sun that bathed her in warmth. The full white light shone in her eyes, pouring around her and girlish laughter filled her throat.

She stepped from the bath.

Her thoughts went black and turned to nothing. She didn't hear the sound of the door beginning to splinter, then shatter and fall apart in a burst of jagged wood as the large muscular body of the Russian shouldered his way into the bathroom.

\*\*\*

# CHAPTER TEN

### *Marxists get up early in the morning*

### The Manchester Herald

IT'S A GOOD PIECE Harry, one of your better efforts, better than you've produced for a while,' the editor proclaimed in his estuary London drawl, a cultivation from his days in Canary Wharf. 'You finding your old Mojo? It'll go out in tonight's edition. The censor gave it a clean bill of health, just a few *t*'s and *i*'s to dot. You should thank yer lucky stars they're not in your office all day.'

That, thought Gates, is the difference between you and me. You're clever enough to work this system and patient enough to deal with it.

'Truly sorry about that,' he said. He wasn't.

Four days had gone past since the visit to Margaret Burns and her sons. Now, he and his editor were sat in the conference room with the rest of the newsroom staff, the hacks, editors, and sub-editors jogging through the news agenda for the next two days. It was the opportunity for the editor to hold court, roll out his ministry and deliver the odd public admonishment. An informal but efficient assembly of twenty or so in shirt sleeves or casual blouses gathered in no order around a long table with coffee mugs and bottles of water, notepads open, ballpoints weirdly doodling until their own time to report or explain arrived. Interest tended to sharpen when a colleague's discomfort surfaced. The smirks and exchanged half-looks across the table would heighten office drama. It was best to be careful though; trouble could arrive at your own door with alarming speed.

Not for the first time Harry realised that by some margin he was the oldest person in the room. Most days he felt it too.

On the wall at one end of the room ran the rolling television news on a large plasma screen. It broadcast twenty-four hours a day, the flashing images generally unnoticed by editors and reporters who had become immune to the displays and announcements. Although, Gates had sometimes thought, if a report of interest appeared on screen, something dramatic or of interest, it was curious the way the room would instinctively fill, as if an invisible sequence of code written into the news staff DNA drew them to gather without the need for summons.

The editor was a young man still, at least fifteen years Gates' junior. He looked it too, despite a head, which being bald on top, presented an early air of maturity to the younger staff. Most of the time Gates felt sorry for him, rather like the Manchester City team that had shipped four goals in Moscow.

The result was never in doubt, yet everyone went through the motions of a fair match. Editing a newspaper was like that.

'You think there's more in this? If so, we could use a couple of in-depth features. Need to make sure it can stick though.' He had a way of tempering praise with warning.

'Maybe.' It was a poor day for journalism when corruption in a union was the best news a front page could offer. It was what it was, thought Gates and went on: 'Seems like Burns was on to something. He may have been popular in some quarters, but he seemed to have made a number of enemies. There were quite a few who didn't like his ideas.'

'Same old story. Nothing surprising there. What's your angle to give it some zip?' asked the editor.

'Give it an institutional feel. Start with opportunism in the lower ranks, corrupt individuals anxious to avoid management scrutiny, cover their tracks—that sort of line.'

'Was Burns involved personally?'

Gates hesitated, but only briefly. 'I'd like to find out more.' He realised something a little more positive might be needed. 'It's going that way, but there are more people I need to speak to.'

The younger man nodded thoughtfully. 'Right, okay Harry, we'll call tonight's effort an intro piece. Take it further, try and see if you can get more on the troublemakers, what they were up to, what was the angle, who stood to gain. For the moment keep it as patriotic stalwart rooting out the greedy bad apples—

until it's not. You get the picture.'

Gates nodded. But he knew the words were mostly theatre, a short rehearsed two-verse drama for the benefit of the meeting.

Earlier, alone in his office, his boss had been as blunt as a pair of rusty scissors in the direction he gave to his staff crime reporter. You have to get this right Harry, or we will both be swinging by our balls, do yer hear me? Gates did, but this was nothing he did not already know. One hint that you are heading anywhere other than low-level corruption by bit-part arseholes, and *they* will be all over us. He didn't elaborate on who *they* were. But Gates could guess. Do what you want with Burns, he's dead so no one will care, we might even make him the finale and anyone else below him, they don't matter. But for Christ's sake don't go near the Party or any leadership—and I don't just mean in print, am I crystal?

Crystal, Gates had repeated.

The meeting moved on crisply, attention passing to others, conforming to the rule that editorial meetings take only thirty minutes—not a second longer. As the business rippled around the table, Gates felt a few curious glances fall his way before attention passed. No one had him down for a crusading reporter, let alone a courageous one.

Everyone knew what happened to them.

LUCY drew him to one side as the meeting closed. The editor

had collected his papers and phone and hurried out munching a chocolate bar for energy, the rest were filing away to their desks.

'You asked me to look out for anything on the Burns family,' she spoke quietly looking up at him, her pert nose wrinkling slightly. He had. He didn't want to keep her at too great a distance from his investigation and she had been eager to help.

She happened to be in the police HQ yesterday, she explained. Just happened, thought Gates, then checked himself, why has everything become so suspicious.

'Well, the son, the eldest one, Jason, I did some checking. One of the police clerks is in my badminton club.'

Gates began to listen carefully wondering where Lucy was going.

'There was a Watch Notice on him, imposed by SB.'

The inflection in her voice caused Gates to stiffen. He wasn't sure whether it was what she was saying or because it was her saying it.

'What did it say?' he asked. He decided to overlook why Lucy had decided to investigate details of his story. He hadn't asked her to.

'No arrest, note all contacts, all locations. There was a list of names of people they wanted to know if he was seen with, mainly ex-soldiers it seems.'

Gates thought about it. It could only mean that the Burns' son was a person of interest to Special Branch, intelligence interest. 'Anything else?'

She nodded. 'It began just over a year ago, a few weeks after his discharge. It seems like he had some suspected links to far-right nationalists, there was probably some radicalisation during military service—it's not uncommon by all accounts. But apparently it was lifted four months ago. Just removed, no further action. I thought that sounded strange? You would know better than me.'

They were alone in the conference room now. On the wall the silent rolling images from the plasma screen television news reports provided a background. A smartly dressed female newscaster was reading some item while behind her a report displayed a silent riot and street violence in some faraway unhappy place.

He heard her words, but his mind had returned to the crushed body in the road and the adult son so aggressive and protective of his father. Almost like he knew, sensed, what was coming. The anger. It seemed more than that expected by loss. A visceral anger that went beyond emotional loss. The heavy rain smacking against the rough tarmac covering the noise of the approaching vehicle. The man deep in thought, a wet dog at his heels just seconds away from the screaming roar that would…

An unseen shudder passed through him.

Lucy was looking at him, her face with a small, puzzled frown waiting for a response.

'Harry, what do you think?'

The thoughts evaporated and Gates came back to what Lucy was saying. The ability to be distracted by thoughts a flaw that had regularly enraged Kate: *'Where the fuck do you go Harry, I'm trying to talk to you...'*

'Yes, it's unusual,' he murmured. Lifting a watch notice? That would be a highly unusual step to take. Once considered a subversive always a subversive. Absence of evidence or even innocence was not enough. The state did not stop.

Unless...

It was told to. Entirely possible under the circumstances. A deal with Special Branch in return for leaving his offspring alone cooperation with them?

'Possible, I suppose if there was a reason. Was there anything else.' She was still looking at him. 'Anything else you want to tell me?'

'I asked the clerk to pull his military record.' She saw the look on Gates' face. 'I was just curious, it's okay the guy wants to fumble with me, so he is willing to pass me the odd favour.'

Gates still looked doubtful, so she laughed. 'Anyway, he's cute, so I might let him.'

'Okay, okay, what did you learn?'

'Two things. One he was up for a gallantry award, a big one. Destroyed a Chinese gun pit and rescued a colleague despite being seriously injured himself. Serious stuff apparently. But it was denied. No explanation. That was before the Watch

Notice. He left the military over a year ago. A medical discharge, honourable but no medal.'

More evidence someone had thought him unreliable for some time, thought Gates. Medals and commendations were cheap inducements to compliance.

The television news had changed to a natural disaster somewhere that could have been India. Surging brown floodwater was roaring through towns, buildings collapsed, cars rolled and popped like tennis balls in the current, people clung to broken trees that hung close to the swirling rush that burst over everything in its way.

'What else, you said two things?'

'Well, there was a recent assault charge against him that was dropped. Two guys were beating up his brother late one night. He injured one of the assailants quite seriously before the cops arrived. He also laid out one of the cops before being taken away.'

Gates said nothing, mulling over the new background to Jason Burns. Obviously being watched over it would seem in return for his father's cooperation. He thought about asking more but the little red Komsomol badge pinned to her woollen jumper flashed under the overhead light and he thought better of it.

'Well, I thought you would want to know,' said Lucy realising the exchange was ending. 'Best be careful with this, but useful background I hope.'

'Good to know Lucy, thanks.' He saw her anxiety and flashed her a quick smile. 'Don't worry. I won't take risks.' He wanted to add, but nor should you, only he wasn't sure whether there was risk for her. Perhaps giving him this information was simply part of the plan.

Gates was suddenly in a hurry to leave, and with a nod that was slightly awkward he walked quickly away to the exit grabbing his coat as he passed his desk; Lucy followed his progress through the newsroom and bit her lip thoughtfully before with workplace smiles to passing colleagues she went back to her cubicle.

Her eyes remained on the exit, and she wondered what would happen next.

HARRY Gates drank vodka and went to bed at ten. He had spent the evening with his thoughts and found them too ugly to continue with. In an attempt to sooth his world he had searched the radio finding a concert with a Bach composition. But he had found it slow and dreary and if anything, the melancholy notes of the cello and violin had made his mood worse.

The concerns over Burns' reliability looked well-founded. Just briefly, despite his scepticism of Dugdale's ideas he had perhaps dared to hope. Perhaps Dugdale did have the means, the keys, the plan. But it looked less likely now. The relentless unpitying machinery of state surveillance and ruthlessness had broken through.

To discover what?

There was something else. Perhaps more worrying.

Sophie.

If Dugdale was compromised, then could he really deliver his promise to extract her?

He had a feeling he was walking a sandy track that was collapsing behind him ever more quickly as he passed. The urge to increase speed to stay ahead of the subsidence, even though he knew it was futile, becoming too strong to resist.

Soon he would be running, and the journey would be out of control.

When he came from an uneasy sleep, the bedroom was almost in darkness save for the pale glow of a nearby streetlight that always lit the far corner of the room. He looked at his wristwatch and saw it was a quarter past five. Blearily he wondered why he was awake. Then the noise of the banging began to filter into his brain, and he knew what had woken him. The urgency of the pounding drove the sleep from his eyes. It was a heavy pounding on the front door to his flat, persistent in the way that the caller knew someone was in there and would just keep banging away no matter what until someone responded.

He felt for his robe and as he wrapped himself in it called through the sitting room: 'Alright, alright, I'm coming.' His mouth felt dry, and he could feel his heartbeat begin to quicken a heavy drumbeat that he told himself could be heard.

The banging slowed, diminishing slightly but continued as a rhythmic rap. He breathed deep, composed his face into an expressionless mask and released the catch and opened the door. He was confronted by a tall well-built man leaning casually with his elbow against the door frame, his hand turned downward with an open warrant card ready to be inspected. The other hand was clenched in a fist and in mid-knock.

Gates had known who it was as soon as he realised someone was outside. Something Shiner was fond of saying came to mind. Marxists get up early to defend their cause.

'Harry Gates?' He waited for Gates to nod that he was. 'DS Barnes. You're coming with me. Some people want a word with you.'

'Am I under arrest,' Gates asked keeping his voice even with effort.

Barnes looked about thirty years old with a smooth-shaven, long face and cool intelligent eyes. Only the warrant card gave his work away, otherwise he could have been anything the better side of a university education that society offered. An establishment man one of the many legions that the nation's education system produced to fulfil its works with unquestioning loyalty and reliability.

'Do you want to be?' he replied coolly. 'Makes no difference to me. Why not get dressed while you're deciding.'

Outside, alongside the pavement was a waiting black BMW saloon. The car's engine ticked over emitting a low powerful grumble. Barnes opened the rear door and beckoned Gates to get in and then followed him into the interior. The car was plush, expensive, and smelt of new leather. A soft green glow came from the dashboard and the vehicle moved effortlessly away, the driver barely touching the controls. Gates almost asked where they were going but decided it was useless. Barnes was not the talking type. Anyway, he decided he already knew.

But he was wrong.

The car headed west into the slumbering city centre away from the police headquarters where he had expected to be taken and passing the dark deserted shops, then accelerated out onto the city's ring road before joining the motorway heading south. The traffic was almost non-existent at this hour, just the first few vehicles starting the day, their drivers bleary eyed. Gates read the sign which put London two hundred miles away.

'We've got a fair drive,' Barnes said over his shoulder while settling himself comfortably into the front seat. 'Feel free to finish your sleep.'

Gates lent back and despite the apprehension he felt, wrapped in the soft leather, he felt his eyes become heavy. Outside the speeding car the cold night began to retreat, and the grey of dawn began to creep over the ant track of vehicles that led to the nation's capital.

THREE and half hours later, the BMW turned down into the Great Scotland Yard entrance to the vast underground car park that lay beneath Whitehall. The first floor of the parking area was practically deserted, and the warm tyres squealed on the dry concrete as they swung to a halt.

The grand Old War Office Building with its Edwardian Baroque construction and placed astride Whitehall was at the centre of the imposing Victorian-era requisitioned buildings used by the Party and dominated the route to a Parliament the Party controlled. The Portland stone interiors were home to the armies of officials and bureaucrats that oiled the political force behind government. When the Party took over, much of the artwork and period furniture had been quietly removed from the old hotels and clubs, much of it pilfered. The War Office stonework and elegant wood panelling had been crudely chiselled and adapted. Now it looked austere, grey, and forbidding.

Leaving the car and walking to the service staircase Gates had noted the lines of identical armoured Mercedes limousines parked discretely in the shadows, red party number plates contrasting with the black and chrome bodywork of the gleaming vehicles.

JOE McBride had been leader of the Amalgamated Electrical and Mechanical Engineering Union for twenty-eight years. It had been suggested that he was possibly the most powerful man in the country eclipsing the influence of the prime minister, although he was at pains to deny any such status within the system from which was drawn the country's political authority.

He would happily ruin the career and lives of anyone who suggested that power in the country had been usurped by unseen and dark forces.

And those that had crossed him had come to rue the day.

Gates had never met the man who to the faithful of the British Communist Party was a legend and, in whose presence, he now found himself. At the age of eighty and with fifty years of leadership behind him he had been honoured with many party awards including land and unvisited houses that had been sequestered by the state from previous undeserving bourgeois owners. His recognition had even extended overseas, as far as Moscow, where it was widely believed he had influence with the General Secretary himself and he counted amongst his personal friends several members of the Soviet Politburo. Stories about regular Black Sea holidays in Sochi were not rumours.

There wasn't much that went on in British political life that McBride did not have a hand in. That meant he was a man to approach and treat with great care. He had a reputation for knowing most things about most people, most of the time.

Gates could feel his shoes sinking into the cream carpet and he felt his palms turn sweaty. He was standing in this man's office. It was still early, barely the start of the working day. He had been escorted from the basement car park via back stairs and made to wait in a dingy waiting room with broken linoleum and an overhead neon light that fizzed. After a while he was taken from the room and they walked on up some stairs and through a fire door the passage became a corridor, the linoleum gave way to carpet and Gates suspected had they were now near the front of the building, on the fourth or fifth floor. In an outer office an official had greeted Gates and his escort without words rising from his desk to open a stout pair of wooden double doors and stood aside for Gates to enter. Barnes did not follow, and Gates found himself on the hideous out of place sea of carpet. Outside, beyond the tall windows covered by the thick opaque sheen of anti-blast net curtain came the low rumble of morning traffic beginning to gather in Whitehall.

Seated at a large desk at the far end of the room sat a hunched figure in a dark suit that for all the skill of the tailor still seemed to hang slightly from his frame.

Like many of the nation's elite, beyond the rumour, little was officially known about McBride beyond the public speeches, which had become rare. It was whispered his wife had dementia and that the devoted pair lived an exiled existence in an apartment that resembled a hospital ward sanitised and purified to defend against harmful pathogens and attended to by a selected band of nursing staff carefully chosen for their skill and loyalty.

But it was deceptive to imagine the man as too tired, old, and shrunken to have lost his menace. He was as dangerous as a crocodile cooling itself beneath the still water of an African swamp and Gates had no idea if such rumours about his domestic regime were true.

Now after Barnes had ushered him in and retreated, he did not know whether to be relieved or whether the uneasy and oily level of fear in his stomach should be rising more quickly to the surface.

Police questioning was not the worst thing that could happen.

He realised that McBride was not alone in the room. Sitting on the sofa in to one side was a figure who Gates recognised. Hallam. The Special Branch chief.

*Think.*

What did they have on him that lead to this? He had been at the site of Burns' murder, a murder they had tried to keep quiet. The visits he had made to London, the flat and Annie Freedman. What else? Shiner? Doubtful. The snippets that Lucy may have put together. Possibly. And of course, the visit to Burns' home; Margaret and Jason Burns. They had seen him there. It didn't seem much to justify hauling him to London to get this level of attention.

Could they know more? Dugdale?

He could only pray they didn't.

But something reassured him.

Cooperation between the upper echelons of the Party and the State's security services was not healthy, the mutual suspicion, politicking and manoeuvring for power bred jealousies and rivalries that kept two powerful institutions in a perpetual wrestle for authority, neither able to land decisive blows on the other, bound together in inosculation, cojoined vascular systems that competed as much as cooperated.

If this was a straight security issue related to Dugdale, there would be no involvement from this man McBride. It would be straight to some police cell for some 'enhanced interrogation'.

It was Hallam who spoke. He pointed to a chair in front of the large desk and said with a trace of irony: 'Thank you for coming all this way. Mr McBride wanted to meet you.'

McBride had not looked up since Gates had entered his eyes. This close, the old man seemed unimpressive, far removed from the dominating titan of the party congress, where he commanded proceedings with iron will and authority, carrying all motions before him. He looked more wizened, his face had sallow loose skin that hung beneath wisps of grey hair carefully collected and organised into a comb over style. His hands were small and wrinkled and he wore heavy gold rings that Gates thought crude and ostentatious.

Now, pulling a moist cloth from his pocket, McBride carefully wiped his hands paying attention to the fingernails and cuticles.

'What price progress.' He looked up from the paper he had been reading straight at Gates. 'I wonder sometimes if we have tried too hard. Do you agree?'

Gates was a little stunned by the remark. 'I suppose so,' he replied. 'I am sure the nation is grateful.'

McBride nodded slowly, accepting the reply but making no

response. 'Yet nation and people are not the same thing,' he said slowly. 'What about you Gates, do you like this country? who we are, what we have become?'

'I hope Comrade McBride knows that I have long been a servant of this country and supporter of the choices it has made.' His mouth felt dryer than ever and to himself his words sounded like a mantra, a neat phrase of loyalty to be rehearsed at appropriate party gatherings or when the prospect of a promotion arises, and all points available have to be scraped together to count.

The old man snorted a short laugh: 'I'd never heard of you until yesterday, so I wouldn't know that.' McBride jerked his head towards Hallam who was looking at Gates expressionless. 'He has though and he's not too sure about you. But let's take you at your word shall we lad.' The gruff vowels somehow seemed at odds with an expensive suit and groomed hair. The caustic sarcasm the same as the bitter jibes of his father. 'Len Burns, you're interested in him, am I right?'

There was no point in denying it. 'Yes Comrade, a most unfortunate occurrence it seems.'

McBride nodded slowly as if agreeing. 'We're lucky in this country you know, so damned lucky. Most people don't realise they are born.'

Gates felt his fingers at the sides of his trousers, his nails digging into his thigh through the fabric. He was being invited to agree with the aging union boss' philosophy here. What was

Hallam's role? Pounce on weakness? identify dissent?

'All we ask is for a little conformity from the people.' He sighed. 'If they give us that then everyone can get on with their personal lives undisturbed, that's reasonable enough I would say.'

Gates said nothing and waited.

'Of course, to many it seems that, that is not enough. They don't understand that to avoid fascism we must first control our capitalist tendencies, live within our means and to the rules that protect us all.'

Again, Gates said nothing.

'Those in our society who disagree with the Party, its *loco parentis* role needs to be identified and re-educated. It's for the good of the many that their influence does not spread, the history of our Movement tells us this.'

What was this, a political theory lesson? or something else? The Latin phrase, carefully pronounced, seemed odd, borrowed, and unusual for a man of his background. The words reminded Gates of the many bearded and corduroy dressed members of the academic intelligentsia who inhabited the late-night news channels with their economic and social theories that were really a load of shit—just no one said so.

He didn't know whether to laugh or cry.

'Sadly, Comrade Burns may have held personal aspirations that were inconsistent with this thinking. He seems to have become corrupted by a desire for personal advancement.

He left much of that duty behind. Do you follow?'

'Yes, Comrade, I think I do. But...what do you require from me?'

'It's quite simple Gates,' interjected Hallam suddenly. 'Comrade McBride is aware of your current assignment to investigate Burns' involvement in corruption. He wishes you have all the background in order that your story reflects the proper truth of why he *may* have been murdered.'

'I see,' said Gates carefully. 'So, we have evidence of why he was killed and by who?' Silly question, he thought. Of course, they do, I'm now part of the cover-up.

Hallam rose and handed Gates a slim unmarked folder about a centimetre thick. For the first time Gates had a good look at the feared detective. Hallam was tall, gaunt and thin. Smooth and shaved, his dark hair was neatly trimmed and even from a few feet away Gates caught the scent of an expensive men's cologne. A lawyer, government official, banker, someone of serious trade, he could have been any of those things. But, he thought, the eyes gave it away, pale, and wide, penetrating, like butterfly valves that allowed detail to enter, but denied escape. The hard eyes of the securocrat.

'Off the record of course. Use it but non-attributable.'

'What is this?' Gates began to leaf through the set of papers inside the buff-coloured plain folder.

McBride spoke from his desk: 'It's your story. The one your editor wants you to write. Spreadsheets, emails, foreign account details. Burns had a number of enrichment projects, and you'll find some bribery and or threats for support. There's more if you want it.'

'The General Secretary has had his suspicions for some months,' said Hallam. 'After some preliminary investigations of his own he decided quite properly to hand the matter over to ourselves. We compiled the rest.

'Burns wasn't investigating corruption he was responsible for it.' Hallam sighed, a small sound of resignation and non-surprise. 'He wasn't the first, he won't be the last.' He shrugged. 'It's regrettable he will evade justice.'

'So, who killed him?'

Hallam shrugged: 'We have not confirmed that yet, but we will. Seems like a falling out among thieves, internal rivalries, you can see a few names in that file if you want to use them.'

Gates assumed they were both lying. 'And how does this involve Special Branch and counter-terrorism?' he blurted out.

Hallam ignored the question and walked to the window to look through the silver-grey blast curtain his back to Gates. 'Not your concern Gates,' he said. 'How the Party coordinates its investigations on behalf of the people is an internal matter. It's best you understand that.'

McBride had returned to studying the paper on his desk. The hum of an air purifying unit sucking and pulling the air around them was the only sound.

Hallam spoke: 'Comrade McBride has given you more than

enough to keep you and your paper happy. Write something good, write something in the public interest and leave it at *that*. It's corruption open and shut.'

Gates thought of what he knew; what Dugdale had told him, what the police had said about Dugdale, what he had learned about Burns and his family. He briefly wondered what they knew about himself. Was this simply a smoke screen, cover up, supporting the official history, a truth that could be believed, would not be challenged, and would close the matter.

'Listen to the commissioner, Gates.' McBride's words were quiet, his eyes on the paper. 'There is no mileage in trying to go elsewhere. Now if you'll please excuse me, I have work to do.'

Hallam was regarding Gates coolly. His voice expressionless and precise. 'You heard what the Comrade General Secretary said Gates, keep the file.'

He may have looked the part of a smooth operator with a sophisticated intellect, but Gates knew that violence came easily to the man, not personally with his own fists driven by ragged emotions of anger and rage, that effort was for others. Hallam's satisfaction came with the cold logic of the mind, knowing the violence was a means to an end. Gates realised he was gripping the file tightly and he felt a muscle flutter in his cheek. He tried to keep his expression impassive.

Hallam's face lifted, suddenly the menace seemed to leave him. It was like he had departed from a script, realised, then checked himself and returned.

'We're on the same side Gates in all of this. The Comrade General Secretary has a union to run and Party responsibilities, I have an investigation to complete, and you have a duty to report. It's all part of the same effort to make the country work. You will do well to realise that.'

Gates said that he did. Except he didn't believe it. McBride was no more an ally of Hallam than he was of Gates. Everyone knew the tension between the Party and State Security was like a battle between an elephant and a whale. There was no way of getting at each other and the result was uncertain even if they could.

Gates turned and left the office without McBride seeming to notice, Barnes was waiting and then Gates realised that Hallam had followed him.

'I'm interested,' said Hallam, 'to know how you came to be at the incident scene the other day?'

Gates looked neutral and said: 'Just a call to the paper.' There was no point in lying. Hallam would have seen the transcript, read the words, scrutinised the timing. 'A tip, it sounded interesting. I went.'

'You see to have found yourself in a number of interesting places recently meet a number of interesting people.'

*Christ*, he thought. *What does he know?*

'You were at the London apartment of Burns the other day.'

*How does he know that?*

'Do you deny it? Where were you before that? You caught

the early High Speed Inter City.'

*He's fishing*, thought Gates. *Someone was at Burns' apartment he is wondering whether it was me.* 'I took my time in the morning, then I went there yes.' The cleaner would recognise him, there was no point lying. 'But I found nothing, I wasn't the first there.'

'What about Annie Freedman, what did you find there?'

'Who?'

'Don't fuck me about Gates. That's where you went afterwards.'

'All right, I did. I didn't learn much, she was in no state to talk. She was drunk, probably high as well. I knew she was Burns' mistress. I just wanted to see what she would say. I told her I would be back when she was in a condition to talk.'

'Don't waste your journey,' said Hallam. 'She's dead. Hanged herself. As you say, the drinks and the drugs were too much for her.'

Inwardly Gates felt shock. Had she really taken her own life, or…the alternative didn't bear thinking about. He thought of the directive from McBride. 'Can I use that,' he said, straining every nerve to keep his voice under control.

Hallam was standing close, very close—close enough to smell the morning cologne the man wore. 'Listen to me. You've been sniffing in murky places, I know where,' he whispered. 'He wants you to help the Party with the story you've been given. That's fine for now, you can be of use to the Party. But when that's done then we'll *talk* again.'

Hallam moved away and looked at Gates levelly.

'Take the file Gates.' The pale eyes dropped away. 'Barnes will show you out.'

Outside, through the windows, a weak sun had risen over London, its light a dim radiance through the battleship-grey cloud.

THAT evening, after his return to the office as the weary-eyed news staff departed from their days work he read the file. It amounted to an investigative journalist's dream conveniently compiled without the inconvenience of an actual investigation. He thought of what he knew of the death and compared it with the evidence he had been given and was supposed to use to report it. The macabre twisting of truth, modern doublespeak, an ugly construction of *Macbeth* proportions. Had his daughter's life not rested on the outcome he would have laughed. He realised that the only thing now keeping him from a cell was the story he would write to protect an old Party tyrant's quest to cling to power.

He opened his computer and wrote:

*Corruption in Union Management.*

He thought about Dugdale. He needed to warn him. There was more danger to his plans than he probably knew. If he did tell him what would happen? There was no way of knowing. He tapped the keys, tak-ta-ta-ta-tak-ta.

*Police continue to investigate the hit and run incident...*

There was no alternative.

Don't make waves, don't be brave, carrying on as normal, pretending to be unknowing to the unseen drama was no longer an option. *Either way your life now changes.* Dugdale's words and he remembered the promise to him on Sophie. *I can get her back.*

Miranda had been very specific: *No telephones no emails, go to this place...* His fingers continued a nimble dance.

Tak-ta-ta-ta-tak-ta.

*Details are emerging which may cast light on...*

He paused and reached across for his phone. He began to key in a street finder search address—then he stopped. Instead, he reached into a drawer found an old city centre map. Fulton Street.

Tomorrow... He returned to the keyboard, pulling the practised phrases from his subconscious swiftly without thought.

*Investigators have subsequently found...*

He rubbed his eyes, tired from the early morning awakening, the adrenalin, the long drive, the fear of what awaited. Think straight, think carefully, he told himself sternly. Outside the filthy Manchester deluge hurled itself against the window. McBride's words: *All we ask is conformity.*

'Fuck you, pal,' he thought to himself. He closed his eyes and inwardly laughed for a few moments forgetting who and where he was.

***

# CHAPTER ELEVEN

*We always clap for birthdays*

**Łódź Voivodeship Poland**

LAST NIGHT SOPHIE HAD dreamt of her mother.

As always, the dream caused her to awake abruptly, her eyes a little wet with tears. She must have been about six, perhaps seven when one night confused and anxious, holding her father's hand, the two of them had left the home in north London behind. She had only her small pink backpack of precious toys and a change of underwear, her father with only the clothes he wore. For once there had been no fight. She had been playing in her bedroom one evening when her father already dressed in his raincoat had entered and told her they were leaving. There hadn't been time to think about what happened. One moment she was on her bedroom floor surrounded by toys, the next she was being bundled into her puffy bright red anorak and her father clutched her little hand as they walked quickly into the night while her mother had watched. She had been upset but after a last look turned away and had forced herself not to think of her mother much since.

She had never been back.

In the dreams that would come later, as they hurried away, her mother was standing there, framed in the dark of the street by the hallway light, tall, slim and beautiful with sleek black hair that fell below her shoulders. Behind her stood a bearded man she had seen a few times before but didn't know who he was, his hand was resting gently on her mother's shoulder. There was a smile on her mouth, one of satisfaction and something else—something as a child she did not recognise, and which confused her, but she now recognised as contempt?

She could not remember quite what happened afterwards. She was too young perhaps; she didn't know how to ask questions and her father did not know how to explain. In a way this was good. Life rebuilds. There was no fear or pain, no complex sorrow. Sophie and her father just started again. She recalled a dingy cold and small house they shared with an old man a long way from London. The old man was gruff, unfriendly, and smelled slightly. He wore damaged clothes and sat every night by a feeble electric fire staring into the orange glow of the filament. She and her father lived with him for a few months where they shared a room and prepared meals with the old man who barely said a word. Don't mind him, said her father, it's just his way.

On her birthday and quite unexpectedly, the old man had given her a doll, made of fine exquisite porcelain, not plastic, delicately painted, and old, beautiful but fragilely dressed in pastel coloured lace that looked like it might crumble to the touch. He had mumbled something about it being his mothers and he wanted her to have it. Then he had retreated, shuffling away, returning to the small warmth of the electric fire and the silence between them all resumed.

It was not long after this that her father announced that his house in Manchester had been returned, well not all of it, but part of it, somewhere for them to live properly. They left and she never saw the old man, who she came to realise was her grandfather, again.

Although over the years she thought less of her mother, the memory of her never did quite disappear, mercifully the hurt did. She had come to realise what the look on her mother's face had meant when they left. Indifference and an absence of emotion that was like the closing of an unloved book, a story to remain on a shelf and never opened.

So, the dream had surprised her, and she wondered what its unwelcome return meant.

It was her third year at the campus and Sophie had been granted unsupervised walk-out privileges. This didn't amount to much except that when classes had finished and before the mandatory evening socialising began, she and a small group of friends were allowed to stroll around the campus area and take walks in the nearby forest. In summer when the evenings were long, they would sit on the long grassy bank that led down to the fence surrounding the campus and there they laughed and chatted under a Polish sky that was mellow blue, washed with butter-coloured clouds.

One day she found it had been decided that they should all change dormitories and the small circle of friends she had made were gone, separated by a new configuration of classes, routines, and timetables. It was time to start over again, try and make new companionship in a resigned awkward circle of introductions tinged with melancholy for the loss of half-formed relationships. No one questioned or thought of opposing this stirring of their society. It was just the way it was.

When the change of season bought colder weather and chilly evenings, the students kept to their blocks. Inside, the corridors were whitewashed brick with linoleum floors and smelt of bleach. Between the regular noticeboards were large posters tacked to the walls, their colourful ideology promoting a mix of pride, comradeship, and personal health. While the others preferred to keep to the warmth of the dormitory with their books, listening to music or collecting around the television to watch Polish documentaries and soaps, Sophie now found herself alone on her walks. She didn't mind, the short respite outside was a chance to breathe air not recycled by others, not filled by the instructional cadences of the tutors who with patient deliberation spent their days explaining the inspiration for the political thought that, the tutors assured them, they all benefited from in their societies. Thoughts that protected them from wasteful liberalism and unnecessary conflict.

Today had been mild and bright for autumn and the sky began to turn oyster grey as the late afternoon waned. In the distance the dark crests of a pine forest began to merge, the tips of the trees like serrated teeth blurred into a thick line that separated the sky from the earth. She paused by a low wall. She was a short, smallish girl with a soft oval face and shoulder-length hair that was dark but lacking the shine of her girlhood. Looking across the open pasture to the trees beyond, the wind rushed across the grass, and she felt it buffet her cheeks. Rough soap, cheap moisturiser and cold water meant the skin on her face stung and felt coarse.

Still after all this time she was not completely sure where she was. She had stopped thinking about it by the end of her first year. Somewhere near a place called Łódź, she remembered being told that much, but it could be hundreds of miles from that city and in any direction. For the first few months she had been angry, almost defiant, furious at what had been done to her, transported across the continent for re-education. Furious because fury was her last defence before understanding. But she had stopped short of non-cooperation her anger receding to a hot sulk.

One day, near the beginning of her stay, a French girl with a few more weeks of experience than Sophie had quietly explained that there were worse places than the classroom to spend the day, or the dormitory rooms in which to spend the nights. But such realisation had only cast her memories in a sharper light, and it would take months before the feelings of repression and loss began to be replaced by something else, something close to acceptance and compliance.

Now, it did not matter to her so much where they had sent her. Sometimes, when her guard was down, her thoughts would wander back to her old life in England, and she wondered when she might see her home again. The image of her father when she had been summoned to the Youth and Family Tribunal Court to explain herself remained with her. He had a look of anguish and fear, a look she could never extinguish. She remembered the dawning feeling that she had been stupid, reckless and that her selfish exuberance, taken a little too far, had placed them both at risk. She hoped he was alright and had recovered from their parting.

You must be grateful, they told her patiently. Your mistakes and poor choices for companions had allowed a lesson to be learnt. Over time she had come to believe her tutors right.

Slowly but surely, the teaching began to make sense and Sophie realised what a fool she had been. She began to understand how her thoughts and emotions had become muddled and confused. It was all straight forward really. The reasons why she had got herself involved in pathetic childish political and social writing now seemed juvenile, misguided, and even embarrassing. Once it had been explained properly and often enough, the philosophies of belonging and contributing to a society, and that being your main purpose with the need for duty to others made perfect sense. So much more sense than being able to run around spreading nonsense, saying what you like, to whomever you liked. That was irresponsible, surely.

Wasn't it?

But then. Somewhere deeper, somewhere in her mind inside a locked cupboard, she still realised that she did not belong to this place, its teaching, and its ways. The feeling of isolation, that she was marooned on a strange planet always returned. She had to be compliant, there was no choice, but the best she could do was to stifle the doubts that would not leave her, their persistence both unwelcome and glorious in equal measure and which came unsummoned.

Just like the dream of her mother did.

When something unsettled her, a return of a memory, or something unusual it felt as if part of her old self was waking.

Something unusual like today.

In the distance a small drone hovered and buzzed in the air, its bold, brash, persistent fizz like a wasp riding the wind's currents as it prowled on some unknown mission. She could just make out the tilting and shifting rotors that moved at blurring speed like an insect's wings. Its lifts, turns and swoops looked aimless although nothing in nature moved aimlessly any more than this mechanical insect did. There is always purpose. Were its patrols to protect the campus grounds from intrusion? Or was it snooping on students making sure they returned from a late walk? Or was its mission unrelated, innocent, something to do with the farmland or forestry that surrounded the campus in all directions for miles? She had no way of knowing.

Behind on the concrete quadrangle, the tannoy made an announcement, a cheerful sing-song female voice telling everyone that the evening movie would begin showing at 7:30 pm. High on their poles alongside the 'safety' cameras, she barely heard their regular announcements, calls to meals, class, seminars, summonses. In the early weeks, the small speaker in her shared room had proved more irritating. It was fixed in the corner attached to the ceiling, where it sat unnoticed until during the daytime and without warning the same four note motif in a never changing octave would sound to introduce uninvited words. But you became used to it of course, tuning out the overlapping announcements, no longer finding them sinister or malevolent. She had read once that humans can get used to anything once they realise that they cannot do anything about it. Their disgust, irritation, anger, and any other feeling of odium fades. Things that would normally cause distaste or repugnance, insects, human filth, even pain slips away to be hidden in the background where the mind simply decides not to deal with it. You had no choice. It was much the same here, they just called it education. In the end, the posters, lectures, tannoy calls, it came to the same thing. You swallowed the slogans recited the texts of books and moved on waiting for the time when you could be alone.

That brought her to today and the unsettling event that caused her to walk alone on an autumn Polish evening. There was an hour remaining before the sun vanished, the still night came, and the distant trees would fall into deep velvet silence.

Earlier that day there had been a parade for a birthday. A girl a couple of years younger than herself, from Italy—Naples, Sophie thought, although she didn't really know. Vaguely, she remembered her arriving some months ago. Hot and surly, a bold-looking girl of about twenty with thick dark unbrushed hair that looked gorgeous. She was traffic-stoppingly beautiful and had regarded her new companions with disdain, her smooth bronzed skin flushed with fury, curses spitting like machine gun bullets as she vainly vented her frustration. How different she was now. Shyly, through the corridor of smiling faces and clapping hands, the girl had paraded with her tutors, dark eyes shining and radiating a golden youthful smile, loving the brief attention, and then blushingly handing out slices of the thick layered cake. Sophie had clapped and smiled too. There were lots of birthdays here and they were all celebrated as a collective, a brief parade and mingling in a tight group in the mess hall before returning to the classroom or community events or sports programme. This one should have been no different.

We always clap for birthdays.

Except it was different.

As she stopped clapping, the noisy attention settling down, everyone patiently waiting for the slice of cake that always looked and tasted the same, she felt someone press something into her hand, folding her fingers around it clamping her fist within theirs as a ball and holding her fingers closed for a few seconds. Somehow the pressure holding her hand closed was not alarming. It was as if the slightest of squeezes was to reassure her somehow. Even when the hand released her own, she kept her hand closed uncertain of what it now contained, unsure whether she should look and see. It was only in the bathroom area of the dormitory in the privacy of a toilet cubicle that she pulled the tightly folded piece of paper from her skirt pocket and with a confused racing heart read the short pencil-written message.

*Grassy bank after social time, we have a message for you.*

Without thinking she dropped the paper into the toilet basin and flushed it away stepping back in concern her heart bumping loudly in her breast. She was confused and thoughtful and, after steadying herself, went back into the dormitory and the cubicle bedroom she shared with Cecile the girl from Norway. Cecile wasn't there and she assumed at this hour she was in the library. Why would anyone give her a message like that? What did anyone want with her? Who were they and what did it mean?

She looked around the dull contents of the space that was home, two lockers with iron beds, a few creased rock star posters that belonged to Cecile, but she found no answers in the glum little space where only the yellow and red duvet covers gave colour to the poverty of the room. It didn't add up.

Message from who? Should she report it?

Probably.

She wondered if the message was a test, a threat, some psychological ruse to measure her progress against some ideological scale of reformed loyalty. The idea made her tremble slightly and she shook herself to control and rid herself of the fear that briefly had gripped her.

She should definitely report it. External contact had to be authorised. Official internal communications came from the tutors or the tannoy. This was way outside of the rules.

Yet the feeling developed that she shouldn't. The feeling grew and irrationally turned into guilt. What was she jeopardising? It made no difference the curiosity to know what it was about remained. In fact, it strengthened and hardened and the emboldened urge to learn the meaning of this contact both excited and frightened her. This place with its lessons, Party slogans and control had not quite claimed her as it should and, perhaps it was the dreams, but she spent more time in the past now than she should. Right or wrong, when her eyes closed the memories of youth and different times would seep back.

Voices came to her from outside of her cubicle, students returning in groups to their personal spaces, and she panicked thinking they would hear her thoughts, discover her new secret.

Don't be stupid, she told herself. They couldn't of course. Nervously reassured, she settled back into her studies with apprehension to wait for the hours to pass.

Work was almost impossible. She sat through two lectures an oily sick feeling sat in her tummy. The time until evening passed slowly, and she navigated the rest of the afternoon in slow motion as if walking underwater or wading through a dream. She felt it gave her a terrible weakness and she was forced to concentrate on each step of the day. She tried to avoid her friends, preferring to be alone. But they sought her out, Cecile chattering about some German rock band, Krisztina from Budapest worried about her poor English and the forthcoming test, both of them maintaining a constant stream of conversation to which Sophie gave the best replies she could muster.

Now as she sat outside, the clouds had dispersed leaving a fresh autumn evening full of scent. The sun had shifted round to begin its evening decline behind the distant line of firs. The sky glowed slightly, and the trees took a more dynamic form like the shadows of primitive dancers. Sunsets were rapid affairs here, and soon only a crimson sash on the horizon would remain of the dying sun. She felt the deeper chill that began to collect around her and pulled the thick cable wool shapeless cardigan she had knitted herself closer around her shoulders.

'Sophie?' The voice came from behind her and was female. 'May I join you; you got the note.'

Sophie turned slightly; her heart banged realising her

nervous wait was over. She found a woman in her thirties settling down on the grass beside her. She nodded in answer to the question.

'What did you do with it?'

Sophie said she had destroyed it.

The woman looked pleased and smiled.

'It will be dark soon; we mustn't be long. You probably have lots of questions, but they will have to wait, at least for now. We can talk again I promise.'

Sophie saw the woman was dressed in jeans with a hooded sweatshirt that looked too young for her. A tawny-blond woman with green-brown eyes. From her pocket she pulled a packet of cigarettes and lit one, the tip glowed as she inhaled. Her chin was angled up delicately and she held the cigarette between slender straight fingers and blew the smoke forcefully away from her face. Her face had a gentle nose with high cheekbones, and lips that were curved into an easy smile. She looks very cool, Sophie thought, pretty, intelligent, and confident. She had spoken in English without an accent and although she had not seen her before Sophie assumed she was a tutor, one of the academic staff. There were so many it was impossible to know everyone.

Her name was Gina and she taught Social Economics Theory. That was all that Sophie needed to know.

'I want to ask you something Sophie and it's important. Do you think you can be honest with me?'

Sophie looked into her face, saw the woman's blue eyes looking at her carefully, waiting for her answer. 'Yes Com—, alright, if I can.' The urge to add the Party salutation into the reply had been instinctive. But she had checked herself. It was curious why in the context of this meeting the salutation should sound odd.

'Do you miss your father, Sophie? Do you miss being with him?

She shrugged, not sure how to answer. 'I suppose s-s-sometimes.' she said with a little hesitancy. Her heart was racing, no one, not once in her entire time at the campus had anyone ever asked about her family. Talk of such things if not actually forbidden was not encouraged. 'Is he okay?' She had never given it a thought that he might be ill or in danger or that some accident had taken place. We do not concern ourselves with families while we are here, someone important had once told them all. There will be time for such matters when your education has been attended to.

Somehow you pushed thoughts of family relationships away even when every genetic fibre in your body screamed at you in frustration and disappointment.

Gina had nodded quickly, responding to the anxious look with a reassuring smile and telling her that her father was fine.

'You can be honest with me. It's not a test, no one but me will ever know what you said.' She looked at Sophie, the green-brown eyes grave and then asked something quite unexpected.

'Sophie...Sophie, dear, would you like to leave this place, get away if you could, go somewhere without the rules or the restrictions? Do you wish you could do what you wanted?'

Sophie did not know what to say. Two years ago, a year maybe, she would have lashed out a reply not worried whether the question was a trap to test her or not. Yes! Get me away from here. She had felt as if her heart had been torn out, her stomach constantly empty and churning with anger. The campus was formed of cells not classrooms, the tutors were warders not teachers. But now, she was less sure. She felt her breath become shallow in her chest and her stomach clenched. Life here, the study, the friends, the small communal rituals was strangely comfortable, life made more sense. Such talk was dangerous, how did she know she could trust this woman? What was this all about? This could still be a trap. Was it some sort of faculty test? A test for loyalty? Or the progress of conditioning?

'I am learning so much here. I...I mean the subjects are quite interesting,' she added, immediately thinking how lame her answer sounded. An unconvincing compromise, that avoided the question. Naturally she wanted to remain here. Why would she risk the progress she had made?

Yet...she felt her own eyes had given the real answer.

The woman looked at her for a while, her lips forming a thin even smile and she stubbed the cigarette out on the sole of her training shoe. 'Not for much longer,' she said in a business-like way. The meek response from Sophie had told her all she needed to know. 'We're going to take you away from here, somewhere safe. But you're going to have to listen very carefully and we're going to have to work together to get this done. Do you understand?'

Sophie felt a peculiar giddiness when she heard these words. Thoughts of freedom and escape suddenly flushed away the months of obedience and acceptance patiently and relentlessly impressed upon her. The giddiness gave way to a sensation of being in a dream that will end at any moment and a nervous thrill flooded through her. She wasn't sure whether to fight to stay asleep or wake up. Can I really leave this place and not have to return? she thought. She had no words. So, she just looked at the woman who smiled at her and calmly smoked another cigarette and Sophie wondered who she was.

In the distance the drone continued its patrol of the landscape turning lazy figures of eight against the darkening twilight blur of the forest.

GATES pushed the shop door open and heard the bell jangle above him. The smell of old wood, tarnished metal and ancient dust greeted him. The interior was small a situation made more so by the collection of wooden crates and boxes set out on the floor and which held household odds and ends that sold as bric-a-brac. He began to wander through the piles of junk roughly stacked and displayed. On the table lay chipped thick glassware, ashtrays, and vases resting amongst school pencil boxes, old military badges, campaign medals and large ugly broaches. Pewter mugs and condiment sets gleamed brightly under the greasy spotlights that blazed harsh light onto the tables. The walls of eroding grey distemper were crowded with faded prints, warped printed replicas of landscapes and portraits. Below them on metal clothes racks were lines of tatty clothing, men's jackets worn shiny, cocktail dresses with seams split and heavy shapeless overcoats that were, Gates suspected, infested with moths' eggs.

It was a depressing collection, thought Gates. More like debris than items of value worthy of purchase. Rubbish that had been flogged and re-flogged gradually relegated down the trading chain to end up here. It was usual to find this type of stock on the street markets, hawked by monstrous women with thick plump forearms which they waved aggressively and with their foul mouths loudly bullied passersby to study the items laid out on their stalls and reach into their pockets for change. It was unusual to see a shop premises operating like this and it made Gates curious.

He browsed into the shop deeper stepping around the boxes and crates and found a glass panelled door above a short step that was ajar. He pushed it open and stepped through into a new room. A further showroom, but somewhat different. He was taken back a little. Here, there were display cases that were clean and polished. He could see immediately that the items, all marked for sale with little white labels on string were more valuable than the clutter at the front of the shop. Delicate porcelain carefully angled so the smooth surfaces shone, decanters that looked as if they were crystal from Ireland rather than dull heavy ornamental glass from eastern German factories. The small watercolours were fresher and looked, and very probably were, originals. At the end of the room was a long glass counter. It served as an illuminated display cabinet that held a sizable collection of watches, rings, broaches, pens. There were also what he thought he might find, small pieces of silver, locket boxes and picture frames. Even one or two items of silver tableware. Silver was rare nowadays. Pretentious, bourgeois signalling decadence that society disapproved of. Some of it of course was hoarded by those with money, hidden from view. Most had been collected under various schemes and melted down for industrial use.

Burns had kept picture frames. He had bought them from here. Careful enough to trigger his meetings with a legitimate purpose.

It dawned on Gates this was not the junk shop first appearances suggested. Outside was a broken dilapidated shopping street with vegetable stalls and cheap hardware. Buried in plain sight hidden amongst the unwanted debris was this place, a pawn broker. A place to raise money. Somewhere to bring those items that were special and loved but ultimately useless in keeping the lights on and food on the table. The piles of junk at the front were just that, a front to keep the curious out of the way. Here towards the back was the place where citizens, many probably of status but without means, resorted to keep afloat.

Yet he had just wandered in.

Regarding him from across the glass counter was the proprietor, a wizened man of some years, winter-white hair, and thick owl-like spectacles, and who looked at him with a neutral smile. His hands were made of fleshy fingers which rested flat on the counter. His shabby smartness that included a tweed jacket, waistcoat and country tie knotted at a frayed collar reminded Gates of the older generation of academics from his university days or perhaps a music tutor driven to teach through insufficient talent to perform but carrying a surfeit of love for the art.

'Can I help you?'

There was a bulge to his nose that spoke of Jewry and behind the distortion of the glasses the pale watery eyes regarding Gates were cautious but not unfriendly. They glinted behind moisture, like a jackdaw, which on glancing around the shop, Gates supposed he was of a type. Interesting, he thought. An elderly man of an unloved race plying a trade on the fringes of legality. How have you survived? he wondered.

Gates let his eyes wander a little more around the room taking in the tiny bits of history that filled the cabinets.

'I was passing,' he said. 'I've seen your shop a number of time and always been curious as to what it was like. Then a friend recommended I should visit and suggested you may be able to help me.'

The old man resettled his glasses on his nose. He did it every few seconds as if they did not quite fit. It made him seem thoughtful, vulnerable. The introduction had been acknowledged, and a message between them had been passed. Seemingly without words the purpose of Gates' visit was understood by the old Jew who nodded understandingly.

'Yes, I see.' The rheumy eyes looked him over. 'Are you thinking of buying or selling?'

Gates' eye was caught by the glint of a small plain picture frame that sat in the glass case. He pointed and the man looked down in the direction of Gates' finger. The frame had plain straight lines with a beaded edge and a small, neat hallmark stamp was etched into the smooth surface.

'A gift for my daughter, something unusual but with a little value. Nothing too extravagant, but generous' he added a little hastily. 'We live in tough times. I had in mind about a hundred pounds.'

'For many, yes. But of course, I see and a hundred pounds gives you some good options. Well, a picture frame is an excellent choice. They never go far from the eye. Was it this one you were interested in? It's a plain design but quite stylish, I think. It will look good anywhere, don't you agree?'

'How much?' asked Gates.

The figure caused Gates to inwardly wince, but he agreed

to take it.

'But wait,' the man peered closely at the reverse of the frame and tutted with irritation, 'I see the retaining clasp is damaged at the rear. I must repair it first. Sorry, I didn't notice this before.' He sighed at his oversight. 'Do you have a card? I can call you when it's ready to collect.'

Gates pulled a business card from his wallet and slid it across the glass. He watched as the man picked it up and studied it. For a moment their eyes held each other, and Gates was again aware of a brief scrutiny. 'Will it take long? As it's for a birthday and I wouldn't want to be late with my gift.'

The small man pursed his lips and shook his head reassuringly. 'No-no, I imagine I'll call you tomorrow with a time. We'll make an appointment, I keep this area closed normally, but I saw you arrive.' He glanced towards the side of the counter where a camera image of the inside of the shop showed the front door. 'Will that be all right?'

It would be fine; he told the shopkeeper.

'Well, nice to have met you,' the older man concluded, the lines of his face expressionless. 'I wish you a good day but suggest you browse for a few more minutes before departing. There are some nice pieces to look at, and I can see you have an eye to appreciate them. If you'll excuse me, I'll see you soon.'

He disappeared into what looked like a workshop come office. The frame did not require any repair and Gates was happy the message had been passed. The pawnbroker would do the rest. He did as he was instructed and spent a few minutes studying the valuable and not so valuable pickings gathered from previous lives that lay around him.

When he left, it had once again started to rain, cold drops that smacked with force against the pavement. He buttoned his coat against the sharp wind that flew down the street and stepped into the hurrying pedestrian stream that pushed past in search of shelter.

***

# CHAPTER TWELVE

*What do you think they know?*

**Manchester**

'SO, HE WAS BEING run. A Russian agent.'

The car interior was in darkness Dugdale rested back in the rear seat and stared out into the night then back towards Gates.

Gates looked back towards him as long as he dared. The clean lined ruddy face from the farmhouse kitchen. He searched the dark eyes and the crinkled skin around them for the smallest tremor, signal of emotion of concern, fear, or relief, but nothing yielded, nothing to betray his thoughts. Gates simply nodded. 'It certainly, seems that way.'

Somewhere across the car park Miranda stood guard, unseen in the cold shadows of the ugly industrial buildings, avoiding the dim puddles of security lighting and the water filled potholes that caught their light in oily reflection. Earlier, she had steered the big Skoda with expertise across the broken yard manoeuvring like a tank cautiously traversing a shell-shattered battlefield. Between buildings she had reversed into a narrow alley which ran as a dank fissure, splitting the abandoned works. Clinging to the building's sides ran a tangled rusty network of fire escapes reaching like black spiders' legs to feel the ground. Tenacious weed, thick, strong, and nourished from the soft damp of rotting woodwork and leaking drains had grown out across the blackened walls forcing the brick and mortar to crumble then fracture.

Dugdale made no response. The Skoda's windows were blurred with rain and misted with condensation. Dugdale looked older than Gates remembered, a pale shadow across his face which gleamed waxy in the near dark.

'We feared as much,' Dugdale said quietly, 'but had to be sure.'

'How bad is this?'

'Enough,' Dugdale said quietly, and he drew his breath, 'but steps have already been taken. We'll pick up the pieces and continue.'

'So, what happens now?' Gates asked.

'Not your concern,' said Dugdale, 'But after his death there will be repercussions. They know who is responsible, we can expect some collateral damage. It will be more random than effective.'

Both men knew how it would work from here. The security services and their Soviet allies would be angry. The loss of an asset would cause them to increase their efforts, pressing harder to recover ground, uncover those involved. They would move quickly, stung by the loss and Inevitably innocent people would be caught as they fished with very big nets. Their methods would not be pretty and there would be no discrimination as to the guilty.

In the dark silence of the car Gates had told Dugdale of his discoveries; the planted girl, evidence of blackmail—the homosexual son—and the older offspring, radicalised but living without any interference, the visits by Special Branch and the Russian involvement. Compelling evidence that only pointed one way. Earlier, while waiting in the rain, he had contemplated how to relate his theory, the idea that had been nagging him. Now in the quiet of the car he picked up his thoughts.

'I think he was going to run,' added Gates sombrely. 'Something, the girl, his wife, and son said. I think he had a plan. I don't think he intended to go along with them. He didn't *want* to betray anyone.'

Dugdale's chin dropped, and he appeared thoughtful. 'He was,' he murmured. 'We knew that he had plans. It wasn't safe to let him go.'

Gates was disappointed, there was not the nod towards redemption he had hoped. 'Did you have to…? It's not just him, his family, the girl, they are all done for…'

He stopped himself. He was theorising to no purpose, he realised—it could go nowhere.

Dugdale was not looking at him. 'It had to be done. There

was too much risk that they would have caught him. Better safe than sorry.'

He's cold, thought Gates. How cold do you have to be to dispose of life simply to mitigate a risk? But he knew he was wrong to judge, and that he couldn't put himself in Dugdale's shoes, but the ruthlessness disturbed him. He wanted to protest, indicate his distaste. The rational pointlessness of doing so held him back.

But his uncertainty must have crossed his face and Dugdale tried to make some form of amends: 'Don't think bad of me Gates, I had no choice, we're too close and too much is at stake. I did what we had to do.' He turned the conversation elsewhere. 'Tell me about your meeting with McBride.'

*Too close. Too close to what?* Gates struggled to keep his look impassive.

'Tell me what that reptile wanted?'

And that was that, Gates thought, realising the futility of grieving over Burns' death. A pointless gesture. Dugdale spoke as f the disposal of a human life was totally normal. Practised every day, if with regret.

So, Gates told him. The presence of Hallam, the folder of evidence, the task he had been given. What was expected of him.

'So, McBride wants Burns' corruption exposed?' Dugdale asked, 'make him useful even in death. What you write will be syndicated, they'll make sure of that, copied by others and the narrative is built.'

'He was clear: "The Party must have corruption exposed. The people must understand that strong leadership will not tolerate such wrongdoing."'

'What about Hallam? I wonder whether McBride even knew that Burns was an asset?' Dugdale answered his own question. 'No, of course he didn't.'

'I don't think Hallam cares about what McBride wants,' said Gates. 'He's after you…and whatever you are planning.'

'Certainly. He is no more an ally of the General Secretary than I am. State Security guards its secrets jealously. They spy on the Party leadership, learn their habits, plans and secrets like they do everyone else. Hallam more likely takes his orders and shares his information with Moscow rather than London. Yet it sounds like McBride may have bought you—and therefore ourselves a little time to regroup. So, you'll need to go to work and write about corruption.'

'You knew Hallam would come for me. Yet you wanted me to investigate anyway.'

'He easily has enough to have you arrested—at least for his purposes. Or the Russians could just take you. That's all quite true. But he won't for a while.'

'What's stopping him?'

'Losing Burns already looks bad, he'll want to retrieve himself a little for his Soviet masters, he wants to see where you can lead him.'

'To you?'

'That's possible. Announce my death. Give you a little latitude with Burns' affairs and see where that leads. He also won't want to risk a silly spat with the Party. You have a use to everyone in the cover up Gates, at least for a short while.'

'And then?'

'Let's say we have a week, possibly ten days, agreed?' Gates was silent, he averted his gaze partly to escape Dugdale's scrutiny, partly to conceal the seeds of excitement that began to grow. 'We have time to get you to safety. There are some plans to put in motion and we'll need to get you some papers and a plan. I'll see that you get word when the pawnbroker is ready.'

In the dimness he turned his face back towards Dugdale. He was wearing his exhausted old overcoat and a cuff button hung loose; he had been waiting for weeks for it finally to part company, the will to repair it routinely forgotten. It was time to remind Dugdale of his promise. He pulled at the button, testing its remaining strength, pausing uncertain how to approach the knowledge he must have; should he be threatening, demanding, he didn't believe in goodwill, the notion that someone as ruthless as Dugdale had proved would be inclined to do the right thing seemed ridiculous. So, Gates reasoned, what did he have to lose. But somehow the appeal to reason seemed more appropriate, the innocent question of progress as if the enquiry was curious, conversational without uncertainty.

'My daughter—Sophie. What about my daughter? We had an agreement. Will you get her back?'

So much was hanging on Dugdale's answer that Gates felt disconcerted. His words had sounded weak, and he tried to console himself that fatigue was affecting him. He could almost feel the heavy rings of tiredness that hung beneath his eyes.

'Ah yes.' Dugdale had become cheerful again, his voice genial. 'Calm yourself, Gates. Your daughter's removal from her place of study is already happening.' He pulled a small photo from the inside of his coat, he looked at it briefly then passed it across to Gates. It was Sophie, a recent picture Gates thought, she looked older than when he had seen her last, her hair longer. Almost a woman, no longer the small girl he had raised alone. She was looking into the camera smiling, something he did not remember in a long time, a spontaneous smile that suggested being caught off guard by the lens. She was outside somewhere sitting on a bank of grass, a winter coat and woollen scarf wrapped around her neck.

'This picture is a week old, taken by a colleague who works where she is staying. That colleague has put herself at great risk for Sophie. But as I promised, she'll leave Poland very soon. She won't be in that internment camp they call a college for much longer. Obviously, she won't come here,' Dugdale continued, picking his words with care. 'Nor anywhere in Europe. It's best I don't tell you more, for her own safety. But you'll join her.'

The thread broke and the button dropped down into the dark of the seat well.

The car was still warm, from somewhere came the tink of metal cooling and the soft hiss of rainwater evaporating from the hot engine surfaces. Gates continued looking at the picture. The image just a few days old and a feeling of extreme relief pulled over him.

'You should believe me when I say we keep our word,' Dugdale added quietly.

FOR a moment, Gates hung there, stood on the stone bridge, the waters of the Irwell worked and wormed their way through the countryside below him. The swollen turbid winter water bought foliage, river debris along with scum to congeal in floating barriers caught by overhanging branches. He stood in the rain his battered overcoat that carried the musty smell of damp wool that no amount of drying and airing would remove shielding him. He felt anger towards Dugdale, anger increased by the callousness of the decision to kill Burns. Dugdale had known Burns may have been working for State Security but had been ignorant of the blackmail as well as knowledge of the girl. He had signed the man's death warrant anyway. He also knew that Burns had been planning to flee.

*How had he known that?*

And now Gates himself was on borrowed time. Hallam was just waiting, biding his time. Unless Dugdale kept his word he could expect arrest and then who knows what. A large car rushed past, the engine roar filling his ears, the distraction caused his thoughts to shift to Sophie and how her fate also lay in the hands of Dugdale.

In his memory he saw him exactly: the cool poise of the man, the calm clear features of his face. The confident words as he wheeled and spun peoples' lives.

Perhaps he can save us, he thought.

It had been late morning when he had left Manchester with its uneven skyline of long apartment blocks ringing the city like a convoy of great liners at sea, beyond them the chimney's that slowly smoked ochre clouds into the heavy sky above. Before leaving his apartment, he had showered but had, had little sleep. The past six days following his meeting with Dugdale had been a restless dream, each night unsettled with his thoughts cluttered by doubts and fears. The evening before he had sent his latest copy to the editor, a further excoriating account of the abuse of power, the narrative of fraud fed and woven from the corruption dossier given to him in McBride's office. His pieces had appeared not only in his own paper but had been reprinted and quoted in the London dailies, each headline praising the union and the Party for their vigilance and swift action in discovering and rooting out cancerous greed.

Lucy had been full of admiration, proofreading his copy, suggesting minor adjustments, cross-checking uncertain facts with fresh research. Both the editor and Lucy had known better than to ask for the source of his information and such was his creative skill in weaving the material as you would a coat into a compelling tale, he had almost become encouraged with his work again. Then he remembered it was a fabrication, a lie bought about to manipulate and deceive and protect the powerful. He gruffly turned away Lucy's praise: 'Christ. It's nothing special, it's just a job, it's what I do. just the work of a hack...'

This morning with daylight his mind had cleared but questions continued to prey and unsettle his mood and he needed to be sure of what he had begun to suspect.

McBride's words: *'There's more if you want it...'*

Dugdale: *'We became aware of the problem...'*

Once clear of the city blocks and towers he had ignored the outer ring road with its Saturday traffic and had headed north until the heavily populated inner-city areas and then the leafy suburbs were behind him, and he entered the half-forgotten hinterland were population ran out but agriculture had not quite begun and the roads became empty, save for the ugly roadside poster boards urging citizens to report suspicious behaviour, join the Army and see the world, enter the lottery, and have the chance to win a Black Sea holiday of a lifetime. The tired wiper blades groaned with the shudder of worn hard rubber on glass and worked furiously to push aside the fat drops of rain. Through the window condensation he had seen glum groups of people, sheltering in bus stops who had watched him drive past, wary of the water forced in their direction from potholes by the car's tyres.

Turning right at a T-junction, he had mounted a rise and there was the fine stone bridge at which he decided to pause easing the unhappy Fiat onto the wet verge. With the impatient driver disappeared into the distance there was not a human soul in sight. Why was he not sensible? A sensible man would have considered his work for Dugdale, and McBride finished. A sensible man would have thrown himself on Dugdale's mercy to get him away from here, wait for word that he had papers and could leave. But for a reason he could not explain that was not an option. He told himself it was because there was nowhere to hide, nowhere to run and that he was too anxious to simply wait for the inevitable whether that was escape or arrest.

But there was something else, a strong instinct that still drove him in a way he had almost forgotten. An instinct that had been dormant but which in the last few days had begun to come alive and seize him more. What he had written, crafted, was a fabrication. A misuse of words and intentions to make people believe what others wanted. But in doing so, in scrolling down the worthless information, messages, dates, figures, he realised he wanted something else. *Truth*. He didn't have the truth or at least enough of it. He felt compelled to know more. He knew that digging further could expose him to even more risk, but in the end, he decided he had no choice.

He returned to the car and made his way into the town of

Great Lever. The dark stone of the church tower with its Gothic spiral loomed above the black crumbling tombs in the graveyard scattered in loose rows like a parade of drunken soldiers. At the lynch gate entrance, a large peeling poster appealed to the local faithful to heed God's word. *Is that where the sinners go or the virtuous?* he thought. He checked his mirror for the umpteenth since leaving the city but there was no sign of the black saloon that had been a companion over the past few days.

Not long after he found himself at the Burns' house. This time there was no car in the drive and no sound of woodcutting from the outbuilding. He drove at a crawl intending to slip his own vehicle into the driveway without announcement. Beams of late morning sun had broken through the drizzle causing the rain drops on the windows to sparkle. A small drift of smoke rose from the red brick chimney, and he saw the front curtains had been drawn, but he still caught the small shadow of movement upstairs that fell away as he watched it, and he wondered for the thousandth time whether this visit was wise. *Truth.* There was so much he did not know.

He ignored the front doorbell confident the chime would not be answered. He had left the car where it could be easily seen in all its battered glory. *Hardly a threat with this heap*, he was trying to say. *The police don't travel in vehicles like that.* The glass in the door was rippled and although he peered in pressing his eye to the cold pane, all he could make out was the distorted shape of hall furniture lit by light that fell through from the kitchen area. He walked around the house to its rear where a stone patio was host to a washing line, a rotary type, folded and heavily beaded with drops of rain. A chainsaw lay abandoned on the stone, wood dust, wet, congealed coated the blade. The day was brightening the rain being chased away by a freshening wind and from the trees came the sound of thrushes shrieking with delight. An outside dog shelter stood as an abandoned sentry post, a few chewed and mauled rubber toys discarded at the entrance along with a large ceramic drinking bowl now overflowing with rainwater. Gates thought of the limp, broken, soaked animal on the country lane.

He tried the door handle, which yielded to his pressure and quietly he slipped inside closing the door after him. He was standing on the tiles of the kitchen floor, and he noticed the ugly modern units not really in keeping with a space that was large and filled with natural light. On the table was a wooden board and the ingredients of a half-made sandwich. He touched the electric kettle, which was just cool, next to it a mug with a waiting teabag and an open bottle of milk.

'Hello,' he called gently. 'Mrs Burns?'

He crossed the kitchen and entered the hall, where he stood listening to the silent rooms that he was sure were not empty. Then he realised the house was not silent and the soft sound of sobbing was drifting towards him. For a moment Gates hesitated, reluctant to follow the sound, anxiety as to what he would find here growing.

'Mrs Burns? I'm sorry to just walk in, I only want to talk,' he called. 'Are you here?'

He softly pushed open the door to the drawing room and there saw the Polish housekeeper sitting on the long sofa facing the fireplace. Her eyes were red with tears, and she looked up at him wordlessly, her body shivering, her lips trembling. She was holding the younger son to her chest, her arms wrapped around his head and his shoulders, the embrace was tight and protective. Within her clutch the boy had been sobbing, his face buried in her bosom, the thick cotton apron she wore soaking away his tears. He took in the scene anxious unease rose inside him.

'What's happened?' Gates asked seeing her dismay and a cold feeling creeping into his stomach.

The question caused the woman's face to contort and shrivel with fresh tears that began to run. There was a look of deep dislike on her face, and he could see that she recognised him, she uncurled her arm from the boy who did not move and through angry sobs told him in halting English to go away, he had no business to be here.

'Where's Jason,' he asked ignoring the tearful order. 'I need to speak to him.'

'He's not here, no one is here. Go away.' The passion in her words and the manner in which she held the youth was surprising. It was obvious that her association with the family was long, deep, and held trust.

'I don't think that's true,' he said. He thought of the abandoned chainsaw and unmade food. There had been boots by the back door too he remembered. Whatever had taken place had been recent. 'I want to talk to him; I don't want anything.'

'This is your fault…you, the…stories you make…so cruel…look what you done.' She sobbed harder and waved dismissively in his direction back through the door. Her face was white and ill, and Gates could see her shaking from shock and anger.

Gates left the room realising with increasing apprehension that something further, something dreadful had happened to this family, something further to be discovered.

He left the drawing room, cautiously climbing the stairs and neither the woman nor the boy objected. There was a corridor that smelt of polish along which were a number of closed doors and one straight ahead that was open slightly, light spilling around it. The door belonged to a room at the front of the house, and he assumed it was the master bedroom.

He pushed it open, but not before something made him first give a soft knock to the wall. But the room was empty of the living. He saw a large ugly bed with a padded pink headboard. In the centre looking ridiculously small lay Margaret Burns. Her clothed frozen body was framed by rich shafts of afternoon sunlight that had poetically appeared. He recognised her from their first meeting, but her death was obvious. A face in death can tell a story. A devoted mother, caring father taken early, a cruel sadist meeting his judgement, or perhaps just the sleep of peace wearily and thankfully anticipated. Margaret Burns' face preserved none of these tales.

She lay on her back, head thrown rearward and congealed vomit had spumed and dried like an old lava flow across the cheek, mouth, and clothes. Beside her on the bedspread lay the empty bottles, half a dozen small, clouded plastic containers with their labels of neat tiny print that told of the pills she had consumed. Jesus, he thought, she had botched it, probably choking to death rather than quietly slipping into endless sleep as she had certainly hoped to do.

Gates turned quickly from the room. He knew Jason was somewhere and began looking throwing doors open and finding just empty rooms, bedrooms, bathrooms a store cupboard his feet scraping on the polished wood floors. Then downstairs, a dining room, panelled with a long glass table and modern chromed chairs. Untouched and cold. A parlour with warm sofas and a television, cluttered with magazines and cushions and finally...a study. A study that was roomy, with bookshelves a desk, cabinets, a leather smoking chair pulled close to a small empty fireplace.

Jason Burns raised his head when Gates entered. He was crouched on the floor closing a safe door and fiddling with the lock. He looked at him with suspicious eyes and his face set like a rock. Just for a second, Gates feared the worst, that he would come for him anger and resentment roaring into a violent attack. But instead, the look turned to defeat the eyes became hollow and beaten. There were no tears like his brother, just that solid resigned bitter look.

It was Gates who broke the silence.

'Your mother...' he said in a soft murmur. 'Oh Christ, what happened? I'm sorry.'

'Ain't it obvious? I hope you're proud of yourself. A good day's reporting for you.'

Gates wanted to protest, He wanted to ask the questions and formed the words: *She did this because of me? You think this was my fault?* But the words wouldn't come because he knew it was probably true.

'You and your filthy stories. Lies about dad, lies about what he was, what he did.' Jason flung the words at him, and Gates sank his rump back against the smoking chair the leather cracking gently under his weight. There was a longish silence as they both considered how to proceed.

Gates thought about what the dead woman had said when they met. The fraternal loyalty, the patronage, and expressions of friendships that she imagined forming around her grief. What he saw now was when reality caught up with theatre. A final realisation that all around you was a grotesque stage. Now was not the time to talk about where the lies began and ended. The boy was not guiltless and probably knew it.

'I was just doing my job,' Gates said hoarsely. 'It's my job to report. I'm sorry, truly.' He heard the words, but they made him sick. He knew Burns was right. He had been used to trample a dead man, create a web of lies for public consumption and to do the Party's bidding. What the fuck have you done, he thought. But guilt was not enough for this consequence. He wanted truth, well here truth was in all its naked ugliness. His words had killed a vulnerable woman and ruined a family. It wasn't the truth he expected, but here it was, full-throated and raw.

'Report what they tell you, you mean.' He gave a little laugh that was venomous. 'Then bring the rest of the wolves down on us.'

Gates knew what he meant, but asked anyway: 'Who, what happened?'

'"What do you know about your husband? Did you know he had a mistress? What do you think he was doing?" All day and most of the night. Fucking hounds chasing your lies for their own story. Then the sinister signals from others, "Sorry, Mrs Burns, your credit card is declined" and "We need to talk to you about your pension eligibility, there is an issue", It drove her to this. She was always weak, but she couldn't take what was about to happen, the humiliation, fear. She knew the Party was behind it, that without him to look after her there was no hope.'

'I'm sorry, when...' Why do I keep saying sorry? He asked himself, you sound ridiculous.

'Her, you mean? This morning. An hour ago, possibly

longer, she found him,' he nodded his head towards the doorway and the drawing room beyond. 'They called me over from the workshop.'

*Truth.* Well, here was more truth to take on board. Another life he had managed to destroy. He was not alone. Others were complicit. But it came back to him. He had used the tools given to him, wielded the knife. With the loss of a husband, the patronage of ideology, she was unable to contemplate a life to be led in half-shame devoid of privilege and utterly without the dependencies she had come to rely on. 'PARTY AND PEOPLE ARE ONE,' ran the familiar slogan that hung in school halls and municipal offices. Except when the Party decides they aren't, thought Gates.

Faintly the sobs still filtered through from the drawing room.

'You've not reported it yet?'

Jason did not answer. Instead, he asked, his tone suspicious: 'Why are you here?'

'I had some questions.'

'What? You've had your story.'

'Your father was not killed by any criminal union rivals Jason. But you know this. Don't you.'

Seeing Margaret Burns had shaken Gates. But he was here for a reason. Burns had now risen from the safe. In his hands, documents, Gates could see passports and pieces of paper. 'You know who killed him, and you know why.'

'I don't know what you're talking about, you should go.'

'Your mother's dead upstairs and you're collecting documents and passports from a safe. Where are you going?'

'It's none of your business,' Jason's shout was almost a sob. 'LEAVE US alone.'

The sound of grief from the sitting room had ceased and Gates realised they were no longer alone in the study. The younger son, Hugo was at the door. He wore a creased linen shirt over jeans and looked young and vulnerable. Tears still filled his eyes, and his face was red and swollen, but he was under control, apparently drawn to the exchange between Gates and his brother. He had a slightly puzzled expression on his face, a questioning look aimed towards them both.

'What's going on?' the boy asked. His face was wide and uncertain. 'What are you doing? What does he want?'

'You knew about the blackmail Jason, didn't you,' said Gates with punch, ignoring the younger boy's appearance. 'What did you do?'

Jason looked between Gates and his brother, then dropped his chin and shook his head. 'Not…not at first. I just discovered he was cooperating with the police. I found out about the blackmail when I went to the apartment.'

'Your dad's apartment in London, you went there after he was killed?' Burns nodded in response. 'Why, what was there?'

'These,' he looked at the passports and papers on the desk. 'He told me where they were. He told me months ago, explained we might need to escape and If anything happened to him, I was to go and get them, take mum and Hugo, and get away as quickly as possible.'

Gates thought back to his own visit to Burns' apartment. The Jamaican cleaner had said someone had been there the day before and Annie Freedman had told him there was a safe.

'Was that all you found?'

Burns shook his head. 'No when I got there, I found pictures in the safe, the ones…'

'Pictures. What pictures?' interjected Hugo.

'You, you fool, you and that stupid boyfriend of yours,' his voice was a growl, 'and those of him and that tart of a girlfriend he kept in London. They were blackmailing him because of you.'

'Who was?' Hugo's face was ashen, his voice hoarse. 'How do you know…'

'He was protecting you, you little prick. He agreed to work for them to protect you.'

'If the photographs were in the safe, why did you hide them where they would be found?'

'I didn't have a plan when I got there last week. I realised what they meant and didn't want to risk being caught with them. I figured anyone who would search the place was responsible for the blackmail anyway. They were no good to me.'

'When was this?'

'The day before you came here last time.'

'I…I don't understand, are saying this is about me?' said Hugo, anguish in his voice, he was confused and lost struggling to understand.

Gates and Jason looked at one another. 'Why don't you explain Jason, Gates said quietly. 'Then you can tell him what you both have to do.'

Jason looked back for a moment and then turned to face his brother. 'Dad was a patriot, he didn't like the government, the union any of it. He wanted to change it get rid of the Party. I helped him a bit, we knew people. He was helping people do that—'

'That's insane,' Hugo broke in, 'why—'

'Let me finish.' Jason cut him off irritably. 'I…I thought he had changed sides; he was meeting Special Branch…Russians. I found out about it and assumed he was giving them information. Then when I found the photographs, I realised he was being forced to work for them. But…but by then—then it was too late…'

What do you mean? Why was it too late? What had you done Jason?

'You don't get away from these people,' his tone was appealing, a cry for understanding, 'nobody gets away, but there are people…people I know of…I—I thought they—'

'Who did you tell, Jason.' Gates thought of what Lucy had told him. Radicals, extremists, military hot heads. Surely— 'Who did you tell that your father was working for the Russians?'

'Someone I served with, I wanted to know what to do.' He saw the look on their faces. 'Look, I was angry, disappointed.

We lost so much for this fucking country, good men dead, men broken, minds and limbs gone and for what? Nothing, that's what. Now I found out that he was selling them out, their sacrifice was for nothing. I was mad. I didn't know what to do so I went for help.'

Gates had wondered how Dugdale had suspected. He didn't know about the blackmail he had never explained where his suspicions had come from. Jason's radicalised companions? That was it. Word had filtered back to Dugdale. Oh Christ, thought Gates.

'And?' asked Hugo.

I went to the apartment, when I saw the photographs, I began to guess the truth, that I was only partly right and that he was doing it to protect you, prevent you being taken.'

'Who, Jason?' There was confusion on the boy's face. 'Who would take me? I don't understand. Tell me.'

'Christ's sake, you tell him,' Jason appealed to Gates.

'State Security, the police,' Gates said slowly with care. It was taking time to sink in with the boy. 'You wer...are in danger. The authorities know about you Hugo, what you are, who you have been seeing, they took the pictures, intimate pictures of you with that kid...your friend. If your father did not give them information, then you would be arrested.' He turned to Jason. 'But it wasn't just him. His cooperation kept you out of jail also, they knew enough about who you were associating with. Your father was trying to protect you both.'

Jason's face was now in his hands. The enormity of what had happened, what he had done, was upon him. Slowly he looked up towards his brother, his eyes appealing. 'I'm sorry Hugo, I'm sorry, but I couldn't just let him betray and destroy everything. The system has caused this, the fucking Party they destroy and ruin everything.'

'You bloody fool,' said the brother. He put his hand to his forehead. 'What the fuck have you done. You're no better than him.'

Jason did not answer. The grief of the two young men made the air heavy with despair.

Gates reached across and took the passports. They were good, very good, not forgeries, inside the boys' documents were State Security exit visas as well as education entry visas issued by the Canadian Embassy. Two other passports were for Len and Margaret Burns exit visas and Swiss tourist entry authorisation. The final passport was a surprise, it was Portuguese issue. Inside, he saw it was Annie Freedman's face that looked back at him. They must have cost a fortune to arrange and would have required considerable influence to acquire. Burns had obviously thought this through. He kept the parent's and Annie Freedman's passports slipping them in his pocket, Jason did not object. We don't want anyone finding them here, he explained.

'What was your father's plan?'

'Flight vouchers for Hugo and myself, Manchester to

Dublin, then international to Toronto. They…would have travelled there separately.'

'When can you go?'

'There's a flight tomorrow. Early 6:30, I—' he looked down. 'I booked three tickets…'

Gates thought fast. 'Do you have somewhere you can stay tonight, away from here? Is there someone you can trust? You don't want to stay here, it's not safe.'

Jason thought then nodded. 'I suppose so, there are places we can crash in the city.'

'Do you have cash?'

He nodded once more.

'Good. Leave here, right now. You know not to use your phone or any cards right, leave as little trace as possible. It might buy you enough time.'

'We can't leave—' began Hugo.

'Yes, you can,' Gates cut in. 'There is nothing you can do for your mother anymore. Tell the housekeeper to go home while you make arrangements. Tell her to come back in the morning after ten. When she gets here, finds you gone and your mother upstairs she will report it. It will be tough for a while, but I doubt anyone will blame her.'

'She and mum were close, she's been with the family for years, we can't abandon her,' said Hugo.

'You have no choice. She can't go with you, telling her anything puts you and her in danger.'

Jason said nothing, he knew. Comprehension seemed to be dawning on his younger brother.

'Look your father knew something like this would possibly happen. He prepared for it; he made a plan. That's what the passports were for. Don't waste your time worrying about what happened, just take this slim opportunity he gave you and improvise. Once they know about your mother, they will come looking for you. Do you both understand? You must be gone before they do.'

Hugo looked upon him with swimming eyes, Jason began to pull the documents together. He appeared wrung out and empty of thought but mixed in the vulnerability Gates could see was strength.

He looked long and hard at Gates and breathed deeply. 'Why don't you just fuck off,' he said.

GATES went home his spirit that of a condemned man facing his final meal. By tomorrow, perhaps earlier, nowhere would be safe for him. Margaret Burns would be found, and Hallam would call time on any temporary pact with the Party, he would fold the whole thing up. He found some whiskey and decided to wait, wait for whatever came next until it was time to visit the pawn broker shop. He removed his shoes and lay on the sofa not wanting to undress, the prospect of arrest creating a curious fear of the indignity of being hauled from his mean little home without clothes. So, he lay there, and his brain turned until his thoughts burned out.

The night came, and he waited for morning, gazing at the ceiling watching street shadows flicker and dance.

\*\*\*

# CHAPTER THIRTEEN

### *A land fit for a king*

**London**

CHRISTOPHER SLADE LOOKED OUT from his office at the grey London skyline. The nineteenth-floor window had been washed last week but already traffic pollution settling across the city had left the drops of dirty rain to form as tiny greasy black specks on the thick glass. Nearby, he could see the grey anonymous office blocks that lined the river, large buildings developed in haste and without thought, already shabby and ugly beyond their twenty years. Down below, across the street was the architecture of older generations, the neoclassical stone colonnades and brick portals of Threadneedle Street and Bishopsgate, merchant houses and trading halls, five storeys high, black as coal with a century of traffic fumes, streaked and fouled by the birds.

There have been soldiers, merchants, and thieves on this spot since Roman times, he thought. Beneath its streets lay the lost coinage of Claudius, Marcus Aurelius, and other emperors whose reach had extended from Rome to the banks of the Thames. Above the fresco and tessellated debris of Roman times had been built the banqueting halls to celebrate, churches to pray and the banks to closet the wealth of the privileged. Gold and coin gathered and protected as the power of the nations and its elites grew into an Empire. Kings and tyrants come, and they go, but there will always be those who serve them here, delivering taxes or loans to pay for their wars or recover their debts. Who do I serve? Slade thought without finding an answer to his question. Far below him, within the ancient foundations of the bank lay the remains of the nation's gold, depleted, and leveraged as never before in the country's history. He turned back to his desk.

The screen of his phone lit briefly with activity. It was a short instant message that blinked its arrival. *Am in the club for dinner tonight if you are free?* The words appeared innocent enough, a comradely invitation to meet up between business colleagues and friends. Conversation, business, and Bordeaux in good measure.

Except it was no such thing.

He read the message two or three times more, digesting the significance of the harmless sounding text.

Then, Slade opened his personal safe and removed three small thumb drive storage devices. Using one of the drives he restarted his laptop computer into a secure non-traceable operating system not connected to the hard drive. The next device was a virtual private wireless hub which took him away from the bank's network and the final drive held one-time use encryption keys.

It had been his birthday last month and despite the arrival of his sixth decade he considered himself extremely adept and up to date with technology. Even his older children, grown and departed the family home were impressed at their banker father's ability with computers, software, networks, and management of data. They may have been surprised at his proficiency with encryption, but this was an area of talent he preferred remained undisclosed to the Slade household.

Such was his skill that in a few minutes his laptop had been isolated from the bank's corporate network and was using an operating system that did not store data and would receive and send only encrypted emails. He was reading one of them now. The innocent phone message had been an invitation to view a deep web mail account to which a few selected individuals held access protocols with encrypted algorithms. It was still an invitation to dinner, but the message carried detail that changed completely the nature of the event.

A meeting had been convened. It was urgent.

Slade felt a mixture of relief and anticipation.

He looked at his watch, closed the computer and returned the three flash drives to his safe. Upon restarting his machine, to the network only a harmless reboot had been registered.

He sat at his desk and thought for a few moments

drumming his fingers, a feeling of excitement growing inside of him.

'Mrs Francis, I shall leave the office slightly early tonight. I'm going to take dinner at the club.'

'Very good Mr Slade,' her voice came back through the intercom. 'Will you be using the car?'

He thought, then: 'No, I'll walk to St James' it will do me good.'

'I'll let the driver know. He's on call should you need him. The Governor's outer office have sent through the agenda for the monthly policy meeting tomorrow. Your briefing is ready.'

He told her to send it through. The Bank of England's monthly meeting was a dry affair even by the standards of banking. It was made more so by the current governor, a humourless German from Thüringen whose absence of character covered the presence of his sharp analytical mind. A technocrat of the kind only produced in Germany. Good news or bad news were all treated with the same dry reasoning and absence of emotion. Although as Deputy to the Governor for over three years and with deep insight into the state's finances, Slade could not recall the last item of real good news that had accompanied the country's economic fortunes.

Slade asked not to be disturbed and for the next hour he worked at his desk absorbing the brief for the policy meeting. He knew there would be no time this evening and phoned his wife to let her know he would be staying at his club due to an early start and not to wait up.

Behind him through his office windows the jumble of shapes of London's buildings darkened, blended, and merged as the winter night fell. The thin city fog came too, blurring the hard lines of buildings, acting as a milky filter to diffuse the orange glow of sodium streetlamps. When it was time to leave, he collected his coat and with his briefcase in hand said goodnight to Mrs Francis who smiled a farewell and returned to her typing.

Outside, at street level, the air was clearer, and he breathed the early night deeply, pleased to feel the evening chill on his face. The pavements glistened like wet liquorice under the dull light, and he strode briskly down Cheapside west towards the city deciding to walk for a while and pick up a cab near St Paul's. Stepping into the cab he realised his heart was thumping a little faster. A request to meet like this in person was rare, it had happened twice in as many years. Slade not only pondered the reason for the summons but was nervous that it either signalled danger or perhaps progress. He was a banker, not a field agent or a spy of any kind. *Keep your routines similar, nothing out of the ordinary. Dine at your club at least once a week and nowhere else that may be unexpected or unusual.*

He had followed this advice carefully over the months, nothing in his personal or professional life would give cause for concern or grievance to anyone watching.

*Always, act normally.*

Easier said than done. But with the passing of time, it somehow did become easier. Over the years he had spent his time building his career in the bank.

*We must act patiently and with nerve.*

Slowly the advancements had come. Junior management giving way to positions of increasing influence. He had been sent away to the commercial sector for a while to manage the foreign exchange of a major overseas bank.

*Don't be concerned, they had told him. It shows they trust you. You'll return.*

The requests they had made to him had always been small, irritatingly small, personnel decisions, some organisational reform, all decisions that fell within his responsibility. But he had understood the need for patience, caution, recognised what the process entailed. Which was just as well as many frustrating years would pass.

Eventually the governorship itself had opened up; he was touted as a candidate.

*No. Stay where you are. Too much risk, you will be too exposed.*

And so, he had, taking the instruction in good part, understanding he had more internal influence where he was, telling his wife it was for the best, and anyway the Party had some dry German wizard earmarked for the role.

The city was quiet as the cab rolled through the damp streets. The driver sensed that his fare did not share a passion for football and so used the short journey to lecture Slade on deviancy of youth; how they didn't stand for their druggy, idle ways in Russia, why they should keep them in the army. Courteous as ever, Slade listened carefully, nodding occasionally while inwardly grateful the rattle of the coarse diesel engine took away many of his words. They passed office workers forming congealed patient lines at bus stops and at the entrances to tube stations. Red buses inched either side of them, the traffic crawling, horns bellowing, their passage slowed to a hobble. He told the driver to take him to Covent Garden tube station, but Shaftsbury Avenue had also become blocked with an oversized wheezing delivery truck that should have known better than to negotiate the cluttered narrow side streets that led into Chinatown. Slade's driver broke free into a side street determined to circle around the ugly worming mass of people and vehicles made slippery by rain.

'Thank you, I'll get out here,' Slade said politely, and paid the driver with change before stepping onto the damp street. The cab pulled away leaving a trail of blue-white vapour that hung in the watery evening air. Around him the pavement shined with rain, and he heard the *shhh* of tyres on the wet road.

He would walk from there to Pall Mall. The photographic recall by London cab drivers of their passengers was on par with their famous understanding of the ancient city's streets. Slade had no reason to believe he was under either suspicion or surveillance—but who could really tell. Informers were everywhere.

Crossing Leicester Square, he joined the convoys of pedestrians. Glancing at the cinema billboards he saw the queue that was forming for the early evening performance of an American romantic comedy that had negotiated the censor. In Trafalgar Square, Nelson remained imperious atop his Corinthian column still dominating London's central heart, his arrogant guard of Barbary lions aloof to the fluttering pigeons who walked in circles pecking at the ground, happy in their filth.

What happens if they never clean its granite and sandstone, he thought, will it all just one day crumble and fall away? When it does, do we all finally wither and follow? He put the bleak thought aside, there was something reassuring that transformation here had been avoided, and it remained an oasis of national heritage. Slade thought of the many examples of social realism that inhabited the city's public places elsewhere. Monuments that had grown in number each year, vulgar exaggerations that littered the green parks to celebrate muscular blood and soil heroism, political advancement, and the crushing of old colonial celebration.

They now seemed so normal they no longer made him shudder.

Curiously much of the old order had just proved stubbornly resistant or too difficult to remove. Grand British public schools still welcomed the children of the elite, the privileged lamented the state of the public health system while checking into the privately run clinics. The church saw its pews filling, a modest evangelical revival, yet it kept its liturgies and social treaties bland and ecumenical, careful to avoid offending the state. The rest was debris surviving by possessing a wiriness that was resistant to authority, like a virus that slyly eradicated its hosts, gently mutating when threatened to become useful accessories.

Hidden amongst these accessories were the few remaining London clubs that had managed to keep their doors open, their existence a thin thread back to the Edwardian values at the height of their power when the nation was vibrant and energetic not crumpled by disease and decay.

Slade was still early, and he slowed his walk, but even so after a few minutes he found himself turning into Waterloo Place and then across Pall Mall into the palladium mansion block that was the Travellers Club, still a grand if faded place, its survival owed to the amalgamation of lesser establishments and the patronage of those with power who found it useful. Someone at the club—he couldn't recall who—had told him the waiting list for membership was now several years.

There were many good reasons Slade liked coming here. Aside from the slightly better food, albeit at a price, a careful eye was kept on the staff to make sure unnecessary loyalties were not imported and the club management had the knack of keeping business conducted within its confines discreet. Slade knew for a fact that the public and private rooms were regularly swept electronically. The membership was carefully balanced, enough commissar-types to keep the authorities happy and enough unspoken club rules to make sure the peculiar Chinese walls of British society exposed none who entered and entertained to risk or harm.

Slade's dining companion was George Faulkes, one of the nation's senior industrialists. A tall but thin man, with a slight stoop and a smile that many found flinty and distant. That the chairman of one of the largest steel and chemical conglomerates in the country should meet with the Deputy Governor of the Bank of England would surprise no one. Faulkes had been a year ahead of Slade at Cambridge in the seventies where they had both read Economics against the backdrop of industrial and financial decline. They made a point of meeting once a month, where common interest in all matters economic gave them material for conversation.

In truth, they did not know each other that well. The regular meetings a chore they endured, waiting for the hours to pass before vying to be the first to get out of the other's company. Both were men who socialised easily with long cultivated skills, but there was something about Faulkes that gently grated with Slade denying true comradeship. An intenseness that below the facade of courteous words, rubbed the wrong way like an unwelcome itch. Faulkes extended his hand his eyes glinted like a lynx, and Slade knew that behind them their view of each other was shared.

But tonight, this did not matter. Slade sensed the collegial affinity the shared summons had delivered. Other unspoken matters concerned them.

In a dining room that was only a quarter occupied, under the flinty marble gaze of engineers of empire they dined agreeably on English lamb. Both drank little, a glass each of a Merlot with an expensive Saint-Émilion label while around them a reliable waiter pecked and fussed protectively. The conversation passed the many topics of business, trade, and politics, flitting and touching down briefly on the conversations of the day. Both lamented the need to raise interest rates, the ministerial change in the Department for Trade and finally fell back on the gossip and rumour that makes its way around the better informed. The Maître d' suggested brandy, which was refused, and they ordered coffee in the smaller of the two drawing rooms where they placed themselves beside the open fire smoking and sipping coffee continuing their conversation without making great progress.

A large mantelpiece clock serenely struck the seconds away. Following its chimes Slade saw it was still only a quarter past nine. Elsewhere in the room two senior members occupied their leather chairs behind the newspapers solving the world's problems and growled their findings at each other.

'Pounds down again,' reported a voice without surprise. 'Coal and steel are looking bad for this year.'

'Nothing is going to be good this year,' said his companion.

Doesn't anyone want to work anymore?' complained the

first speaker with the frustration of the moneyed whose energy in life was directed towards his share value.

Slade resisted the temptation to drum his fingers impatiently on the leather arm of his chair and opened a new flank to his own conversation. He was bored with the affairs of the nation and found it irritating when two men who didn't really care for each other could only find themselves in agreement.

'How is the family George,' he asked lightly, 'those kids of yours having fun at university?'

Faulkes briefly caught the theme, lobbing the question back like a tennis ball with an enquiry as to Slade's eldest daughter and her family cosily happy in some Sussex village.

'Any children there Christopher?' he asked.

'Too many,' Slade replied with a laugh, 'permanently pregnant, fortune in birthdays.'

And there it died. Talk of family seemed not to interest him either.

The two of them gamely kept their conversation going until just before the hour when the steward from earlier approached and quietly announced: 'The Maitland Room was ready,' and invited them to use the main stairs to the first floor.

Today was Thursday, traditionally this was a quiet evening in the club. No one was around to watch the two men as they ascended the broad stairs crossed a landing and made their way along a corridor that was only dimly lit with feeble table lamps and on the walls of which were old water colours of

Middle Eastern trade trails and scenes of Asian tundra, donated by long forgotten members mistaken in believing their generosity would be remembered. The end of the passage was in darkness with enough shadow in an alcove for Slade to believe he detected movement and just for a moment his stomach turned wondering what was waiting for them. Then he relaxed, the shadow soundlessly retreating, the unseen figure of a guardian carefully observing the corridor for movement.

The Maitland Suite was towards the end of the corridor and Faulkes knocked softly, and the door opened slightly. Dugdale himself gazed out, recognition followed, and he then opened the door fully.

'My dear Faulkes, Slade. Come in, we're expecting you of course.'

Slade and Faulkes stepped into the room while Dugdale paused in the doorway seeming to nod to the shadow in the alcove then closed the door. Dugdale shook their hands and led them across the room. It looked more like a place used by the club staff than paying members and had a slightly scruffy appearance, the sideboard showed the debris of used coffee cups and side plates from an earlier gathering. The heavy curtains were drawn, and the room was stuffy and warm.

They were surprised to find that Dugdale was not alone. Standing at the far end of the meeting table was a solidly built middle-aged man with crew cut hair and who wore a blazer, light-coloured slacks, and a blue button-down shirt with pale tie.

There was a light frost of age at his temples. In one large fleshy hand he held a coffee cup while his other fist was pushed into his pocket. He looked at the newcomers with rigid impassivity and Slade knew instantly he was an American, the clothes, the jawline, the clear-eyed smile. All traits of that race.

We look every inch the secret cabal, a fugitive meeting to plot alternative political and economic futures. Slade recalled where the original term *cabal* had come from—Charles II and his cohort of extra-legal advisers. That did not end so well, he thought.

'Christopher, George,' said Dugdale, 'thank you for coming, this is Alan Weiss, he's a friend from Washington, we need say no more. We've asked you here because the time has come to make a decision.'

Weiss raised his free hand briefly in a gesture of greeting, his face crackled into a wrinkled small smile, but there were no words or offers to shake hands.

'A decision,' continued Dugdale, 'that will decisively and forever, change this country.'

THERE is no etiquette for conspirators who do not know each other well to greet, especially when the circumstances are those of a seedy hidden meeting room. Whatever inward emotions Dugdale's declaration may have brought forth in the two men, there was no occasion for either celebration or formality. Reliving this scene later, a thing Slade would do often in the light of the conflicting emotions that being there when the decision was taken, he was constantly struck by how unremarkable the surroundings, the theatre and the words all were.

He turned his attention to Dugdale who he had not seen for two years. There seemed to be an ageless appeal to the man who was still dapper and smoothly good looking for someone of his years. In different times he could imagine much younger women being caught on the spell of his good looks, and roguish smile. It was as much a reason he held belief in his plans as any other. he couldn't help but be impressed by the man, who, he thought, held a zeal, energy, and fearlessness. If anyone can drag us out of this situation, he had decided, this man can.

'Before we start, let me reassure you it's okay to speak freely. We can talk here,' said Dugdale, 'the room has been cleared.' It had been a room like this that he had first met Dugdale, Slade remembered—just the two of them—a contrived meeting that first afternoon. Dugdale nudging him, sounding him out, warily, tenderly pawing at him like a fox considering what to do with the chicken he had cornered, knowing he was in control.

*You can't be happy with this country,* Dugdale had announced in his amused drawl, as if disagreement was unthinkable, his pronouncement beyond debate. *We deserve so much more as a nation. You know this, this is why you stayed, I think.*

Slade had heard of Dugdale without ever realising his role in the organisation that had carefully guided him since his early days at the Bank.

"The greatest crime is to do nothing because we fear we can do nothing."

He had wondered how Dugdale had known so much about him. Did he know that he, Slade admired French philosophy, or was it just a rhetorical flourish, a clever phrase restored from his political days.

*We have a special role for you Slade, one upon which the salvation of many, indeed, probably our nation rests.*

This night, the room smelt of dust and slightly stale air. It fell to Faulkes who could no longer hold his fascination to ask the question that had been on both their minds. The question they had actively resisted asking each other over dinner, where they had forced their talk far away from their reason for being here. 'There are reports you have been killed. Why are the authorities reporting that you are dead?'

Dugdale, as so often, avoided the direct answer, the cool glinting eyes already looking beyond the simple quest for answers to the lonely and devious trail that lay ahead.

*Be patient, avoid frustration, the time will come.* As he had been bidden Slade had watched the Party tighten its control, extend its authoritarianism grip, and had without the need for courage played his part, avoiding the politics, as best he could, sticking to the world of finance, keeping the flows of money moving to industries which became increasingly sick with decline. He knew within the system he served his standing was good and with loyalty and dedication came privilege. Years before, before meeting Dugdale his faith had wavered and he had quietly discussed with his wife departing, to Canada or Australia, in the days when such flight was still possible. But he had held back, the powerful pull of some small piece of patriotic loyalty telling him to stay, convincing him he would be of use one day.

Seniority had brought him his introduction to Dugdale. How had Dugdale at that meeting seemed to know those thoughts? he wondered. He certainly had never confided in anyone else. Had he just read his man carefully, identified the coming value?

Perhaps.

It was true that after meeting Dugdale his own weariness at life had given way to new clarity. He felt sure that Faulkes' motivation was the same. There were others involved, waiting like himself. Some, a very few, like Faulkes, he knew, there were a couple he suspected, but the majority he did not. They were sitting there, somewhere, ghostlike, hidden in the various layers of power. Restless or maybe supremely patient, perhaps confused, and uncertain or with all the clarity they needed. But Slade felt they probably had all shared the same craving; an eagerness for word that they were finally needed.

If only it was that easy.

Was this what Dugdale's meeting, carefully arranged and concealed was about?

'Clearly I'm not,' Dugdale was saying, 'but we will assume

the story was a further attempt to flush us out, sow seeds of doubt. Create some panic. That's one of the reasons, although not the main one for talking to you and the others, reassuring you that everything continues to move forward.'

'That's good news,' Slade heard himself saying.

They must have entered through one of the club's service entrances, Slade thought, smuggled through streets hidden from closed circuit television earlier in the evening to be sheltered discreetly, probably on the upper floors while below, the club management looked the other way. Bold coming here even so, moving with such impunity around the Capital and to a location frequented by many without allegiance.

He's done it for us, thought Slade. Put himself at risk coming here to keep our routines ordinary.

There was a tray with a coffee pot that smoked ever so gently, cups and a quaint touch of a plate of after-dinner mints.

Faulkes asked: 'Any idea how much the authorities may know?'

Slade and Faulkes declined coffee and Dugdale poured for himself and more for Weiss, Then he sat and nibbled absently on one of the mints, folding the foil sleeve wrapper carefully into a thin flat strip that betrayed an ancient dinner party habit.

'You will both know of the death of Mr Len Burns.'

They did and wanted to know what happened.

'Regrettably, Burns' allegiances had become compromised. Our...' he spoke carefully, 'shared assessment is that forcing Burns into their camp was the limit of their success. We can never be sure of course, but the resources available to our cousins are mighty and we believe the threat has passed. Therefore, with the support of our cousins,' he glanced slightly towards Wiess who dropped his eyes slightly in agreement, 'then we have concluded we can proceed.'

'In fact,' cut in Weiss, 'time is important. The Burns affair, and the police and security moves against Dugdale here suggest an upscaling in their efforts. We can't risk further compromise. Washington is keen for a firm timetable.'

He wants to be in charge, thought Slade, the American impatience and aggression surfacing to make it clear where power resided. Dugdale sipped at his coffee and made a face that suggested the liquid was a little too bitter but may have been something else. 'You see our point gentlemen,' Weiss continued, 'if there were any further infiltration it would put the entire plan at risk.'

They are not, thought Slade, a race replete with patience as a quality as we know it. But they must be nervous? Worried that they could still be outmanoeuvred, the long decades of the Cold War passing as a magnificent chess match. Years spent agonising over the single move of a pawn and now the chance beckons to slide the Queen in a deep sweep into the opponent's territory, seizing back the centre of the board. Provided they have not been out thought.

'Alan is right of course,' Dugdale agreeing quietly with the

American, 'Years of work and effort, not to mention lives would be lost.'

There was a sound of movement outside in the corridor. Soft footfall on the carpet that caused the boards to creek, and which quickly faded.

Both men wanted to know more. Only a lifetime of instinct held back Slade's questions, sensing that Dugdale would arrive in his own good time and would not be rushed. Instead, he saw the excitement on Faulkes' face who asked: 'What does this mean?' He asked. 'Do we move soon?'

Dugdale had begun to doodle absently with a silver pen on a leather pad with gold corners, its nib forming looping curling patterns. But it was Weiss that answered. The educated east coast accent was easy and suddenly relaxed.

'Washington wants to leave it up to you people. Dugdale here has a time frame, it's up to you guys to say if it works. Y'all say it's fine that suits us and we'll go with it.'

Slade managed a ghostly smile while Dugdale regarded them both. Key components in a plot dormant for so long and whose time was fast approaching. Slade found himself saying, 'Yes.' It was only a word, but they all understood what it meant. He heard Faulkes quietly agree and both men saw the small, crooked smile form on the American's lips.

Now the questions fell to Dugdale. 'I take it there is no change to your situation and your role in what we need?'

The years of professional financial and political caution

would not hold Slade back now. There could be no more hesitancy, secret scoping and plotting, cautious assessments of success or failure. Dugdale and his American overlord had made it clear the dawn of action was soon to be upon them.

'None,' said Slade, with confidence. 'If the international markets can be made to stop lending, then the Bank will be forced to restrict the money supply. The country has almost nothing in the way of reserves and economically Britain grinds to a halt. Will they do that?'

'Oh yes,' Dugdale replied quite lightly as if stopping a country's economy was something he did every day. He twirled the pen in his fingers, mesmerised by the glint it made in the light, 'the Americans and Japanese will see to it. How long do you think?' Weiss was slowly nodding in agreement.

Slade gave a small shrug of his shoulder. 'After that, not long, a couple of weeks. The cupboard is literally bare. But—' he gave an anxious look in Dugdale's direction— 'we talked about the preconditions necessary for us to be sure. It would be easier without the present Governor. I can make certain technical decisions on timings and interventions into the markets that would ensure a collapse.'

'That will be taken care of Christopher. You will be fully in position to do what's necessary.'

'He's not a bad man, I don't mean—'

'—It will be discreet; but please don't concern yourself with that,' there was a certain snappishness to his reply, 'we will give you the space you need.'

Slade nodded. He felt foolish for raising an objection. He thought of Burns and wondered about his death. But there was too much at stake to be squeamish about a fat little German technocrat who disliked England and the English and suffered the work only out of obedience to the Party.

'At that point we are left with only printing money, which may work for a while but with nothing to back it up rapid and massive inflation will follow. Price of foreign goods will go beyond the reach of cash and borrowing, and the country will be on its knees.'

Dugdale was pleased with this answer and nodded in agreement. His attention and that of Weiss turned to the industrialist.

'Can we hear your thought's, George?'

Faulkes sat with long bony fingers extended on the tabletop. He seemed in thought about the scenario Slade had set out, although it was one, he had considered often. His reply was grave. 'Shutting down the banks,' he shot a dependent glance at Slade, 'well, it will destroy industry. Without the banks and lending, no materials, no export or import, no wages. Coal, steel, shipbuilding will collapse.' He licked his lips, pausing for thought, then offered his cigarette case which all three men declined, so he lit one himself and drew deeply. His pale complexion became paler, but not from fear or concern, Slade saw the same excitement he felt within himself. 'Workers can be ordered to work, they may even do so for a while,` but there will be nothing to produce. Transport will stop. As Christopher said, it will be chaos.' He added quietly: 'It could get pretty rough. This country can't feed itself. People will get desperate. We don't know what the Government may do in this situation.'

'It won't come to that,' Dugdale said, almost with gentleness. 'We want the crisis but not complete collapse.'

'Can that be judged? Can we control the slide once it begins? We have no brakes,' said Slade. He regretted his words immediately, sensing that now was not the time for doubts, for inner fears to surface. He watched Dugdale continue to twirl the pen, debating the question, recognising that anxiety was natural, unavoidable. He suspected Dugdale shared the concern and wore the authority and confidence like a suit, perhaps reluctantly but certainly as a duty. For this reason, he watched Dugdale gather himself, pull his thoughts together and prepare to respond with a statement, rally their doubts and turn them into confidence in the way that truly inspirational leaders can. Someone who desires neither to be liked or pitied but realises that the man he must be is the man without doubts.

'Once the impossibility of the situation is known to the Party, once they see the country grid-locked, shops empty, transport halted, industry at a standstill and hundreds of thousands of people are in the streets, it will be clear to them they have no answers. Controlling the police will not be enough. then we take charge and mobilise the people. Quietly and decisively, we take hold of the various levers of power. At that point then, the lights will come back on. It's going to be all about the timing, as you know.'

Hungary in fifty-six? thought Slade or Prague in sixty-eight? Could this country be different? Possibly, he thought—different times, different places, different people. Those were spontaneous revolutions by the people, opportunities that were seized. They were always doomed in the face of ruthless authority. That was not the scenario here. Political and economic authority itself has been corrupted and undermined? Could the levers of the state be made impotent to respond? Was this different from earlier attempts at national attempts for freedom?

'But there will be violence. The Party will not cede control without a fight. Protest alone will not be enough.' Slade realised the words were his own.

Dugdale just said simply: 'Yes, there will be violence, on both sides and yes, those plans are made.'

Both Slade and Faulkes knew however trusted and critical to the plan they were, there were others, key appointments placed or nurtured elsewhere, ready to play their part in removing obstacles. But if the authorities ever identified them, then their fate was certain. Only the tight cell-like compartments of knowledge and responsibility kept them and the plans safe. The Burns' affair was a warning. He prayed that the authorities would not be ready for them.

'So, James,' asked Faulkes whose cigarette had burnt low, and he wandered across to the far side of the room looking for an ashtray among the coffee debris, 'when does all this happen?' He turned to Weiss. 'I respect that you and your colleagues in Washington are impatient Mr Weiss, so you must have a date, an event in mind to act as a catalyst. I assume you won't want to be seen to be involved from the start, that would be interfering in Bloc affairs. It would be international madness and I seem to remember someone once said: "Rest not your hope on foreign nations"?'

Slade watched Dugdale ponder Faulkes' words as if he was reluctant to answer, so used to holding his secrets he was reluctant even now to share.

'It was Jefferson Davis,' Weiss said, 'who issued that warning, and, rather aptly, he was talking about falsely relying on the British. 'Tell them Dugdale,' said Weiss quietly. 'Let's get this show going.'

Dugdale smiled and his eyes held the same glint that Gates had seen the week before, flinty, and cold.

'Waiting will only increase the risk of the authorities and the Soviets of learning more. Our preparations and the situation are as good as they are going to get.' All three men were looking at him, waiting for the words. 'The political and economic can be made no more favourable than they are at present. We can control communications, the military and therefore in turn control the seats of power. There is only one ingredient that we need to ensure success and for that we must wait just a little longer.'

Slade was puzzled, what did he mean?

'Three months,' continued Dugdale. 'That's when the next opportunity presents itself and the stars align for the best chance of success. When the government is distracted, and the nation's guard is down and when legitimacy reveals itself.'

For a moment there was no sound except faraway traffic from the street below although Slade swore that he could hear the soft tread of feet on carpet outside the door as the guardian patrolled a solitary beat.

'We start in three months, and it will be over in four. We begin to open the Lionheart network. Time to put it to work.'

Dugdale saw their surprised look and laughed. A roguish rich laugh of the conspirator and Slade had a ridiculous vision of how Guy Fawkes must have felt on learning of the gunpowder plot. Was this the same?

'Our new Monarch has returned to us from California. He's come home to serve his country, possibly because the others won't take the job but all the same...I think our new King deserves a new country to go with his coronation. Don't you agree?'

'Good God,' said Slade, the significance of the timing and the implication suddenly apparent. He looked towards Faulkes who stared back at him.

Neither knew what to say.

Alan Weiss' ploughed face turned into a broad grin. 'God save the King,' he said.

***

# CHAPTER FOURTEEN

*Down in darkest Lambeth*

**South London**

THE HOUSE SMELT DAMP; its musty odour hung like a gas filling the narrow hallway. Deeper inside the pungency grew becoming something else as it ripened with the added evil mix of dust, old vomit, and rotten food. It was the middle of the day; however, the hallway would have been as dark as a tomb had it not been for the weak illumination of a naked light bulb hanging from the ceiling.

Outside, the street was Lambeth at its seediest. The once smart Victorian suburbs had been left to decay and crumble, a long row of large unloved terraces, their window frames sick with rot and with walls made of red brick that were crumbling from a century of traffic pollution. Weary rows of London plane trees lined the road stooping like old sentries still faithfully attending their posts long after their duty should have ended. Their roots erupted through the tarmac while from their branches dropped early by disease, sticky catkins formed a slippery carpet. In the road a group of feral kids played football scrapping around a ball, oblivious to the cars that timidly edged past. Surly young men from Africa leaned against walls and smoked as they looked out, protecting their territory, suspicious of anyone who crossed their border, their wary cold eyes following the paths of the few passersby who hurried along wordlessly, their faces kept down and looks averted. Beyond their sentry posts lay the overgrown gardens, laced with metal and debris, half-hidden rusting scrap from car parts and kitchen appliances to abandoned supermarket trolleys and fouled mattresses. The terraces themselves backed up against an elevated section of railway line. The concrete stanchions were decorated with urban graffiti, ugly, bubbly letters in the spray can ballooned style that appeared on every bare wall across the city.

Shiner had travelled here from his home in North London.

'You'll have to get out here,' the Hungarian driver had called cheerfully through the glass partition still a quarter mile from Shiner's destination. 'They are a law unto themselves in this area and they don't take kindly to people from elsewhere.' The warning made Shiner grimly realise that he would be counted as one of those from elsewhere. The journey across the city had been spent listening to the driver explaining how difficult life in the capital had become, especially for immigrants. He had listened without interest, responding with random grunts of sympathy between the old Magyar's grumbles while reading messages on his phone and preferring not to watch the pavements slide deeper into filth. South of the river the city was close to economic and social collapse. Unless you were someone like Shiner, with business, you only really went there if you had to or had nowhere else to go.

It was the end of the line.

For a moment his mind returned to the telephone call that had interrupted his morning. *Can you find time for a trip to south London?* He had been reluctant but recognising the number he had agreed.

Leaving his taxi, he had made his way along cracked pavements, avoiding a drunk collapsed on a step, buried in flea-ridden clothes, his head nodding in and out of sleep, his foul breath burbling with gas and incoherent fears. Finally freed from its owner's grip an empty vodka bottle rolled and clinked rhythmically against a concrete step.

The sights no longer disturbed Shiner, his resignation at society's decay long complete.

He had pushed open with uncertainty the front door of the three-storey sprawl of a house that lay partially hidden amongst a small jungle of weed. It had swung creakily open, unlocked, and sagged on its hinges.

The hallway of the house had two doors off the corridor that were open and a further door at the end that was closed. A narrow set of stairs led up into an uninviting dark cave that was the next floor. From out of its mouth the small sound of a radio filtered tinnily, with it the occasional bump and thud of furniture being dragged across a floor. Shiner could see that one of the open doors on the ground floor belonged to a bathroom of grimy white porcelain fittings pasted with congealed soap and toothpaste, the light in here didn't work and Shiner considered it a relief he could see no more. The smell was disgusting.

*Won't take long*, the caller had encouraged, sensing his hesitation. *It'll be worth your while.* Looking at the scene before him, he could not see how.

Peering through the other doorway into a smallish bedroom he could see long strips of peeling blue wallpaper that curled away from the damp walls to dangle freely, curtains hung limply as frayed and thin as ancient shrouds and a collapsed and stained mattress lay in the centre of the floor on which was heaped a tangled mass of unwashed bedding and clothes. The floor around it was strewn with drink cans, food wrappers and dirty plates. From the corner of his eye, he caught the scurry of movement and he saw two fat cockroaches investigating the discarded treasures. Four or five syringes lay scattered to one side of the mattress, and he felt his throat clench at the dense atmosphere.

Engrossed in the scene that confronted him, the sudden sound of a chuckle from behind him startled him.

'I wouldn't go in there if I were you.' The voice was male, youthful, south London. 'You won't come out the same dude.'

Shiner's heart jumped at the voice, and he quickly turned

and with relief recognised the lean man in his early thirties with curly dark tousled hair, brown leather jacket and blue jeans. He was leaning against the now open third doorway and with relief Shiner recognised the man whose phone call had summoned him. Alex Corbett had a smile on his face, but it was humourless, the grim smile of the career cynic who can find humour where others might only find pity or despair. Shiner was here because when Corbett called it was usually worth his time to listen.

Around the two men the walls of the house shook, vibrating to the approach of a thunderous train beginning to decelerate, brakes screeching and protesting as it began to pull the last mile into Waterloo Station. They waited for the noise and rattle of windows to subside. Across the yard, through a collapsed fence Shiner glimpsed the coaches rushing and lurching past, more ballooned graffiti, blurred but distinguishable, scrawled on their sides as they raced past.

Although Shiner tried to return the smile, the tightness of his throat turned it into a gulp. He had a feeling he was about to be shown. There wasn't a corner of this city he didn't know, but being summoned somewhere without warning or knowing why, was unnerving.

Responding to these types of invitation might be a mistake?

Taking personal risk was what he paid people like Corbett for.

And, he reminded himself, Corbett was different. He could be a gold mine.

For a few, even in these difficult modern times, police work remained a vocation or at least a job which offered variety and interest. To most it was a way of gaining privilege. Shiner considered Corbett a rarity in the world of criminal investigation. A policeman who was not only bright and quick witted, but educated, abilities which had made him a detective, quickly singled out from the ranks of the truncheon wielding cannon fodder. A detective in the London force was a person of power and influence, while the city was a source of opportunity. Junior police pay being what it was, Corbett was a rare breed and had the brain and ability to put the two together. He was smart and his relationships with the worlds of drugs and prostitution was profitable and art-like.

For Shiner's part, the impressive stable of contacts that served his needs came from the widest assortment of society and walks of life. From the privileged and connected to prostitutes and porters. He found them because they were useful and loyal, a quality he returned, paying generously, and granting helpful favours. The information he gathered, he sold, some of it for news, some of it because it gave leverage and some of it—well because people would pay to keep it secret.

Of all his informer ranks, he rated Corbett amongst his best and liked him for it. When corruption is a way of life other qualities come to the fore. Most police officers were simple brutes, thugs given power in return for obedience. Somehow Corbett was different, corrupt certainly, but not without humanity.

Two years earlier, he had pursued the killer of a street prostitute when no one else in the department, the press or the public had shown any interest. The girl had been tortured, raped, and finally beaten to death. She was sixteen and a lone fallen girl at the mercy of the streets. The discarded and abused body had been found naked with her head crushed, a casualty of a society without responsibility mourned by no one except confused and bewildered parents who grieved without hope or recourse to justice. It had taken Corbett six months, six months of patient detective work on his own time, but the killer, a middle-aged air force officer with no connection to the girl, just a twisted need for gratification while on leave and a misplaced sense of entitlement, had kept an appointment with the gallows.

Corbett's reward had been to be given a medal and an assignment of his choice, after which the matter was swiftly forgotten.

She was far from the only unfortunate one to fall prey to violent streets and would not be the last. Shiner had wondered what had made the detective take that particular task on. There was no need to, he hadn't been ordered to and no one expected it of him, yet he did.

Shiner still wondered.

'In here,' said Corbett, ignoring the dubious look on Shiner's face. 'Come and meet the current tenants, they'll be thrilled to meet you.'

'If I must,' Shiner replied without enthusiasm and reluctantly followed the policeman into the next room. 'What's this place?' Corbett's call had given no details. Not that he had expected him to.

'Charity owned,' Corbett replied. 'In theory a safe place they put the homeless and the vulnerable.' His laugh was bitter. 'More realistically it's a magnet for drug dealers and crackheads. Local Party and residents have given up trying to close such places down, they just sprout up somewhere else. The charity dumps them in here, claims they are safe and collects the city grant for cleaning up the streets.'

He followed Corbett into the main room and Shiner was surprised to find that the living area was not as bad as elsewhere. A collapsed sofa, music system on the floor, plates, cans, food debris and a broken smack pipe its dark resin contents spilling onto the already ruined carpet. More peeling walls and stained ceilings. But the smell was almost gone, an open window allowing the cool outside air to billow the grimy net curtains inward and circulate into the room. The furniture was roughly in order, and nothing seemed to be crawling around. There was even a picture, faded away by sunlight in a plastic frame and hanging askew, brown, and blue splashes and strokes of somewhere that may have been the Lake District, but could have been many other places as well. Shiner was grateful it wasn't a repeat of the other rooms but nevertheless he wanted to leave very much, the house was oppressive, decayed and ruined.

Corbett stood in the middle of the room. 'Then they forget all about them and the gangs and the dealers take over.' Shiner said nothing. Over his shoulder, Corbett glanced at Shiner, and saw Shiner's uncertain face. 'No one checks so it's a nice little scam,' Corbett concluded.

Corbett sank into a large armchair that sighed and creaked with his weight and threw his legs casually over the arm. From his jacket he produced a small metal box and from inside he took a filmy cigarette paper and a small pile of tobacco. He rolled it expertly licking delicately the paper and lit it immediately huffing deeply and blowing blue rings towards the cracked ceiling. 'Meet Jamie a well-bred English fellow who is accompanied by his American girlfriend Nancy here, two lovebirds enjoying a city break.'

Lying at opposite ends of the sofa, collapsed and unconscious were a boy and a girl both around twenty years of age. The boy was lean and thin with extended limbs yet to gather the muscle of adulthood and long black waved hair that fell in a greasy curtain forward over his forehead. His skin had a lipid glisten, and his chin and cheeks wore a dark shadow that betrayed days without shaving.

There were too many like this in the city to feel pity

anymore, thought Shiner. Wandering tribes of young people who failed to conform to the system but who had nowhere to take their frustration. Shiner was not sure what saddened him more, these drug-riddled outcasts with little hope, or the congress halls full of zealots moulded into the political, economic, and educational culture of the Soviet system and patterned to the requirements of the State. It was true British culture had avoided the ordered discipline of the mass games, perhaps socialist transition had come too late, perhaps it was still too early to expect such areas as culture, art, and youth discipline to be imposed in the way it was elsewhere in Europe. The televising of the Czech *Spartakiad*—at least privately—did not bring forth the admiration and enthusiasm the authorities probably wished for. Shiner took the view that while political and social repression had proved possible, the disinterest the British felt towards central order would forever prevent the type of conformity seen across the Eastern European satellite states.

Corbett resumed, his tone matter of fact: 'Actually, I know it's difficult to believe, but the girl is quite pretty, when she's not in this condition.'

Shiner looked down at her. He found it difficult to imagine that youthful beauty graced the wasted female body curled into a loose ball, unconscious and oblivious to his gaze. She was painfully thin with long tangled blonde hair that fell across her face. It was lank and needed washing. A thin dirty yellow vomit stain had dried into her purple t-shirt between her shallow cleavage. It was not impossible, he supposed, that she was girlishly attractive, once made presentable and fed properly, but her current state made it difficult to tell. Shiner thought of the youthful good looks, wasted talent, the unused capacity in the two sick bodies before him. It was not nice to see.

He turned his attention back to the policeman and put his revulsion for the scene behind him. Corbett's apparent amusement for the situation was irritating him. He decided he didn't need mystery or a dramatic build up. 'What's the story Alex?' he said a little impatiently. 'Why am I in some Lambeth shithole looking at two druggies? I've got better things in my diary.'

Corbett gave a look that seemed to agree but went on: 'I know but stay with me. I think you will be interested.' Corbett puffed on the cigarette and began to explain. 'Jamie and Nancy are two privileged little fucks who with a few other wannabe bohemians hide themselves away every so often in this pigsty. She's truant from her highly respectable finishing school in Surrey and he should be in his university art class, painting whatever shit they call art nowadays. Instead, when they can find the cash, they pick up drugs, take off from their comfortable homes and lives to cosy themselves here for a few days, perhaps a week.' He waved the cigarette towards the unconscious pair in circular roll of blue smoke. 'Now, nothing remarkable so far but keep following me. These two, or I should say the girl, are a little bit special. Not only do they have parents that for some reason will at some point come and take them back, clean them up, at least until they do it again, but can, at least in her case, protect them from the authorities.'

'How do you mean? what are they to you?' Shiner said. 'I'm still not following.'

From outside came the angry bark of a large dog, there was shouting and the revving of a motorcycle an altercation on the street. Men began to shout joined by the hysterical angry screaming of a woman. Bloodcurdling, Shiner thought, what must the area become like at night. What drove these two kids to spend their time here? He asked himself. Only complete desperation, he supposed. He thought of his own bolt hole the sixty-foot old Dutch tug that sat in the estuary marsh lands.

'I'm getting there. So, I have an arrangement with the dealer they use, he keeps me sweet, I give him some cover, it's a good thing we have going. These two, were cashless and tried to angle some crack or something, anything in fact that they could get in exchange for some items they claimed were valuable.'

The boy started to cough and puke a little. As he shifted on the sofa the smell of sweat, unwashed clothes and excrement lifted from him.

'Oh Christ,' Shiner covered his mouth with the back of his hand. 'How can you sit there in this filth?'

'Anyway, the dealer called me, thought I might be interested,' said Corbett ignoring the protest. 'He said they were trying to peddle some documents; he thought I might be interested.' With relief Shiner saw the point Corbett was getting to in sight, while deep in nothingness, a dark void beyond dreams, the lifeless couple remained unheeding to the conversation taking place about them. 'Now, forget the boy for the moment, concentrate on Nancy here,' and he waved an open palm towards the youth that dismissed him to be alone in his stupor.

Abruptly, the policeman swung his legs off the chair and leaned forward, elbows on his knees, hands clasped straight as if in prayer, his eyes following the burning cigarette which he pointed arrow straight at the girl.

'Her dad is a big wheel, and I mean very big wheel diplomat at the U.S. Embassy. I know this because she's turned up here before, as well as a few other god-awful little dens nearby. She even has a diplomatic passport, and I know this because she's tried to sell it to my contact once or twice.'

Shiner did not react, but the explanation erased his irritation at being dragged across London to a rat-infested slum, something began to stir his interest. 'Go on.' He had no fascination regarding drugs or degenerate youth, there was nothing he could do about it, and no one was there to thank him even if he could. But intrigue amongst the powerful—that he could work with.

'This tender delight of a daughter decided that her craving

for some smack enjoyment time was best financed by a raid on her father's possessions. Not the first time she's tried a stunt like this, so her folks are wise to attempts to exchange family treasure for drugs and most of the valuable stuff was safely kept beyond her reach, although if you like *Čapek* I know where there is a highly prized first edition going begging. I am still considering that for myself,' he explained in his dry way.

Shiner always forgot this side of Corbett and remembered now there was an artist in the younger man, a lonely fondness for painting, literature and probably music that few shared and seemed strange for a man in his profession.

'If she's a risk, what's she doing in the country? Surely, they should have shipped her back to the States.'

'You'd think so wouldn't you,' replied Corbett. 'Especially as her old man is the Embassy number two in London. So, only a couple of scenarios can answer that question.'

This was too much for Shiner. 'Oh, my Christ,' he remonstrated, his voice rising. 'What the fuck are you doing, they must be searching high and low for her.'

Corbett seemed remarkably calm and smoked more. 'Well, they're not, at least not yet and not officially. My guess is that Daddy is keeping quiet about wayward daughter and his bosses don't know about this and well our own gallant faithful guardians are not in a rush to burn him. In fact…that's kind of interesting isn't it. I wonder why?' his eyes glinted with something knowing, a secret he had yet to reveal.

Shiner hesitated, frowned, then seemed to wake to the intrigue, then his eyes settled on the girl, drawn by that inner magnet of curiosity that lodges with every journalist. 'What did she take?' he said in an interested voice.

Corbett gave him a cool look and didn't answer immediately. Instead, he moved over to where the old music system sat on the floor kicked it carelessly to one side and reached down behind it. From there he recovered a large document wallet, zipped, and made of good quality leather. He passed it to Shiner who with an uncertain glance at the policeman took it.

'What's in it?' He felt a reluctance to investigate without warning, without some knowledge of what he might discover.

Corbett puffed his cheeks and held up his hands in a defensive gesture. 'Take a look. I peeked and thought only of you.'

The purpose of Shiner's summons had been arrived at.

Shiner emptied the case out. There was a sheaf of communiques, internal memos, he glanced quickly through these. They may have been sensitive but he could see they didn't amount to much. Shiner became puzzled. He could understand the desperation of a drug seized young girl in believing such material was of value, but what had Corbett seen that made him call him?

Then he found it.

An anonymous manila envelope unmarked nor stamped.

Its flap closed by the small piece of string wrapped around the cardboard buckle. It bulged slightly and looked more promising than anything else in the document case. He uncurled the string and glanced inside the open flap. A passport. A Russian passport. Shiner's breath leaped and he pulled it free quickly flicking it open he saw the owner was a Russian businessman: one *Dimitri Igorovi.*

The photograph.

The small black and white passport image of unsmiling man of middle years. Short hair cropped and with a centre parting. Broad shoulders.

'Her father?' Shiner asked, his heart beating fast.

Corbett nodded. 'Mr Alan Weiss, number two in the U.S. mission to the United Kingdom, a position more widely recognised to be the CIA Resident here.'

'Holy fuck does this mean—' Shiner's brain was spinning.

'—I don't know,' Corbett chuckled, 'I don't really want to. But you should keep looking.'

Shiner began to leaf through the other papers. All were prepared in the Cyrillic script of the Soviet State, the complicated orthography conjuncted with the seals and stamps of officialdom that told Shiner they were permits and travel papers all prepared in the same name as the passport. Shiner took stock of what he was looking at and surmised he was looking at a complete identity. In front of him were the complete set of bureaucratic and administrative tools that were necessary

# LIONHEART

to step into a new existence far from here.

There was a small brown pocket diary embossed with the seal of the U.S. State Department. He flicked through the pages but it was empty apart from an asterisk marked on a page every few weeks. Not just an asterisk, an asterisk placed after the capital letters CB.

It was the next set of documents that caused his breathing to stop. He read the opening page.

**EMBASSY OF THE UNITED STATES OF AMERICA**

**(TOP SECRET)**

**NOFORN**

**SUBJECT:** High level meeting convened by CLOUD BURST

| | |
|---|---|
| Source Evaluation | A |
| Intelligence Evaluation | 1 |
| Dissemination | 5 (NO DISSEMINATION) |

**REPORT**

| Source | | Evaluation (SID) |
|---|---|---|
| Case Officer | **RE: LIONHEART ACTIVATION** Source cell wishes you to be aware: 1.0 CLOUD BURST will be convening meeting of key actors between 16-19th of this | A/1/5 |

month.

He read no further and bundled the papers back together into the envelope. He realised he was looking at intelligence reports, memos, assessments.

'Jesus Christ,' Shiner swore again, 'Have you read these?' he asked looking at Corbett.

'No...at least, not properly. I saw where they came from but nothing more.' Shiner wasn't sure whether he was lying or not. He concluded it didn't matter. If either of them were caught with such material, they were in jail for a long time and perhaps worse.

'When did she bring all of this?' he asked.

'Last night. Dealer called me straight away and I came over a few hours ago. I called you.'

'Why have you left this stuff here? Wouldn't it be safer elsewhere?'

Corbett stared at him as if he was mad and chortled. 'I don't want anything to do with them. Weiss must realise by now, or very soon, what she has done. He's in trouble, this can't be hidden. That stuff is no use to me. I prefer to keep away from it. Before it goes back, I wondered if you wanted to see it.'

The answer made sense.

'Did she say anything?'

'He said she was awake when he got here, drunk, or high

but still with it. She told him: "He's a bastard, it's all yours for a hundred." "What's in it?" I ask. "You'll see," she says. "Where did you get it?" She didn't answer that, so, I am guessing a briefcase raid, hunt through study drawers, must be something like that. Probably her father got careless at home, and she was in so quick and before he had time to store them properly. You know how resourceful these druggies are—clever and fast if they see an opportunity.'

'Anything else?'

Corbett blew out his cheeks again and shrugged.

'Only that the parents haven't reported her missing yet, officially. If I had material like that, that I knew was missing, I would be looking for help to get it back and that starts with her.'

A girl with an American intelligence chief for a father missing with a complete Russian identity and intelligence material. Someone would be looking for her.

Like most people Shiner knew a little Russian. If I was sixteen, I would know more, he thought. Learning Russian was compulsory from ten years of age. He scanned the other documents which appeared to be various official notifications of social security, educational and professional qualifications, an apartment lease, and local police registration, even pension entitlement—a generous one. There were also some bank cards, new and unsigned from Bank of Moscow and even American Express.

This wasn't just a cover, it looked like an escape.

Did he want to get involved in this? He was reluctant. Selling gossip to editors and blackmailing the powerful to keep them to account was one thing, but this looked dangerous and a different league. It was espionage.

People with more power than he could imagine would soon be involved.

He couldn't keep the documents. Someone would come looking.

What about Corbett? Did he trust him completely? He thought he did. But... That's the trouble with deception, its layers and folds begin to overwhelm the mind, sending reason and imagination into paradoxes impossible to resolve.

Gates.

He thought of his last conversation the two of them had, had at breakfast when Gates visited London. The hint of plans for change, conspiracy theories he had assumed. The country was full of those, everyone had one. Dark shadows always being chased by the police and security services. *Was he a good communist?* Had there been more in that question than he realised? Was he right to have been so dismissive? Perhaps Gates' line of questioning had held more than he knew.

Shiner nodded towards the comatose pair on the sofa. 'What can you do with them?'

Corbett laughed. 'Well, if I'm quick and get her back to her father, he'll gratefully receive those and her back with no questions.' Shiner could tell he already had a plan worked out. A plan based upon return and reward. 'If others find those documents before him, he's in big shit, so there'll be a price to claim to make sure it stays quiet.'

'What about him?'

Corbett looked coldly at the boy. 'Couldn't care less,' he said without feeling.

Another train thundered past, and the walls shook once more. Shiner looked at his watch. It was two in the afternoon. He needed a drink but knew there was no pub within two miles that he would be prepared to enter.

'And this?' Shiner indicated the papers.

'It'll have to stay with the girl.'

Shiner thought it over. Corbett was right.

'Can you keep them here a few hours longer? Until first thing, while I get this copied? With a little luck he won't be in rush to say anything about their loss until he knows they are definitely gone.'

Corbett nodded. He had already thought this scenario through. 'Easy enough, I'll supply a little more junk, let me know when you're done. I'll get in touch with the father, feed him some bullshit to stop him doing anything silly.'

'What about—'

The service cost, of course. Shiner pondered; Corbett hadn't called him here for free. 'Let me know what the owner of this pile agrees for its return. I'll give you fifty percent of that for the copies. Will that do?'

Corbett didn't even think the offer over and said it would and they shook hands.

As they parted, Shiner turned and said: 'The dealer who these two approached...?'

'Don't worry,' said Corbett, 'I've got that. He can disappear for a while.'

'No one can get to him except you?' Shiner wanted to be certain there would be no loose ends, no trails that might be followed.

Corbett shrugged. 'Take a look out in that street, no one is going to find him around here except me.'

LATER, on his way home, Shiner bought a brown parcel box, strong tape and Christmas wrapping paper from a newsagent. He also bought a tourist postcard that had rested there unsold for years. A saucy scene of a fat red-cheeked policeman being tempted with an ice cream by two bikini-clad blondes.

'Nothing like getting sorted early,' chuckled the cheerful shopkeeper. 'Sending off to the family already?'

'Can't be too organised,' Shiner had replied entertaining the joke. 'You know what the post is like,' and they both laughed at the unspoken but widely held bleak view of the postal service.

'Well, as long as it's not valuable, you'll be okay.' And the two men laughed again.

He made one more stop at a photo and print shop he

knew, one which would ask no questions. The stops meant it was gone five o'clock by the time he entered his top floor flat. He placed the now copied pile of papers on his desk and pulled the curtains tightly closed. Then he poured himself a large drink. The flat was cold, and he turned on the electric wall heater and while he waited for the temperature to rise, he sat in an armchair and contemplated the materials that sat on his desk. He also looked towards the telephone and wondered whether he should call first. Warn of what was coming. *Everyone's a good communist...*

In the end he decided against the phone. Too risky. He would have preferred to meet and explain but the instincts of his trade kept him in check.

He pulled out the small diary. It was a standard U.S. State Department issue with the first few pages full of usual information: moon and sunrises, a country currency index and U.S. national holidays. The diary itself was a week to two pages and he flicked through the dates. The only entries were those dates marked with 'CB*' inscribed in pencil. They were random and there was nothing else. Why have an empty diary with only these entries. Who uses a paper diary? Someone who doesn't want an electronic record perhaps. CB. What was that? Initials, a person…location?

He re-read the latest assessment report.

|  |  |  |
|---|---|---|
|  | ...the meeting date and location is not disclosed.<br>1.1 CLOUD BURST will inform them that political authorisation for LIONHEART to be activated coincident with the occasion of the Royal Coronation next year ... |  |
| Case Officer | 2.0 **OPERATIONAL COMPROMISE**<br>2.1 CLOUD BURST reports that operational security of LIONHEART plans have not been compromised by internal dissident activity... | A/1/5 |

CLOUD BURST...CB that was it. It became obvious. CB was a person. That was who he was meeting. Intriguingly, the last diary entry matched the date in the assessment.

The report went on to say the potential threat had been successfully identified and removed without serious knowledge of plans being disclosed.

"...the Party official and trade union leader was not sufficiently aware of the operational timetable to affect operational execution of LIONHEART..."

Burns. Len Burns. Shiner thought of his conversation with Gates. Who else could they mean?

All of this was in the last few days. He knew there were big gaps in his knowledge, but from what he held and what he had read, it seemed like the American was working for the Soviets and was informing on some secret plan, the nature of which he had no idea. The reference to Burns meant that Gates was involved, although how he had no way of knowing.

When does a man become a traitor? Is it to a cause, his country, or his wife? He fixed upon the passport picture with an intensity reserved for the immigration official. *Everyone's a good communist.*

He bundled the American papers back together and then continued to think through what he would do.

Revitalised by the cigarette and the drink and with the room now pleasantly warm, he wrapped the documents immersing them first in Christmas wrapping and then placing the package in the parcel box and taping it. It was a snug fit, and he was pleased. At his desk he took the postcard and turning it over drew a small child-like picture of a rising sun above a sailboat, wrote a six-word message and a telephone number. He put the card and the half of the ten-pound note in an envelope and wrote a Manchester address. Tomorrow the package would be secured safely far from here, and the originals given back to Corbett to allow him to claim his prize. It was for others to play the game, whatever it was.

He refreshed his glass and sat down once more, loosening his collar, slipping off his shoes and began to relax a little. His eyes began to close but he forced them open, jolting himself to stay awake. The evening was early, and he needed to be sure of what he was doing, confident before he let relaxation claim him.

He was sure he had covered his tracks; the only link was Corbett, and he would just have to assume Corbett was not a threat. He took his drink out onto the Juliet balcony which clung to the side of his building and provided just enough space to wedge himself into the night air while the tobacco filled his lungs. A fat old woman wobbled her small toy dog along the street, pausing before she kicked its dirt into the gutter. Despite such carelessness, to Shiner the city seemed better at night, less dirty and corrupt. The street softened in the gentle streetlight and was all shadow. Attic skylights bled little squares of light into the night illuminating chimney pots bejewelled with television aerials. At the end of the street the small park had become refreshed, tingled to life by the cold moisture. There should be stars to complete the scene, but all were blanked out by the haze above the city.

Nevertheless, it would be wise to stay low for a while, off the scene and just see what materialised.

He wanted company and called the boy who came as he always did. Later they lay there, and Shiner told him he would be away for a while and the boy who was peaceful and slender, thin hipped and with mother-loving eyes and who had known Shiner for a long time knew better than to ask more questions. He would give him some money, a clean phone from his small supply and told him what to say if it rang. He then told him to post the Manchester envelope tomorrow using a distant post box.

Outside, seeing the light in Shiner's flat extinguish, the two men thankfully started the BMW's engine grateful for the heat that soon began to creep around their shoes. With a low growl the car slowly eased from the kerb and prowled down the street. When dawn broke and before the street's occupants arose and Shiner's boy crept from his bed it would have returned.

***

# CHAPTER FIFTEEN

*I'm just a sleeper*

**Manchester**

THE NEXT TWENTY-FOUR HOURS would prove a suspenseful time. After discovering the death of Margaret Burns and leaving the grief-stricken house, Harry had no idea whether the sons had been successful in their escape. Whatever happened to them he was sure his own arrest would follow at some point, probably soon after the housekeeper reported the body. There was no time to lose. On returning to Manchester, he had intended heading back to the newsroom. He knew going back there was to take a risk. Every crumb of logic of the situation told him they could be watching for him there, waiting for him to reveal something, anything that may help them draw their nets tighter. Nearly thirty years of living in a surveillance society shouted 'caution' at him. But he was sure he had not been trailed from the Burns' house. At the moment they weren't locked on to him. But very soon would arrive the last chance to slip away. If it didn't work, then it was probably all over.

Tomorrow was the day Dugdale had told him his papers would be ready.

He decided to go to the newsroom. Feign normality for as long as possible. Every hour in which he did not raise a suspicion, or a question could be critical.

In the *Herald* newsroom he had tried to focus on work. He returned the hails and greetings from the staff as he passed the desks. He's back, the smiles directed his way, seemed to say, strong journalism waving the paper's flag. Amongst the emails was an instruction from the editor. *Give the union and Burns corruption story one last piece.* His boss obviously wasn't aware of the death of Margaret Burns and wouldn't understand the significance of its occurrence if he had. Gates began to write without enthusiasm, in his gut he knew his words would not survive contact with the sensor, may not even reach them. Hallam and McBride would soon know she was dead and that the sons had gone. With their departure Gates' own usefulness to the Party would end was over, Hallam would set about clearing up the loose strands arising from Burns' death and Gates was a dead end of no value.

Lucy was not at her desk. Her absence pleased him. She had a habit of looking at him in conversation that always made him think there was something she knew, some secret or insight that gave her an advantage. It was just a feeling. A casual enquiry led to his discovery that she had called in sick and was not expected to be in for a day or two.

The internal mail made its second round at three, still circulated and distributed on a trolley, a strange and curious anachronism of newspaper houses that apparently defied the march of email and messaging. Gates had no idea why. Maybe because the authorities only expected mischief in electronic form these days and believed it was too much trouble to open mail. An envelope was put on his desk, it had a hand-written address and London postmark. Inside was Shiner's postcard and the torn half of a ten-pound note both of which he spread flat on his desk. The picture he understood, and he took the other half of the note from his wallet matching it thoughtfully noting the perfect fit which he knew it would be. He memorised the phone number and then crumpled the card and the two halves of the ten-pound note ready for disposal.

He realised his heart had quickened and his fingers were trembling.

THE door to Gates' apartment hung splintered and smashed. Inside was silent, the air made dusty by the fury of the search. He had realised before he entered his building something had happened. The old hags standing at their stalls were silent, he felt their watchful eyes on him. Climbing the stairs, he had passed the quarrelling young couple clinging together next to their door, the silent baby held tight against the woman's breast and previous anger forgotten as their fearful eyes followed him into the hallway. The rest of the house was also silent, although he knew it was not empty, its residents presumably hidden, preying whatever had taken place would not reach into their own sanctuaries.

His apartment had been searched thoroughly, and with brutishness. His belongings, pitiful and few when seen together, had been thrown into a heap in the centre of the living room—books, cushions, papers, clothes, electrical items the complete debris of his life lay collected into a pyre only awaiting the match to ignite it. He was not surprised; it was only a matter of time. On leaving the newsroom he had toyed with the option of not going home, finding a hotel, going to ground but had rejected the idea. Now he considered whether that decision had been wise. His only comfort was that whoever had wreaked the damage upon his apartment was no longer here, their work done.

He reached down and pulled the only photograph he had of Sophie, the glass cracked, and the cheap wooden frame splintered as rough fingers had forced it open to look behind the image. Sophie had been about eight and smiling self-consciously into the lens of the camera. He remembered it being taken on a spring day in the park when the two of them had just about got themselves back on their feet after leaving London. 'Smile,' he had encouraged her, coaxing the image that he wanted so much of her with the impish dimpled shy smile he loved and wearing the light summer dress he had bought her.

What did that smile mean now, he thought.

He folded the photograph and put it into his pocket and tossed the broken frame back onto the pile.

If it had been a tornado, it would have done less damage, he had no real idea what if anything they were looking for. He suspected it was the start of the process that would lead ultimately to arrest, sending him a message that his life was not his own. Such tactics were not uncommon. But he also reasoned the search meant they weren't coming for him immediately and perhaps that would be their mistake.

But for now, there was nowhere to go. They didn't want to arrest him yet, if they did, they would still be here, so he may as well wait in the apartment. He pushed the door back in place and forced himself to leave the unsmashed vodka untouched and pulling the remains of the bed together he pulled off his shoes without untying the shoelaces and then lay on the mattress. There followed a nervous sequence of hours passing in semi-darkness where Gates slipped into sleep deep enough only for his dreams to form around his fears, their vividness jolting him awake again.

In the morning the dawn was delayed by fog which formed a grey wall across the streets. He hunted through the havoc in the living room and found fresh clothes. The kitchen had been left mostly intact, which was both careless and fortunate. Because he did not know what the day would bring, he unscrewed the small fixings that held the work top to the kitchen cabinets, then with a large heave pulled it clear a few inches from the wall. Reaching down behind the cabinet he pulled free a slim envelope wrapped in a plastic food bag. Three hundred U.S. dollars in twenty and ten-dollar bills, the small supply of foreign currency that every household that could, struggled to put together, just in case. It was hardly a war chest, but it would suffice for a while. Then he ate some bread and drank some tea, carefully cleaning the draining board after he had finished. Irrationally, given the way his home had been ransacked, he didn't like the idea of the mice, ever bolder, assuming control of the flat even if he didn't return. There was no milk, but he had drunk the tea anyway thinking as he did: *What now.* What would happen after he left this place? Arrest, escape? Perhaps neither—more time to be spent in limbo. And, what of Sophie? They were questions he could not answer. But the tension they created spread like a nervous thrill through his body.

He looked around the room something telling him it was probably for the last time. An image of Sophie playing with a doll under the window with sunlight falling upon her came to him. Eating the small birthday cake with giggles of delight, her small cheeks flushed and full of the effort of forming a bellow to blow out the candle. He brushed the images away and jamming the door in its frame as best he could, he descended the stairs. He did not look back and no one watched him leave.

He decided the best option was to spend the day on the move. He rang the newsroom and told them he was taking the morning to do some early Christmas shopping. He drove his car to a nearby railway station, bought a ticket from a machine for a local destination, Oldham. Then he walked away back from the station and caught a bus in the opposite direction, towards the city centre. Leaving the station car park, he checked his watch. He had five hours before he was expected. He had a lot of time to kill. So, he did what he had told the newsroom he was going to do. He spent the day moving in stages. A bus, a taxi, walk a bit. He sauntered into the major shopping centres, aimlessly entering shops, turning back on his route, and even returning to previously visited shops, listening to the syrupy music that followed him wherever he turned. Buy time, don't set a pattern, he thought, keep your mind sharp. He spent forty-five minutes with coffee in a shopping centre coffee house watching the heavily coated passersby criss-cross the floor between shops with varying degrees of purpose and urgency. He bought stamps at a post office, a box of Christmas cards. At the Intercontinental Hotel he entered the glittering lobby and sat for a while as if waiting for a colleague to arrive. Looking around he was sure that his random movements and purchases had been successful in confusing any potential watcher.

Eventually, the time came, he made his way into the eastern section of the city taking a slow circular loop. The smog had stayed throughout the day, reluctant to leave and the streets which glistened like liquorice. The darkening blankness of the day made the pedestrians slow shadows against the grey mist. The cars and vans had their lights on easing through the mist at crawling speed in long convoys, tyres crackling on the wet surface. Away from the shopping centres the shops diminished in quality, bright fashions and Cuban coffee shops turning to the utility of haberdashers, ironmongers, and greasy cafes. The remnants of the fog and slow traffic were a blessing. Impossible to follow him by car and difficult to keep track of him amongst the pedestrian crush—even if they had realised he had left his desk.

He weaved, ducked, and double backed a few times. He was not an expert and had no illusions that he would have thrown off a professional team, supported by the city's web of cameras, the experience with Miranda had confirmed that. But he made the effort, it was all he could do. He dropped to tie his shoelace, glanced into shop windows to catch a hostile reflection, read headlines in newsagents, diverted through a small shopping centre, where workmen were clustered around the broken teeth of an escalator which allowed him to use the stairs and then exit through the car park entry barrier. Back on the shopping street around him, pedestrians hurried past, the declining weather a spur to their journeys. Ahead a security van was pulled beside a bank, a squad of helmeted security guards stood barring the pavement and for a sickening moment Gates thought it might be for him, a backstop preventing flight and he had a nervous vision of an arrest squad moving on him from behind. He listened for the heavy rapid footfall. None came and he crossed the road moving on, this time plunging towards his destination.

He entered a narrow street hung with the occasional sodium lamp and he kept walking passing a shoe-repair kiosk, a grubby pub and a sex-shop, its windows blacked out, the services to be found within were trumpeted only by a crimson blaze of the neon block that flashed the brash curves of the caricature topless showgirl. He was alone, he was sure. Loitering in the shadow of the street he waited for the last few minutes to pass and began to shiver in the cold air. A dog barked, he could hear nearby traffic and overhead planes went by dropping steadily to the airport miles distant.

He moved on and two streets later he saw the pawnbroker shop opposite. Its front was palely lit by yellow light from inside. He saw the white and blue broadband engineer van parked astride the pavement in defiance of the prohibitive yellow lines. A small barricade of plastic barriers was erected next to it and a group of fluorescent jacketed workers conferred and stared down into a minor street excavation undertaken amongst the paving stones and he relaxed.

Gates went to cross the line of traffic road, seeking a gap between the white van that lurched through the vapour, its dipped headlights glittering through the mist and the empty bus that followed it. The draught of the bus sucked at him strongly as it passed. The pawnbroker's door had a notice that said 'TUESDAY TO FRIDAY 08.30-17.00. SATURDAY 09.00-16.00. SUNDAYS BY APPOINTMENT ONLY'. It was exactly four o'clock, and in the door the CLOSED sign was displayed. When he entered the little bell above the door jangled shrilly, like a dowager's summons to afternoon tea. Inside the same sad odours of old things greeted him, musty paper, worn fabric, decayed polish and dust forced between aging wood and metal. Gates made his way through the clutter to the rear of the shop and the glass door that led into the inner sanctum of small treasures, gathered like the gifts to a departing pharaoh.

He pressed the door handle to enter his brain registering too late that a shadow waited on the other side. Gates spun, attempting to turn away, but he was too slow, his fingers were still clamped around the handle and the door was yanked inward; off-balance he stumbled through, losing his footing as he tripped into the room. Then a large burly figure was on him, grabbing his collar and the back of his coat to fling him deep into the shop room towards the presentation cabinets that glittered with silver and glass. In a bent-over stumbling run propelled by his own momentum his head made contact, bursting the display case open and the glass smashed around him. He tried to turn, struggling to move, tangled in his own clothing and the debris, feebly realising he must offer some resistance, but the man had already grabbed him by the shoulder spinning him around and suddenly his body exploded in excruciating pain as a heavy fist made two rapid solid punches into his liver. It felt like a pile driver had been forced into him. Through a red mist he felt himself being hauled on his back out of the display cabinet presumably in order that his assailant could have unrestricted access to swing his fists, his head cracked against the ruined cabinet frame and the red mist and waves of pain deepened, smothering him.

The man fell on top of him, a punch to the midriff that drove the wind from his stomach and then a powerful, practised hand gripped his throat, turning his head while the other fist pummelled the side of his face. Gates felt a tooth give way and blood filled his mouth. He flailed desperately, twisting and writhing trying to get from under the man's weight, waving his arms vaguely and lifting his legs to unseat his assailant and get free. But there was no force in his arms, no power to provide grip to his fingers and Gates felt consciousness begin to leave him. The man's fingers were grinding his throat forcing his windpipe closed and he could neither breathe or see, he began to surrender to the pain that wracked him, his movements slowing becoming feeble and a blackness rushed upon him.

The torture ended suddenly with a bang, a report like a firecracker and the fist poised above Gates' head never arrived, the grip on his throat slackened and immediately Gates' vision began to return. Through a pink mist gasping and coughing he saw the man begin to lean sideways, and he felt the crushing weight lift and slide from his body. There appeared to be blood flowing freely from the back of his head and he seemed to be trying to turn to raise an arm in defence. Gates half raised himself but was still caught under the collapsed bulk of the man still astride him. He heard a loud sickly smack. A brass poker, heavy, solid, swung through the air in a wide arc to impact against the man's temple. Gates saw the eyes turn white and vacant and with the deflation of a slowly punctured balloon, the body slumped to the floor where it lay deathly still as if frozen.

Gates struggled under the immense weight of his pain to raise himself onto his elbow and pulled his legs free from the motionless body and hauled himself groggily to one knee but could go no further. He looked at his attacker and through eyes that swam with tears he saw thick blood was oozing steadily and quickly from the back of the head forming a dark viscous pool and the skin on the man's face had turned as white as snow.

Above the unconscious body stood Lucy; the brass poker—the man's blood dripping from the tip—held with both hands in the upper arc of a golf swing grip. She stood breathing deeply, her feet planted firmly, ready to descend the poker with all the force she could muster if he moved again. Gates didn't think he would ever move again.

THE pain was thumping like rapid explosions: his ribs, cracked, throat, head and most intensely his liver which pulsed and twisted with the deepest pain Gates could imagine.

'We have to leave, there are more of them outside,' said Lucy, with urgency and she passed him a silver polishing cloth which he pressed against the wound to his head. She looked ashen and was shaking slightly but seemed in control.

Gates struggled to understand what was happening. 'W-What are you doing here? What's going on?' Gates gasped, his voice came with difficulty, his lungs still empty, his windpipe wheezing, he felt giddy and sick, his vision fuzzy at the edges.

'No time to explain, come on, you have to try and pull yourself together, we can get out the back if we are quick, but we must go *now*.'

The adrenalin began to kick in and Gates knew she was right. He pulled himself to his feet and with Lucy holding his arm at the elbow stumbled around the counter towards the inner workshop. In the back amongst the tools lay the old pawnbroker. He lay on the floor eyes open, but sightless staring glassily upwards towards the yellow ceiling. He was neatly dressed, a burgundy cardigan, faded shirt, and knitted tie, even his snowy hair looked combed. There was no blood, but his head looked a strange angle to his shoulders, the knot of the tie almost under his ear. They stepped around him and made for the rear door and the courtyard beyond. Through the clouds of pain that caused him to reel the sight of the old pawnbroker in death bought forward the realisation that this was more than an ambush against himself. They knew about the pawnbroker, his appointment, *fuck*, so they probably knew about a great deal more.

Outside, Gates began to follow the path that led through heaped and abandoned ironmongery, there seemed to be a gate at the far end. He began to stumble in its direction.

'Not that way,' hissed Lucy, yanking on his arm and pulling him in a different direction, this time onto a coal bunker and he realised she meant for him to scale a fence considerably taller than himself. He wasn't sure in his state that, that was realistic but somehow, he managed to haul himself up onto the rough concrete, as he did so he discovered a new pain announce itself at the base of his spine.

'The back will be covered; we go this way.'

There was no time to argue, and Gates followed Lucy, rolling painfully across the top of the fence. Above him he fleetingly saw another plane emerging from the low cloud the landing lights winking through the gloom. In the second that the silver airliner passed overhead like a gliding albatross Gates thought of the passengers packed together each with their individual lives full of worry, love, guilt, and work, remote and separate from each other all blissfully unaware that beneath them, right now his own life hung by a thread. The idea struck him briefly as fantastic and absurd. From somewhere else he heard cries and shouts and noises that could be men running. Then, somehow, he was moving again through the semi-darkness guided by Lucy's arm.

They stumbled into a kitchen full of heat and so brightly lit it hurt his eyes. The smell of spices, rice, and frying meat caught his throat and told him it was Chinese restaurant. A door was held open for them and they went through into some living quarters and then out of another back door. The pain had dulled a little and Gates began to understand they were following a route. A route that was planned. She knew where she was going. Outside again and two fence gates were open and then they were in a darkened service area full of industrial waste bins and vehicles before heading for the entrance and returning to the main road.

'Don't look back,' she muttered, 'it's not far, keep going.'

Gates looked anyway. The broadband van had its doors open and the engineers had turned into a black suited SWAT team, the hole in the pavement forgotten. In the distance he could now hear sirens and was aware of reflected blue lights forcing a route through the slow-moving vehicles that clogged their way. They crossed the road judging the gap in the traffic which had come to a crawl and then found themselves in a side street where after a couple of hundred metres Lucy opened the passenger door of a blue saloon and pushed Gates inside, ignoring the groans of pain that twisting his body into the passenger seat caused.

'Phone,' she hissed and held out her hand. He must have looked at her a little dumbly because she repeated the order with more venom. This time Gates understood and gave it to her, watching as she pulled the SIM card and the battery clear, snapping the first and throwing the second through the car window.

'Where are we going,' he managed to wheeze.

'We don't have long before they lock this area down,' she

said, gunning the engine. 'We need to focus on getting clear of the city. We still need some luck.' She reached across clipped his seat belt and then let in the clutch and they were on their way.

Gates fell back in the seat. He felt drowsy but forced his eyes open. He looked across at Lucy whose eyes darted between the road in front and the rear-view mirror. The adrenalin had made her cheeks shiny and her eyes bright. She seemed more adult, more serious than he remembered. Gone was the Party office zealot and cheerleader. A very different Lucy sat next to him, scared, but in control; someone he would never have imagined. The questions were beginning to find their way through the pain and the mist and forming a queue.

He was quiet for five minutes as Lucy drove north weaving their way into the drabness of the suburbs. She was watching the headlamps that switched between each other as they approached suspicious of anything that moved beyond commuter sedateness. Then he asked: 'Do you know where you are going?' He became aware that Lucy was now trembling slightly holding the steering wheel in a tight grip, breathing a little deeply as the realisation of what had happened, the luck of their escape came up upon her. The emotion had begun to catch up. 'Where are we going?'

'Later,' was all she said, her voice tense.

The car was a Fiat but bigger than Gates' with a more powerful engine. Lucy was a good driver, keeping the car speed down and the steering and power balanced. He had never seen her drive, he thought. Never been in a car with her. What else did he not know about her? Quite a lot, it seemed.

They drove on in silence.

Lucy continued to make careful progress: north onto the ring road initially towards the airport but passing the entrance slip roads before heading west towards the country. The traffic began to lighten, and the city lights fell away behind them. She left the motorway with its cameras, and they found themselves on the rural roads. In the quiet of the country the traffic seemed normal and inside the car without saying anything they both began to relax a little, the adrenalin from the escape retreating. They appeared to be safe for the moment. Gates' pain had subsided, and they could gather themselves to talk about the situation.

'We have to head south—London,' said Lucy. 'The car is good until we reach the outskirts. We shouldn't risk it further too many cameras. We can take a local train from there; I have travel cards.'

'What are we going to do in London?' asked Gates. He was unsure whether he was being saved or sacrificed. The events at the pawnbroker told him that an expected rescue from arrest by Special Branch by Dugdale's organisation now seemed remote. London seemed risky. But he had no plan, no idea of what to do now. His scheme had ended with getting to the pawnbroker without being arrested. He thought of the message from Shiner.

Somehow, he began to think his only hope lay in that direction.

The headlights of a passing vehicle illuminated Lucy's face. Gates was pleased to see it was now calm and composed.

'We follow protocol, we're going to make contact with Dugdale's people and find out what's gone wrong,' she said. 'This was meant to be an extraction not a lucky escape.'

'What's going on Lucy? I hurt like hell, I have no idea what's happening to me or why you are anything to do with it. What do you know about Dugdale for Christ's sake.'

She glanced across and must have seen the bewilderment and the rising anger in him. She took the cue that explanations were in order. There was a turn off ahead and a lay-by. Dark trees hung their branches above a few parked heavy goods vehicles. Although still reasonably early, the curtained cab windows were already dark and silent as the drivers began an evening of solitude. It was quiet and she breathed deeply before pulling over the car and closed the engine.

She turned to face him. The pawnbroker, she explained, should have been the route out of their situation. She was there to take charge of their travel and paperwork from the old man and take Gates away. She had been informed the previous night that Gates would be arrested soon, and she should no longer put herself in danger. Her association with Gates was too close, there could be questions. She was ordered to use the escape protocol.

Something, she had no idea what, had gone badly wrong,

they were waiting.

She had arrived twenty minutes before Gates and realised the shop was under surveillance. Gates hadn't been followed up until then because they knew where he would go. He interrupted her to tell her about the apartment. She shrugged, probably to make you panic, escape early, who really knows. She resumed and said that she had used the escape route through the Chinese restaurant to enter from the rear and there she had seen the pawnbroker already dead. Realising the assailant was in the front of the shop waiting for Gates, that he was unlikely to be alone and that she was undetected she had hidden in the rear store to see what would happen.

'Then you arrived and the rest you know.'

'Not exactly. What has any of this got to do with you?' He was impressed at her bravery and tenacity but remained terribly confused. His head throbbed, his ribs ached at the slightest movement, and he was sure that the pain deep inside meant that his liver had burst. He searched his pockets and realised with relief his cigarette packet if crushed was at least complete. He lit one and wound down the window.

'The life story we can do another time. But we *are* on the same side.'

'You work for Dugdale?'

She frowned and then gave a short laugh. 'A long way down the food chain, I don't know him, only heard about him by keeping my ears open, but yes. I play my part, which up until now has not been very much. Now your turn. What's going on that's suddenly made my life so expendable?'

The news of Lucy's involvement raised many more questions than it answered to Gates. He decided the rest could wait until they were somewhere more secure. 'Well, that depends on what you already know?'

She replied a little bitterly and her lucid grey eyes had lost their innocence. 'Not much. I was just told my work at the *Herald* was done. Something like you I am just a commodity in all this. Willing and complicit, but a commodity to be used bought or traded nonetheless.'

He thought about what he owed her. She had saved his life almost certainly. The thug waiting for him had not been messing about. He would have killed him. The flight from the scene had been a close-run thing, evading arrest by their fingernails. 'What do you want to know?'

'Everything. Why you are investigating the death of a union official. Why you have been writing Party nonsense. Why Special Branch are after you, just to be clear that *was* a Special Branch goon at the shop who almost killed you, so let's share shall we?'

'Oh that, yes I guessed...' He grimaced at the recollection of the beating and wondered again what he would have done if Lucy had not been there. Nothing. He would be dead or as good as, held in a Special Branch cell spitting out more teeth onto the floor. He leaned back in the seat and felt weary. She wanted to know, it seemed he had nothing to lose. So, he told her.

'Len Burns was a double agent, he was working for both sides,' he began. 'He was killed on Dugdale's orders because he suspected the truth about Burns, that he had become an informer for…the Soviets—or at least I think that's what he was doing.'

He then told her everything he knew. He started with the death of Burns. He told of his meetings with Dugdale. He told her about the blackmail of Burns and the girl and her death. He told her about Margaret Burns and how he had found her and the realisation that it was the eldest son that had informed on his own father. He told her that he thought whatever Dugdale was planning was not far away. He even told her about Shiner and the cryptic message and that he thought it must be important and possibly related to their situation. Finally, he told her about Sophie and why he had agreed to help. When he had finished, he concluded to himself he felt better. Something about unburdening himself, he concluded.

Part explanation part confessional, he wasn't sure which.

They both sat silent for a while in the darkened space of the car, each putting the pieces together with their own knowledge. 'I was a sleeper, in the paper,' said Lucy, taking her turn to explain. 'Just the occasional report on what went on waiting for when I could be useful. I mentioned your name as potentially useful a couple of years back.' She had been monitoring the news activity, the comings, and goings of people to the *Herald, as* well *as* the Party meetings that took place in the vast grey buildings across the city between minor bureaucrats and officials. She had reported anything interesting or unusual passing information discretely occasionally through the pawnbroker. It had been routine for as long as she had worked at the *Herald*. When the Burns' death took place, she sensed it was important, significant, but not why. Her instructions had simply been to stay close to Gates, be helpful, if she needed to assist him, she would receive instructions.

'Spying on me,' complained Gates wryly, 'checking I was doing as instructed.'

Hardly. She had no idea what he had been told to do. Anyway, welcome to Great Britain, everyone spies on everyone. She had just undertaken her own research and watched and waited. She knew his corruption investigation was a cover, but it was plausible. Everyone had bought it, even the editor. It made for good Party relations.

That was funny. She let out a false, nervous laugh and ran her hand through her hair. 'You made good work of the story. Very detailed.'

'I had help.'

'Where from?'

He told her. He recounted his meeting with Hallam and McBride.

'Oh Christ,' she said. 'Do you think they knew who you were informing to?'

'No idea. I don't think Hallam cares. He was running an operation on Burns and with him dead wants the loose ends disposed of. I'm one of them.'

'But they knew of the local network, they knew of the pawnbroker, your meeting.'

'Yes, they did,' said Gates grimly. 'Which means what's going on is probably much more than loose ends.'

'That means we are in danger if we make contact. We can't use protocol.'

'I suspect so.'

'What shall we do?'

'We hide, while we find out what's going on. We can't trust any escape plans now; it could be compromised. Any ideas?'

She thought. Yes, there was a friend's place, empty in the east end of the city.

'Then that's where we go for now. You try and let them know what's happened and I'll try to find Shiner and see if what he wants to tell me is connected.'

'Then what?'

He looked through the glass of the car window, a mist of condensation had formed, and he had the urge to run his finger through it, hear the squeak of his skin against hard smooth glass.

'Then we improvise.'

Gates finished his cigarette and threw it out of the window. He wished he had more faith and could offer a better way forward. For the moment he decided on getting to London and going to ground, then take it from there.

Lucy drummed her fingers on the steering wheel, already preparing to resume the driving. He noticed her fingers wrapped around the soft plastic—slim, manicured, no jewellery and very steady. She was under control.

He felt a little better and looked around the car. Then he froze. On the back seat tucked under a gym sports bag was a fleece jacket, black with chequered livery. On it he could just make out the three letters: P-O-L. His heart stopped and he must have let out a start because Lucy turned quickly to see what alarmed him.

'Who owns this—' he began.

Lucy laughed at his fright, a nervous tension reliving giggle.

'Badminton club,' she announced. 'He lent me the car for the weekend.'

THE drive to London was something of an anti-climax. They stayed away from the motorway and used A roads to make surprisingly quick progress south. It was Friday evening and the post-work rush from the offices and factories was over. The towns and villages they passed through had settled into cold sleepy early winter evenings. Nobody paid any attention to the Fiat driven by a woman with a passenger, and it occurred to Gates that there was no reason for anyone to be looking for Lucy at the moment. There was a brief unease as they passed a police patrol car sleepily observing traffic from the mouth of a side street. But it did not pull out to follow them and Gates assumed once more that if they had made a routine check it would show only a respectable police officer owner. Gates tried to keep himself awake for Lucy's sake, but eventually the effort was too much. He wedged his head between the headrest and the window and for a while escaped.

They threaded their way into London at nearly eleven in the evening, Lucy with a skill that Gates could not help but admire, kept to the residential rat-runs until into the northern fringes of London where they entered a multi-story car park. There they left the Fiat and made towards the station. At the bank of telephone boxes opposite the entrance Lucy told him to wait while she made a call. He did as he was told thankful the area was quiet and almost deserted at this time of night. Nevertheless, it was a tense few minutes while he waited for Lucy to return. When she did, she wore a grim look that was not reassuring.

'Okay, I got a response, but no news or instructions other than to just stay put, don't move, and continue normally. Not much use to us, is it, it's just a general instruction. We should get to Docklands, no one knows about that place. Let's go.'

An hour later Gates found himself in a single room in a tiny apartment deep in the jungle of a tower block estate only a stone's throw from the river. The flat was at the top of a large block and would once have been smart, but the block seemed worn and decayed. But it was clean and anonymous within the concrete tenements. A friend from university, wealthy parents had bought it for her. She was in Paris, Lucy explained. His room was warm, stifling in fact, all the heat of the floors below seemed to have risen and been funnelled into the few rooms. In the dim light of the tiny bedroom, he undressed and inspected his bruised body. A vivid red and purple rash circled his throat. The side of his face was turning a jaundiced yellow and the skin around his liver and ribs had become almost black. His throat hurt like hell, and the muscles in his neck moved and twisted like hot wires, but his breathing was okay. Everywhere hurt to the touch, but he was relieved to find there was nothing serious or that there was no evidence of internal damage, he suspected a rib was cracked but that was all.

From down the hall he could hear the shower raining lukewarm water as Lucy cleansed herself in the bathroom. Dawn was hours away and the new day would take care of itself. He sank into the narrow single bed with relief, he knew full well there was danger in this city but for the moment all that he could think of was sleep. Exhaustion claimed him. His last thoughts were on Shiner's cryptic message. *I have something.* A message calling him to meet, to meet for reasons he could only believe were linked in a way not yet apparent to the present circumstances.

## JAMES MACLAREN

Beyond his window far from his unconscious state and the streetlights below that cast their long, strange shadows, the oily flow of the Thames sullenly murmured through the small hours.

\*\*\*

# CHAPTER SIXTEEN

### *Sunrise*

**London**

'WHAT'S HE GOING TO say that we don't already know?'

From the television screen the new King looked a little self-consciously towards the camera as he rose to stand before a bank of microphones in the banqueting hall, the full red beard not quite attaching maturity to his rank. Behind him gracefully furled, were a row of union flags which under the glare of the powerful television lights provided a regal backdrop. There was a rumble of chairs as the guests took their seats, the brief murmur of their conversations receding and fading to respectful silence as the great and the powerful awaited the young Monarch's words.

'Whatever they've written for him,' Gates replied drily. He didn't envy the young man and had wondered what compelled him to accept the Crown. Following the death of a grandmother, a voluntary exile due to illness and the stripping of personal wealth, the line of succession had been reduced to a farce. In earlier times there would have been a constitutional crisis, but the point of worrying about such matters had been well-passed. Monarchy took the final tottering steps to symbolism and if people cared, for whatever reason they did not show it.

Gates and Lucy were preparing to spend their second night in the city. That morning, when day had broken Lucy had briefly left the tenement to make a phone call and gather some food. Gates had offered to go, but she had looked at him saw the bruises and the way he limped and told him to stay where he was and to get more rest. She also made the point that, unlike Gates, she still wasn't, at least not yet, being hunted. Lucy returned with some basic provisions for their stay but not much else. She had reported that they were safe for the moment and the response had been to sit tight, check back in forty-eight hours. And with that news they began their wait.

Their new home was just by the Wapping Wharf. Outside of the apartment windows it was evening, a nearby church clock struck eight and the street below was dimly lit, full of shadows. Above the city the moon rose to appear as a crescent in the evening sky, the night closing over the sounds of the cold streets.

The television on which the Monarch appeared was large, an imported flat screen model that sent a blue-white glow into the dark room. Lucy was sitting on the floor her back against the sofa, knees drawn up under her chin with her arms wrapped around her legs. The images from the screen were reflected in the large round lens of her glasses. She seemed genuinely interested in the drawled words as the King began to talk about the great future awaiting "our country" with "its powerful alliances" and "courageous friends and allies".

'"Powerful alliances"? Why do people swallow all this nonsense?'

Gates remained by the window cautiously looking down into the street below. The contempt in her voice startled him a little. This was a different Lucy to the committed dedicated reporter with her Komsomol badge of Party loyalty. He had only ever known her as the loyal Party organiser, countless hours spent recording dreary proceedings of endless committee meetings. The enthusiastic organiser of weekend bowling, volleyball, and hiking. Producer of lists, reminders, and mini-bus bookings. When he thought about it, he recalled that like many of her generation she had conducted her conversations in accepted mantras, bouquets of Party slogans and cliches to be repeated and chanted.

That she was something else, some form of undercover mole, an agent awaiting political change still left him disconcerted and unsure, not knowing quite what to say.

'Who says they do,' was all he could manage. 'You talk like a revolutionary,' he then added, which, he thought, made him the same thing. She did not reply.

'Do we just wait here?' he asked.

There was no answer. For a moment he thought he had

offended her, the categorisation of 'revolutionary' taken to mean something he had not intended. Then she said: 'Nothing else for it. We wait until we are told what to do and when to move. Simple as that.'

'Okay.' Gates stood slightly away from the window. Although he could hear the television his eyes were on the street. There was a little traffic and only a few passersby going about their business. An entwined couple, merry with a lover's celebration of some kind, wandered down the street, cheerily waving to a hurrying man with a briefcase who ignored them.

Were any of them Special Branch, Security Service or even KGB? He didn't think so, but who knows.

His speech complete, the new King had sat down to thunderous applause that rolled in waves, his young shy smile acknowledging the reception and he shared something amusing and intimate with the high Party official on his right.

The camera shifted to a dark suited newsreader who now filled the screen; behind him a picture of the King as a lowlier duke meeting the Cuban President during last year's state visit.

Lucy went to make tea and Gates heard the electric kettle begin to whistle and boil. 'It's difficult I know.' She had realised her reply had been a little short and tried to make amends. 'We are okay here, at least it looks like it. Most of these places have stayed privately owned, they have influential or foreign owners. But we don't want to move around much, there's supplies for a few days. I think we should stay here.'

'Are you that sure it's safe?'

'We're still here aren't we. Look, I don't have the faintest idea of what has gone on. Perhaps it was a local operation rolling up a cell and pulling up the roots. Let's hope so. That would be bad but not fatal, I guess. If it's anything else...well, then we are on our own and I don't have any ideas for that scenario. Do you?'

Gates turned from the window to take the offered mug of tea. He would have preferred something stronger, but an earlier hopeful search of the cupboards had yielded nothing. 'It may not be too late for you,' he said. 'As far as we know no one is looking for you yet. It's the weekend, you were reported ill you could pick up on Monday with no one noticing.'

She looked at him through her glasses as she sipped the tea. The frames made her eyes look large and soft; the hot tea caused a small brief smear of condensation on the lens'. She shook her head. 'We both know it's too late for that. After what happened they will be relentless in piecing it together. Anyway, my usefulness is over, so all that is left is to follow protocol.'

'What made you become part of all of this?' he asked. She seemed happy to accept the situation and possibly her fate.

She had sat back down on the carpet, putting her head forward between her knees and returned to hugging her knees. He knew she was twenty-seven years old. She only knew things as they had been, with no experience of a political system or society other than the one that existed now. Her rescue of him from the pawnbrokers had done more than surprise him, it had shaken him. He realised that actually he knew absolutely nothing about her. Everything he had thought had been assumed. Nothing was any longer what it had seemed, and he wondered what to believe in anymore.

'I told you, I'm very small fry. One of the tiny gears that waits instruction to turn.'

'But what motivated you to get into this. The Movement, working in secret.'

She picked up her cup and regarded him across the tea, blowing the steam away. It was if she was contemplating whether to explain, open up on her story. Was this something she wanted to explore, information she wanted to share? Internal resolution came and she began: 'It didn't feel right even when I was young. My dad was a civil servant, not senior or anything important, just an administrator, my mother was a nurse. They did nothing wrong, just did their jobs. He worked in pensions and with each new reform he realised he was helping to slice them away, devaluing them, reducing entitlements, taking away incomes. My mother worked at a local hospital and just watched the buildings collapse around her, medicines become shorter, harder to qualify for, unless you knew someone, had a friend that could help you, or could buy on the black market.' She bit her lip. 'They were good ordinary honest people and to see society become first corrupted and then fractured practically bewildered them. "It has happened so fast," he told me one day. I remember he looked beaten. "A generation, that's all," he said, "what this country built, fought for, stood for, is slipping away so fast." Lived experience we call it, don't we. Well, what happened to them and worse to others made me realise how fragile society is.'

'What did they do?'

Lucy shrugged simply. 'Nothing. What can ordinary people ever do. They kept quiet, did as they were told. Kept out of trouble and spent all their energy protecting me.'

'Was that all? Parental disappointment? Was that enough to put yourself in danger?'

'No, not all. Grief and anger.' She shrugged and Gates could see the anger. 'I lost a brother in the first Afghan war. I never really knew him, I was a young girl when he died, summer nineteen ninety-eight. His tank was attacked and exploded, he burned alive. His death destroyed my parents. They were already disillusioned, their health all but ruined, and this completely broke them. Those sorts of circumstances make you angry, bitter, losing a brother and watching your parents rot, caught between despondency and their broken hearts. How many people have had to suffer like that since?'

Gates had no idea, but he was confident it was not a small number.

'Go on.'

'At university I would have turned radical, nearly did, I mean properly radical, there were people who would march protest, get into trouble with the authorities. But it didn't turn out like that.'

Gates thought of Sophie, her rebellious student acts of small defiance. There had been others who had gone further. 'Why not?'

Lucy sighed. 'My tutor. I assume he saw something, identified my anger early. Persuaded me that protest would go nowhere. All that lay that way was conflict, trouble with the authorities, probably prison or worse. I was reading journalism and he said there was a better idea. After that it became clear there was. I didn't fully understand, still don't. The message was always the same, be patient, be ready. But it just seemed natural to become involved.'

'The *Herald*? You always seemed so dedicated. A team player.'

'Of course.' She looked at him almost surprised that he didn't understand how the roles worked. 'That's the idea. Be trusted, conform and eventually you grow useful. "Your day will come." That's what I was told, and it has.' She sipped her tea. 'Not in the way I expected, but when does life ever go in the way you expect.'

'What will happen if we get away?'

'To me? I have no idea. Resettlement, exile, refugee, whatever you want to call it I suppose. Canada has programmes to take in people. I'm not sure what the options or the quotas are but there'll be something. What about you?'

He shrugged. Some reunion somewhere with Sophie was as far as his hopes went. He didn't want to spoil the moment by saying how unlikely escape seemed.

'Well let's hope that's somewhere not around here. That won't be very joyous,' she said with a grim laugh.

He was taken back by the gallows humour and his mouth felt a little slack. She looked at him coolly, calmly as if the decision was about two models of dishwasher in a show room, comparing their various merits and deficiencies, features, efficiencies, colour, so matter of fact. She was right of course. They had to hope that Dugdale's resistance would protect them. The alternative was unthinkable.

It was then he reminded her about Shiner. Who he was and the message he had sent him. Why he thought he may know something relevant.

'You think this is important,' she asked.

'I do. I think he knows something that may help all of us make sense of what's happening, you, me and Dugdale. It may even help if we can use it somehow.'

'What are you suggesting we do?'

Gates told her he should go and find Shiner. It was better than sitting here.

She thought about it. It was breaking the protocol, but it also made sense. 'You said he's in the estuary marshlands to the east. How will you go?'

It was his turn to think. Public transport was to be avoided.

'There's an underground car park.' He thought of his own solid Fiat abandoned in Manchester. He'd fired that into life with a screwdriver a number of times and a decent car thief would have had its door open with a wire hanger in ninety seconds, so Gates expected he'd only need a couple of minutes more. 'There'll be something crude enough to liberate.'

'I'll come with you.'

'No, that's silly, too risky. We'll be more obvious, and you need to stay put here in case there are instructions.'

'You're not going to come back.'

'Yes, I am, of course I am. It's just more sensible on my own.' He sensed sudden vulnerability in her, the thought of being alone and waiting was unwelcome.

But then Lucy nodded and gave no more argument. 'Okay, go. But don't be long.'

The television picture was fading to an image of the union flag with its embedded sickle that filled the screen and slowly waved in an unseen studio breeze. The scene turned solemn, majestic; the background lights turned soft. A long drum roll began the national anthem, and a choir began to sing the words.

*God save our gracious King*
*Long live our noble King...*

He swore he saw Lucy's lips moving silently as she watched the screen. But there was no sound just a moistening of the eyes.

THE next day he found his vehicle, not quite believing his luck. A small Fiat parked in a corner of the basement, similar to his own, with a thin coating of dust covering the body. He also saw one of the tyres was slightly soft and concluded the vehicle was not in regular use. The coat hanger he had brought with him, raised the door lock with a satisfying click and fifteen minutes of inexpert fiddling was enough to fire the engine into life. Further pleasure was found in a half-full tank of fuel, and trailing blue smoke behind it, the tough little car throatily exited the car park ramp into the outside world.

The city was deserted, a cold sun and the peace of a Sunday morning kept the streets clear of people except those who could sleep and those in need of a church. The few pedestrians moved as slow shadows against a morning winter mist which rose from the river. Traffic was light and he used the Rotherhithe tunnel to cross under the Thames and then struck east following the main route that pointed out of London. A frost had appeared overnight and the few cars that were around drove with their lights on, their tyres crackling lightly on the crusted surface. He thought about his destination. *It's pretty wild out there, but people mind their own business, they don't attract trouble*, Shiner had explained once, when Gates had asked him why he kept a boat in a half city made of outcasts and travellers; *no surveillance, easy place to keep secrets.*

The carriageways stayed empty, and the main route he was following would have taken him without hindrance to the south coast. Instead, he took a slip road and without warning he found himself in the wasted miles of estuary land, used untidily for industry, scrap yards, workshops, tyre distributors and car repairs, most of the area was long bankrupt and mostly abandoned and the desolation grew around him. On his left, he passed a wharf area containing derelict sheds that sat in the shadow of a ruptured cargo freighter, its decks rose three storeys high and were streaked with long fingers of rust. Glancing in his mirror he caught the drunken spires of cranes etched against the grey sky, their thin useless limbs not yet devoured for scrap.

Gates was feeling his way. He had rung the number on Shiner's card and the boy had answered. *Look for the cafe, The Happy Kettle. They'll direct you, that's all he told me to say.* Gates did as he was told and began looking for the cafe although finding refreshment in this confused wilderness of nature and industrial decay seemed unlikely.

He bumped over a railway track and the rusting hulks of more coastal cargo ships came closer. He realised that people did live here, there were small groups of shabby caravans and huts with peeling paint, and which had been converted to dwellings. Amongst them children played in the dirt and ran between clothing that fluttered on washing lines like untidy flags at a regatta. Thin beams of sunlight broke through the mist, and he began to crawl through the avenue of temporary buildings each with grimed and dusty windows and with relief he caught sight of two container buildings parked and joined together, resting on large breeze blocks. A red neon sign proclaimed 'CAFE', underneath a jaunty coloured sketch of a whistling kettle and a chalked smudged menu board stood guard at its entrance, in the window a smaller sign saying, 'OPEN'. *He said you might call,* the boy had said. *He'll be there on the river,* the young man, used to being used by Shiner and discarded but loving him all the same. *It's where he goes when he has had enough of me or someone's chasing him for revenge or money.* The boy had rung off, his duty complete. Gates wondered who he was that Shiner would trust with his privacy and could think of no-good answer.

He pushed open the door and found the place empty, surprisingly clean, the plastic and Formica fittings shiny and glistening. Behind a counter at the end of the cabin a pretty young woman with long dark hair and smooth olive skin looked up from a magazine and regarded him neutrally, a woollen shawl of crocheted colours around her shoulders. Behind her a water boiler popped and whistled, and an old, large fridge hummed and clicked.

'I'm looking for someone, they have a vessel, the *Sunrise*, can you help me?' Gates asked in a polite tone that he hoped was a casual enquiry.

'Who do you want?' she replied with a smile in an accent that sounded sweet, eastern Europe. 'We'll see. Might depend upon whether they want to be found.' Her eyes twinkled but were guarded at the same time. Her voice was rich and musical, the Romanian accent adding romance to the rigid English words, a weird, imagined image of her traversing an ancient marketplace or singing from a balcony came into his head.

Gates gave her the name.

A bead curtain rattled, and a man joined her from what Gates presumed was the kitchen, older, unshaven, heavy tattoos on thick arms, large, knuckled hands the callouses washed white from dishwater and detergent. They spoke together and Gates now recognised a few Romanian words. The last ones were directed towards himself.

'He probably won't want to see you,' the girl translated. 'People here don't like strangers,' she added, her eyes grave and she gave a small shrug.

Gates laughed to give reassurance. 'He will want to see me,' he said confidently. 'I owe him money. I've come to pay him.'

The old man grunted and said some words in Romanian. The dull suspicious eyes glinted but there was amusement too. The girl also laughed.

'He says you are not like his usual men; you are much older and more scruffy, and you don't look like a policeman,' she paused and became serious as the thought he might be occurred to her. 'You're not, are you?'

I am not, he assured her. 'How long since you have seen him?'

The girl repeated the question in Romanian looking up at the man. Her father, Gates decided. Her fair skinned sweet smoothness was still waiting for the ravages of gravity and time while his body had become twisted, flabby, and contorted with years of alcohol, comfort food and the grind of finding a living. But despite the interval of years the resemblance was clear. There was a conference between the two.

'Two days ago,' the girl announced at its conclusion. 'He came by to pick up the key to his boat.'

'By himself? I don't want to disturb him if...if he has company.'

She shook her head. 'We weren't here. My brother gave him the key. We keep it for him, and he hasn't returned it.'

'Good he's probably there then. Where is his boat? Is it far?' The shanty areas went on for miles, abandoned wharfs and warehouses, merged with marshes and murderous tidal waters that fused an abandoned economy and the hash ingress of the North Sea into an environment fit only for the migrant groups that collected there.

'No, not far,' she said, shaking her head. 'About a mile. Turn towards the water at the blue containers, just a few metres further on there's a collection of house boats. Look for the Dutch barge. That's his.'

As she finished speaking three men entered the cafe and waved to the father and daughter team. They wore worker clothes and smelt of tobacco and sweat. It was just mid-day, and the Romanian father grunted a return greeting and found beer cans in a fridge which he held up in a salutation to his new customers. The group huddled in a far corner of the cabin around the plastic tables sitting on the patio chairs and began to smoke and talk. Gates decided it was time to leave. He was sure from the description the girl had given he could find Shiner's hideaway.

He thanked the girl and turned towards the exit, then stopped hearing something that the men began to mutter. Their accents were thick, but they spoke English, the international common denominator of communication when different nationalities converge. He caught the words 'kops', 'immigration' and 'customs'.

'Where was this?' he broke in and they looked up in surprise, seeing him for the first time. Suspicion and mistrust immediately directed his way. 'Sorry, I overhead.' He excused himself. 'Has there been a raid? It's alright,' he added hurriedly, seeing their faces, 'I'm not with the authorities of any kind. Just looking for an old friend.'

One of the men shrugged and swilled his beer. 'Some goons arrived from the city.'

There was silence for a moment. 'It happens,' another added.

'Do you know what they wanted? When was this?'

'Couldn't say, but they knew where they were going, happened about five this morning, well before daylight.'

'Many of them?'

'Just one car, but probably more around, I'm guessing.'

Gates did not need to know more, his stomach sank, but he smiled and muttered his thanks and left hurriedly. Jamming the car into gear and ignoring the protesting suspension he headed along the broken road in the direction the girl had told him. The road disintegrated further and the thud and clatter from the front of the car told him he was going too fast. He saw the blue containers suddenly, turning a corner he came upon the collapsed pile of blue rusting metal, old shipping containers that had toppled over to form an unlikely but prominent and effective traffic roundabout. He pulled to their left and followed the deeply pitted road back towards the shore and after a couple of hundred metres saw the masts of half a dozen vessels moored or abandoned against rotten wharfs. Through the tall reed he glimpsed the brown water that slapped and rippled in the wind. There were several river and coastal vessels floating and beached, but he instinctively knew the stub upright wheelhouse of the one vessel was the Dutch barge he sought. It was the only one that looked like it had not been abandoned. He stopped at the side of the road which was now little more than a track that ran a few metres above the water's edge. He left the car and dropping down on the mud path through the reeds he found the barge pulled tight against a broken jetty that had seen far better days. On the bow was the name, *Sunrise*. Its paintwork was worn and some of the deck timber looked split and warped. But the ropes appeared in good condition, the visible metalwork was bright, pulleys greased, and the vessel rode well in the water.

Gates realised that the mooring was in an inlet set off from the main channel, the tide pulling the mud and silt away to form an unlikely harbour, the ugly exposed bank of silt showing the tidal reach to come. On the far side he could make out a group of men and youths gathered at the shore who appeared to be fishing, too noisily Gates suspected, for great success, the sound of their raucous shouting and laughter drifting across the water. Behind them was a group of caravans loosely pulled together in an encampment that was possibly temporary but was transitioning into something more permanent. A flight of water birds lifted from the water and in formation headed east, arrow straight for the open sea a few miles distant.

Gates hauled himself aboard and found himself on the deck. The vessel appeared deserted and apart from the creak of moving wood appeared completely silent. The barge wasn't large, possibly sixty feet, but its stubby beam was broad, built for stability in the blunt short waves of the coastal waters of the North Sea. There were only two entrances into the interior that he could see. The door at the rear of the wheelhouse was locked. The curtained windows were all drawn as were the small portholes. At the stern was a deck hatch which was also locked, and he thought was bolted from the inside. Of the two options the wheelhouse door offered the better prospect, and he began to look around for a means of prying the lock. A rusty chisel abandoned on top of a locker provided the means and Gates levered the lock easily, the door swinging open. Inside it was dark except for the weak light bleed that filtered around the drawn curtains. There was a buzz and whizz in front of his face, and he swiped ineffectively at the flight of flies which, annoyed at the disturbance to their peace, scattered like a formation of fighters surprised in a dogfight.

He realised there was a cold sweat on his back that made his shirt cling to his skin. He called anxiously down into the darkness, 'Shiner, Shiner, Tom, are you there?' there was no reply. A hatch and entrance led down into the interior blackness. The atmosphere smelt dense and musty from trapped hot air and human sweat and something else, something that was slightly sweet and sickly. He stumbled down the steps and felt for a light switch. Not finding one he lit a match. The flame flickered briefly in the small space on the soft furnishings, the wood edges, before it died, he saw the slope of the hull and reached to pull back a port hole curtain and grey light fell into the cabin.

The living space and sleeping area beyond was destroyed, sea locker lids forced from their hinges, cushions ripped apart with their feathers still drifting lazily in the still fetid air. In the corner a small old-fashioned iron potbellied stove had been pushed over, the soot and ash spilling through the round open top across the rug like a flow of volcanic lava then kicked off.

Books had been pulled from the shelves and the contents of the tiny galley cupboards, tins, and packets, lay mashed and thrown together. Everything that could be pulled apart had been. In the centre of it Gates recognised the body of Shiner.

He was naked and had been tied to a chair by the wrists and ankles, his head thrown back, glassy eyes staring lifelessly at the ceiling a few inches above his head. A mix of congealed blood and dried vomit lay across his chest dripping towards his groin. The sickly-sweet smell of congealed blood and vomit was now overpowering, and Gates reached for his handkerchief to muffle his nostrils. The white flesh, its middle-aged muscle folded from his frame drooped sadly from his shoulders and on his flanks. His skin was mottled with black bruising that reached across his body as a macabre dreadful map. In the grey sideways light of the port hole, he looked a broken and pitiful sack of skin held in position only by the powerful black plastic zip ties that held him upright in the chair. The single bullet hole to the forehead told Gates the end finally had been swift. Probably fired at close range, it had shattered the contents of his skull onto the bulkhead behind to create a grim mosaic of blood, hair, shreds of brain and skin.

New formations of flies had gathered grouped and regrouped, to gorge and feast on the livid flesh.

Why was he not more shocked?

Shiner had tried to hide, tried to hide in his secret little retreat buried in the middle of a ghetto of the unwashed and they had found him anyway, probably, thought Gates, because they knew exactly where to look. The realisation somehow did not surprise Gates, what he wasn't sure of was why, but he knew in his heart that it was connected to himself. It was more evidence to support his growing fear that the pawn shop had not been an isolated operation. They knew more and that meant they could know about Lucy, where they were hiding, Dugdale, anything was possible. He felt his hand shaking and he had an urge to run, leave the scene as quickly as he could, put as much distance as possible between him and this place as he could. But he steadied himself, forced himself not to panic. He sucked in his breath forced the shaking to stop and surveyed the scene again, this time more methodically, willing his mind to act rationally, to try and make sense of what was going on.

Shiner had wanted to tell him something, or give him something, something he knew Gates would consider important. An extraordinary calm descended over him, a lucidity that almost a relief. He lent back against the narrow door frame and though through what must have happened. They didn't know he had planned to meet Gates, otherwise why not just wait, and catch them both. Why had they killed him, tortured him, left him like this? There were other options, plenty of detention facilities they could have used. He could just have been disappeared. But he knew the answer as he asked himself the question. The thugs that had done this were in a hurry with no time for legal niceties or conformities, even with the wide-ranging discretion the law in the country offered. These, he decided, were assassins, outside the local law, Russians? Quite likely, and almost certainly KGB. Had they found what they were looking for? The destruction seemed total. Shiner's life had been dispensed with. Whatever Shiner had wanted to pass to him, whatever secret these people had wanted, was gone, he could assume gone with the people who would do this to a human being.

There was nothing to be gained by staying here.

He left the carnage with relief climbing into the grey sunlight sucking in the moist air taking it deep into his lungs. The tidal flow had caused the *Sunrise* to rise a little in the water which was becoming choppier. Across the bay the group fishing at the water's edge had noticed his arrival and were shouting and calling, although what they were saying, was indistinguishable, the noise carried away on the wind. But he could see they were beginning to move his way and the sounds and calls were becoming louder and more strident as they gathered to follow the track along the far shore to come around the inlet and investigate. There was about ten minutes, he calculated before they would cross the neck of the inlet and could prevent him returning the way he had come. Gates had the sense it was better to avoid any involvement and turned towards his car, scrambling back up the bank, feeling the soil slide away beneath his shoes. Somewhere was the path he had used to get to the boat but in his haste, he had mislaid the way and made direct for the vehicle over the coarse muddy grass.

Amazingly from the line of river boats rotting alongside the sinking jetties heads had begun to appear, white faces, previously hidden, realising that this was not authority returning and now pulled from their solitude with curiosity overcoming their fear. He reached his vehicle and pulled the door open. Then something caused him to halt. Someone was already there on the far side of the car waiting for him. A head of dark hair and face of dark skin, her eyes just visible above the line of the roof, and with surprise he recognised the girl from the cafe. Her appearance momentarily stunned him, and he wondered what she wanted, why she was there.

'Is he dead?' she asked.

He nodded and her head dropped. When she looked up, she gulped a little, her eyes nervous and uncertain. 'Get out of here, quickly, you must go, there is nothing you can do,' he said, and turned towards the car door.

'Wait,' she blurted, 'I have something. It's for you. Probably I think what they came after him for.' The noise of the approaching crowd was growing louder. Gates hesitated only briefly then as if finding agreement, they circled the car towards each other meeting at the rear. Without words she offered a brown paper wrapped package carefully presented, heavily taped. He turned it over in his hands and saw it was unmarked. He looked at it then at her, his eyes asking the question.

'He gave it to my papa. Just said you may come for it. Give

it to no one else.' She stopped, seeing his bewilderment. 'Papa sent me after you, he realised it must be you who he meant.'

A final precaution. Too late and too small to save his life. How had he not told them? The noise and shouting had now reached the neck of the inlet. The girl looked nervously in the direction of a small but growing crowd that was heading their way. 'Take it, quickly, I think you had better go.' She looked back past the *Sunrise* which rocked gently against the jetty. 'You can carry on around the way you are facing. It will loop back onto the road. It's only a track from this point but your car will make it, just keep going.'

From the approaching crowd he could hear a man call in accented English: 'What's he found? Who is he? What does he want?'

Gates nodded and took the package. He indicated towards the approaching crowd. 'What are they after?'

She looked unhappily towards the group moving around the edge of the inlet. 'Camp travellers, they are new here, they arrived a few weeks ago. They bring only trouble, they would have seen what happened this morning now they want to pick the bones, see if anything has been left. We try to live a quiet life around here, we give no one trouble. These people just draw attention to us before they pick up and move on. Now you really, better go.'

Gates looked at the girl's face and saw concern in the soft eyes. He pulled open the door of the car. 'Thank your father for me. Look after yourselves.'

She nodded, gave a brief thin smile, and turned back into the bushes. Gates ground the car into gear and without reaching second followed the track around the marshy foreshore taking care to avoid the water filled potholes that threatened to remove the exhaust. The car was not young and the grinding from the suspension had become ominous. In the end it took twenty minutes to work his way back onto the main road and point the vehicle west back towards the city. It was now afternoon and dark piles of cloud had arrived to sink low across the city scape, the air was sharp with cold and damp.

Gates drove on. Behind him large fat seagulls swooped and glided over the estuary shore patrolling the decay and debris that blanketed the shoreline stretching as far as one could see.

***

# CHAPTER SEVENTEEN

*Arise ye workers...*

**Poland**

> *"Arise ye workers from your slumbers*
> *Arise ye prisoners of want"*

THE FIRST TWO LINES of *The Internationale* rose with enthusiasm from the hundred or so throats and lifted into the rafters of the student assembly hall. The bright and breathy female voices with their high notes melding with young male baritones to form a rendition of the anthem that would have pleased the spirit of its French revolutionary creator.

> *"We'll change henceforth the old tradition*
> *And spurn the dust to win the prize"*

The emotional words of the epic composition rang out and the air fizzed with enthusiasm and youthful belief. With cropped or pony-tailed hair and crisp white shirts topped with red scarfs, the large group of students looked every inch the model of healthy and happy communist youth conducting their final assembly before a rare departure away from confines of the college campus.

Later in the one of the staff common rooms, the instructor in charge of the assembly would beam with pride and proclaim to colleagues how effective they had been in the rehabilitation of troublesome youth. Social control bringing about educational and behavioural outcomes that would make these young people model citizens back in their own countries. Very few would ever again stray far from compliance with authority.

'Excellent,' the instructor intoned after the rousing words had died away. 'Time for the buses. The Baltic Komsomol Congress awaits. Now, collect your things and be ready to board in one hour. We have a long drive to Warsaw and then a longer train journey to Vilnius.'

The students filed out noisily, a scraping of chairs mixing with excited chatter. Above the exit a large portrait of Lenin gazing sternly into the distance watched over the assembly. Sophie filed out with them, linking arms with her friend Cecile. Cecile was excited, she was looking forward to the adventure of the bus and train journey with her friend, and then the Congress with the singing and cheering and seeing in person important Party officials who had travelled from all parts of democratic Europe to be with them, inspire them. It occurred to her that Sophie seemed less thrilled at the prospect, She wondered why Sophie did not appear to quite share her excitement and it seemed to her that her friend was a little subdued. Was it her period time? No, she would have told her. Nevertheless, she looked fraught and a little haunted and Cecile worried about her.

Cecile squeezed her friend's arms gently and nodded towards the side of the vestibule as they began to file out into sunlight. 'That woman is looking at you. She's faculty, right?'

Sophie followed Cecile's glance and looked across to the fair-skinned young woman in jeans and a large leather jacket with fur collar, too warm for the inside, but a useful precaution against the Polish winter climate approaching, and who appeared to be watching them. 'Oh, yes, tutor from my ethics class.' Sophie said hurriedly, 'Listen, I need a word with her before we go. I'll catch up with you later.' She kissed her friend who frowned slightly at Sophie attracting someone else's attention, but Cecile moved on continuing with the jabbering throng to collect luggage and packs of sandwiches. She had decided she would talk to Sophie when they got to Vilnius about how she felt about her, she had been meaning to for weeks but had no idea where to begin. Finally, she had concluded that four days in a foreign city was just the right time for their friendship to blossom into something more and tell Sophie exactly what her feelings were.

Gina was leaning with her back against a heavy iron radiator. 'Hello Sophie,' she said with a broad open smile, 'walk with me a while, we won't be long, I know you are leaving soon. Let's go somewhere private.'

They strolled across the large open quadrangle towards a block of empty classrooms and tutor halls set behind the main newer complex. A hundred metres from them, a batch of students were being put through a physical education class under a cold sky by a stern female instructor who barked encouragement and simultaneously scolded them, the students anxiously twisting and jumping to comply with the shouted commands and the shrill whistle that hung never far from her lips.

Sophie had seen Gina only twice since meeting outside on the grass four weeks ago. The first time had been a chance meeting in a corridor between classes.

The Baltic Komsomol Congress will take place in Lithuania next month, Gina had told her as they once again sat on the same grass bank. You're a third-year student, and therefore eligible, apply for a place, name me as a sponsor and we'll see what happens.

So, she had and had been surprised when a place on the much sought after delegation had been allocated to her. Gina had found her again shortly after the news, seeking her out as she left a lecture and had looked satisfied when Sophie told her what she already knew. What will happen? she had asked. Gina had only told her that it was good news, an opportunity perhaps. But it was for others to decide. After that until today, there had been nothing and Sophie assumed she would return from Vilnius and remain at the campus, carrying around her secret, attempting to remain normal while her mind aired all sorts of doubts, questions, and fears. Without news of a plan, she had not really been looking forward to the Congress and had found herself unable to match the enthusiasm of her Norwegian friend, Cecile.

Turning away from the exercising students, Gina went behind one of the large single-storey buildings and used a fire door to lead Sophie into the front of a deserted classroom. It was an older classroom block, little-used now, gloomy with dark floors and peeling walls. The windows were long slits high on the walls while the wooden desks and metal chairs had been cleared and stacked at the rear of the room. Only the tutors fixed long console station at the front of the classroom remained.

Gina lit a cigarette and with the filter between her lips went behind the console and bent down to open one of the storage cupboards. 'We haven't got long,' came her voice from below the desk. 'Here, you'll need this.' She stood up pulling a regulation black student rucksack, exactly like the one that sat packed and ready waiting on her bed to be collected. This one was full too. Gina drew on the cigarette and waved a hand over the bag which she put at Sophie's feet. 'This has all you need. There are new papers in there but leave them alone for now. Keep your current identity documents on you, you'll need them for the train in Warsaw. Don't worry about this bag, I will get rid of it later.'

Sophie nodded. Realisation what was happening dawned upon her.

'Nothing personal, Sophie, do you understand.' Her voice had a sharp edge 'Take nothing sentimental or anything that identifies you, no photographs or momentous. It won't take long to move you, but it will be risky, and you may be stopped, and your papers checked.'

Sophie nodded again.

She gave Sophie further brief instructions and then looked into the girl's apprehensive face.

'Trust me, Sophie. Just do exactly as I say, and everything will be fine. There will be someone with you all the time, you won't be doing this on your own. Then you will be free just as we said. You won't be coming back here or anywhere like it.'

Sophie could feel her stomach tightening in apprehension.

'Where am I going?'

'I can't tell you that love. If something went wrong…well, it'd be dangerous for others.' Gina saw the look that spread across the young girl's face. She said quietly: 'You do trust me Sophie—you trust me, don't you? I am on your side.' Gina took the girl by the shoulders and looked deeply into her face. 'You need to say yes with your voice not just your eyes.'

She did so. 'Will I see my dad?' she asked.

Gina nodded. 'That's the plan sweetheart, but I don't know how or when. But you will very soon, I am sure.' She reached across and stroked the girl's hair reassuringly.

Sophie gulped, nodded, and reached down to pick up the replacement bag. She then looked up into the face of the taller woman. Her look was a little more confident, determined. 'I'm ready,' she said.

Gina smiled and unexpectedly kissed her on the forehead. Sophie could smell the warm fug of cigarettes and perfume and felt the salty splash of a tear fall on her skin.

'That's my girl, now go, and good luck.'

Sophie picked up the rucksack, went back into the quadrangle to mingle with the student throng and board the waiting line of bland white buses.

## **London**

THE streets around Limehouse were quiet and Gates stopped the car. It was a short walk back to the apartment block, but he now hesitated uncertain what may await him and considered what to do. On the return drive he had switched on the radio, searching for the news. The airwaves were clear of reports of any manhunt or arrests, there were no warnings of counter-revolutionary activity or foiled plots. The BBC was replaying a recent speech by the new King. '*...it is time for the nation to ensure we pull together, pool our talent and our loyalties in our renewed efforts to serve this country, creating greater success...*' Broadcasting the King was no surprise, nor was the call for national loyalty and coming together. But normally the media would be ablaze with such news of successful action by the authorities against traitors or foreign agents.

Around him lay old tenement flats and wasteland, semi-abandoned basins, and dockland buildings. Dozens of other vehicles were parked without discipline, mounted on kerbs, across verges, tightly packed. Gates judged it would be sometime before anyone noticed the car left here let alone investigated it. Leaving the vehicle, he walked towards the river where a kilometre away as dusk began to fall the shore lights of Canary Wharf formed a yellow ribbon that brightened the point between where river ended, and concrete began. He lit another cigarette; God knows how many he had smoked in the last forty-eight hours. On a bridge over a basin inlet some youths were playing on bikes and skateboards. They were too far away to take an interest in him. A bench sat overlooking the river and he paused despite the river's chill to sit and look across the water towards the chrome and steel buildings. As he smoked, he thought about what would come next.

It was still secret.

Whatever the Soviets and their Special Branch colleagues were doing to destroy Dugdale's plans they were doing without involving the police or local authorities. That would hamper them a while. Did the secret lay in the brown parcel he now held and which Shiner had given his life for?

Lucy.

She was alone and waiting a short distance away, desperate for news from Gates, trusting in help from allies that would no longer come. Her short life had been carefully devoted to a cause that Gates believed was now doomed. He wondered if they had been to the flat already. He had to check. And what about Sophie? Where did this leave the plan to extract her? What had happened to her? He dreaded to think and tried to put the dark thoughts that clouded his mind away. The noise of the skateboarding youths moved away, and Gates decided the time had come to move to leave the solemn river with its inky musings behind.

BEHIND the door Gates could hear the soft murmur of a television. There were no other sounds but obviously Lucy was waiting for him. His knock on the door was greeted after a couple of seconds by a rattle of bolts and it swung open to reveal her standing in the hallway. There were no lights except for the glow of the television on which news pictures flickered. Gates guessed she had barely moved from the sagging sofa from where she could concentrate on the images.

'How did you know it was me?'

She gave a slight wry smile. 'Who else? And if it was the police, what was I supposed to do?' was her fatalist reply.

She had made coffee and poured him a cup and asked him what had happened, her eyes grave. In response he held up the brown wrapped parcel and told her about Shiner's death.

'Dead?' her eyes took on worry, but they were both past any more shock. 'Oh my God, that must have been horrible, who…'

'I am guessing KGB, it wasn't pretty.' Said Gates and sighed. 'If this is what I think it is, then we are in danger and probably don't have much time. Lucy we can't rely on rescue.'

Gates realised he was sweating and that it was not the enforced heat of the apartment causing it. He wiped his hands on his handkerchief and then began to tear and rip at the brown paper pulling it free. He paused, momentarily puzzled when he saw the Christmas paper, but only briefly and ripped that aside to reveal the sheafs of neatly photocopied paper. He placed them onto the coffee table neatly aligning the edges to match the table's angles, then hesitated, almost unwilling to discover what they contained.

'Look at these,' he said grimly. Lucy took a seat beside him, and they both studied the pile before them. Then Gates began to lift the papers one by one inspecting them quickly before handing across to Lucy who also scanned the content before placing it face down. Her eyes were large and her look uncertain. Both could feel the excitement that they were looking at something of importance.

'These are identity documents,' he said slowly, 'Russian identity documents. But who do they belong to? Who is this man?' She held up the copy of the passport with the man's photograph. 'I have never seen him.'

'Nor me,' said Gates, and continued lifting the papers, looking at them thoughtfully. 'But look at this, it's not just an identity, it's a complete new life ready and waiting in Moscow.'

'How could he have come by all of this? Who would have given it to him?'

Gates blew out his cheeks. 'No idea. He is…was…a very resourceful man with a great many contacts. But this…this is beyond his usual trade.'

'So, what should we do with them?' Lucy asked, a question that irritated Gates slightly, as if he could have an answer to that yet! 'What do they tell us?'

Gates did not answer. His heart had stopped and then he realised his breathing had ceased as well. He was looking at the next sheaf of papers under the identity documents.

'Oh Christ,' he whispered, struggling to believe his eyes. 'Jesus, no wonder they went after him like they did.' Slowly he passed the American intelligence assessment across to Lucy who looked at it uncomprehendingly. How, the fuck had Shiner come by this, thought Gates. The implications…too great to imagine.

Lucy was still behind, 'I don't understand, what is all this?'

| Case Officer | SECSTATE confirms negotiations and guarantees with monarch representatives ongoing. Wording and form of national address subject to POTUSREP/KINGREP agreement. |

| CLOUDBURST (CB) | CB provided strategic overview & SITREP on opening LIONHEART Network and transfer of authority preparation: |
|---|---|
| | COMMS CONTROL: GREEN (BBC) |
| | MILAUTH: GREEN (Defence Council) |
| | STRAT TRANSPORT: GREEN. ATC, Rail, Ports, Type A routes |
| | ECON: GREEN, (BoE) |
| | GOV COGS: GREEN (Gov CIS restriction) (secure key sites) |
| | CIVPOL: AMBER. Note as assessed concern over police & security service loyalty to SOV. Executive measures on identified target list include covert pre-op target tracking. U.S. INT/OPS cooperation measures agreed |
| | SOV LEGIT: GREEN (See above) |

'Burns wasn't the double-agent, we thought.' It was coming to him now, a horrible realisation. A realisation they had followed entirely the wrong route, pecked at the breadcrumb trail exactly as Hallam and his Soviet superiors had planned for them. 'I was wrong, I think he was the decoy. The real source, the leak to the operation was with the Americans.'

Lucy seemed unsure. 'How can you be so certain? Burns was definitely implicated, what about his sons?'

'I don't think they'd have got anything from Burns. If they did it was a bonus.' The excitement in him rose further. 'He planned to escape rather than be trapped. No, the purpose was to make Dugdale, who then made me, look in the wrong direction. This—' he scrabbled amongst the papers and held up the passport photocopy. 'This is who they wanted to protect.' He breathed heavily; his head was spinning as the knots of the situation he had been in quickly unravelled. 'Dugdale, me, we fell for it, all of it. It was an elaborate disinformation plan. They gave Dugdale a traitor to clean up which gave Dugdale and the Americans the confidence to proceed.' Gates slapped his forehead with the palm of his hand three or four times. 'Stupid, stupid, so stupid. Fuck, they've played us all. They've had a source all along, we were just meant to believe it was Burns.'

Lucy fingered the thin sheaf of intelligence reports. 'What about those, what do they mean?'

'It means they know everything...well as much as they probably need. They have access to an American intelligence source. They've known what's been planned all along. They haven't been trying to stop Dugdale's plan, they've just been waiting for him to try.'

'The sleepers...the names, everything?'

'Depends, what this guy had access to. My guess is Dugdale, and others were more cautious than that. It would be more compartmentalised, but I'm only guessing. But strategic plans, timetable—yes. They seem to have that.'

'So why have they moved now, why are they arresting and killing people?'

Gates considered that. 'Because of this.' He tapped the sheaf of papers with his index finger bearing down hard. A light bulb that had been flickering for a while, the current and the light not stable now began to burn with more intensity. 'Their agent's blown, somehow Shiner, God help him, intercepted or was given this material. He knew I had been in touch with Dugdale but didn't know why. He was trying to get this to me. When the Soviets realised it was missing, there was no point in waiting any longer.'

'So, what do we do? We must warn Dugdale?'

'Easier said than done. He's not a man you pick up the phone to. He's practically a ghost. We left the only means I had of contacting him dead on the floor of his pawnshop.'

It was Lucy's turn to stand up. 'I'll go and call in. Warn them, get a meeting.'

'No,' he said sharply, 'you're not thinking straight. We've no idea who we can trust. We have no idea what's happening. In fact...' he looked at her, the implications dawning on him. Then he looked around the small bleak apartment. 'We don't know what's compromised and have no idea whether we are safe here anymore. We should leave.'

'Where do we go? We must tell someone, Dugdale, the Americans, who? Do you have a plan?'

Gates reached in his pocket for a cigarette but realised he

had none left. His fingers had curled around the photograph of a young Sophie. He couldn't bear to pull it free, and he forced his thoughts away. But his fingers were still in his pocket, and he found something else... Maybe... Maybe there could be a plan.

The thought for a moment leaving her question hanging. Then.

'Not a good one. But possibly'.

## *Vilnius Lithuania*

SOPHIE watched as the stick-figures worked their way to safety—then suddenly the rails were vibrating, there was a rush of wind, and the view was cut off by the sleeper train to Moscow, accelerating out of the central Vilnius station. The double-decker dining cars and sleeping compartments were like a cliff and took half a minute to pass and by the time it had cleared the small column of drifters had vanished silently into the orangey dark. She held her breath too frightened to exhale and although noise was all around her the air felt eerily silent. These were the sprawling marshalling yards that covered the eastern side of the city, linking the Baltic Sea and the teeming container port with the vast never-ending Eurasian rail network, a nerve map of metal track that could carry goods from the ice-bound port of Vladivostok on the Pacific coast to the thin artery of the English Channel faraway in the west.

Sophie had been waiting in the darkness for nearly half an hour although the time felt much longer. Behind her, distant and towards the bright lights of the main passenger terminus came the muffled platform announcements. In the opposite direction, east, deep into the darkness came the loud solid clanks of couplings, wheels, metal on metal as points turned and engaged. The sounds were magnified by the dark and her fears. *Please God*, she thought, *please make me brave*...and she huddled crouching herself down between the trunnions of two carriages of rolling stock that lay silent and bleak in a long black snake. Out of the darkness just inches away she could hear the raspy breathing of her guide, a young boy with tousled hair, and smell his stale breath. She was impatient, counting her own rapid pulsebeats. He must have sensed her nervousness. Stay calm, came the whisper. It won't be long.

'Who are they?' she whispered back, grateful for the reassurance, turning her mind to the line of dark coated figures that slipped away to disperse into the ink of the night and wondering who else was inhabiting this barren inhospitable lake of stone, metal, and machinery. She needed to pee, investigating the movement of the rapidly disappearing figures took her mind off it.

'Drifters, vagrants, transients,' came the quiet reply. 'They hide under the carriages looking for shelter, avoiding the rail police. Every so often the kops try, but they can't get rid of them. They're useful to us. If anyone does see us, they'll just think we are one of them.'

She watched a last little body that had been left behind

move along a line of goods trailers, attempting to catch up with the departing column. The figure kept low moving in short crouching dashes before darting quickly into a gap to disappear from sight. It looked desperate and pitiful and made her realise what her own escape must look much the same.

She had been here a while now and the cold was beginning to bite.

The soft knock on her tiny hostel room door had come just over two hours ago as the small travel clock by the bed blinked 8:30 pm. The accented young male voice had asked her name and she had given it, her heart in her mouth. We need to leave, don't worry, you're safe. Just do as I say, it'll be fine. Take nothing.

So, she had, with only a passing regret at not being able to say goodbye to Cecile, whose conversation at dinner had been strangely quiet as if something was on her mind. She could not suspect, thought Sophie, but was nevertheless sorry that there was no chance of goodbye. *Absolutely no one must know anything, not a word, not a hint or any suggestion.* Gina's instructions had been clear. There was an evening lecture due to take place in the hotel conference room in twenty minutes, she might be missed during that, but it was unlikely they were looking at attendance too closely, there were delegations from across Europe, it would be a maelstrom of young people. After that, if she had not appeared her friends would ask questions, then the tutors would be involved, after which… she had a couple of hours she supposed before the alert was raised.

In a side street she had got into the rear of a small French-built van. It had smelt of oil, machinery parts, old rope and tools and was very dark, too dark to see anything and only a slim bead of light that shone around the bulkhead partition to the driver broke the blackness. Don't worry, her guide said softly, it's not far maybe thirty minutes. I work at the yards I know where I am going. As the engine started, she sensed another person slip into the passenger seat, she eased herself to sit on the spare wheel which lay loose on the floor and then reached out with a hand to steady herself as the van had begun to trundle away bumping over the cobble of the city's Old Town its shock absorbers creaking, lurching, and rattling into the Vilnius evening traffic.

Now, in the rail yard she sensed her guide shift and heard him speak urgently but softly: 'Look, over there, that's our signal, we go.'

A white stab of light flickered out of the darkness in their direction. It winked at her like a lighthouse, a brief flicker of safety to guide her. 'Where are we going?' Sophie whispered. Her stomach felt hollow, and her heart was in her mouth.

'You'll be hidden in a shipping container heading for a Swedish ship. It's waiting to be loaded. Don't worry, once you are aboard and the ship has left port someone will let you out,' he explained, in good English. 'They will have papers for you, and you will arrive as a passenger. The Swedish authorities will not ask difficult questions. Someone will meet you there. Just stay calm and do as these people say. Good luck my young friend.'

The light flickered again. Rapid white spots of light and then they were moving. Behind them, distant on the cold night air the terminus announcements continued to echo, and the sodium orange lights of the marshalling yards cast a silver glow under the low cloud. The old world with its restrictions, control, and cruelty, yet strangely familiar and comforting lay in that direction. Ahead, the white pinpoint of light beckoned out of the inky lake of darkness that surrounded it, uncertainty, the unknown and danger, but also hope. She pulled her coat around her and wrapped her scarf tighter. Trying to avoid colliding with the broken timber and steel track or stumbling on the loose gravel she fixed on the point where the light had last shone and began to walk into the dark.

### *Canary Wharf, London*

CANARY Wharf was a blaze of lights. Around it the city had sprawled and crumbled. To the east the battered and tormented docklands and the feral communities of immigrants and illegals that followed the estuary to the coast. To the north and west the chic suburbs filled with the wealthy and the powerful the masters of Party and business. There, the elites rubbed shoulders with bohemianism the tolerated unconventional lifestyle of the arts that somehow was allowed to thrive, even celebrated in a way that was peculiarly British, an eccentricity that even a relentless shift into authoritarianism could not erase. To the south the dreary endless suburbs of corralled workers that stretched deep into the southern counties, legions of minor bureaucrats and officials, teachers, hospital workers, clerks, and secretaries. In these communities their children learned Russian in schools as a second language, the parents drove budget French, Italian or Czech cars, saved for German washing machines and dreamed of affording holidays on the Black Sea.

In the middle of this city, sat Canary Wharf. A not quite gleaming patch of capitalism with its steel and glass that was tolerated because even if something of an ideological embarrassment it was useful. As time passed an international financial centre had attractions for the many secret deals that its non-political status could broker. Far eclipsed in financial power by New York or Tokyo, nevertheless it provided a trading portal for the East, a seat at the global table of finance. A useful oasis that fed the metropolitan elites who unblushingly denounced capitalist greed while quietly protecting the systems which gave them wealth and provided the private schools for their children. Russian, Japanese, and American financiers and investors weaved their money magic here while British bankers and lawyers made large sums as middlemen and carefully and smoothly bribed officials to leave them alone.

Below the glittering mezzanines was a small parade of single unit shops that occupied a passageway the only purpose of which was to lead to the car park. The shops included a dry cleaner, key cutting service, a men's barber shop and an all-night pharmacy. The pharmacy was Indian run, a family operation that saw the overstocked interior open long hours. Lucy entered while Gates walked deeper into the main shopping area where he found a travel and hardware store and bought a medium sized suitcase. He also found a modelling scalpel and a heavy-duty sewing kit. Inside, the pharmacy Lucy spent some time selecting hair products, dyes, and colourants. She also bought a mirror, scissors, and a hair dryer.

They left and walked back onto the central mezzanine. The area was full of restaurants busy even on a Sunday with couples dining, pubs with groups of young men drinking and an American-styled family eatery from which a choir of young voices gustily chorused 'Happy Birthday'. Nobody, as far as Gates could detect showed any interest in them. Nevertheless, they wore their collars turned up and their scarves tight around their faces.

It was ten o'clock in the evening. With their purchases complete they returned to the apartment, pleased to feel safe once more and out of the stare of a cold moon.

'WHAT about you?' Lucy looked at him with her wide eyes. Only it didn't look like Lucy. Her hair was several shades darker and ruler straight, the hair extensions falling smoothly to her back. Her skin was also darker than before more olive in colour, the result of careful spray tanning. False eyelashes gave her eyes a more rounded look. The face that regarded him was pretty much Annie Freedman. She stood wrapped only in a large towel, the ingredients she had bought at the pharmacy all round her, an inky black liquid stained the bottom of the bathroom basin.

He had knocked on the open door, discreetly, conscious of the intimacy of a woman's bathroom. She had been leaning across the basin peering into the mirror, the open Portuguese passport that Len Burns had procured for his girlfriend propped open below.

'Don't worry about me, I'll be fine,' he said.

Later, dressed, she came into the sitting room and Gates was impressed at the change and the likeness she had achieved. She was taller than Annie Freedman, but only a couple of inches, a difference that could not be helped but, he thought, was unlikely to be challenged. He was using the scalpel knife and thread on the case they had bought earlier, the documents now concealed in the lining.

'Will this work,' she asked nervously.

'Yes, of course. Just be calm, your papers are good, and no one will stop you.'

'Harry, what about you?'

'I'll be fine. We will have to get out separately. I'll head north, get to Liverpool, I've friends there,' he lied, 'there'll be a way out on a ship or something. It may take a little time to organise, but I'll be safe.'

He could see she did not believe him.

'That's not true, is it. Let me come with you.'

He decided not to argue. 'We've been through this. *You* have an exit and entry visa to Lisbon that no one is going to question. It's the safest way for you *and* the evidence to go.' He hoped his confidence was not misplaced, but something told him that Burns' preparations for flight would have been thorough.

'Okay.' She nodded glumly.

'And in Lisbon?'

'I'll head to the Canadian Embassy, ask to speak to the Resident and say I have information and documentation regarding Mr James Dugdale.'

'Exactly, that I assume, will wake a few people up and then give them the file and say you need help.'

'Will they believe it; will they act on it?'

The doubt had grown in his mind too.

'Maybe,' he said uncertainly. 'Something will happen. But my priority is to get you safe. That's why the Canadian and not the American Embassy. If there is a leak from the U.S. side, we don't know how far or where that runs. The Canadians will look after you, the rest we'll have to wait and see. Dugdale's plan is finished, it's a question of saving what's left.'

She began a small lament about the number of people in danger and the moral responsibility. 'They can't ignore them. The Party and the Soviets will hunt them all down. They will have to try and save them.'

She sounded defiant, courage and confidence returning. 'For what it's worth I don't see the country staying as it is,' she continued, the hope rising in her voice. 'There are cracks everywhere and not just here. Even if the Soviets do succeed in crushing this attempt, there will be others, two, five perhaps ten years and it will crumble. All authoritarian states go that way.'

Gates couldn't think of a reply.

SHE left just after daybreak. Both had been awake for hours and had separately watched the half night lighten the windows. Dawn came and with it a red edge that had briefly made the London sky beautiful, then it was gone.

'You have everything?'

'Yes.' She had just finished retouching her make up. A blue silk scarf wrapped around her neck obscuring her face, a style that could be religious or cultural.

'Not the nearest tube station, walk towards the city you have plenty of time.'

'I know.'

'Who are you? When were you born?'

She answered correctly.

'Purpose of travel?'

'I'm visiting my Portuguese grandmother. She's sick.'

'And if someone asks to see inside the case and finds the documents?'

The case was filled with layers of old clothes, light flimsy items of no weight. To find the documents they would have to remove the lining. A professional search would see Gates' attempt at restitching the inside seam.

She looked back at him and said simply. 'Then it's over.'

'Exactly, so be careful right until you are on that aircraft. No nerves, make yourself as cool as you can. And Lucy, thank-you if it wasn't for you, I'd already be dead. I wish there was more I could do.'

They had looked at each other briefly. She hadn't wanted to reply to that. Instead, she reached up and kissed him delicately on the cheek.

When the time came, she left quietly by the rear door and using the outside metal steps to the alley below. There was a moment of comic theatre as the large suitcase almost refused the space through the kitchen door and the fire escape platform and Gates hoped the rest of their planning would prove better attention to detail. She struggled down the steps without looking back and then the slight figure with the oversized case was gone, the low rumble of the wheels on paving stones disappearing until he could hear it no more.

\*\*\*

# CHAPTER EIGHTEEN

### *Run*

ALONE IN THE FLAT, Gates considered the future. It wasn't pretty. There was no plan for himself; he had nowhere to go, but he had to give Lucy time. If they found him, then it would not take long to learn of the deception and hunt down Lucy with her bag of secrets. He didn't feel safe here either. If Hallam was looking for him, despite being careful, there were enough cameras in this part of the world they couldn't keep the hunt a secret for too long. More people and organisations would be drawn in, evidence collected, sightings investigated. He wanted to leave the city far behind, lay low for a day or so and then…well, 'then' didn't matter, but Lucy would be away. But he couldn't leave the city yet. One more task lay before him. He knew his best option was to keep moving. If he stayed still, they *would* find him.

Taking a black bag, he began to clean up the flat. There wasn't much but the debris of Lucy's disguise, papers, wrappings, tape, anything that might be a clue to where they had been, or their onward movements needed to be disposed of. There was a road map they had bought with them from the car journey south. On this he ringed two towns east of Manchester and a random location on the A1 Road north. He put that in cupboard hoping it looked like it had been overlooked in the clean-up and wondered whether anyone who came later would fall for such a ruse. When he was finished, he pushed aside the net curtains and observed the street for a while. It seemed normal, traffic a few people, but nothing he could see as not ordinary. He didn't want to stay longer and gathering his coat made his way downstairs and left by a rear fire exit.

At the rear of the apartments were the waste area. There were mattresses and old furniture, almost a barricade, as well as the line of overflowing black and green rubbish bins. He pushed the black sack of the debris from their stay deep into one of them. There was a broken wooden mop handle, and he used it to push the sack further into the stinking contents of the bin, drowning it below the pungent filth of sanitary waste, rotting food, greasy liquid, and sodden cardboard.

THE car was where Gates had left it, anonymous amongst the various other vehicles carelessly parked. The long screwdriver he had used to start it still concealed in the exhaust pipe tail. Once again, he had decided that without a full manhunt in progress, he should keep on the move trusting that Hallam and the security services did not want the entire Metropolitan Police Force stomping over their operation. He would drive out of the dismal city and sit in some nice quiet piece of countryside until he was sure Lucy was safe, enjoy a few hours solitude, that would probably be his last.

He got in through the unlocked rear door and the screwdriver worked its magic on the crude ignition electrics and the car fired into life. He still wasn't sure where to go. He imagined Lucy was beginning to make her way to London's southern airport now. They had agreed she would take a long route, slow trains but give herself plenty of time. He himself had half-decided to travel north for an hour or so, it was the shortest and quickest route out of the city and once away from the main roads there would be somewhere quiet to stop, stop and think. But there was no rush and he sat there while the engine gradually began to warm the car. He felt tired but sleep was the last thing on his mind, even if he had been occupying a soft bed safe in a warm comfortable room, sleep would have evaded him. All his thoughts were pushed like an excited football crowd straining against a barrier, to the front of his head. In a way it was a blessing, without space to flourish the vanished days of a peaceful life with Sophie and what had happened to her could not seize his mind with melancholy and dread. It was better to let the anger he felt bubble inside of him and live with the fear it created. He leaned his head back against the headrest and for a few moments escaped.

Turning the car, he set off leaving the housing estate with its dejected municipal blocks and turned onto a busy main route, the road lined by parades of shops on either side.

It was now his luck would change.

Maybe the suspension on the car from the flight from the estuary was damaged, perhaps he was looking through the rear-view mirror just when he should have been paying attention to the traffic ahead or it was the van driver's fault for turning out of side road without looking. Whatever the cause, there was a violent lunge and ear-splitting crash that shook the car to a standstill followed by the rattle of small pieces of debris flung against the windscreen and Gates' brain registered the collision with the thought: *What the fuck was that.* He was aware of pedestrians turning their heads, startled at the noise. Neither vehicle had been travelling fast, but his head had whipped forward. Now he saw his windscreen was filled with the shape of a large white van and he also saw the shocked face of the driver, a pimply youth, mouth open, eyes wide. *Shit.* He got out of the vehicle and inspected the damage; the youth was still in the cab of his vehicle, his face shocked and fumbling on his dashboard pulling his mobile phone towards him. He heard an unseen voice shout from somewhere behind him: 'Are you alright?' Across the road someone had stopped and was holding a phone towards the scene. The youth was out of his vehicle and was shouting something about look where you are going. Gates anxiously looked around, cars were parked either side of the street, traffic which was beginning to back up behind him. and the first horns began to sound.

*Dump it, run.* He was thinking quickly. *Get away from the vehicle as far as you can.* More people were beginning to gather. He raised his hands to the van driver and began to back towards the rear of the vehicle, more horns were blaring and looking down the street, Gates saw the scene was in full view of a traffic camera. He found the pavement dodging between two parked cars putting himself out of sight of the van driver and began to walk before the small crowd of witnesses to the incident became organised and recognised the participants. *The police will be on their way very soon.* He walked faster, searching for a side street, found one and broke into a brief jog. He felt a cold sweat on his back and a pounding anger in his breast. How stupid, *stupid*, to get caught by a traffic accident!

Twenty minutes later, he was well clear of the scene, and he found a cafe and pushed through into the interior. It was empty save for the proprietor who was watching the television attached high on the wall. Gates ordered coffee and then found a table to wait. When it came time to pay, Gates realised he had no money except for the balance of the war chest in U.S. dollars. *You idiot*, he thought. *What else will go wrong today*. He offered a ten-dollar note to the proprietor who looked at it blankly.

'I can't change that,' he said.

'Take it,' said Harry. 'My fault.'

The proprietor looked at Harry doubtfully but took the note. Gates sipped his coffee and thought about the next few hours.

The news was reporting a major demonstration gathering in central London. Students, activists, militants, intent on making trouble, the newscaster was talking about police preparations and warning people to stay clear of the area. The protesters were expected to be angry, and the police were prepared for trouble. Gates could imagine what that meant. The news moved on and Gates froze. The picture was of his car abandoned on the street, police cars with blue lights and images of the white van. Then a photograph of himself. The police want to question this man, reported the television, he was reported to be linked to dissident activity and had nearly been apprehended after being involved in a road traffic accident. He glanced towards the proprietor, but he was busy cleaning the large gushing coffee machine that did everything, practically speaking Italian. Any information on this man, who should not be approached, should be reported immediately. Gates felt a loss pour over him. There was no nimble footwork to be had now, every set of eyes, human and mechanical, every camera and every entry device in the most surveillance intensive city in the world would be looking for him. Now the fear began to grip him. He knew what reserves of courage he had ever possessed were close to exhaustion as the inevitable moved closer towards him. There was only one more task to complete, one small plea to humanity that he must find time to make. *Please God, give me a little more time*, he silently prayed.

The proprietor turned from his cleaning duties, his

gleaming hissing pride and joy once again returned to peak condition. He thought the over generous payment by his only customer merited some light conversation and looked to engage the stranger with some topic of the day.

But the table was empty, and the coffee stood untouched, gently steaming on the table.

GATES heard the disturbance long before he saw it. It came as a long, muffled growl reverberating off the streets to reach him. He checked his watch. It was twenty past four, already the sun was lowering causing the narrow side streets to darken into shadow. The noise of the protest barrelled down the roadways, the angry rhythm of the marchers rolling and echoing off the indifferent brick and glass. Students, a Sovereign march demonstrating against poor conditions, health, food, some overseas war, who the hell knew what. The police would be waiting and unlikely to be in a mood to listen. Towards the disturbance lay confusion, chaos, and cover from which he may be able to make his escape.

Behind him the street was empty, but he realised that Hallam would be trying to track him. He looked up, there on the side of a wall two storeys up was a CCTV camera pointing towards where the street entered onto Holborn. There would have been more cameras somewhere on his route and it was only time before Hallam's officers vectored in on him. He had crossed most of central London on foot to hide himself in this melee.

*Hide in plain sight, hide where they have too many other things to look at.*

He headed towards the banners and the sounds, passing small groups of young people on the way, grouped into doorways, pulling hoods or bandannas around their faces and gloves onto hands. They were talking excitedly, and Gates sensed the adrenalin beginning to coarse through their veins at the prospect of what was to come.

He found the main street crackling with tension. It was difficult to tell but he thought he had joined a jeering jostling crowd of at least a thousand students possibly more, or agitators who wished they were still students, slowly moving across the broad thoroughfare in the direction of Kingsway and the Strand. The street had been cleared to allow them to progress, but Gates had joined sufficiently close to the head of the slow noisy melee to see deep lines of riot police forming in their path, a thick dark wall of plastic suited officers who looked as if they meant business. Gates had heard that the London riot squads were on bonuses for arrests, and he could already see the arc of batons swinging as an advance guard of protesters clashed with the first rank of troopers. Beyond the officers a lake of blue lights rapidly strobed the afternoon air their flickering warning amplified by the glass of tall buildings. The mood of the crowd was ugly and already a few long-range missiles were looping through the air towards the police ranks, falling short as the artillerymen began to seek their range.

Gates knew that his cover here was temporary and it would be foolish to remain too long. He was likely to get swept up by the police tactics which would be brutal, and he was trying to escape arrest, not find it by alternative means. The police wall was close now and he could feel the momentum of the crowd increase, pressure being applied to close with their opponents. Gates was becoming trapped and crushed. The din was immense, loud chants of: 'SOVEREIGN', 'PIGS-PIGS-PIGS', roared from the angry marchers. At the flanks Gates could just observe the organisers. Detached from the mass, sunglasses, faces well-hidden, some with megaphones repeating instructions urging encouragement, while marshalling what had become a mob towards the police files. Gates recalled the small, organised groups he had passed earlier away from the march route. It dawned upon him that they were the professional agitators, seasoned activists that would congeal with the students at the last moment and whose purpose was anarchy, intent on whipping up anger to create a frenzy. The students were cannon fodder, the foot soldiers in their violent game.

A police snatch squad had cut off and cornered two battered students who were being bundled into a police van. But the mini operation had been executed too slowly and enraged by the abduction of two of their numbers, part of the mob had struck forward outflanking and outnumbering the small arrest detachment which was now isolated. The officers were overwhelmed, and the van began to rock the flashing blue overhead lights arcing wildly like some macabre stage performance. There was a loud bang and a lick of flame appeared followed by a black spiral of smoke that began to rise from the scene. Gates thought he glimpsed the two captured students, fists raised in triumph released and returning to the fight amidst wild cheers from the protesters.

Next to him was a fiery young woman in jeans and with long straight hair. In the noise Gates could not make out her words but the set of her jaw and the way her long painted fingernails flashed indicated furious defiance and he glimpsed the glass bottles part-filled with amber liquid inside her leather jacket. Above but some distance away he could hear the clatter of helicopter rotors beating the air and he knew that long-range lens would be pointing this way, identifying individuals, hot spots of activity and keeping the flanks of the police lines secure. Above, a drone hovered fifty metres above the police line, its unblinking lens spiralling on its gimble. A few missiles were sent its way but fell far short and then red points of light began to flicker around the machine and on the buildings and windows of the street as intense lasers were directed at the lens. It was mostly too agile to catch, and Gates knew enough to know that facial recognition was within its capabilities. He had visions of Hallam's men already entering the command vehicle somewhere in that sea of blue lights. Like everyone else he had his face covered by a scarf that also wound around his ears.

While the protest continued in all its fury and the streets were full, he had cover. But he knew it would not last, at some point he would need to break away. For an hour he hid himself deep in the anger, avoiding the front lines criss-crossing the street and ahead of him the noise became louder, the sound of collisions, shouted voices and the smashing of glass. A pall of oily smoke appeared, although he could not see where it sprang from. It was a stalemate and Gates sensed the crowd was wearying, the police ahead too organised and too stubborn to give way before the charges and assaults. He saw some combatants beginning to fall back drag themselves behind him nursing battered limbs or holding makeshift dressings against bloody gashes.

Almost surreally a priest in clerical coat and collar appeared and walked calmly by at the side of the crowd regarding the situation sternly, his long white beard glowing in the fading afternoon sun. With him were two medics from the St John's Ambulance, large yellow fluorescent jackets and red medical rucksacks. One went into the crowd to alerted to a man on his knees blood pouring from his head, a stray missile, Gates supposed, the priest, a large man went to help holding back the crowd around the scene while the medic gave attention.

The police ranks broke briefly, and water canon erupted in hard powerful spurts scattering soaked youths who fled amid jeers and whistles. Many were coated in blue dye that would mark them for future identification. But the police counterattack seemed to spur them, energise them and they soon reformed, hurriedly adorning goggles and soaking their bandannas in water ready for the tear gas they expected to follow. They understood that the police charge was an attempt to create stand-off, a gap, before breaking them up with tear gas. The rioters weren't going to let that happen. They were as prepared and disciplined as the police they faced.

Time to go, he thought.

The other medic had knelt in a doorway to adjust a boot. Gates saw it was a woman somewhere in her thirties. Her attention diverted he came up behind her and pushed her to the floor. As she tried to straighten and get up and with regret he hit her, hard a well-placed blow to the jaw. She sank back jaw slack and eyes glassy. As the crowd pulsed past him in the doorway, he pulled off the large yellow coat that dwarfed her and put it on himself and then he shouldered the red medic rucksack. He hoped he had not hurt her too badly and saw with relief there was still colour in her cheeks.

He began to force his way back into the crowd looking for a side street. Behind him was a series of sharp cracks and a current seemed to move through the crowd that was part noise, part movement. A quick glance behind towards the police and he saw a thin pall of wispy white smoke drifting gently his way. The tear gas had arrived. With no little effort, he was gasping for breath and had a sudden admiration for the paramedic that he had assaulted when he realised the weight of the pack he had taken from her, Gates pushed and barged his way through the mob keeping to the edge of the crowd until he found a street heading west that would begin a route to the Covent Garden area of the city. The students' anger and intent was rising with the certainty of water reaching boiling point on a stove. He wondered what issue had caused the protest to spark and form, what could cause such behaviour and then realised that the cause was insignificant, it was the system they wanted to attack.

He escaped through the flanks just as the protesters closed-up tight against the police shields, a hard physical collision as the troopers pressed their thick plastic shields against the kicking. Immediately off the side streets he found other groups of young men, Party supporters attracted by the noise and excitement, youth less hostile to the police or perhaps just staying out of the melee but who watched curiously, with satisfaction and amusement.

As he moved away through the streets with their doors and windows tightly closed, he found more squads of police standing calm but apprehensively behind their shields, thick plastic visors hiding their features, forming up, held in depth ready to advance into the sides of the protesting snake of people. They ignored him, a lone freewheeling individual with a medical kit, all awaiting the order to assemble into formation and advance, fingering their batons which were already extended and ready. He passed them behind leaving them chewing gum concentrating on the orders from their squad leaders.

Shortly after in the quiet of two side streets he found the logistics of the authorities' response, long columns of ambulances, parked, and waiting patiently. Drivers and paramedics in green coveralls standing by their cabs, faces glum and worried talking to one another nervously. Calm, rapid radio chatter drifted from the cabs of the vehicles. The authorities were prepared, and these responders knew they would be needed. They did not appear to relish the prospect that awaited them.

He began to move a little more quickly conscious that the fury of the demonstration receding behind him had created only a temporary lull in his pursuit. He needed to keep moving, circle first north away from the centre of the riot now in full swing.

He felt rage towards Hallam and what he represented, fury that his own plans were being undermined by the unseen hand of the intelligence services that had somehow been one step ahead of them all: the Americans, Dugdale, him, over the last few days.

Three large police vans swept past him, the sirens, blue lights, and the powerful draught of air that sucked at him as the convoy passed, startled him and he felt a cold pool of oil fill his stomach. As the shock passed and the realisation their mission was not him, a vision of Hallam and others with Lucy, or perhaps it was Sophie, lying beaten in a police detention suite, crawled into his mind. The nightly news: *'Terrorist dissidents apprehended by police officers...the captured woman is currently being questioned at an undisclosed location...'* It would be his fault. They were following him and rounding others up as they went. He was like the carrier of smallpox infecting everyone he came close to.

He recalled snippets of previous conversations, words that pecked at him persistently, without let up—

Shiner: *'I think I have what you need, but it will put a target on your back.'*

Dugdale: *'Truth and belief are everything... You saw something that wasn't a fiction.'*

Burns junior: *'Nobody gets away from these people. Nobody.'*

The streets were becoming quieter as he hurried further from the scene. The protest had sucked in police and responders and driven ordinary people from the area. He knew he had to leave the main routes that led back to the disturbance; he was just too conspicuous in this heavily monitored area of the city. He turned north and headed towards Regent's Park and residential areas where temporary shelter may be easier to find, street surveillance less intense. After a while, the houses became more mansion like, set back from the road hidden behind shrubbery and tall hedges with basements and approached by imposing stone steps that you had to climb. There was only one thing left to do and that was a couple of miles away. He decided to keep low until dark.

'HARRY, what the actual fuck.'

The house was one of the smart mansions in Bloomsbury, set elegantly on a leafy street, the road lined with gleaming German saloons resting comfortably for the night under the streetlights. The glossy black door had opened quickly, the hostess not wishing to leave her guests standing on the steps on a cold evening looked down upon him from two steps above. From inside came the sound of glass tinkling and the mumble of conversation and laughter.

She was tall and Cheltenham Ladies College and looked at Harry with surprise that turned to unhappy amusement in an instant. 'You are an unexpected surprise. Don't think I invited you,' she declared drily. 'I hope you're not going to make a scene; I don't like ghosts at my feasts,' she added. She glanced down the street and Harry guessed there were more guests planned for whatever function his ex-wife was hosting.

'No, I'm not for that. I just really need to talk to you, please, just for a moment. Then I'll be gone. I promise.'

She looked at him for a moment, she was wearing something red, silky, and thin and she shivered slightly in the night air. Then she said wearily: 'If we must, Harry. If we must,' and she turned for Gates to follow her into the hall and up the stairs. They walked past the drawing room entrance and Gates saw it was full of a smart younger set looking groomed, spilling with laughter and with glasses being filled by young short-skirted waitresses in white blouses. Beyond the chattering crowd Harry glimpsed a dining table with silver candlestick holders armed with long tapered candles.

Along the corridor they were ambushed by a young, beautiful woman coming the other way smoothing down a black cocktail number that was wrapped around her more like a bandage than a dress, her fluted glass with a lipstick smear balanced aloft on a slender arm.

'Kate, darling,' the woman gushed, 'will you be long, I need a gossip. 'We haven't had a moment yet and I haven't seen you for absolute ages, where's Keith, I haven't seen him either.' Her voice was rich with Champagne bubbles, while cool eyes fixed on Gates trailing behind with only momentary interest.

'Lecturing somewhere, Georgia darling, but let's be honest, who really knows.' Kate said airily and without pausing, 'I'll be back soon,' she said over her shoulder, and she led Harry on and into the kitchen.

Two waiters were arranging Champagne bottles on the island, ready to transport them into the drawing room and quench the thirst of expectant guests. A chef was supervising the ordered in food and Gates could smell the rich juices and the rosemary of the lamb that rested on trays, ready for the order to be devoured.

'Oh God, not here,' said Kate, looking around and realising her error. She led him quickly through to the rear stairs where they descended to the ground floor study. There, they surprised two guests a man and a woman entwined in an intimate conversation while their real partners mingled upstairs. 'Jonty, be a love can I have the room? Take Susan somewhere else, will you?' The couple left sheepishly, hastily making embarrassed apologies and Kate looked at Harry: 'Wait here a moment while I make some excuses then you can tell me what this is about.'

She was only gone a couple of minutes and when she returned, she shut the door and Kate and Harry stood and silently looked at one another. It was Kate who asked: 'Well, what is it? Nearly two years since last time, really Harry, can't you stay away?' she said provocatively. She went to the desk found cigarettes and lit one. 'And you pick your moments, you can see I'm busy,' she added, picking a piece of stray tobacco from her teeth. She then waited, her face impassive, arms folded.

'It's Sophie, Kate, I'm only asking you to look out for her. She doesn't need much, she's nearly grown. But you need someone in this world, and you are all she has.'

Above the fireplace stood a large, elegant mantel clock in a period walnut case and with roman numerals. Harry saw the time was 7:20 pm. Across London, Lucy's flight should be ready for departure. Once airborne it would be about twenty-five minutes into international airspace. All the time her chances increased. He supposed they could still stop her at the Lisbon airport, but they would have to be very careful. Portugal was independent, neutral. Just to be safe he preferred to evade capture for another four maybe five hours.

Kate's question returned him to the present. 'Why Harry, what's wrong,' she laughed rapturously, 'you moving on? big promotion?' her expression remained one of amusement and her words those of dry cynic, 'or have the two of you fallen out,' she added a little more venomously. The scorn in her voice made Gates wonder what it was he had ever seen in her. There wasn't an ounce of caring or compassion beyond that required for her own needs anywhere in her body.

But he could only plead, it was all he had left. 'I...I just want to know, that if I'm not around you will be there for her. Look, it's not much to ask. Somewhere to live, a little money until she gets straight.'

She said nothing for a few moments and just looked thoughtfully with a slight smile at her former husband. She was still a good-looking woman, aging well, slim, her chestnut brown hair that could have been from a shampoo commercial bundled on top, with delicately arranged strands falling to her shoulder, the effect held together by a large ornate pin that looked Asian and probably cost a worker's weekly pay packet. From across the small room, he could smell her expensive French scent. But behind the grimly mocking smile the pale eyes were cold and hard.

Then she let out a false, angry laugh. 'Oh, Harry! You are being ridiculous, you're far too sentimental altogether. What's happened to your little darling, didn't like having some sense worked into her in Poland? Try not to worry, I'm sure they'll find her soon.'

'She won't be there forever, I'm not in a position to help, although I want to.'

Kate stared at him. Uncertain as to what his words were suggesting. 'Are you ill, Harry? Is that it? Health gone with the booze, cigarettes. Or is it something else? The politics again?' She drew deeply on the cigarette and regarded his slumped form leaning against the desk, like a doll with its limbs extended into unnatural shapes unable to accept balance. Then she stood squarely and faced him, hands on hips, and those big pale eyes dangerous and dark. 'It was always the politics that would be your undoing, Harry. You could never accept things for how they were. You always thought it wrong, miss-shaped, or badly applied, *unjust.*' She almost spat the last word out.

She couldn't resist herself, thought Gates, the cruel cynical jibes. Where was the kinder socialism that had been promised all those years ago, where, without the evils of capitalist enrichment, people would care for one another, share resources. It was all a myth, human nature drove people not ideology, the abuse of power for personal gain by those that can, wherever their politics lay.

He was too exhausted to continue. Too tired to argue or plead more and he had developed an unearthly composure, he needed to disconnect. He saw Kate glance toward the door, something flickered in the dark void of her eyes. 'I better go,' he said quietly. 'This was a mistake.' He turned and took a step towards the door.

'Wait...' cried Kate quickly, 'I'm sorry, look, that was mean of me. Just take your time tell me why you think I could help. I never wanted the child Harry; I made no secret of that. You can't expect me to give my life to something I didn't want.'

'I never asked you to,' he whispered.

'But I did have her and if she needs help, well...the least I can do is talk about it.' This time her voice was gentle, conciliatory and the eyes as if on a switch had turned bright almost innocent in their appeal. Harry could think of no obvious reason for the change of heart.

The clock gently chimed the half-hour and Harry looked across the room at a face suddenly containing a sympathy he never remembered. He recalled the fights, snarling, furious, vicious affairs that shook the house and left the young child rigid with fear. He had spent the last two decades full of guilt, remorse and shame regretting all of that time, a regret made worse by the knowledge that she had shared no such remorse. Far away he could still hear the murmur of laughter and conversation from the early stages of the dinner party above. The house was grander, smarter now, the decor more subtle, he imagined the guests were more sophisticated, less of the bearded activist brigade more of the egalitarian elite with tastes to match. He thought of Shiner's words: *There are socialist and there are clever socialists. The socialists do what the clever socialists tell them.*

Kate was definitely amongst the clever socialists. The hindrance of an unwanted child, frustration at Gates' descent into morose frustration, determination to be on the top of the pile where the important people worked and played. Could she really regret how she had abandoned Sophie?

He stood on the thick Afghan rug and tried to explain. 'I'll be going away, not sure for how long. I know you can't forgive or like me, Kate, and I know what you think about Sophie, but she *is* a part of you, and you owe her *something* if only for that. I wouldn't ask if I didn't have to.'

Kate was nodding, suddenly all sympathy. 'Fair enough, I can talk with Keith,' she said, 'perhaps there is a route to some leniency, bring her back into the fold...'

She was smiling, and the eyes still looked soft as if comprehension had dawned. But...

'...There'll be conditions of course, but the people I know can be reasonable about these things.'

*Will we ever see mummy again?* Sophie's wide-eyed question from childhood. *Why does she hate us...?*

The memory of Sophie's words whispered to him one cold Manchester evening returned. Kate was still talking; he had no idea of how long he had stood there now. Her words, the sincerity, the sudden lucid admission of motherhood...it was wrong, of course it was wrong. Then her words stopped abruptly, and she must have seen the suspicion creep onto his face.

'Look, I'll go. I'll work something out,' and he went towards the door.

She moved to intercept him, even reaching with her hand for his. 'Not yet, we can work this out, can't we?' her voice barely suppressing the anxiety. 'Why not stay and have a drink? To be honest you look like you need it.'

The clock chimed again. 7:40 pm. He looked at her. This wasn't Kate. He shook his hand free and saw the anxious look appear in her eyes. He realised then the house had become silent. The murmuring and laughter of dinner party chatter had gone, no clink of glass or chink of plate from the kitchen. *You bitch*, he thought angrily, *you callous heartless bitch*.

He flung open the study door and headed for the front entrance and he heard Kate's unaltered pleading voice calling him back, urging him to talk more. He ignored her and moving quickly, he went through into the night air. The front door had been open; why was it open on a cold night, and he nearly lost his balance as he began to take the steps down to the pavement too quickly. He stumbled, then as he felt the pain burst through his head, he realised he had not stumbled there had been a blow, a tackle from someone that had been waiting for him. He caught the glimpse of a heavy black uniform boot that pushed into his side and propelled him down the steps to the pavement. From there he gazed up at the stars and above him framed against the wide night sky was the unsmiling face of the Special

Branch detective Barnes. In what seemed like slow motion he raised a large meaty fist above Gates' face. He could see the detail of the man's knuckles, the gold glint of a heavy cygnet ring...

Before the blow descended, the pause was long enough for Gates to hear Kate's voice: 'Take him away, get him away from here. He's a disgrace to the Movement. He's a traitor...'

***

# CHAPTER NINETEEN

*Then raise the scarlet standard high*

**Sunningdale, Surrey**

THE fire glinted in the study of Christopher Slade. A grand old patron of empire cast in marble regarded him impassively from the corner of the room and he raised his glass before taking another sip of the excellent single malt that he had poured for himself.

Earlier he had walked the house, looking in all the rooms spending time reminding himself of the furniture, how it was arranged, the pictures on the walls, noting the areas he and his wife had talked about improving. Modernising or restyling. Finally, he was happy that he had as good a memory of their home as he could, and he went looking for his family.

He had found his daughter lying on her stomach on her bed, music player clamped over her ears, a magazine opened under her nose. Slade had watched her for a while from the doorway not interrupting the late afternoon peace of youth. She must have caught sight of him because she had turned and lifted the earpiece.

'Everything alright Dad? she asked. She looked at him questioningly.

He smiled, slightly embarrassed, momentarily flustered that his gaze may have been too adoring. Everything was fine, he said, adding: 'Love you Poppet.'

'Love you too, Dad,' and she beamed at him as he stood in the doorway, thinking nothing of it.

He wanted to kiss her gently on the forehead but was afraid it might overdo the moment. He left his daughter replacing her headphones returning to her music and thought how beautiful and innocent she looked, the unconcerned teenager amongst her posters and the colourful clutter of a teenage bedroom.

His wife was downstairs in the snug, sitting comfortably, close to the fire. A pot of tea steamed at her side, and she too was reading a magazine. She looked up, pleased to see him, and offered a warm smile.

'Hello Christopher, dear. There you are. Are you busy? Would you like to join me for some tea?'

He smiled back at her and said he would. So, for ten minutes he listened to the trivia of family life, how their daughter was getting on with schoolwork and she was sorry, but the latest vet's bill for the pony would arrive this week, she was also thinking her car would need changing in the new year. Would that be possible? He nodded and said he was sure it would be.

They discussed family plans for the following month, relatives had asked to visit, when should she suggest, was he going to be very busy at work? After a while, fully updated on family business and with reunion and visit plans made he rose from his chair and announced that unfortunately he had a few things to do in his study. Taking the two steps across to her chair he leaned over and kissed her gently but firmly on the mouth. She was surprised but pleased and he felt the willing response from her lips.

'That's nice dear,' she said, enjoying the kiss. 'Is everything all right?' she asked wondering where the unasked-for piece of affection had come from.

'Perfectly my love, I'll be in my study for a while if you need me.'

She smiled back at him, and he thought with melancholy sadness how incredibly beautiful the two most important people in his life were.

On his desk the laptop computer was still open, the encrypted flash drives lay on the desk. On the screen was the deep web email message that he had received just over an hour ago:

> "Operations compromised. Lionheart network to close. Destroy all classified equipment and material. Remain in place. Wait for next contact. Good luck. God Save the King."

It was the message he hoped he would never read, and his heart had sunk when he first read it and he found himself trembling, he felt cheated and angry. Dugdale himself had phoned him, breaking the protocol because he must. The quick call of someone busy and moving, but he had verified the message. Something had gone horribly, catastrophically wrong, but he had no way of knowing what. All he could do now was follow the protocol and the protocol was clear. There was to be no communication, no movement, no resistance. That way, whatever survived could be remapped, possibly over time, even repaired. To be part of this was to operate alone, never able to share the close atmosphere of conspiracy. To fail, meant the consequences must also be shared alone.

That they would come for him, he was sure. Others, with lesser knowledge would be rounded up. Offices and homes would already be being raided; more would follow. But most that they arrested would have had no instructions, no knowledge, just a willingness to be a part and the patience to wait. They may be able to describe perhaps one person, a voice on a phone, someone else they thought may be involved, and then the trail would run dry, like water into sand. The security services would end up with lots of people to punish and make examples of, but they would all be dead ends.

But Slade knew more and was more valuable. *We can get you out, but you must move now*, Dugdale had phoned him two hours ago. *My family?* he had asked. There had been simply silence to his question. Slade had contacts, knowledge of communications, an idea of the plan, the great silent coup that would break the country free of the jaws of communism. He could lead the authorities into places from which Lionheart could never be rebuilt. *Don't concern yourself,* he had told Dugdale, *I have my own arrangements.*

It was not possible for him to take the risk of capture, nor did he wish to involve his family in a futile and hurried escape attempt. Innocence was their survival. That left the unwritten oath, the oath, he, and a few others had never been asked for but which they had all made.

He placed three large dry logs on the fire which rejuvenated immediately begin to burn and crackle happily. First, he took the flash drives and buried them among the flaring logs. He watched them curl and melt, flare briefly and then congeal into small unrecognisable scabs of plastic. Then, he slipped the hard drive from the computer and taking a heavy marble paper weight, subjected it to three or four heavy blows which fractured the case, and exposed the inner plastic. This too went on the fire to melt away. A filthy chemical smell rose for a while from the fire until the destruction was complete.

There was nothing else. Any other knowledge was in his head, and that would be beyond their reach.

He sat at his desk and sipped the whisky the mellow lingering flavour somehow giving the settled calmness he needed and craved. All he could do now was wait.

He heard the cars pull on to the driveway outside. There were no sirens, no screeching of wheels and rush of heavy booted feet. Just a simple pulling up and the opening and closing of car doors. He heard the doorbell chime and a few minutes later the door to his study opened and his wife anxiously appeared. There are men at the door, she said. Policemen. One of them said his name was Hallam. They want to speak to you. Is everything all right? Why are they here? What do they want?

He smiled at her and told her not to worry, pleased at how calm his voice was. It was a bank matter. He straightened his tie, shuffled some papers into order and said to show them into the main drawing room, he would be right through to sort it out, he'd just put these papers somewhere safe. She nodded only partially reassured, but reluctantly left him to follow her.

When she was gone Slade opened the lowest drawer of the mahogany desk. He drew out the Browning 9mm pistol. There was no need to check the clip or make the weapon ready. He had done that immediately after reading the email message.

He took a breath, looked at the picture of his wife and youngest daughter for the last time, then carefully placed the muzzle under his chin feeling the cold metal press hard into his skin. Then with a final thought for how much he loved his wife and daughters he pulled the trigger.

## Paddington

GATES shivered, his teeth clicking together rapidly like a clockwork motor, yet he also felt feverish the pain that racked his entire body made him burn with a slow deep ache that was relentless in the grip it had taken of his muscles and bones. He pulled himself painfully to hunch, knees drawn up, against the damp brick in the corner of his cell, and when he had rolled himself into a position, he thought he could endure, he gasped his breathing back into a rhythm that staved off the palpitations that came from the pain.

He had no idea of time. He thought it had been hours, but he suspected not. Having found him, they were now after Lucy, and they knew they had no time to waste. Once in a cell they had not bothered with the preliminaries of questioning. The big detective Barnes had just used his practised fists with force. As his vision blurred under a red mist curtain, he had seen the square dark glass window, and he guessed behind it watching impassive but impatient were other, probably Hallam and who knows who else. Russians?

Earlier, they had bundled him from the pavement and dragged him to the waiting car. Kate had delivered the coup de grâce of the arrest with a phlegmy spit to his face and had watched with satisfaction as he had been driven off. The journey across London had not taken long and they had swung into the underground car park beneath the fortified compound of a central London high security facility after no more than fifteen minutes. From there he had been bundled to the harshly lit cells, hoisted between two Special Branch detectives, his feet hardly in contact with the ground.

There had been a clock above the reception desk in the station. Through his panting breath he had noted the time. If all had gone to plan Lucy would be airborne now, safely speeding through international air space. The papers with their message of an American mole winging their way to exposure. But he wanted to be sure, certain, if possible, that there was no reception committee waiting for her when she landed. When it started, he thought, think of other things, fill your mind with images as far away from what they want to know as you can. He didn't think it would take them long, he was no spy or soldier, and he was as aware of his limits as they probably were. After all, they were experts. But he would try.

The girl. Where is she?

Who do you mean?

Massive blow to the ribs and he felt bone split. Almost dreamily he noticed the hard face centimetres away from his own.

You had papers, information from your nonce newspaper friend. Where are they?

Which nonce? I have lots of friends.

Smash to the kidneys and he felt boiling pain pulse through his body.

*Not bad*, he thought to himself, *it doesn't hurt so much after a while, perhaps they're not the experts I thought*. The thought was funny, and he laughed, then a blow to the face caused him to bite without restraint his tongue, and his mouth filled with thick salty blood.

When did you meet James Dugdale?

Who? What? You mean the man you said was dead?

The hook to the chin sent stars whizzing around his head and he felt blackness descend across him, but consciousness stubbornly remained.

Don't be a smart-arse, Gates.

He spat a fat wad of blood onto the floor.

Why did you go to your ex-wife's home?

It's almost Christmas, the season of goodwill, he panted the words. This is becoming easy he thought, it just doesn't hurt anymore. They're rushing, in a hurry, with more time they'd be more careful and methodical. But he knew his body was failing, the retreat of pain just a sign that his senses were giving up.

They gave it twenty more minutes; questions then more blows then repeated questions. At one point he lay on the floor on his side still in the chair. He felt the cold linoleum on his cheek and watched with detached fascination as his own blood slowly seeped across the floor in front of his eyes. He knew he had bones broken, ribs and fingers that were agony to move. But out of the corner of his eye he saw Barnes, now in shirt sleeves and perspiring heavily look towards the dark window and give a grim shake of his head. Gates felt himself smile, he knew that, this far at least, he had won—even though his body was ruined and there was nowhere left to go, the only thing they had left was to finish him and he knew that was now a certainty.

THERE were gaps in what they knew. They knew about the identity, the passport, loss of papers. And they knew all about Shiner. Gates thought or rather discerned that they had been in control of that. But someone had blundered, Gates guessed. With the material stolen, they knew their own operation was blown. They must have been using Shiner to reel Gates and probably Dugdale in, but something had gone wrong, some minor misjudgement or miscalculation somewhere, he would never know. He assumed they knew all about Burns, but they didn't ask anything about Dugdale. What did that mean? That they already knew all they needed? Or they knew nothing and that could mean Dugdale's plans were damaged, seriously, even, but still intact. They were ripping up what they could.

There was something else they didn't know. He had missed it at the time. *Have they found her yet?* Kate's taunting words came back to him. That could only mean Sophie wasn't in that camp anymore. It was a tiny slip that in the heat of the moment, the fear the adrenalin could have been overlooked. But it had come back to him, and he knew what it meant. Dugdale had kept his word. And right now, that was all that mattered to Gates.

He thought about all of this as he shivered in the cell waiting to see what would happen next.

They dragged him back to the interrogation room and he steeled himself waiting for the fists to fall. But Barnes was nowhere in sight. Instead, an older man in smart blue suit who carried a black case entered. He barked an order to one of the lounging minders to get Gates in a chair. He also ordered water, as well as towels. Before the goon left, he told him to bring tea, hot sweet tea. From his bag he took cotton wool and antiseptic and quickly cleaned up Gates' face. Then he firmly, without violence, rotated Gates' head and shown a torch into his eyes. He ordered Gates to drink the tea and sat and watched while Gates gulped the hot liquid down his throat. He lit a cigarette passed another across the table and waited, calmly observing his patient recover. The tea and the tobacco had an effect and Gates marvelled at how fast he appeared to recover. His heat rate, breathing, focus began to equalise, although his body ached dully and to move bought howls of pain.

After a while the doctor was ready and the goons grabbed his arm pinning it by the wrist and elbow to the table, they freed the cuff and ripped the sleeve away from the soft skin of his arm. While they did the doctor pulled the syringe from his bag, he held the clear liquid under the light and flicked the needle. Gates squinted trying to focus and saw that the doctor had been replaced by a face he knew. It was Hallam, who looked at him calmly, the violence hidden by the intelligent eyes. Behind him was someone else, a large figure with straight Slavic features a crude jaw and hard eyes.

'You're at the end of the road Gates,' said Hallam softly. 'Potassium. In this quantity it will induce heart failure, a heart attack that regrettably occurred during enhanced questioning. It happens, and the coroner will understand. But before you go, before your heart bursts, my friend here wants to know where the girl is, where are the papers you stole. Dugdale is finished, you know that but before we clean that up, we want our property back. Tell us.'

Gates tried to laugh. He heaved, gulped trying to summon what snot and phlegm he could to throw it in the face of the policeman. But he didn't have the strength and all that came was a thick viscous dribble mixed with blood that spluttered from his mouth and hung from his open lip.

Hallam shook his head turning away and Gates could see that he thought enough time had been wasted. Gates pulled uselessly but the doctor had returned into view and the needle was slid professionally and accurately into his vein. He felt his body soften, his brain relax, and its grip on his thoughts and his vision became blurry. In his mind he thought he was laughing. But it was the effect of the drugs. His face was frozen, and he could feel his nerves jangle and dance, his heart rate rising. *You've never mentioned Sophie*, he thought. They've never threatened me with what they will do to her. She's gone and if they had found her, they would use that fact to make me talk.

Then the laugh did come, and he saw Hallam's face twitch with suppressed anger. Behind him the Russian shook his head and glanced down to his feet and the low Russian expletives reached his ears. *You went too fast*, Gates thought, *you haven't crushed it, Lionheart is still out there, bruised very broken, but still there.* Then the pain in his chest expanded like a balloon and his body stiffened, his limbs straining against the cuffs that held him to the chair. He saw light, he saw Lucy, he saw Sophie, he knew they were out of reach and if that was true then there was hope.

Then the blackness, complete and warm and welcoming, closed over him for good.

## Lisbon, Portugal

LISBON was waiting patiently for the mild months of winter to pass. A fresh wind breathed off the mountains into the hill-cradled bay to propel the *fragatas* going about their lighterage. An early afternoon sun lit the many balconies and vistas of the *miradouros* and the Tagus River smelt of the sea a few miles distant.

Lucy had arrived late the previous night taking the bus into the city where she found a small hotel in a Moorish quarter hidden in the ancient *Cidade Biaixa* district. The shabby hotel had an interior courtyard, gilded banisters, and oversized plants in large stone urns. It boasted the barest of amenities and the time of year meant the hotel was quiet, almost deserted. In her room she took a bath and nearly fell asleep in it. When she did place herself between the sheets, sleep eluded her as she thought of what had become of Harry, the *Herald*, and others, others that she did not know in whose hands so much of their fate had rested. She wanted peace. She wanted to gaze up at the mountains that surrounded the city, and where she could hear a distant unseen storm pursue its feud against the blue hills, or to watch the silent freighters slip though the dark waters towards the ocean. But her little balcony only looked down onto a dark street where the houses opposite were so close, she believed if she reached out, she could touch them. Instead, she had lain on the bed listening to the night sounds through an open window. The storm grumbled further away leaving the hills rain-lashed but intact. *I am a messenger hiding from the storm*, she thought. The bad-tempered retreat of the storm was replaced by the melancholy hooting of barges crossing the bay, and the sorrowful notes of a *fado* melody drifting from a nearby bar.

Eventually, sleep did claim her and nothing on the planet, an earthquake, volcano, or hurricane could have woken her. The morning was well advanced when she came awake to the sound of weathered old bells chiming to each other like old men bickering at chess and she felt chilled by the open window but refreshed by the bright sunlight that fell through from the balcony.

She dressed, and then with some thought and ingenuity she hid the papers with their secrets and their story carefully in her room. Satisfied they would be safe until she returned, she wandered out into the narrow streets avoiding the roaming *varinas* in their long black skirts, their baskets of fish carefully balanced above their heads and boarded a clanking trolleybus that with slow jerky progress inched her towards the more modern quarters of the city's commercial and administrative districts. She had never been out of England, and she liked what she saw in this old city that was bright with life that too place under a mellow sky and cotton wool clouds. I can take my time, she thought, let me just enjoy somewhere beautiful and peaceful, just for an hour.

So, she did and happily wandered enjoying the streets and the sun.

When the time came, the Embassy block was grey, square, and anonymous, the Maple Leaf flag hung from a staff motionless, and she wondered what awaited her once she entered. But she paused only a few moments and then went up to the security guard who stood at the door and who she realised had been watching her for the last few minutes.

She gave her true name, nationality and that she was requesting asylum. 'I have important and urgent information for the Canadian Government,' she said calmly and firmly. 'I am travelling under an assumed identity, and I wish to speak to someone in authority. Could you assist me?'

The security guard looked at her impassively taken aback by the request not sure how to respond. The silence became a stand-off, and it was Lucy who broke it.

## JAMES MACLAREN

'Tell them it concerns James Dugdale.'

***

# CHAPTER TWENTY

### *Escape*

**Atlantic Ocean**

'APPROACHING STATION.'

'Aye. Sonar, surface contacts?'

'Sonar, multiple small contacts six nautical miles north, stationary or small revolutions, mechanical winch noise, fishing vessels sir.'

'Officer of the Deck, what's the sea state above?'

'Estimate three to four sir, a little choppy.'

Commander Karl Herrera took a swig of water and ruefully hoped that his crew hadn't eaten too much for lunch. Like all submariners in the U.S. Navy, he knew they were partial to the all-American slider heaped with relish. A period of time stationary at periscope death in a moderate sea state was not a comfortable place to be for a digestive system.

'Nav, confirm position.'

'Right here sir' – the young lieutenant pointed to the illuminated plot – 'just off the twelve-mile limit.'

'Quartermaster, sounding?'

'Sounding is nine-ze-ro fathoms beneath the keel.'

'Very well, rig for red, periscope depth diving officer trim the boat, make your bubble 1.5°. We're gonna be here a while, let's all try and hold our lunches down.

'Navigation, watch those fishing vessels, if any of them begin to drift our way let me know don't want to go anywhere near their nets.

'Chief of the Boat, have our head 'rigger' report to the conn.'

Herrera and his Los Angeles class attack submarine, the U.S.S. *Santa Fe* had just arrived on station in the western Mediterranean when fresh orders were received from Norfolk in Virginia. Proceed at once to a point two hundred miles west of the French port of Brest and take on board a SEAL team. He had thought it odd. It had been a devil of a job to slip into the Mediterranean undetected, clinging as close as he dared to the stern of a Syrian tanker, that had been unaware of its Ramora imitating companion as it chugged through the narrow Straits of Gibraltar. Having avoided the Spanish navy picket boats in a tense four-hour silent transit, no sooner had he arrived than he was ordered to turn around. The rendezvous with the SEAL team was the clue to the conflicting orders.

Through the infra-red of the scope Herrera could make out the distinctive feature of McGrath's point on the County Kerry coast and the toothed coastline that fell away to the south. The intense magnification of the scope meant he could even at this distance see the speckles of light that was the surf crashing upon the jagged rocks. He found the bearing to the coast he was looking for and called for the 'mark'. Swivelling round, he quickly found the twinkling lights of the fishing fleet to the north. To the west the Atlantic Ocean extended uninterrupted into the vastness beyond.

Apart from the fishing boats they were alone.

He gave up the scope to the officer of the deck leaving instructions for an air watch.

'Officer of the Deck, permission to cross the conn, sir.'

Permission granted a mountain of a man in military fatigues who despite his size nimbly squeezed past the banks of electronics with the practise of one well-used to submerged confined spaces.

The head 'rigger' or non-crew member was a stocky grizzled looking lieutenant who, with an age similar to his own, Herrera concluded had come to his modest rank the hard way through the ranks with the experience to boot. He was already dressed and ready for his mission. The *Santa Fe* was neither designed nor adapted for special forces operations however, the seven-man group, none of them strangers to submarine life, had hardly noticed and had spent the time since transferring aboard huddled in the torpedo room, checking, and rechecking their equipment.

'For the next couple of hours Lieutenant, we work for you.

The shore signal could come at any time. You and your RIBs will have about a twelve-mile run. Bring the two pax back and try not to say hello to anyone on the way. We'll cover your back as best we can. We'll slip back down to periscope depth and await your signal that you're on your way back. We good?'

'Aye sir, we'll be as qui–'

'Contact on the mark, bearing Xe-ro-niner-six true. White light.'

'And right on cue.' Herrera gave a quick smile. 'Good luck Lieutenant. See you in a couple of hours, please don't be longer. We are on the edge of neutral territory, and we are unwelcome. Scopes are clear at present, but it may not stay that way.'

Herrera had no idea who he had been sent to collect. All he knew was that it was some Brit that Washington considered important and who they wanted rescuing and bought back home. Ireland was officially a neutral country not directly in the Soviet's orbit. But that didn't really tell the whole story. If there was someone on the run who had made it from Britain into Ireland, then that didn't make them safe. The Finlandization of Ireland was just a fact of realpolitik. Whatever the runaways had to contend with in evading capture, Herrera knew he had his own problems in evading detection. The Atlantic west of Ireland was regularly patrolled by long range patrol aircraft. Two perhaps three Russian subs would be operating in the Atlantic approaches. Naval intelligence had told him that a British warship was on station west of Donegal. They would welcome the chance of pinning an American sub in the shallow coastal waters. The *Santa Fe* was used to snooping around unwelcoming coastlines—still he wished this operation hadn't been so rushed. He would have liked another twenty-four hours taking a look at whether the *Santa Fe* was *really* alone or just thought it was.

No point thinking about that now. The SEAL team needed time to launch the Zodiac boats stored in the outer casing lockers pick up their packages and get back to the *Santa Fe*.

'Make all preparation to surface.'

'Stand by lookouts to the bridge.'

The Diving Officer reported ready in all respects.

Herrera thought of the of the seven SEALs ready to leap onto the sleek, wet and rolling outer casing as soon as the hatches were open. It was pitch black out there, even with their night vision goggles. He didn't envy them. Be quick guys, he thought. If someone is tracking whoever is on that beach, they may just have thought of this as an escape route.

'Surface.'

THE next sixty minutes passed without incident. Returning to periscope depth the control room crew watched and waited. Herrera drank the strong black coffee that never seemed to run out and hunched over the plot table reviewing and pondering his escape route.

'Con, Radio. Tac burst on the high beam. Reports party

inbound.'

'Con aye. Okay people let's get ready to take them back on board. Officer of the Deck range?'

'Nine thousand yards. Two contacts inbound, also multiple lights onshore.'

Herrera took the scope. He found the Zodiacs pushing through the swell, ignoring the buffeting waves that gathered around the sleek boats, expanding themselves for their crashing assault on the coast and the small beach that had been selected for pick up. The coastline, dark an hour ago, now contained tiny points of light that moved and flared in the infra-red, some of them he could tell were vehicles. If the team had them, it was only just in time. But it also meant that whoever was pursuing them knew there was an offshore rendezvous.

A few more minutes passed, and the two RIBs grew bigger converging on their position. Six or seven minutes he estimated. They were making a big wake through the rolling sea. If radar was looking their way, they were being easily tracked. Herrea guessed that the Lieutenant's decision for speed rather stealth meant pursuit was taking place. It was now a straight-forward race.

'Prepare to—'

'Con, Combat,' the announcement interrupted him, the call was urgent, excited, 'contact on the ESM broadband, large turbo prop seventeen thousand yards, designate Sierra One. Possible air contact. Possible bearing two eight fi-yiv.

Herrera already knew what it was. Fuck, he thought, patrol aircraft probably a long-range Tupolov moving up from the south. Unless he was very lucky it would probably have detected the *Santa Fe's* scope, certainly the RIBs would have been spotted. There was no choice now, they were in international waters, he would brazen it out. Three minutes he estimated. With luck spotting them was not the same as doing anything about it.

'Sonar?'

'Sonar, clear sir no surface or sub-surface contacts.'

'Chief of the Boat supervise recovery. Make it very fast. Dump all equipment just get our people below.'

'Prepare to surface. Dive, don't show too much of the deck, just enough not to let the water in.'

A tense few minutes followed as the distance between the fast-approaching inflatables and safety narrowed. The patrol aircraft was a nuisance, but unless it actually attacked them in international waters, they would be okay.

'Con, Sonar, new contacts fourteen thousand yards, designate sonar buoys.'

The Tupolov had dropped a pattern of buoys to the west against the ocean. Herrera could see they were trying to pin his submarine against the coast, keep it in the shallow water probably while gathering other resources to chase, frighten or drive him off.

'Estimate three minutes to rendezvous sir.'

'Surface, open rear hatches, keep the lookouts below. We'll go down fast when the party is aboard.'

'Con, Sonar, new contact, high speed, designate Sierra 2. Course thuh-ree fo-wer niner. Nine thousand yards. Making revolutions for twenty-three knots.'

'Sonar, it's a Type-23 Duke-Class Royal Navy, bearing down through the fishing fleet. He's gone active, he's pinging us.'

Herrera knew, he could hear it. He guessed the sonobuoys from the patrol aircraft had worked out where they were, and the ambush had been the British frigate ghosting the other side of the fishing fleet using them as cover—just as he had.

'Con, Chief of the Watch, party coming aboard, all complete.'

'Sonar, range to target?'

'Six thousand yards, deck noise, Duke's launching a helo.'

'Bridge, Chief of the Watch, last man down compartment and hatch secured.'

That was the news Herrera had been waiting for. They had been helpless sitting on the surface, pinned and vulnerable. He had no idea what the warship intended to do; they were in international waters—just. But he didn't want to wait to find out.

'Very good. Dive the boat. Ahead flank, cavitate. Steer 096.' We'll let them know we're departing, thought Herrera, see whether they have stomach or orders for a chase. Then we can lose them in the Atlantic depths. 'Nav find me deep water and some very international water at that.'

IT took forty minutes for Herrera to conclude they were safe. When he was sure they could secure from action stations, he left the bridge and returned to his stateroom. The sonar sounds of angry propellers and the pulsing throbs of sonar waves receded as the *Santa Fee* slid smoothly down into the cold dark of the deep Atlantic.

He found an elderly man and a younger woman sitting at the table. They still wore damp outer clothing, and each had thick Navy issue blankets around their shoulders, both gripped mugs of hot coffee which they sipped gratefully. They looked robust enough, he thought, but being collected from an isolated beach by a team of Seals and bounced across a choppy sea in the dead of night could not have been a pleasant experience. Herrera was relieved to see colour was returning to their cheeks and he was keen to learn who these people were that the Pentagon was prepared to risk a multi-million-dollar submarine for.

'Karl Herrera, I'm the Captain. Welcome aboard, looks like we got to you just in time.'

The older man smiled ruefully and shook the hand that Herrera had extended.

'And we are very pleased to see you, Commander. I want to thank you and your crew for meeting us like this, I know you have taken some great risks to retrieve us. I'm James Dugdale and this is my colleague, Miranda.'

Something about her looked tough, a wire of a woman. But she produced a weak smile that was both gratitude and exhaustion. She's shattered, Herrera thought. Looks like she needs to sleep for a week.

'So, Mr Dugdale, what's your story? Are we going to be chased back across the pond?'

Herrera listened while Dugdale briefly outlined the long drive from London north to Scotland. Not sure whether they were being followed, changing cars and drivers three times at the dead of night, the wide circuitous weaving route avoiding towns until arriving at the fishing port of Campbell Town on the Scottish east coast. The trawler journey and a new drive across the Irish countryside. They had nearly made it too, passing into the Irish Republic near the town of Strabane when their luck ran out and a Garda patrol had briefly stopped them. They might still have got away, the officer had let them go, but Miranda had thought a plain clothes officer leaning against a car away from the checkpoint had seemed to take an interest. He must have phoned the report in, concluded Dugdale. They had arrived at the beach realising they were being pursued and that the authorities were closing in on them.

Herrera sympathised. He guessed the Russians, or the British had not had much time to mobilise to intercept them. But it was clear he and his crew had arrived just in time. He didn't need to speculate on what Dugdale, and this young woman had been up to. They looked an unlikely pair, but the world of subterfuge and international politics was one he knew little about.

Dugdale sipped his coffee and eased his shoulders back, seeming to relax, probably, thought Herrera, for the first time in days.

'Can I ask what are your orders, Commander? Where have you been told to take us?'

The *Santa Fe* had already signalled Norfolk that the 'packages' were aboard and that they were charting a passage at best speed for the East Coast.

'Halifax, Nova Scotia, I have orders to pass you on to the Canadians after that, no idea. We'll be leaving you there and be heading down to New London, Connecticut. I hope that's what you wanted to hear.'

Dugdale nodded thoughtfully and looked across at Miranda whose head was dropping with fatigue, she was close to collapse. At least she'll be safe now, he thought. Thank goodness.

'Well Commander,' he said briskly, his smile was iron, and the flinty eyes had regathered their glint, 'as quick as you can please. We have much work to return to.'

## Baltic Sea, Stockholm Archipelago

THE lightest of land breezes pulled at Sophie's hair and she breathed the salt air deeply and with satisfaction. The darkness was receding, and from where she stood on the side of the freighter, she could see the black-inked irregular silhouette of the Swedish coast slide past her. The channel was so deep, and the land was so close she could almost touch the pines which reached together and grew thick and tall in dark velvet silence from the shoreline. Small whisps of mist had begun to gather among the shore rocks that spoke of a beautiful day to follow and above, the black of night was turning a mellow blue, the stars almost departed, leaving the moon hanging as a cool silver disk.

The container had been as cold as an icebox and pitch dark. It had been filled with large immovable wooden cases that smelt of grease and machine oil. There were pallets of cans that contained some form of lubricant. She had followed the guides instructions nervously but steeled herself when she was told to get inside. When the doors had closed and she heard the metallic clacking of the seals being re-applied, she prayed she would see daylight again and that this cold, dark little world would not be her tomb. It took all her self-control to steel herself, control her fears and attempt to relax. She had a small pencil torch and found the small space that had been cleared for her, hidden a few pallets back into the container. There was a bottle of water and bread, wrapped in greaseproof paper. They had been placed in an otherwise empty bucket the purpose of which she was able to correctly guess. What followed, was to be a nervous few hours, in which, to begin at least, the darkness began to make her a little mad, for she had always been slightly claustrophobic. At one point her heart had jumped as she gained the sensation of lifting and moving, she thought she heard the murmur of voices and she had strained to listen. But the sound had vanished and only the silence remained. But the panic did not come and once she was used to the isolation, she found herself at a kind of peace. She felt safe enough, like she was in the womb and when light returned it would bring her rebirth.

The hours passed and she lost all sensation of time. She wore no watch. Despite the cold and the tension, she felt her eyes became heavy and she had begun to doze. When she woke, she had no idea of how long she had slept and it had taken a few seconds to realise her eyes were open, she blinked several times to test them. Then she realised there was no light to reach the photoreceptors and her brain could not receive the electrical signals that they would recognise as images. She had eaten the bread, sipped at the water and resisted the invitation of the bucket. All she could do was wait.

She heard the bolts and stood up, fearful of who might enter. Night air rushed in, and she heard a voice softly call her. 'It's okay you can come out now, you're safe.' The accented English belonged to a young man in an officer's uniform. He had helped her out, taken her to a cabin where she had been given food and coffee. 'We're just entering Swedish waters,' he said. 'We'll be in Stockholm in a couple of hours. Stay here until then, you'll be more comfortable.'

She had the urge for freedom to feel and taste the night air. 'Can I go on deck?' she asked, suddenly excited.

He hesitated, he had kind eyes and was tall and good-looking with the clean sharp features and thick, untidy blonde hair of a Scandinavian. Then he smiled. 'While it's dark, for sure.'

So it was that she now marvelled at the beauty of the coast that slid gently past and the sweetness of the air that reeked deliciously of salt and pine and something else that may just have been the scent of freedom. The night was trying to linger but was unable to resist the spreading dawn whose grey light continued to brighten, and which glinted flint-like on the first frost as the stark angular shadows narrowed and dissolved. Nothing moved except the first birds and the gentle lap of water against the rocks. The officer stood by her again and they both contemplated the beauty of the scene.

'Where will you go?' he asked. 'Now that you are out.'

She thought, did not immediately reply and in the darkness her smile was unseen. Then: 'I have no idea,' she said.

**THE END**

Printed in Great Britain
by Amazon